Muir's Gambit

ALSO BY MICHAEL FROST BECKNER

HITLER'S LOKI
Berlin Mesa

SPY GAME
The Aiken Trilogy
Muir's Gambit
Bishop's Endgame
Aiken in Check

A NATION DIVIDED
Volume I: Episodes 101–104
Volume II: Episodes 105–108
Volume III: Episodes 109–112

Muir's Gambit

Book I
The Aiken Trilogy

Michael Frost Beckner

Los Angeles
2022

This is a work of fiction. Apart from the well-known actual people, events, and locales that figure in the narrative, all names, characters, places, and incidents are the product of the author's imagination or are used fictitiously, and any resemblance to actual persons, living or dead, businesses, companies, government agencies, events, or locales is entirely coincidental.

Published in the United States by Montrose Station Press LLC, Los Angeles.

Library of Congress Control Number:
2022901296

ISBN 9798985597400 (hardcover)
ISBN 9798985597417 (paperback)
ISBN 9798985597424 (ebook)

Printed in the United States of America
First Edition

Cover design by Andrew Frost Beckner
Book design by Michael Grossman

For Christopher,
loyalty up, loyalty down
&
For Tony,
who taught me the most important First Rule of Thumb:
trust your gut

Acknowledgments

At the age of ten, my Favorite Colonel made a leap of faith through a third-story window from the back bedroom of a stranger's house. Uninvited, he'd fled inside to avoid being murdered. Second best to having wings to lift him, he had a fertilizer cart to break his fall and hide him. In that way, he escaped Hitler's SS, who hours earlier had captured his village. Fifty years later, retired from his nation's military intelligence service attached to NATO headquarters, he spent three snowy days with me touring the great Bastogne battlefields and local towns. Acting as translator, he provided me with introductions and the interviews I collected for a "child's view of war" that now, thirty-some years later, I still have yet to fully absorb and find a place of peace from which to write its horrors.

The fourth day with him was Christmas Eve. He invited me to dinner with his enormous and jocular family. As night fell with cotton-ball snowflakes unlike any I'd ever seen before or since, he slipped with me into the white and woodsy garden of his daughter's home to catch a smoke. He said, "Not now, but one day after I'm gone, if you're not afraid to write something dangerous, listen to me and I will tell you about GLADIO. What I know, what I didn't know; what I learned and what I did."

From this, a small measure of my Favorite Colonel lives inside Tom Bishop, Russell Aiken, and Nathan Muir within the pages of this book. They are characters whom I have brought to life by a hundred small measures of a hundred stories of "what I know and what I did" that have been shared with me over the years. I am indebted to the many CIA officers, and officers of both our American allies and those escaped of our enemies' intelligence services, whom I have had the honor to meet and to have been trusted by over the course of my professional career. Without their insight and guidance, this book and my earlier film *Spy Game* (to which this is a prequel) would not have been born.

Foremost among those I can thank by name are Antonio and Jonna Mendez. Professionally they have been my mentors, and personally, dear friends. True American heroes, they are prime examples of the best the CIA produces; although Tony is no longer with us, he inspires me daily as, whenever I lift my eyes from my screen, I am greeted by his beautiful and moving oil painting of Burnside Bridge as it appears on the Antietam battlefield, forever alive in the fullness of spring.

I am equally thankful to retired Operations Officer Chase Brandon, who invited me into Langley and welcomed me into his home, where he shared professional and personal details of his life and career. Of the men and women whom he introduced me to and convinced to share their experiences, I would like to thank two by name: former CIA Director George Tenet and retired Operations Officer and Deputy Director of the Counterterrorism Center Hank Crumpton.

Many thanks as well to Shannon Spann not only for the experience of her CIA career but for her memories of her honored fallen-hero husband, Johnny Michael Spann (the first American killed in combat during the United States invasion of Afghanistan in 2001, fighting hand to hand and alone at the Qala-i-Jangi fortress in a Taliban prison riot); if there is any true nobility in my characters, I found it in all she shared with me of Mike.

I have never served in Cyprus; Mike Buscher, CIA Operations Officer (ret.) has, and his expertise on that region, its people, tensions, and the espionage activity that take place in that island nation was invaluable.

There is Sabi, who in Tel Aviv was my doorway into the Middle East; and his agent Flady, who was not in Tel Aviv and who could go straight from a perfect bootlegger's turn at 70 mph, laughing as we escaped an Arab machine-gun position, to undercover in everything but dress, belly dancing on a table inside an Arab fishermen's tavern—two incidences I'm sure I wasn't supposed to witness—a brave and talented woman who knew more about the life of a spy during the Lebanese Civil War than can be found in any book yet written.

Thanks also go to the late Lieutenant Colonel Thomas D. Ferran III, founder of the USMC Scout/Sniper Association, whose willingness to share technical and historical knowledge from his experience as a sniper in Vietnam was matched only by his desire to discuss the psychological costs—emotional, spiritual, and interpersonal—that the military sniper in both war and peace lives and pays.

Books I found particularly helpful for historical reference and whose authors' scholarship informs the pages of this novel are: *The Korean War: The West Confronts Communism* by Michael Hickey (Overlook, 2000); *The Frozen Chosen: The 1st Marine Division and the Battle of the Chosin Reservoir* by Thomas McKelvey Cleaver (Osprey, 2017); *Chosin: Heroic Ordeal of the Korean War* by Eric Hammel (Presidio, 1981); *Breakout: The Chosin Reservoir Campaign, Korea 1950* by Martin Russ (Fromm, 1999); *The EOKA Cause: Nationalism and the Failure of Cypriot Enosis* by Andrew R. Novo (I.B. Tauris, 2020); *The Cyprus Conspiracy: America, Espionage and the Turkish Invasion* by Brendan O'Malley and Ian Craig (I.B. Tauris, 1999); *Cyprus: A Troubled Island* by Andrew Borowiec (Praeger, 2000);

Captive in the Congo: A Consul's Return to the Heart of Darkness by Michael P.E. Hoyt (Naval Institute Press, 2000); *Bye-Bye Babylon: Beirut 1975-1979* by Lamia Ziade (Interlink, 2011); *Beirut Outtakes: A TV Correspondent's Portrait of America's Encounter with Terror* by Larry Pintak (Lexington, 1988); *Battleground Berlin: CIA vs. KGB in the Cold War* by David E. Murphy, Sergei A. Kodrashev, and George Bailey (Yale University Press, 1997); *The Last Hot Battle of the Cold War: Decision at Cuito Cuanavale and the Battle for Angola, 1987-1988* by Peter Polack (Casemate, 2013); *Angola: Promises and Lies* by Karl Maier (Serif, 1996); and the indispensable 30,000 foot overview *Inside the CIA: Revealing the Secrets of the World's Most Powerful Spy Agency* by Ronald Kessler (Pocket Books, 1992). Any historical inaccuracies within the pages of *Muir's Gambit* belong entirely to me.

Special thanks go to Joel Kassay, my creative muse or daemon (depending on my mood) editor for all my work—big screen, television, and fiction—for near twenty years.

Thank you, Kara, for your unceasing love, and for teaching me to stop reflexively saying no to every promising idea I'm offered, and for reading every page of every draft with fresh eyes and open heart every time.

Thanks are due my copy editor Heather Sangster and my proofreader Rebecca Millar. They are, as always, indispensable.

Special thanks to my brother, John, for every time he's said, "It's not like that, it's like *this*," always eager and available to help my fiction while never taking his eye off his own real-world intelligence work where soon he will be catching the bad guys from outer space. Likewise special in my thanks is Charlie Lyons of Beacon Pictures, my champion on *Spy Game* since the very first FADE IN:.

My final thanks go to Murray Weiss of Catalyst Literary Management for his tireless and thoughtful work on my behalf. I couldn't ask for better representation.

Muir's Gambit

This day September 30, 1991

LETTER AGREEMENT

Re: Russell Aiken, legal counsel to the Central Intelligence Agency, United States of America

This letter agreement ("Agreement") will confirm the terms and conditions of the agreement between RUSSELL AIKEN ("Me" [insert language: notwithstanding and without limitation to all other personal pronouns associated with "Me"]*) and the sum total of the success, joy, and personal happiness; the dignity, honor, and pride that, bracketed by the failures, embarrassments, and regrets owned and owed ("Life"), with respect to My free admission that in Life honesty and morality have never been, are not now, nor will ever be mutually inclusive.*

1. *CONDITIONS PRECEDENT: All of My obligations hereunder are conditioned on the following:*
   - 1.1. *God creates Life.*
   - 1.2. *Humankind takes all the credit.*
   - 1.3. *All goodness in Life enjoyed by humankind is a material derivative of God and created by God, given freely of him in perpetuity unto the Public Domain.*
     - 1.3.1. *That the nature of humankind is such that willfully or ignorantly we dishonestly claim ownership of and credit for all goodness in Life.*
   - 1.4. *All evil in Life is a material derivative of humankind abhorrent to God, who in no way*

created or has neither involvement in nor control over.

1.4.1. That the nature of humankind is such that willfully or ignorantly we dishonestly deny ownership of and credit for all evil in Life.

1.5. God's nature is honest; humankind's nature is dishonest.

1.6. Legal documents exist for the sole purpose of compelling something from someone else that they would rather not choose to do, or to be held accountable for seeing through.

1.7. God doesn't believe in paper contracts.

2. *COMPENSATION:*

   2.1. A chance to live with myself.

3. *INDEMNIFICATION: None. I'm tired of indemnification. I'm tired of its mockery, as the above mockery of my life's (*lowercase *m*, lowercase *l) work stands as a drunken immature proof thereof* [sidebar: as practitioners of law we're taught that a word like *thereof* is greater and more clear than the sum of its separate parts, but every time I've compounded *there-of*, my inner voice inserts parenthetical language: "deception indicator, beware what has preceded and all that now will follow"].

PART ONE

PROFESSION

"Words, as is well known, are the great foes of reality."

—Joseph Conrad, *Under Western Eyes*

1

Charlie March is dead. On a day that promised perfection to the hero of the CIA, an eighteen-minute countdown was all he got to enjoy it once he turned the ignition key and sent an electric spark to his sailboat's engine. He'd arrived early, first light golden upon the water, this second-to-last morning in September. Halyards clanged against masts like bells summoning the faithful. It was a habit he had, on days like that, to be first on the water, but even old age and retirement don't assassin-proof spies.

Habits kill.

He backed his yacht from slip 29 at the Pelican Landing Marina in Key Largo, passed the jetty, and turned toward open sea.

No hat was found. He'd never been a ball-cap kind of guy, having had a mane of tawny hair—stark white since he'd left the Agency—wild and thick, that precluded a hat's sun-blocking necessity. He knew his hair made him look like a lion and he worked it just so.

Beneath all his soft genius, his crackerjack heroics, and courteous affability, March was a vain son of a bitch.

His old man's stoop had yet to begin. It never would, but his arms were loose-skinned, stringy-muscled, age-blotched, and knobby-comical as he unfurled his main sail and fed it to the wind. He breathed deeply, thankful to be alive to experience this moment, the moment before his last when the bomb hidden aboard his boat exploded.

A Harbor Patrol skiff operated by two officers of the US Coast Guard arrived at the wreckage less than ten minutes after the big *ba-boom*. One fished Charlie March's body from the wreckage with a gaff and pulled it onto the deck. The other manned the helm and worked the radio.

Burned so badly as to be unrecognizable as himself or any of the countless men he'd posed as in life, Charlie March gurgled out, "Thank Nathan for me... Thank him and tell him that."

"Tell him what, sir?"

"He never murdered a soul."

"Who's Nathan? We don't know Nathan, sir. Did he do this to you?"

"Too old for this. Made a mistake."

It does not matter what they asked him next. They have reported those questions, but March chose to stop speaking after the thing about "murder" and "mistake," so their further interrogatory line is irrelevant to us and to my mission. With the realization he'd said too much, Charlie March waited for death. His large, dark eyes stared lucidly, if not downright defiantly, at the intrusive Coast Guardsman from a face charred black and flaking away in the wind like pieces of a trampled papier-mâché mask.

I've read somewhere that, even after the heart and lungs cease function, the brain continues a minute or two.

Mine, right now, pictures a French Revolution Madame La Guillotine and a pair of Madeline eyes blinking over the head-basket edge, full knowledge of what's become severed from what.

So, though clinically dead, "Some shit way to go, man" were the last words of a last remark heard by a dead Charlie March, one Coast Guardsman to the other.

Having lived the life he'd chosen, I don't think Charlie March agreed with the sentiment.

"AND," NATHAN MUIR said as he poured me into my rental car—I having clutched twice for the door armrest without any sober measure of success—"Charlie March got exactly what Charlie March wanted."

"Died proud, huh?"

I wanted to show Muir that while I hadn't learned to hold my liquor the way he held his, I'd managed to pick up some of his sarcasm. I hadn't. I sounded pissy. I sounded bruised.

"He delivered you here. Now we've split his silver."

Muir was right. I gripped the steering wheel, scowling because I didn't want any of March's Tyrian shekels.

Here was the house Muir rented each September along a stretch of swamp and back bay on Florida's Captiva Island.

He smiled, muzzle-flash bright, and stepped away from my car, the matador letting the bull think it actually has a chance of leaving the ring alive. But I had what I'd come for: signed documents for the Agency; the truth about Charlie March to keep me warm; the stone cold truth about Nathan Muir. And in those muzzle-flash expressions fired in silent ambush between his words, I took recognition that my truth, as dishonestly lived as any part of either of his and Charlie March's truths, was a deception operation I'd perpetrated upon myself my entire adult life.

I left him there. Forever, I hope. I drove fast, tires kicking wet clay and ground-seashell muck I wished would spray his white linen pants and blue chambray sport shirt made in Vietnam to look French.

Here's mud in your *eye.*

I drove drunk to the airport, hoping to gain enough time between now and my expected arrival back at headquarters tomorrow to commit a murder of my own. A murder that when done would drop, as Muir's own admitted murders seem to imply, a shroud of balance over the muddled body of a life poorly lived.

I get ahead of myself.

I'm drunk. Still. And keeping it that way. I'm on the airplane home, writing an ending that is still only anticipation. I've left off the beginning. Anxious to get to my own story, I have left out Muir's confession that, I suppose, is justification for everything I'll do from here on out. I'm going to tell this like it happened. Out one side of his mouth, the other of mine.

Yes, Mr. Director—or yes, gentlemen—or Your Honor—or Detective Inspector Blabitty-Blah, whoever the hell ends up reading this. All of you. Yes. This is my admission that he poured me into my car. Hammered.

This is my admission that I left him of my own free, calculated will, but doesn't that also allow me the argument that at the point I arrived to Muir I might have been clear-thinking, sent and sober? You bet it does, and that's what you want to know. That everything I did up until Florida was of my own free will. So here it is. I was thirteen years dry when I parked the car on the crushed-clamshell drive, got out into a downpour, and stared at the house. Two broad white concrete and glass rectangles stacked askew, the upper floor extended to cover the wraparound porch, all of it balanced upon rocket-fin pylons and stretching into jungle toward a point in time when the sixties were still the future. Muir met me with a challenge across the drenched gray air:

"Don't tell me you're the best Harker and his Young Turks could muster to assassinate me."

"Mr. Muir, Executive Order 11905 specifically forbids the CIA or any other intelligence or military service of the United States of America from engaging in assassination," I said, already as wet as the bottom of a puddle.

On the covered porch, Muir, aged sixty-two back on March 21, hit his cigarette. He sipped his scotch. He considered my response a moment, or more likely considered the taste of his drink. The next thing he did was extend his tumbler over the porch railing to collect some rain.

"Glad to hear that," he said. "Matter of fact, there's about a dozen fellas I met over the years who'd've been really glad to hear it."

"Would one of these fellas happen to be Charlie March?"

Muir toasted me with a grin that lit the shadows. He drank more before saying, "Why not?"

My heart leapt—my purpose for being there—but reflecting off his grin was the question mark fish-hooking the end of his statement. A question is not a confession. A question admits nothing.

Hidden on three sides by dense tropical foliage, the house's fourth side faced the windward and beach-less—so mostly undeveloped—western side of the island, where the storm-tossed whitecaps swatted at seabird wingtips with foamy paws.

Now, if you'd seen Charlie March in his prime, all large hands and feet and shoulders attached to a narrow frame with a funny potbelly that appeared after meals due to a serious lack of sit-ups, earthy and disheveled, and utterly common with the vast majority of men, your intellect would tell you: "This is what real spies look like."

When you see Nathan Muir, as I saw him on that porch, tall and sculpted, blond and fearlessly blue-eyed, the coolest version of handsome with a smile that spoke an entire language of its own, your heart would tell you: "This is how spies should look." This gut reaction is why Muir *is* the best. He gets the job done while you're still marveling at how good he looks doing it. Breaks always favor the handsome man with the winning smile.

I'm handsome enough. I guess. In decent shape, with curly dark hair that doesn't do anything for or against me. But my mouth is crooked. Madeline teases about my smile. "You're better off when you don't. Just be happy you drown girls with your eyes."

My best feature: big, brown, romantically hopeless eyes.

Without an umbrella, I'd been drowning for about a minute since getting out of my rental car and retrieving my saddlebag briefcase, not knowing how to begin the questioning, and worried about other things—

Madeline. Shit. Shit. Shit.

—when Muir appeared at the porch railing and began the interrogation for me with the assassination accusation.

I remained steadfast in the deluge, as if that proved anything.

"Too easy—going for Charlie March right out the gate—even for you. How 'bout a drink? Got everything, long as it's scotch and rainwater."

"You know I don't drink, Mr. Muir."

He gave just enough pause to let me know how inadequate my statement made me before he said, "Stop standing down there like a dog too dumb to come out of the rain. Come on up here and make your lawyer's assassination—the character kind not covered by Order 11905. Maybe by then I'll have changed your mind."

I trudged to the front steps. Muir met me, putting a hand across my soggy back to take my shoulder.

Friendly gesture. Also a control.

He moved me beneath the covered porch, along to the side of the house, where his bottle of Macallan twenty-five-year-old single malt waited, his cigarette packs lined up like soldiers, his kitchen matches like prisoners in a ceramic holder stolen from a Vientiane bistro, and his view of the Gulf—if not for the obscuring rain.

"Drop your bag."

Bag sounded a lot like *gun*. I dropped it where I stood.

"Sit." He lowered me into a heavily cushioned rattan sofa.

"Comfortable. Surprisingly so." I was quick to make small talk.

"Belongs to the guy I rent from. Ugliest furniture I've ever seen."

Muir walked around the glass coffee table and all that shit ordered upon it he's been trying to kill himself with since long before I ever met him. He took the matching chair to the sofa and sat across from me.

He smiled to himself briefly before grabbing the bottle. "My dog comment was uncalled for. Extra asshole of me. Sorry," he allowed, refreshing his drink.

"Two comments: *dumb dog* and *sit*."

He'd coupled *sit* with that disobedient-dog press into the chair that was the most offensive, but I knew Muir was counting and had added up two comments and a push into one specifically to bug me.

"Fine. Just don't want you to think I consider you my bitch."

"Three."

True count: four.

"Actually, I've always been fond of you, boy."

That's all he thinks of me? I'm a dog—God, am I? Hell.

"Find you completely spineless," he added. "Brave on paper, though."

He set down his glass and poured a small amount of the scotch from the bottle into a coffee mug he had waiting for me. Scotch I was dead set against drinking.

Don't feed him at the table.

The mug? Fanciful housecats lazed around it. Typical Muir: I'm supposed to be here for Charlie March and he's got me bitched up about dogs, and now he throws cats and whiskey at me to spin my head on a tangent of whether the dog-cat thing is a coincidence or Muir's purpose to get me off track to drink with him.

He topped the mug with fresh rainwater. "Seem to recall you having a problem with tap water fluoridation."

He'd made the same remark to me April 1, 1970, twenty-one years earlier. I'd been a pre-law senior, majoring in philosophy at George Washington University. Muir, a visiting department professor teaching a mythology elective, running into me as I was running late to class, convinced me to play hooky. By some lucky accident, he found us a revival showing of *Dr. Strangelove.*

Sterling Hayden as the treasonous General Ripper sits on the sofa beside Peter Sellers's terrified British Group Captain Mandrake. He puts his arm around Mandrake. In the background, machine-gun fire crackles as the world moves toward satirical annihilation.

Ripper asks Mandrake if he's "ever heard of a substance called fluoridations"?

Because Mandrake is not insane—going along to get along—he soothingly reassures him that he has, yes, but, "No, no," he doesn't know a thing about it.

Because Ripper is insane, he gives it to Mandrake rainwater and grain alcohol straight: fluoridation is the most odious communist plot ever conceived and exploited by the Soviet Union against the bodily purities of the United States of America.

The lucky accident of the movie was neither. On those rare but not completely elusive days when Muir cut classes with a student, *Strangelove* would always be playing. Just as the characters never changed in the film, the same eleven "characters" in the audience would be there as well. Too few to allow you to absorb into the crowd; too many to allow you to think that the showing was all about you: just enough to make you feel you shared something special. Everyone laughed on cue or murmured knowingly at moments selected by Muir for his young and impressionable guest to notice. I know because three years later, while I still looked up to him, I'd done a stint in the audience.

Muir's pitch that followed would always begin at the end credits, Vera Lynn singing "We'll Meet Again" to humankind's annihilation of all life on the planet.

"Suffice it to say, the Soviets don't have a Doomsday Machine," Muir said.

I grinned, my future bright and impressionable before him.

"We do." He wasn't joking. "Up near the North Pole."

My eyes were the same wide as those of his every prospective recruit at this shared confidence. Muir laughed as he always would, only to backtrack. Keep his target off balance. "Bullshit, by the way. The Soviets *do* have one. Naw, bullshit again, not really." Another laugh. "You know, try never to believe anything I say, by the way, except this"—Prospective recruit outside the theater, he'd finish the scruttles at the bottom of his popcorn bag, go for the steely-eyed kill—"What the Soviets have is worldwide terrorism in the form of nuclear proliferation and now's as good a time as any to let you know that people who dedicate their lives to making sure something like that idiotic 'Doomsday Machine' never happens…"

Crumples bag. The toss, two points—three-pointers not yet invented—into the wire trash basket. The city-sidewalk basket always there. Always half full. The basket: always a recent newspaper, folded so an appropriate Cold War horror headline peeked out for the most observant of his student candidates.

"They have asked me what I"—he points to himself—"think of you."

And the finger turns on the target—hopeful brown-eyed, crooked-mouthed me, that day back in 1970, having just glimpsed corn kernels scatter across the top of the *New York Times:* "U.S.S.R. SENDS NUCLEAR-ARMED SUB INTO BAY OF BENGAL"—a bull's-eye straight for my heart.

Though, like I said, I wasn't the only one.

There was Tom Bishop.

He didn't see the movie but bought the Muir ticket just the same.

Bishop: the best of Muir's recruits. And where is he today? Estranged from Muir, running black bag ops out of Hong Kong station. Tom Bishop, the one to whom Muir would like to give the other half of "Charlie March's silver;" Tom Bishop, whom Muir recruited in Vietnam and in Germany, and wasted in Lebanon; Tom Bishop, who replaced me as the apple of Nathan Muir's eye the moment Muir found him sharing a bowl of grilled dog ears on rice in an ARVN sniper's hooch near the Laotian border in Vietnam.

BACK TO the porch. Back to the scotch. The thing about it, the Macallan that is, is that I realize the year of its distillation—as opposed to the no-year little plastic Johnnie Walkers the flight attendant (whom Muir would pointedly call "stewardess" yet manage to take to bed) is feeding me—is the year of Madeline's birth.

Have I mentioned Madeline?

Only fair I should.

Oh yeah. Scrolled back. Chopped off her head in absentia a few pages ago.

Madeline's easy. At least she was, screwing her brains out a lifetime of two nights ago.

She's my lovely wife.

The man watching her fuck him wasn't me. (Read it twice to feel my revulsion.) I was the guy pointing the other kind of gun straight at the back of her head.

2

CAMP PEARY, VIRGINIA, is the home of the Department of Defense's Armed Forces Experimental Training Activity, a US military installation where the CIA quaintly doesn't acknowledge the existence of their top-secret training facility known the world over as The Farm. It has changed substantially in the seventeen years since I passed through. This due to Watergate and Senator Frank Church's committee, which turned the Agency inside out until men like March and Muir found ways to inside-out the inside out and get the Clandestine Service right-side-outted again. All future CIA officers undergo training within its confines.

Classroom study, tradecraft, fieldwork, black bag, and paramilitary: the amount of each and level of intensity determined by the future role for which you already—but don't know it—have been assigned. One program they claim dropped, which probably means it hasn't, is practical interrogation resistance. They work this in as a sort of pre-graduation surprise party. The thinking behind it was—whether you were to be the highest level, cloak-and-dagger, behind-the-lines operative or the lowliest "In-Out" basket clerk—the very fact that you are CIA makes you a perennial high-risk abduction target.

So although I'm an attorney forever ensconced at headquarters serving the Office of General Counsel where my chance of capture by anything but boredom is nonexistent, late one night toward the end of training I found myself rousted from my billet at The Farm and subjected to a didn't-feel-simulated simulated capture and all that followed.

Still follows me.

They hauled me outside and hustled me on foot for an hour through forest and swamp to a mock prison I'd not seen before. They put me into one of ten cells. Doors barred, lined in a row like you'd see in a prison. A little rough, but a little fun and games too. At first.

There were no other prisoners.

I'd been yelled at in Russian. Beat up a bit in the international language of fists, saps, boots. Sleep-deprived, but no one asked any questions. Just me alone and banged up in my dummy cell.

You go through gobs of psychological profiling at The Farm, where, since you're competing for success, nobody volunteers his or her deepest phobia for discussion or even notation. I certainly didn't. Mine is childish. A nightmare I'd had throughout childhood after viewing a movie on television I'd been expressly forbidden to view, mention, or think about.

A jail cell with a barred gate is psychologically disconcerting to me but not disabling. My imprisonment lasted about twenty hours, which I spent listening to happenings outside. A loud construction vehicle. The intermittent movement of supplies, equipment, or something. Voices in a Russian dialect using words that mostly weren't covered in the brief language course I'd been given. The ring of hammers on nails. All orchestrated to punch in volume with sudden and horrific male or female screams if I started to drift off to sleep.

Over time, the sounds diminished so sleep might have been possible, but as I had become aware that the screams and hammering were my only human connection, and had grown hungry to figure out what was happening, I couldn't have slept if I tried. The quieter they became, the harder I strained to hear them. Shortly after I deduced a certain crunch and scraping I'd been hearing were people engaged in digging, the power cut out and the prison went completely dark.

More of the rough stuff. More Slavic curse words. I was zip-tied and leg-manacled, dragged into another night, shoved into the back of a van.

The simulation aspect of my situation was wearing thin. I rationalized it to exhaustion, starvation, physical abuse. I knew I hadn't really been captured, but being treated exactly as if I had made it exactly the same. I was breaking. I knew that too. I'd been instructed I would and been taught to expect it.

The interior of the van was originally white. There was nothing inside the cargo area but me. There were no windows, and no sound came through the wall of the cab. For the first few hours, the ride was smooth. This allowed me—rather, forced me—to study my surroundings. The jail cell had been fifteen square feet with the open barred front. The van's dimensions were about twelve feet deep and seven wide. I mention the white paint because in a number of areas much of it was gone. The longer I studied the scrapes and scuffs, the clearer it became to me that they were the scouring of leg irons. The abrasions of kicks. The clawings and poundings of prisoners at the doors. There was desperation and suffering in these patterns; as my own desperation and suffering surged and grew, the easy ride became violent.

I don't know whether we went into a quarry or across a lava field; I was convinced the wheels were equipped with square tires. The van pounded for hours over rock and debris and I pounded like a ball bearing shaken inside an empty coffee can.

Grunts became my shouting became my screaming and moaning and gouging and flailing of the leg chains.

We'd stop for prolonged periods of time. The engine never shut off. Then Mr. Toad's Wild Ride would resume. The violence and pain crashed my mental state. Frustration and anger morphed into hatred and fury. Self-pity followed regret and preceded hopelessness. We did hours of winding roads to the sudden and blaring accompaniment of Cuban political anthems. All I had to hold on to was my admission that without a minute of interrogation, they'd fully broken me and I belonged to my captors.

We stopped. The doors flung open. It was night again. Different captors, these in civilian garb more frightening than the uniforms I'd seen before. It added a deeper dimension of unaccountability. I was in the driveway to a house on a neighborhood street.

I tried to yell for help. I was brutally gagged and hooded.

Jostled inside, they forced me down narrow stairs.

Hood removed, I was kicked into a ten-by-ten cellar smelling of feces, urine, and vomit. Neither too dark nor too light. Neither too hot nor too cold. No music. No voices and no sounds outside. Just one more diminishing step into smaller confinement. One more diminishing step into subtracted contact with the outside world. Each captivity was safer in concept and location, yet each further concealed me from that more desirable outside world. The cellar offered none of the psychological mind-fucking or sleep-deprivation techniques I'd experienced before. They didn't have to use them.

I wasn't alone in that cellar.

That childhood fear-fest movie I mentioned earlier, you might guess, was about claustrophobia. It was called *Barnaby's Closet*, a retelling of Poe's "The Cask of Amontillado" B-movie updated to 1956 London and an assortment evil children with oh-so-proper high-voiced English accents doing the brick work.

I shared the space with a steel cage. Rectangular and low. The kind you might use to transport an alligator. Or lower it into a vat of acid. The cage was empty. Its door was open.

Did they expect me to crawl into it? Clearly, with the smaller and smaller containments, the crew at The Farm knew my phobia.

How?

They were better at their job than I was at concealing my private thoughts.

I would never get inside that cage. Any cage. Ever. That was for sure.

Screw you, CIA! Screw your job offer, Nathan!

I shouted that in all its variations once or one thousand times. Only in my head. I would not give them the satisfaction to hear me make another sound out loud.

For almost eighteen fidgeting, hyperventilating, food-and-stimulation-deprived hours, I defied the cage, until it dawned on me what my trainers sought. So simple I wanted to laugh but fearing punishment if I didn't maintain a properly broken decorum, I choked back chuckles and proved I had conquered my terror of confinement.

At sixty-eight hours and forty-four minutes from my original abduction, I willingly crawled inside an animal cage.

Two hours after that, I crushed my eyelids together and—violently quaking—pulled shut the gate. I locked it.

Six hours later, after my urine had long since dried, four men entered the room. They didn't congratulate me. They didn't set me free. There was no shouting, no answering my reborn cries and pleas, no speaking by them at all. They carried me into the night inside my cage.

The first snowflakes of winter's first storm sifted down night's black shroud. Silent, secret snowflakes lighting through the bars of my cage, they put me beside some tools, beside some wood.

The backhoe idled nearby.

I knew where I was. I'd heard the machine before. The tools. The stacking of the wood. I'd heard the digging. Understood the hammering. Without seeing it, I knew what they'd dug. I thrashed. I babbled: incoherent terror for the length of time it took them to construct my coffin. Next to the fresh-covered graves of the sixteen other trainees in my section. I struggled inside my cage as they dropped me into the box and hammered it closed. I lost all sanity when they lowered me into the pit.

Hours, minutes, seconds, eternity: the concept of time utterly lost to me. The only fight left was to breathe because I somehow couldn't do it automatically any longer. There was air, but I was fighting myself to take it in, explosive gasps that horrified and humiliated me.

The scratch of a phonograph stylus like the jab of an interrogation needle and violins began with plaintive complaint, introduction to *The Voice*: Frank Sinatra—outside my coffin, above my grave—plaintive and coaxing, monaurally urging me to "Try a Little Tenderness."

3

At the beginning of the interrogation section at The Farm, trainers pay a great deal of critical classroom attention to the study of torture. They teach you that no one is capable of holding out to torture. Everyone will talk. No one is expected not to talk. Nothing you give up, they comfort, will lose the war, end civilization, destroy the planet with a Death Star bang. No one is expected to be Superman; and contrary to one's own ego, an individual's secrets aren't the be-all end-all backed against a flat Earth's edge in a lonely dump truck. Pull the latch. Drop the load. All gone. Bye-bye.

Nope.

What's required of an unlucky officer is a level of dedication to holding out long enough for your capture to be registered and emergency contingency plans made operational.

But if everyone breaks, how does anyone hold out?

You hold out, they tell you, by holding on to the most precious secret you have. The one secret the enemy can never get out of you. The impossible secret they don't want and wouldn't know to go after. A secret belonging only to you. For many, it's a personal detail or a confidence about their spouse or their children. For others, it might be a youthful triumph or a private ambition. Or the time you felt imagination take physical wing when you flew your first kite.

A secret love.

A treasured keepsake.

You do not write it down.

You do not tell a soul.

This secret will buy, they urge you—*you must understand*—this secret will buy the Agency, your assets, your agent networks, the protection of a spy's most uncontrollable commodity: time.

Codes can be changed. Plans redesigned. Teams redeployed, individuals exfiltrated, invasions called off—well, not really that one; in practice, overwhelming force is the child of overweening ego—but time is the one thing only you can save that can't be manipulated, transformed, reshaped. It cannot be stopped. It is up to you to protect it as long as you can. You accomplish that by protecting your secret they aren't asking for until you know you're about to give it up to them, unasked and unmasked, just to stop the pain and the horror.

Never give it up. That's when to break instead. Choose your breaking point.

Does that mean cooperate? Hell no. It just means you don't have to voluntarily go down with the ship of your life. If dying were necessary, you'd have been equipped with and already used your L (for Lethal) pill.

Afterward, after you've given up your professional secrets, afterward: you'll still have beaten them by saving yourself. You'll have protected the secret most important to who you are. It becomes the first building block of your dignity, the cornerstone to the reconstruction of your broken psyche.

My secret of secrets was associated with my father. He was a long-haul trucker who spent twenty-five years driving the hated Los Angeles–Rust Belt, Rust Belt–New England, New England–L.A. loop. An uneducated man who worked without respite so that his wife could have a house and his children private, wholesome, Christian educations.

He burned to death among sunflowers.

A lovelorn, suicidal teen drove a Dodge Dart head-on into Dad's Peterbilt. Dad's chemical load ruptured. Escaping fumes ignited by a spark. It all happened in a field just outside of a no-place, Bible-thump-t'nowhere called Quinter, Kansas.

That's not my precious secret.

My precious secret is the records Dad played every night he came home. On those nights, after my sisters (I have two, both older) and I would be packed off to bed, Dad would put on a record from his Sinatra collection—"They're grown-up records, Rusty, and I'll know if you've touched these while I'm out"—and he and Mom would drink André Cold Duck and they would dance.

Dad sang each song closer to her ear until the first, second, sometimes third-side of his chosen and sacred albums ended, the diamond tip of the stylus scratching out the rough, rhythmic, wave-sucking-back-from-the-shore crackle of the center label. He would take her by the hand and into their bedroom. Their love sounds, sighs, and childish giggles (I never, at least consciously, heard anything lurid) would fill me with affection.

Happy and family-safe.

I'd slip from my hiding place behind my door, climb into my upper bunk bed, and pull up my blanket. Within the confines of the little back sun porch that Dad had converted for me, with the green-tinted glass roof where, post-*Barnaby*, I could watch the stars or the clouds in my "open air" ("So what if it's odd? The kid's scared") bedroom: I would be safe.

I've never told a soul any of that. This writing is the first time I've revealed it to anyone, anywhere, in any form or manner. In high school, college, in law school, and when I passed through The Farm in 1974, I didn't own or listen to—by choice or by accident—any music made, composed, or performed by Frank Sinatra.

They knew anyway. That night at The Farm, they *knew*.

Dog comments and cat cups.

And that's how they thought best to teach me that there is complete and total hopelessness. There is complete and total desolation, shame and fool-terror ignominy in capture. What happens isn't about duty, honor, country. Are you fucking serious? What happens isn't about spilling your guts. What happens isn't about being brave and brave-you pulling up a warm fuzzy secret to your tender throat. It isn't about mental or physical pain.

What happens is about crushing everything inside you.

Crushing everything that is the last piece of privacy within your heart that no one but you would value or even want.

Then they stomp on it. And they don't give a shit what it is.

This is a double confession. "Try a Little Tenderness."

They didn't bury me. I'm a pussy: it was a simulation. The music didn't even play the length of the song. Point made, it was stopped. The coffin raised, the crowbars crowed. Cage unlocked, I was lifted out, neither roughly nor gently, and no one said a word. There was no hail-fellow-well-met, we're all good brothers, fraternity ritual night revelatory chug-a-lug, gooey-eyed and somewhat queer "now you're one of us."

You're on your own. One of nobody.

A black guy in a parka, jeans, and muddy boots drove me back to my billet and let me off out front. He told me to get some rest and "Report for PT at reveille as usual, Mr. Aiken."

I opened the door and stepped inside. I felt a small object beneath my foot: a green marble. I didn't question how or why it was there. Over the years, I'd learned not to. I pocketed it. I found my bed. I went to sleep.

THE FINAL WEEK of my training at The Farm, I sat for the last two psychological counseling sessions. The same as required over the first five weeks of my course. The doctor never brought up any part of the simulation.

I wasn't about to. I told myself that if I'd cracked in a permanent way, I'd have left. I stayed, *ergo*, I hadn't humpty-dumptied.

Proof of that? Easy. Two nights ago I listened to Sinatra. The Voice.

"Try a Little Tenderness" is track three, side two, of his *Nice 'n' Easy* vinyl album, track nine on the CD between "She's Funny That Way" and "Embraceable You." That's what I listened to in my car—CD not vinyl, obviously—its front bumper poking around the corner just up the street and across from the 1938 brick-built Tenleytown, American Traditional townhouse Madeline fell in love with the first week after we started dating. I bought it for her as a wedding present two years ago. Here, at the point in the song where Frank allows that women who may be weary, do get weary, my wife, twenty-five years old, Madeline, was anything but, and her dress, a skintight Dolce & Gabbana: nothing shabby about it. I'd recently purchased it when she'd made a Sunday-sudden decision to change her look and style, and I made the decision she was cheating on me. That bald, bearded American University marketing professor she'd been seeing since the summer semester, and was now going to drunk-fuck in our home. He had the zipper down her back. She unlocked our door. She must have left her shoes in her little SUV where I saw his bike—tucked behind the hatch—presumably for the secret getaway he wouldn't make tonight.

In June I'd followed him as he'd ridden it pedal-pedal-ugly-asshole, scooting away from a cherry-picking assignation with my wife, he in his tight black-and-yellow cycling costume like some kind of sex-drunk bumblebee.

Madeline's bare foot kicked our front door shut behind them.

The lights remained out and I remained outside, peering through my windshield but inwardly picturing what was happening inside.

Her breasts.

He'd go for them first. First with the pudgy hands and then, her hands on the back of his sweaty dome, with his bristly face on her soft cleavage, sluggy fingers of his other hand crawling up under her dress to make sticky trails on her inner thighs.

In 1973—before I'd even gone through The Farm and unbeknownst to me—Nathan Muir declared me unfit for the Clandestine Service. Didn't think I was a guy who could make the "split of a moment" decision to pull the trigger on a human life. Eighteen years later, I was about to put the answer to that straight to bed before my wife and Beardy-Baldy got to the bedroom.

I grabbed the .22 automatic pistol that Uncle George had given Mom to protect us kids after Dad lost his life. My sister Paulette had found it a year ago when Mom died. She shipped it to me. I grabbed that little sucker and left the car running, crossed the street, lyrics about her waiting and anticipating amplified in silent crescendo inside my head to the beat of my heart.

I let myself into our foyer. I peered into the dark of our living room. I watched my wife and Beardy-Baldy finish undressing. And now, seeing him in neither bumblebee spandex nor the *Dead Poets Society* elbow-patched corduroy he'd worn from campus to car to my front door a few minutes ago—seeing him ass-naked but for a gold chain dangling a medallion—I understood he bicycled for other reasons than fitness. Hippos carry pregnancies better than Beardy-Baldy his gut. To him, bicycling was about the costumes, the equipment; the magazines—dozens you'll find in his apartment along with the Tour de France recorded off his cable TV. Beardy-Baldy bicycled because he's a fad guy.

I hate fads.

"You're sure your husband isn't home?" Beardy-Baldy fucking-fatboy said between dog licks of Madeline's cheeks and neck, one hand disheveling her thick, dark hair, the other between her long, firm calves.

Her calves. Not mine anymore—

"I told you, never mention him."

She punched his flabby butt particularly hard, almost spiteful.

She'd never done that to me.

"Ow! Sorry."

He seemed to like it.

"I don't want sorry, I want you in me."

He did just that. My wife helped him. My stomach lurched and my skin crawled as every bit of me down to my blood cells howled at their animal rutting. The raging desire to put something into both of them. Two precise shots. The first eliciting Madeline's yelp of shock. The second blending with it, lead passing through tanned animal skin and blowing fragments to ricochet and burst a ceramic lamp.

Earplugged on the range, the sound of a gunshot is about as loud as gunshots on TV with normal volume. In your own living room, from your own hand at the woman you pledged your life to, heart and soul, and who did the same to you but didn't include her genitalia, gunshots are the loudest thing you'll ever hear. I've read that the first volley of cannon fire at Gettysburg before Pickett's useless charge was louder than the nuclear tests in Nevada and Bikini combined.

Try shooting your wife for a bang.

The explosion of everything that makes up your *before* carrying an echo that reverberates through and defines your *ever after*.

Outside, without knowing how I'm already there, I just miss a tree. I can smell it and the grass around it, wet from sprinklers. Feel a brush of bark on my turning cheek.

Neighbors' lights go on. Both sides of the street.

Fuck.

Front shoe airborne in front of me as my back shoe propels me off the curb.

Car: fumbling keys.

Slapping the steering wheel, engine revving—unmoving, *why am I going nowhere?*—until, neither soft nor gentle, but oh, so easily, I wrench back the shifter and glide into darkness.

I HADN'T STARTED drinking yet. Like I've said: until Muir, I'd been thirteen years sober. But I'm blacked out to how I got to the parking loop inside Fort Marcy Park. Only that I was in my car beneath the dark, spanning arms of the oaks and the hanging vines. "Try a Little Tenderness" played on a loop. I bellowed like an Eskimo-spear-stuck seal, between sobs drafting out loud the Letter Agreement I have previously written, and which you will find, and may refer to for clarity, at the beginning of this double confession.

"This letter agreement confirms the terms and conditions of an agreement between Russell Aiken and the sum total of the success, joy, and personal happiness—"

I put the pistol to my temple.

"Dignity, honor, and pride that, bracketed by the failures, embarrassments, and regrets owned and owed—"

I shoved it into my mouth, the slide clicking, hurting my teeth.

I tried to pull the trigger, pushing the barrel up under my tearstained chin as I hollered, "With respect to my free admission that in life honesty and morality have never been, are not now, nor will ever be mutually inclusive!"

I tried to wedge the gun around the back of my neck to the base of my skull so I didn't have to see it. I wasn't about to provide later satisfaction to anyone noticing I'd shut my eyes.

Split of a moment.

Muir said that about me.

Well, it's *spur of the moment*. That's the phrase. The proper wording.

Muir throws out verbiage without thinking. And words are important, and words mean exact things, and somehow people are always hearing his and ignoring mine even when I write them down precisely and perfectly and soberly reasoned, and I can't, I can't do this split-spur-fucking-fuck-of-a-second finger-twitch thing to myself.

I hurled the gun into the passenger footwell. I screamed about God's nature. About humankind's evil. I pounded the steering wheel with my fists, folded up and kicked the dashboard until—*Nice 'n' Easy* ejecting and cracking into pieces—I broke the CD player that I'd spent too much money on in the first place. Goddamn German product. I hated myself for what I'd done tonight but didn't hate bravely enough to do what I should do to pay for it. Yet.

"Chrissakes: out all night or what?" said Jeremy Harker the Third, accompanying his words with one of those irritating golfer pantomime swings.

Another fad boy.

He'd been new to Clearasil and destined to spend the next four years as their best acne-cream customer when I was busy being deep-sixed to Frank Sinatra. Harker today is all slicked-back, Ivy League, hand-tailored ambition who at thirty-five is the youngest deputy director of operations in CIA history.

I was a dirty, unkempt wreck who'd abandoned my car in the park, not knowing I'd done that until I was climbing out of the taxicab I'd called to the service station located where the George Washington Memorial Parkway exits onto Dolley

Madison Boulevard, and I had been driven the mile and a half to headquarters.

I presented myself at the main gate, fully expecting a Metro police cruiser to be awaiting me.

There was not.

I was reprimanded for the taxi, non-verbally ridiculed for my appearance, and escorted to the pristine, green-glass New Headquarters Building, where I'd recently been moved into my own cell-sized office. One of four offices situated off a common paralegal and secretarial suite. I am allowed to keep my door open—which staff believes is out of a spirit of openness, not claustrophobic, buried alive fear.

Harker stood inside my doorway pretend-golfing and furious beneath his Chiclet-toothed smile.

I said, "Had some car trouble. Sorry."

"You didn't ask security for any help with your car when you stumbled up to Campus gates—which, as you must know, is *verboten*."

Not "know" but "*must* know," as if I'm some kind of moron who might not. I grunted with purposeful moronity.

Oh, and "Campus"? Let's get this straight. No one but Harker calls Langley *Campus*. He says for security reasons, but really because he knows how much it rankles every officer who earned his stripes the Cold War hard way. Me included. Nothing collegial about my stripes.

I didn't rate a full sofa.

Instead, I had a generic government love seat that Harker impatiently motioned me into. He shut my door, boxing us in. On the side table, a *Top Secret*–stamped folder waited for me. The red and yellow bars along the edge told me the type of file contained inside without having to open it. Nothing, thankfully, incriminating or personally dangerous. At least that's what I thought yesterday, at the time.

"Forget your car and you're stumbling around—inside your head and out. You have something else to do. Takes precedent over any personal bullshit you're wasting Agency time on."

"None of my personal bullshit is—"

I shut my mouth before I slipped on the bullshit about to come out of it. Harker ordered me to open the file.

As I'd visually ascertained, it was an Agency service jacket. In all circumstances, this is a single-page summary, an official cheat sheet of an officer's personal statistics, postings, operations, briefings and debriefings, dates, and directorate cross-tabs, all with the appropriate central file reference numbers and clearances needed to pursue any notation to its logical and/or stunningly illogical illuminations and conclusions.

In Charlie March's case (whose file record this was), due to the extent of his Company work, his summary filled three pages and bled onto a fourth. Paperclipped to the edge of the back cover were two photographs. The first one, taken during the Berlin Airlift in 1949, depicted March, late twenties: square-jawed, but noticeably plain, dressed as a civilian, and grinning predatory teeth. The second one was more recent: Charlie March standing upon the eagle-and-shield seal of the CIA, accepting an award from former Director William Webster. Clenching his now-jowled jaw to square it out. But for his rangy mane, his plainness had aged him into spies' twilight innocuousness.

"Public Affairs trotting out a 'Hero of the Past' Trailblazer *'Profiles in Courage'* to counter some bad press ready to come out?" I said.

Just to make words. I am a lawyer. Words are important. Words are my life.

Alcohol: provide me.

"Charlie March is dead," said Harker.

"He *was* getting on in years."

"And whoever planted the bomb on his yacht in Key Largo this morning agreed."

"Who'd kill Charlie March? Cold War's over. He's been in the open all this time. Wrote a bestselling autobiography."

"Which we're happy to let the FBI read. What won't make us happy is them digging through forty years of our secrets. I shouldn't need to remind you."

"Remind me what?" I asked.

"We're a kinder and gentler America."

"Coming from the only president to have previously served as Director of Central Intelligence; I thought Poppy Bush meant it as an inside joke."

Harker gave me his best sourpuss.

I said, "Look: is there something about this that the Seventh Floor needs protected?"

"Hardly. It's a Cold War hiccup—he's dead—who gives a fuck?"

Not knowing where this was going, how or why it had anything to do with me, I grew impatient. I lowered the file into my lap. "I don't understand what you need from me. Likewise, knowing you have zero respect for what I do here, Mr. Harker, I'm a bit baffled why you're discussing it *with* me…"

I stood up and offered Charlie March's file jacket back to him. After all, it was my office. I was certain my phone would soon start ringing and the attention I'd be receiving, civilian though it might be, would supersede whatever involvement Harker imagined I should have with the old hero's murder.

"Sit down. If this incident didn't tangentially involve you, you're damn right I wouldn't have you here making me hate sofas because you're on one."

"This involves me?"

"March mentioned a name."

"It wouldn't be mine. I only met the man twice, sir. To shake hands. Not to talk—no talking."

"He mentioned," Harker began, then set his mouth as if his next words were poison, "Nathan Muir."

He gave that a second to poison me.

"Old bastard decided to take his country down with the ship by asking the Coast Guard—and I quote—'Thank Nathan for me and tell him he never murdered a soul.'"

"That doesn't mean anything." Hardly confident, I added, "What do *you* think it means?"

"Who in Christ knows? Except Muir. Meaning, you have to get to Muir, debrief him, and lock his mouth before the FBI get their dicks down his throat."

"You don't like me…"

"That's right, Aiken."

"Muir hates my guts."

"Yet, you're the only 'legal mind' within the Agency he's ever taken advice from."

I frowned. "Muir's on sabbatical. He could be anywhere."

"He's not."

"Where is he?"

"Captiva Island."

"Florida?" I asked, my heart sinking faster than Charlie March's sailing yacht.

Harker stretched his mouth with a humorless grin. "Imagery Analysis says Muir could have practically seen the explosion from his back porch."

4

I'VE GOTTEN OFF TRACK, mired in me when my destination is Muir. Where was I? Macallan–Madeline–twenty-five. Rainwater. Muir offering me the kitty cup.

"Mister Muir, did I not just tell you 'No, thank you'?"

"You're lying." He jammed the mug into my open palm. My hand reflexively closed around it.

"You know what Charlie March would say?"

Not once during our two days together did Muir ever refer to March by anything other than both names at once: Charlie March.

I placed the mug on the table. Muir looked askance.

"What I'm here for," I said. "And no thank you. I do not drink. I don't want to drink. It wouldn't be good for me."

"'Good?' You think I'm trying to make you the better of something?"

"Of what? It wouldn't be good for *me*."

"I'm not deaf. Hell, Aiken, I'm trying to bring you down to my level. Suit yourself." Muir finished his, pounded back mine, refilled both.

Scotch and rainfall.

He lit a cigarette. Thrusting it for accent, as if he were warming up for darts, he said, "If you asked Charlie March, he'd tell you that what happened to him out on the water this morning was simply the returning echo of his first infant cry."

Sterling Hayden, who played General Jack T. Ripper in *Dr. Strangelove*, was one of us. Served as an undercover OSS (Office of Strategic Services, precursor to my CIA) officer, infiltrating Yugoslavia and—fuck you, Nathan Muir, because this is the double edge of bringing it up today—committing *assassinations* in Occupied Croatia during the Second World War.

"Echo-infant-bullshit, Muir. I'm here to make you understand that we are facing potentially serious FBI blowback on account of Mr. March's mention of your name."

"Shut up and listen for once because this is important. Because—and not to put too fine a point on this—you're boring. I'd rather listen to seagulls fart in the rain than listen to you drop your bird-turd comments all over my ears." He drank and gauged me for umbrage I couldn't muster.

I'd been sent to get Muir's confession, followed by his resignation signed in ink, whether he'd killed March or not.

I said nothing.

"You don't find the first part of Charlie March's statement a bit curious?" he said.

"What statement?"

"Charlie March made it—maybe not to the Coast Guard but at least enough for us to know what he was saying in his head."

I'd never heard Muir make so little sense. He made sure to always make sense, which meant this nonsense made a kind of perfect, coded sense I had better decipher.

"We all got an inner dialogue. That is, if you're normal."

"Screw you, Mr. Muir."

"*And* if you drink. Hell, 'specially if you drink. Me, for example. Clear as I can remember, my inner dialogue began the day I recognized myself in the mirror at age three. 'Why, *you're* that Nathan everyone's fussing about all this time.'"

"Three seems a little old for that."

"Some of us don't have your acuity. But if you don't believe I was acquainted with Charlie March well enough after more than forty years of being *his* bitch to recognize what his inner voice would be telling him at the telling moment of his life, then drop back a few years to the time he made the statement out loud."

I huffed exasperation. "You're making no sense."

"You're just too sober to understand me. I remember it exactly: me and Charlie March. And that poisoner, Fred—whose real name we told people was Solomon—the guy Langley'd sent us to help make a permanent alteration to President Patrice Lumumba's health."

"1961? Who cares? Shut up. I'm here about today."

"Solomon. Sent to assassinate the poor Lumumba whom Charlie March had worked so hard to put into power. That's right: '61. Down there in the Congo, where we watched him go commie, like all good dictators must, and begin building an army rather than cleaning up his fucking yard. He, by the way—poisoner Solomon that is—died at Langley not too long after that. This is before your time—"

"What would I know? I was eleven."

"And you thought three was late." Muir rolled his cigarette between his fingers. "Happened in a chemistry lab in the basement. Cut his foot on a tiny shard of glass had something unclean on it. What he was doing in his socks at work... well, it's all very mysterious."

To be truthful, there was a poisoner sent by Langley to Muir and March in the Congo... yes, in 1961... when things down there started going bad.

"That scientist's name was Ezra and you, and Mr. March, were supposed to call him Solomon—not Fred—and there are not now, nor have ever been in the past, basement poison labs at Langley and you know that."

Muir ran a finger around the crystal edge of his glass. It made an appropriately spooky sound.

"Come to think of it, when Charlie March said it, he was only repeating the words the Baluba juju-man said to us; 'Hear that, Nathan? My death will be nothing more than the returning echo of my infant cry.'"

Muir lit a fresh cigarette from the butt of his previous. He dropped the butt out of sight.

"Mr. Muir, I am not interested in long-ago Congolese witch doctors."

"Grow interested. See, the Baluba believe that contained within that first gasp of air—our first infant cry—is the story of our entire lives. We're born and we cry out, and that cry echoes from hut or hospital or home, from behind the plow-ox, rice paddy, taxicab, or whorehouse—wherever we're born—across time and space. It echoes all the way to heaven, where heard by God it is judged imperfect as all of us are—even you, fancy that—and He returns it to earth, where it echoes along the path of our lives until it finds us and slays us."

"Does their god ever judge a baby's cry perfect?" I said.

"Don't be stupid. It's not 'their' God. It's God. God, Aiken—His one and only—it's what we're all in business to fight over. And no, He does not. He did once, but mankind made sure that didn't work out. Lynched that fella up on the cross they talk so much about."

"If that isn't the most nihilistic view…"

"Are you listening to me?" He nudged the mug closer to me with the tip of a finger. "I am speaking of a Congo juju-man. A witch doctor, like you said. The kind of headshrinker who really shrinks heads. This guy read Charlie March's fortune from a bunch of bird bones and charred teeth and dung marbles he threw in the dirt from a little leather bag he'd sewn from some dead schmuck's scrotum."

"Christ, Muir, you're drunk and you're out of your mind. We'll take this up in the morning."

Muir spreads his hands as if to admit he never tried to prove otherwise.

I didn't stand.

He shook his head and turned away from me to the darkness. He didn't face me at all until he'd drunk half his current drink, smoked the rest of his cigarette, and stubbed out the butt with his toe. Putting the flattened filter by itself on the table, he considered me, smiling broadly as if seeing me for the first time and delighted in my presence.

"Rusty Aiken," he said expansively.

"It's Russell." I soft-pedaled. "Please."

"Russell now? Always thought Rusty was better the name of a nail or some woman's Airedale that gets hit by a car and turns her into a lesbian."

"Your third wife showed Airedales, didn't she, Muir?"

"Lesbianism wasn't the problem between us."

"Oh, right. That was Tom Bishop."

In my mind's eye, the rain froze in midair at the withering look he shot me.

"We're not talking about Tom Bishop. We're talking about booze."

"Jesus Christ! Focus: we're talking about March. About blowback. He died speaking *your* name. What the fuck happened to Charlie March and why did he say your name with his murder?"

"Aren't you here to tell me?"

"No. He linked you to his death and he was publicly known to have worked for us."

"Charlie March: the original Cold War hero." Muir's last word dripped with an insinuation that made heroism a vulgarity.

"Mr. March was publicly recognized as a Trailblazer. It's our highest award. Only fifty of them ever given," I said. Then, in self-pity, I opened my guard. "At the time I thought you deserved the honor more than he."

Laughter in Muir's eyes. "Next."

Angry, indignant, the least bit humiliated, I averted my gaze. It had only one place to go: the coffee mug.

When Muir spoke again, which was that very moment but felt like the time it takes a baby's cry to echo its way to God and back, he sounded every one of his sixty-two years. "Your problem, Russell, is you believe things."

I lifted the coffee mug. Hating Muir, I toasted him. "I wish I'd never believed in you. Or in myself the way you taught me to disbelieve."

Muir sized me up and damn it if he wasn't proud of me. "Now that I will drink to."

Stalling the drink I'd known since I'd arrived I was going to hell on anyway, I said, "You know, after the Wall came down, I only stayed with the job out of a sense of obligation to you."

And to Bishop. But I didn't tell him that. He'd done enough to Tom Bishop—things Bishop didn't even know had been done to him. Things I hoped Bishop would never find out. Bishop: the one person we could agree was the better of us both.

I said, "You know what kind of shit staying on for you has gotten me, Muir? Both professionally and personally?"

I wanted so badly to put down that mug. I wanted even more to drink it.

"Awww, Wittle Wusty Aiken, bwaiming Big, Bad Nat'an Mewer for wuining his wife."

God dammit. He knows.

"What—did you bang her too?"

"Watch your mouth."

Truly angry, Muir snatched the coffee mug from my hand. I snatched it back and drank my whiskey in one big gulp. Only I did this without benefit of the years of constant practice Muir carried under his belt. I coughed and spluttered and forced myself to swallow back the rush of vomit.

"There. Bet you feel better now."

I wiped my lips and nostrils. "Yes. I'll remember, in fact, to recommend it."

"With or *sans* cigarette butt?"

I blinked. Had something gone down with the whiskey? I thought something had. I gaped at the table. There was only the second butt. I gaped at the floor. The first butt wasn't there.

I faced Muir. He showed me two empty hands. Both sides.

"You're an asshole," I said.

"Yep. But never the way you think."

He passed one hand over the other and the missing butt reappeared.

"I didn't sleep with Madeline. You're a worthless piece of shit to even think it. That you expressed it out loud defiles you, and me, and Madeline—*again*, if I understand you correctly."

I bit my tongue, afraid to speak, to reveal.

Muir chose to push. "Tell me this—and then I'll drop it. You loved Madeline the instant you saw her?"

"You know I did."

"Okay, then. When we're done with the business at hand, I'll sort that out for you too. I promise."

Muir lifted an ashtray from a windowsill behind his shoulder. It was already half full. Had he been planning the disappearing butt the whole time?

I'm that predictable.

I spread-finger swept the alcohol sweat from my brow into my wet hair.

Fuck you, Nathan Muir. Fuck you, and fuck Madeline, and fuck Mel Finley—Double-D: Dr. at one end, PhD at the other like a bra clutching his gynecomastia between. Fuck you for reminding me of my essential truth and daring me with your black-souled but oh-so-wanted day-late dollar-short hope.

All I did was smirk. "In legal terms, that offer could be considered a bribe."

Muir loved it when a protégé, or in my case protégé-turned-betrayer, managed a hit in verbal fencing.

"It could be. And it is. Doesn't mean I don't genuinely care about you."

At an earlier point in our relationship, his riposte would have stabbed me right in the heart as intended, but it didn't today because Nathan Muir is incapable of—strike that, willfully disinterested in—genuine compassion.

Or affection.

Or even the rigmarole of decency.

I'd always marveled at this because in spite of all that, Nathan Muir commanded more respect, more loyalty, more honor in the men and women he recruited (and, yes, I'm still—ef me—one of them) than any other operations officer I'd ever come in contact with at CIA. He watched this go on in my face and he smoked.

The rain drummed.

"'You can walk back everything but your words, Russell. It's one of the Nathan Muir—"

"Rules of Thumb."

"'Rules of Thumb.' You'd be smart to remember that."

It sounded stupid when he said it, but it was the one "rule" I'd chosen to follow well and, because of that, made Muir decide

I'd best serve the Agency as a legal counsel rather than as the ops officer I'd been so desperate to become.

The alcohol was doing the trick. I'd not wanted it to do this to me for thirteen years and yet desperately I loved it. As I gathered my senses in remembered ways, I admitted to myself I was ashamed to be at Muir's house. Ashamed that not only had I come to finish him off by getting his confession, but that I had volunteered a plan to the Young Turks—the nickname Muir called DDO Harker (the real boss) and Director Folger (the appointed-anointed one) to their faces, but that I only had courage to call them behind their backs and then only in my mind—to finish him off with the Company completely without having been asked to volunteer a plan for that at all. But that's what we do as lawyers. Work behind people's backs. Muir had been asking for it to echo back at him all those years ago since he bore me for the Agency and forced the deadening dead-end job onto me.

5

I SCOFF NOW at Muir's Baluba jujube tarot reader, but had I known of this Congo-bongo back around the time of the American Bicentennial, I'd have invested in hat pins and had Muir's swami airmail me his very best Tom Bishop voodoo doll.

My first meeting with Bishop took place illegally and on-paper, not in-person, whereupon I hated him on printed sight. An operations officer of the Clandestine Service is never caught with papers on him; I'm caught if I don't have all the relevant papers on me all the time.

I eat, drink, sleep, and drown in paper.

I drown in words.

By the Bicentennial, Tom Bishop was turning up in too much of my paper. Taking more words than, I reasoned, his fair share.

My division, the Office of General Counsel, is the least liked internally. When Muir stuffed me into it, I was one of fourteen lawyers in an open workroom-style building last used in the Second World War for who knows what, constructed in the Civil War for what more, and who knows?

It's changing now.

We've been moved into the green-glass goblin monstrosity of the New Headquarters Building since the Monday after Muir's birthday, this year. That would be March 25, 1991. There are now almost one hundred and fifty employees in the OGC, sixty of them lawyers. Me still ranked—but for Muir's stubborn care and my stubborn capitulation—fourteenth from the top.

The problem with this job. The problem I scratch—or beat—my head at, depending on the day, and depending on the laws that need subversion that day—*id est*, the act of subverting (not overthrowing) governments (although that's what a lot of it's for, which kind of makes my point, doesn't it?)—the problem is: the CIA exists to break laws, not to follow them. While the laws that the CIA break are those of foreign countries, our country holds that we keep and enforce laws that govern the how, to whom, and why, and the in-what-method, where-the-fuck-fore, there-the-fuck me of-we who can be allowed to break them. All so we can force foreign entry and stay inside, invisible, stealing secrets in the bliss of enemy ignorance and continuous divulgence.

On July 4, 1976, three years since DCI Schlesinger's wing-clipping reports known as the Family Jewels—commissioned in response to the Company's involvement in the Watergate scandal that revealed the Agency's direct violations of its charter with its illegal wiretapping, domestic surveillance, assassination plots, and human experimentation—they *mea culpa*-ed those skeletons in our closet in an attempt to lock the closet door on the rest of them. Three months since the Achilles tendon-clipping external Church Committee published their six books, pulling out said skeletons and re-fleshing their bones with our attempts to assassinate foreign leaders (including, but not limited to, Patrice Lumumba of the Congo, Rafael Trujillo of the Dominican Republic, Ngo Dinh Diem of Vietnam, General René Schneider of Chile, and Fidel Castro of Cuba), President Ford—effective in his affable ineffectiveness—released the books and issued Executive Order 11905, Muir's favorite, banning US-sanctioned assassinations of foreign leaders.

July 4, 1976. The day we'd Yankee-Doodled ourselves into Bicentennial fever, the day of the Tall Ships sailing into New York Harbor, the day that culminated with the dumbest fireworks display in our nation's capital the world cast its eyes to our feet to witness.

Two words: ground displays. Yep, flags, and eagles, and that rascally fife-and-drum trio of walking wounded all ignited and illuminated. For the earth worms.

While everyone was looking down at the flashing of fire above the flattened sidewalk gum in Washington, that night in West Berlin, Muir launched his operation to flush out Ambassador Cathcart's wife as an East German Stasi asset. In true Muir fashion, he accomplished this by letting it slip to the woman across a one-night-stand goose-down pillow—a long-necked kinduva goose herself—that he was smuggling an East German economist, Dr. Ivan Gridenko, across the East-West line. The officer Muir sent to do the exfiltration, Thomas Bishop, was called off at the very last minute. Muir forced Bishop to abandon Gridenko to certain execution. But the mere threat of Gridenko's defection possibly exposing Ann Cathcart's treason proved too much for the ambassador's wife, who fled across the Iron Curtain into the arms of her East German lover and Stasi handler, Heinz Trettin.

Her murder one morning, as she stepped outside of the Pankow district Gethsemane Church into an assassin's crosshairs, was investigated neither East nor West. Her usefulness having met its "use by" date, ready to be poured down the drain. Both sides happy. Crime never solved. Buy a new carton of milk and get a new down pillow.

Do geese see God?

Muir engaged my services—after the fact, I might add—to make sure the mission documentation (LACE PICKLE aka *The Cathcart Affair*) reflected an operation *whereby* the loss of Gridenko was unplanned and enacted to protect the life and freedom of Muir's operative—read Tom Bishop—rather than Muir's true and original plan to let Gridenko take a bullet to trap Ann Cathcart. In other words, I dutifully executed pre-dated paperwork that explained the exposure of Ann Cathcart as collateral and accidental to a botched Gridenko extraction, rather than the purpose of the whole damn thing all along.

Any other way, Tom Bishop, and by extension Nathan Muir, would have been complicit in the premeditated murder of one Dr. Gridenko, defector. Bad for business, terrible for congressional oversight of the CIA charter—and would have triggered investigation into the assassination of the long-necked Mrs. Ambassador Ann Cathcart.

I know Tom killed her. No one cares. Except him. And Gridenko and Gridenko's children. And Muir, because it bagged him Bishop's soul.

I didn't hate Tom Bishop for that.

But *The Cathcart Affair* wasn't the first time his name had come across my desk with Muir's operational paperwork in need of legal sanitization. I'd ignored Bishop the first time. After all, he wasn't CIA when Muir had resourced him as a sniper from the Marine Corps for a Phoenix Program late hit in Vietnam, when his go-to hitter, a regular Sergeant York name of Binh, caught a mortar round with his teeth and Muir had come up short for a cross-border grand slam inside Laos.

I didn't hate Bishop for *that*.

It began with the combination of the two, and how a Marine with nothing going for him but a long gun with a nifty scope got from a Xuan Loc hooch to Checkpoint Charlie, Berlin, as a full-employed, scrubbed-behind-the-ears, salaried, benefited, insured, and indemnified, capital-*C* Company man who supplanted me as the apple of Muir's eye. I hated Tom Bishop because Thomas Bishop got my ticket. He got to be the Muir-promise-reneged *me*.

I hated the job I had-slash-have. When I'd first accepted it with bold, crooked-smiling brown-eyed disappointment, Muir had sworn the lawyering would be a short bench before I'd join him in the field in one way or another.

I didn't believe him, but I'd wanted to.

I pretended to.

That kind of loyalty is supposed to buy you something. But I knew, once I sat down at my little desk beneath ironwork rafters sooted by World War Two government-free Lucky Strike cigarettes and shat on by "Johnny Comes Marching Home" pigeons, I was behind the desk until Muir smoked himself dead or I laid an egg. I took my seat—no complaints from Trusty Rusty—to impress Muir with my dedication. To him. To *his* CIA.

I am profoundly experienced at sitting.

It's not that I'm disturbed he didn't pick me. It's that he'd been cheating behind my back. With some socio-psycho friend-and-family-less shooter—psych profile stolen and read: no father, Boy Scouts, unaccompanied to the rifle range—little Tommy Bishop.

Don't think I was jealous. Jealousy had nothing to do with this. Jealousy implies envy. Envy—the desire to have a quality, a possession, or other desirable attribute(s) belonging to Bishop—was not mine.

Give me a flippin' break.

I didn't want anything of Bishop's. Nothing he could ever give me. Nothing I would ever dream to take. Everything he was, did, had—inside and out—I dismissed in hand and out. Would've been, would've done, possessed, exhibited all other things that Tom Bishop could want, think of, or comprehend. No desire. In perpetuity. I wanted what was due *me*. What was *mine*.

Or should've supposed to have been.

He preferred to drink only beer. It was in Muir's recruitment prospectus, inside the larger profile set: training records, psych (I've mentioned), personal, administrative, payroll, you-name-it profile.

I peeked.

No jealousy. No envy. I swore off beer the minute I read that tidbit. Tossed the twelve pack of Natty Bohs from the trunk of my car that afternoon before I even drove onto the expressway; the case I had in the kitchen I gave to the cute nurses—Cutie and Perky—in the apartment down the hall. Beer had always been the periodical stops interrupting the flow of real beverages, anyway. The clear ones of my clarity. I am a lawyer—you should see how far I can run on commas and ice—or up with a twist—not choosy. Weren't then either.

And not a single accident. Not a single ticket driving or walking or laid out in an alley. Not a single hangover since before college. Never got caught up in sloppy dorm-life stupid alcohol hijinks. I'd passed that danger zone of behavior safely before I was eighteen and an adult and could do any real damage to myself and others.

And drinking wasn't as frowned on in the workplace as it is now.

There were plenty of office drink cart, bottom desk drawer, flask-in-pocket imbibers at headquarters as there were in the field. If it didn't interfere with the work, sometimes it helped.

There are nine employee AA groups offered by the Office of Personnel at Langley, but there are far more employee groups who gather for, take your pick: California wine tasting, Burgundies and Bordeauxes, Single Malts of the Highlands, Single-Barrel Bourbons of Kentucky, German Beers, Island Rums, "Some Like 'Em Cold" Sakes—every desk and territory getting in on the act, in fact. And never was there a successful agency alcoholic who found themselves frowned upon for drinking. It was when the drinking started frowning upon you that you either lost it all or got lost all in it.

TWO YEARS AFTER the self-inflicted castration of our Agency independence, Muir and I were drinking tequila inside what would be the fifty-second suite of the Roosevelt Hotel, New York City, had this suite suited a publicly displayed number. Accessed by private elevator at the end of the long-ago-sealed walking tunnel from Grand Central Station, this suite has belonged to the CIA since 1968, *suite* quickly having become a generous term in the context of the fine hotel it was hidden within. Neither of us cared too much for tequila, too sweet, but Muir had brought it anyway.

The room is uncomfortably functional: a worn sitting area, a dining room with mismatched utilitarian table and chairs. There is a stained coffee maker atop a well-stocked mid-century modern cocktail cabinet. Stimulants or depressants depending on need. An old refrigerator chugs along in a corner. The second bathroom is fitted out as a functioning medical bay. Ashtrays are everywhere. In parlance, a safe house. Good for debriefings, clandestine meetings, or those stifling waits for the ring of a phone. We weren't supposed to be checked in there. Not Muir and certainly not me—hence his BYOB. How he'd gotten access, I didn't know and I didn't question.

Whenever Muir faces a lock, he always has the key.

I never went into either of the bedrooms, so they may have been first class like the rest of the hotel. But I doubt it. Safe houses are designed for begrudged discomfort. The definition of *guest* always carefully balanced for everyone's private acknowledgment on the tenuous ledge of *prisoner*.

I was there at Muir's behest. Pens, legal pads, typewriter, boilerplate docs with fill-in-the-blanks for justifying the unjustifiable and legalizing the criminal. Muir had made me his go-to attorney, flattering twenty-eight-year-old me into more loyalty by telling me, "Rusty, the general attitude of the General Counsel Office is to say no to ops and to take as long as possible to say it. I've found with you that you can work it not to say *no*, but to say *yes if* or *no but* and help people like me do what we want to do by stretching the constricting sleeves of the law long past the knuckles of illegal overreach."

Mainly, this involved me finding ways to convert Muir's *covert actions* that the law Carter-cum-Ford-cum-Senator Church-cum Directors Colby-Schlesinger required reported to Congress within five days, convert them into *intelligence operations* the law didn't require reported to anyone. I dissembled the whole Achilles heel remark.

The fact you can't remember what that "Achilles heel remark" was without looking back is an object lesson in how good I am at this dissembling. Don't like it? Sue me.

My writing I have made my own Clandestine Service. My words are my spies and assassins and thieves. They break the law, steal as much meaning as they can, and set murder onto truth literally under your nose and in plain sight. The page is the field of battle, the words my agents of subterfuge. Born in my head, alive in black and white silence, my cold, unmoving, seemingly inert words commit their deceptions in the loud living color of the very real world. To write what isn't seen, to make what happens next invisible.

Muir told me this would be one of those op plans with the added legal problem that CIA's very charter we all worked under needed to be bypassed so that Muir's officer in New York could operate freely on home turf.

"Otherwise," Muir said, "how's the kid gonna relax?"

My Bishop sonar should have pinged at "the kid." He used to call me that, but now Bishop was his youngest protégé.

Yet Tom Bishop was in Berlin.

I know because I kept an unlawful eye on his agent payouts and personal expenditures through a sweet data input secretary in the Office of Accounting. Hometown beauty-queen kinda woman named Nancy. Nancy the Numbers Numbskull. Through her veritable twin, Derrick in personnel, I kept track of Bishop's performance reviews and his most recent posting request, which is Moscow. Derrick the Numbskull Numbskull. I achieved their complicity by assuring them that Seventh Floor was grooming Bishop for great things, great things Muir—whom they feared more than the director—was rewiring to make Bishop look bad and them incompetent.

They weren't and he wasn't, but they didn't know that, and it's loyalty up, loyalty down. I told them, "When Muir gets caught popping his boner, I won't let you take the black eye from it."

So, with my ass counting the sofa springs, my materials spread out on the cigarette-burned coffee table, I was confident that the clandestine officer coming through the door would not be Tom Bishop.

"You're in Berlin," I blurted to the man who, at 8 p.m., March 13, 1978, stepped into the room from the elevator.

He gave Muir—who grinned canary feathers—a cock-eyed look, then smiled pleasantly and sniped me with sarcasm: "Absolutely. Just flew in from New York." He offered me his hand. "Tom Bishop."

6

WHO DOESN'T RISE to an offered hand? Naturally, I came to my feet, but this was *his* hand, so, unnaturally, I started back down, thought how stupid I looked, and split the difference. I clutched at his firm grip, bent but un-fawning. "Russell Aiken?"

"You askin' or telling? Know all aboutcha. The prudent jurist who keeps the boss here out of all the trouble he makes for me," said Bishop.

"Just trying to save the world for my kids," Muir said.

Bishop hadn't stopped looking at me. "Jus' having fun with you, Mr. Aiken."

What's with the "Mister"? I am only 10,226 hours—that's 426 days—older than you.

"Ever it said, I'm ever the good sport, *Mr.* Bishop."

"Said never by me," Muir scoffed.

"What you've 'said' for *me*, I can't thank you enough for the hours you put in on my behalf. Muir talks."

"Everyone talks," said Muir. "Don't either of you forget it."

My cage. My coffin. My country.

He was rugged and natural. He had a fucking great inner light that was dead-on honest. Dead-on real. Fuck. You shook Tom Bishop's hand and you wanted to be friends with him. No, not that. This: you shook hands with Tom Bishop and you felt his greatest desire was to be friends with you.

This is when I gave in to my hatred.

He gestured if he could sit down next to me. I scooched over obediently.

"I'm just an overgrown Boy Scout," he said, "but I believe in the 'Loyalty up, loyalty down' this agency asks for."

The SOB mocked me without even trying. Mocked my private thoughts inside my mind as if I'd given him permission. And, like everything, it came effortlessly to Tom Bishop.

He folded his long legs between the sofa and table—which I pushed to make room—"And I see no better model of it than in the loyalty Nathan carries for you, Mr. Aiken, and that you obviously hold for him."

I am not obvious. I hold nothing. Ever.

"Hey, just call me Rusty."

I hate Rusty! Why am I slobbering?!

Muir rolled his eyes. "Ace the Wonder Dog starring in *The Adventures of Rusty!*"

I gave a crooked smirk. I'd been teased over those old *Lassie* rip-offs every day after KTLA Channel Five broadcast them in afterschool rerun, and I let my mind go to a half-dozen great comebacks I couldn't quite think of then (or right now), but while I wandered the hollow halls of my head, Tom Bishop struck back:

"Don't know the dog one, Muir. How 'bout Rusty Staub, best designated hitter in the Major League, plays for Detroit, only player with five hundred hits for four different teams; or Rusty Crawford, hockey Hall-of-Famer; there's Rusty Tillman, Washington Redskins Special Teams captain—? Oh, got another one: Rusty Bryant, alto sax sideman for Sonny Phillips."

"Well? Better to be eaten to death by rust than scoured to nothing with perpetual motion—as they say." Muir shook a spear back at him.

"You know, I'm fine with Russell too."

Bishop shouldered off a beat-up leather kit bag, not unlike the briefcase I'd planned to start carrying. Copycat. He reached inside it. "Mr. Aiken. What's your favorite book?"

I gave Muir a vexatious look I'd been storing up for years.

"Yes, Rusty, it is a real question."

Bishop gripped a well-thumbed paperback. I couldn't see its title.

"I guess, uh, classics, um, Dickens. *A Tale of Two Cities*. It sounds dry, but it's literature's best espionage story. I like it. A lot."

Muir chuckled. He did this in his throat, which made it sound that much more derogatory. "A drunk lawyer book."

Bishop: "For or about?"

"Both." Muir poured and offered a tequila. "Speaking of which?"

Bishop took it. Drank a little. Put down the glass—never touched the tequila again—but said, "Something you can't get overseas in Manhattan." He winked at me. "Reminds me of home."

"Mexico?" I babbled.

"Los Angeles. San Fernando Valley. Muir says you're from the other valley—San Gabriel?"

I nodded. I flicked a finger at his hand. "Book?"

He handed it to me. Stephen King's *The Shining*. "You like scary, this'll kill ya."

I didn't read books like this—

"Thanks. I love this author. This'll be good."

—pulp horror? Give me a break.

"Cool. I'll look at the *Cities* one. Might've been assigned in school once, but I copied on the test. Teacher should have said it was lawyers and spies. No wonder you love your job."

God, I hate sincerity. Madeline oozes it.

We got down to business. Muir mapped out the operation's CONPLAN, for which he saw two legal hurdles.

There were seven.

At noon the next day, the Israeli ambassador to the UN would address the Security Council. Afterward, he would answer the press in the First Basement Conference Room 4 directly below the General Assembly Hall. Agents of Libya, Syria, Lebanon, and the PLO would be among the press and delegate member protesters. Bishop, posing as press, would provoke a negative encounter with one or more of aforementioned enemy agents. In the scuffle, he would lose a notebook, abandoning it for them to find. Bishop departs. Notebook is analyzed and found to contain Israeli intelligence. Buried within said intelligence will be a piece of actionable false intel that it is Muir's intention they act upon.

"This operation falls under Middle East Section purview," I said. "Why you? Why Bishop?"

"My question exactly." Bishop wanted me to know he could pay attention.

"Simple. The intelligence we're passing falls under my Eastern Bloc operations. It pertains solely to Soviet interference through their East German proxies."

"Okay," I said. "But why Bishop?"

Muir grinned. "Tom is anxious to transit to Moscow. Cherry on top of the Cold War sundae. This mission, providing it goes off without a hitch, seals the deal for him."

Bishop flashed a look appropriately thankful.

Muir continued, "Two birds, one stone."

The specifics of the mission—the precise nature of the false intel Muir desired the enemy to "capture," being need-to-know, I wasn't BIGOT-listed to know it. It wasn't offered and I did not request as I didn't even rate an extra spoon for a taste.

I should have. A lot of who I am and whom I've become was happening in that room. Instead, I offered my best legal opinion.

"This is a clusterfuck of epic proportions waiting to happen, and you know it, Mr. Muir."

"He only slaps *me* with a 'mister' when he's scolding."

Bishop crosshaired me with his eyes. "I'm okay with the cluster. Explain the fuck."

Before I could, Muir jumped in, jumping as you would to stomp out a hot foot. I let him. He'd given me plenty of matches. Muir said to Bishop, "Both the posing as press and the operating inside US borders go against our charter." He said to me, "I think I can walk us around those. So, clickety-clack?" He pantomimed fingers on a typewriter.

"That's just two. I have five more. One: espionage enacted against an ally."

"Informal ally. We do not have a recognized alliance with Israel. Hell, 1965—they've not kept it a secret they stole six hundred pounds of highly enriched weapons-grade uranium from the Apollo facility in Pittsburgh."

Bishop's gaze tripped back to Muir. "They did?" Muir nodded. "That must have been a fun smash-and-grab."

Muir just looked at me.

"'Two wrongs *make* a right' is not an argument we want to be forced into," I said. "Regarding our allied position or not: Harry Truman recognized Israel eleven minutes after its declaration of independence. The United States and Israel have had a special relationship, which has evolved over time into a web of military, economic, academic, bureaucratic, and personal connections at the local, state, and federal levels. Israel and the United States signed a secret memorandum of understanding thirteen years ago, *in 1965*, which marked the beginning of this strategic alliance. I cannot argue before any assembled legal body that we are anything but close political, military, and social-cultural-spiritual allies."

Bishop leaned back, the smirk on his face letting Muir know he liked seeing me outmaneuver him. The fool. As if this spy business were a game.

"It would be easier if I list the rest *in toto*, then knock them off in bulk—minimize stones, maximize birds," I said.

Counting Muir's first two—*illegal press cover* and *operating inside US borders*—and my first, *espionage against an ally* (number three to the total)—I'd identified four more legal hurdles, for a grand total of seven. They were as follows:

1. (4). Conducting a Covert Operation ("Mission") without congressional reporting.
2. (5). Transporting Secret/Top Secret intelligence ("Material") outside of a secure location in the execution of the Mission.
3. (6). Supplying the Material to known and identified agents of an enemy service in the execution of the Mission.
4. (7). Through the provoked, intended, and assumed foreign acquirement and analysis of the Material deliberately provided in the execution of the Mission, the revealing of Sources and Methods.

"All right," Muir said. He checked for a cigarette in his Marlboro soft pack.

I'd watched him fish out the last one some minutes before. He had, as he always did, fingered around inside, verifying that the pack was empty. And, as always, he checked again now, crumpled the empty pack, opened a fresh one, lit up.

"Over time, that's going to kill me," said Bishop.

In 1978, we hadn't heard much about, or at least paid attention to, the questionable dangers of secondhand smoke. But even then, that kind of busybodying was juvenile, unsubstantiated, and annoying. Readying another tick against Bishop, I was surprised and, I'll say it now, amused by what he said next.

"You know the fucking things are empty. You want me to keep working with you, you stop the stingy finger-fishing routine and just get on to the next pack before I die from the tired routine."

The fucker was a little bit funny. Muir never did it again. That entire day. I poured us—me and Muir—tequila shots and silently toasted myself a pledge to make this legal process as difficult for both of them as I could.

"All right, all right. These birds you're stoning: cassowaries or doves?" said Muir.

"I'm sorry?" I said.

"The cassowary is the most dangerous bird on the planet," said Bishop. "Along with being one of the largest. Taller than me, they can slice you completely in half with one kick."

"Oh. *That* cassowary. Never see him coming before it's too late." I leaned into my ignorance.

"They're fast, sure." Bishop deadpanned right back. "But in the Australian outback you'd see 'em—like I said, they're big, comical-looking—you'd see 'em coming. 'Course, in the New Guinea rainforest—" He must have judged my frustration with him to be at the spewing-out point because he added, "And I'm just messing with ya again. Look, I don't want to have to shoot my way out of this thing tomorrow. You *can* fix Muir's brilliant plan, right? I'm counting on you, Mr. Rusty Russell Aiken. Just nervous about getting dead over it."

Damn him, if his stacking of my names like that hinted not at patronization but fondness. How's a guy get away with *that*?

I ditched the game, retreating to the arms of expertise. "By removing all covert op elements from the plan, we get rid of half our problems. We achieve that by having Bishop receive the notebook from a 'Brief Encounter' cutout at the press event. Therefore, two-five, three-six, and four-seven are eliminated."

"Talk normal, Aiken. I know the way you're saying it is for some mystifying reason more clear to you. But five, six, and seven is best for us. How does adding a cutout achieve this?" said Muir.

"The material—" I said.

"The intel in the notebook," said Muir.

"Yes. Bishop enters the UN basement empty-handed to *receive* intel. He's not carrying anything. The cutout is not revealed—I'll leave that up to you, but it needs to be someone whose identity can be legitimately redacted so that, were they revealed, it would not compromise sources and methods of other ongoing operations of superseding national security."

Muir flicked ash like snapping his fingers. "Doable."

"One stone, three birds." Bishop's eyes shined with amusement.

"Getting around the press pass is easy," I said. "Office of Technical Services can make up something as simple as a delivery service, or janitorial, or foreign official badge look exactly like a press pass to anyone who's been checking a whole fleet of them and glassy-eyed from it. Just can't say the word *press* or name any real or invented journalistic outlet."

CIA never creates cover ID with press, Red Cross, medical, or religious order. Allows the real ones not to get killed so much. At least in theory.

I consulted my notes. "Here's a cassowary."

Okay, I *was* into the game. I had another drink. I have to admit, I was having fun and the tequila, I decided, I'd been previously unfair to in its entire classification of alcohol. This tequila was tasty. "Big and stupid-looking, your second hitch is the one that can kick us."

Muir poured himself one. Offered the bottle to Bishop.

"Naw. I'm cool."

I said, "It's got the kick because it goes straight to our *raison d'être.*"

"Stop with the French talk. I hate it," said Muir.

I said, "Roosevelt only allowed the OSS charter—against incredible resistance from J. Edgar Hoover—only if operations were restricted to foreign soil. The FBI and DOJ are the only entities allowed intelligence operations in the United States. This was the first condition in the creation and chartering of the CIA."

"I got this," Bishop said. "All embassies, consulates, and missions—the UN being the largest—are foreign soil. I just have to make sure my scuffle doesn't get pushed to the street before I drop the material."

"He's right," Muir said.

"You're both wrong. And I don't have a way around it. Article 22, Vienna Convention on Diplomatic Relations 1961. To paraphrase from sections one through three: '*The premises of the mission shall be inviolable... The receiving State is under a special duty to take all appropriate steps to protect the premises of the mission against any intrusion or damage and to prevent any disturbance of the peace of the mission or impairment of its dignity. The premises of the mission... shall be immune from search, requisition, attachment, or execution.*'

"It's a determination of immunity, not sovereignty. The Vienna Convention does not state that the property belongs to the embassy's country. In the case of the UN, what country would you even assign it? The United Nations is protected and is considered UN property, but the territory does not belong to any state other than the United States."

That got them. I took another drink. In other company, it might have appeared excessive, but I was both a spy and an attorney. Separately, each are drinking vocations. Joined together, drinking becomes a spiritual calling of the highest drinking order.

"Anyone but you know this?" Muir frowned, but he was proud of me. I could tell.

"In the House Select and Senate Select Committees on Intelligence, if I assume they've watched more television and movies than studied Article 22 of the VCDR of '61… and my assumption borders on certainty… No. FBI and Justice? They exist to know this."

"I don't want to sound like a pussy—" said Bishop.

"Then don't ever start a sentence with 'I don't want to sound like a pussy,'" Muir said, pouring himself and me a shot.

"However," I said, "here's where the recent exposure of our Family Jewels—namely within the pages of the Rockefeller Report—give us our leeway. That report goes out of its way to note that in enacting the National Security Act of 1947, 'Congress contemplated that the CIA would be involved in *all* aspects'—emphasis mine—'of foreign intelligence, including collection.' Meaning: while Congress does not wish to have us interfere with the authorities of the FBI, nor become a secret police unit akin to the Gestapo in Nazi Germany, and recognizes that the Act limits the expanse of CIA activities to foreign intelligence and counterintelligence, as opposed to domestic intelligence, neither these provisions, nor any other portion of the Act, restrict the Agency's intelligence collection activities solely to overseas endeavors. Indeed, Rockefeller's commission points out that the Act's legislative history indicates Congress expects the CIA to collect intelligence inside the United States. To be clear: the Rockefeller Report *reaffirms*—"

"Emphasis yours?" said Muir, bored. Satisfied.

"Emphasis Rockefeller's, *ergo*, Congress. Reaffirms this operation is within our right. It doesn't need to go in the Concept Plan, but I'll hardwire it into the final OPLAN. We just can't step on Federal feet while Bishop is 'live.' If we don't, they'll happily dance on the other side of the ballroom. Feds have no choice."

We all three raised our glasses to that. Bishop, pussy, didn't drink.

He repeated, "I don't want to sound like a pussy, but if my mother found out I'd been busted by the FBI, I'm already lying to her about everything else in my life."

"I'd never do anything to upset Mrs. Bishop," Muir said. "Russell, I don't think it'll ever get to DOJ, but if it does, my favor account has enough of a balance to cover this one."

He took a drag and continued, "Okay, we've taken care of my two, and your five through seven. And then your other one. That's six," he said, blowing smoke. "I thought you said 'seven.'"

"Three-three," Bishop said with good-natured approval. "'Espionage enacted against an ally.' It's the most important element of Mr. Aiken's CONPLAN, why he left it for last, I'm guessing. And since, if you'd been listening, it's where the two sets of numbers meet, I'd say Russell is identifying the symmetry of my op is in this crux. Makes perfect sense why Mr. Aiken organized the numbers the way he did." He gave me a nod, hard and confident.

Son of a bitch, he'd seen my crossworded syllogism. Where three meets three... and pairs.

Muir regarded us as a couple of Jupiterians fallen from outer space. "Seems stupid. But I'll let you two own that."

Obvious to Bishop, Muir didn't see it. It is, though, how and why I'd done it that way. This Tom Bishop was sharp. A lot sharper than his files showed. They'd all missed this about Bishop.

But not me, and what is hatred but the active destruction of any admirational possibility for its subject allowing a fertile field for friendship to grow?

"Yes," I said. "Espionage enacted against an ally. Excellent. Without knowing the nature of the material or the intention behind its compromise, I will only say this, if it is *not* counterfeit material, then you will be passing our ally's secrets to our ally's enemy. If Israel discovers this—"

"No way they can," Muir said.

"—will the outcome be worth the blowback and will that blowback be something the Seventh Floor will withstand… *and*… stand by us?"

A worry line dropped between Bishop's eyebrows. He and I studied Muir, as Jupiterians might, for both artifice and confidence.

"Unequivocally," he said. "Yes."

"Then the way around it is crucial: you must appear to be protecting it; they must appear to be stealing it." I collected my materials and stood. "In that way, you will have 'enacted' nothing. I'll type this into the CONPLAN—takes ten, fifteen minutes, your signature, Muir, on that and you're good to go. Then I'll expand it into the official OPLAN. You can sign now on a blank signature page, or after it's done."

"Blanks are fine. I'll sign both now."

He followed me to the table and my typewriter. I found the appropriate sheets. It was after 11 p.m.

Muir signed twice.

He went to the phone. He called the Office of Technical Service officer standing by in the city, made arrangements for the not-a-press press pass. I cringed when he requested OTS print it in English and Hebrew. Delivery of the cover identity kit arranged, Muir grabbed his jacket. He said he'd leave the key card with me in case I wanted to go out for something to eat, but that I was to cut it up the middle, then cut both pieces across the center where the holes were and to throw out the pieces in various airport trashcans before my flight home.

I told him I didn't have scissors.

He told me to stop being a jackass. "Operational improvisation: buy some."

When I'd finished both documents, I was to lock them in the safe. He gave me the combination, had me memorize it, then memorize the number to call that would signal his courier. He stepped into the waiting elevator.

"Muir, what's the operation name?"

"SHINING CITIES."

Bishop shot me a two-finger pistol wave, more Steve McQueen than John Wayne, and joined Muir. The elevator door shut. The car descended to its escape tunnel.

I made a tall drink, mixing the tequila with a Squirt no one would miss from the cabinet. The CONPLAN was twelve minutes' work. The OPLAN took me five hours to write it all up—an hour break for a late-night snack/early breakfast and a new bottle of tequila—and type a clean copy. I passed out for a couple vacant hours. By that time, the Israeli ambassador to the UN would be beginning his address.

I was out of tequila again.

I locked the finished documents in the safe and dialed the courier. It rang four times before it was disconnected at the other end.

Job over, services rendered.

I was supposed to head back to Langley, but I wanted to stop somewhere first. Which I did, at 42nd Street and 1st Avenue. But not for a drink. It's a UN address.

I passed the Café Austria and entered First Basement Conference Room 4. In violation of a dozen of rules, protocols, acts, statutes, and probably the law, I took a position where I stood a better than reasonable chance to watch Bishop run his op. That's the precise moment that I saw Numbskull Nancy move.

What was she doing here?

She possessed even less ops training than I. And when every spy in the crowd beheld her awkward brush pass with withering contempt, the deaths of more than two hundred and fifty people, including almost myself, were secured.

I'd already written it up and handed Muir the blank-check blank-page dotted lines to sign for it.

7

I'D MADE A BAD DECISION.

A breach of confidence.

A protocol violation.

A stain on my personal record. In all good conscience and, not to mention, all of good law properly argued, a direct and applicable violation of: Title 50 U.S. Code § 3121—*Protection of identities of certain United States undercover intelligence officers, agents, informants, and sources*

Sections:

(a) Disclosure of information by persons having or having had access to classified information that identifies covert agents;
(b) Disclosure of information by persons who learn identity of covert agents as result of having access to classified information;
(c) Disclosure of information by persons in course of pattern of activities intended to identify and expose covert agents;

under Title 18 these with fines and/or imprisonment for fifteen, ten, and three years, which, [according to section (d)]: *Imposition of consecutive sentences*, could lock me up for twenty-eight years—I was giving myself a "yes" tick in each of those boxes by virtue of showing up uninvited, unwanted, uncredentialed, and unwarranted to the United Nations, First Basement Conference Room, Israeli Q&A follow-up to the Israeli UN ambassador's address to the Security Council that was the stage for Nathan Muir's Bishop operation.

Why, Nancy? Why Nancy?

At least I'd walked and not taken a taxi, thereby roping in some hapless cab driver and his family into the ruination of their lives.

These things were on my mind when I slipped in with the most obnoxious school tour group I could find, then slipped away with the old gangway-for-the-restroom pity-the-teacher head fake, my mind consumed with the doctrine of *scienter*. That I, the offending party, possessed knowledge of the "wrongness" of my actions prior to committing them—provable *malum in se*, wrong in essence, or *malum prohibitum*, wrong by prohibition—that is, that I knew what the statute requires or, at a minimum, could have discovered what the statute requires with a reasonable amount of effort before I traipsed off to 405 East 42nd Street.

Could have known/discovered: like back in law school.

Like in further-instruction-upon-employment and completion-of-training: within the CIA Office of General Counsel.

Even were I to use Steve Martin's January 21 of this year, on the *SNL* record, two-word precedent defense against the commission of a "foul crime," *arguendo videre licet*—

"Two simple words: '*Excuuuuuse me!*'"

Under most statutes, to win a conviction, the government must prove beyond a reasonable doubt that the defendant acted "knowingly." Courts routinely conclude that one can be convicted of a crime for having acted knowingly (that is, purposefully doing an act) without requiring the government to prove that the defendant sought to achieve a particular end or to violate a known legal duty contained in a statute or regulation.

The assumption of foreknowledge of fucking-my-whole-life myself existed *a priori* before I'd left the Roosevelt and I would be prosecuted to the fullest extent were I to be caught screwing—or even caught *not* screwing—things up.

Excuuuuse me! running through my head, and "Excuse me… Excuse me, thank you… excuse me" running from my lips for once in sync with my inner dialogue, I took position at the back of the gathering of press and protesters.

We stand with history at the tail end of the Israeli-Palestinian conflict—if we're to believe it will be settled next month with the Peace Conferences in Madrid. Today's he-killed, she-killed bully pulpit UN bluster centered on eighteen-year-old Miss Dalal Mughrabi, and eleven Palestinian and Lebanese Fatah militants who landed their boat on the coast near Tel Aviv, killed an American tourist unlucky enough to have been taking holiday pictures on that spit of sand, then hijacked a bus on the Coastal Road near Haifa. En route to Tel Aviv to attack the Israeli Ministry of Defense, Dalal and her crew hijacked a second bus—over seventy hostages by then, and IDF forces in hot pursuit—leading to an extended shootout, the killing of thirty-eight Israeli civilians, including thirteen children, seventy-six wounded, with Dalal and her cell KIA as well. That's what the shouting was all about.

I wasn't paying too much attention to the cowboys and Indians of all of that. The tomato-tomahto, martyr-murderer, *latkas-kuku sibzamini*, let's call the whole thing on.

I was paying attention to Nancy.

My first thought was: Muir knows I've been raiding Bishop's files.

My second thought: Muir couldn't possibly have known I'd be here to see this.

And third: It's Muir. Of course he'd know.

With Nancy, he'd chosen the most redactable individual to make a failed handoff possible. Even without access to the identities of those she made payoffs to, the number of accounts, indexed by station and amount, Nancy's day-to-day work revealed a deep-level template of CIA sources and methods across multiple areas of operation.

Not too casually, her eyes searched the agitated crowd for Bishop. My mind made the jump from ledgers to motel rooms. To comforter wet spots. How do you think I got her to put out with the Bishop product? I put out in rented beds.

The lady was insatiable.

Enjoyable but insatiable. So, yeah, I fucked her to get the goods on Bishop. Now I wondered, What did Muir do to get her here? Wasn't jealous—I don't get jealous—and what the hell was I doing thinking that shit, as if it mattered here, or anymore for her, or for me, if she screwed this? Up. Screwed this up.

Nancy was scared witless. Her corn silk Dorothy Hamill sweeping side-banged hair framed a face bloodless pale. Her right hand held a top spiral notebook slightly larger than a reporter's pad, thick and vibrating like one of her big-girl toys. Guaranteed already noted by every hostile state actor on the lookout, on duty or off, as soon as it left her hand for Bishop's—if that was even still the plan—she would be marked forever. And depending on how successful Muir's endgame played, her life will have gotten a mortal timestamp.

Warn her. Save her. White-knight something for once in your life.

I rooted to my spot. The Q&A was deteriorating from shouting and shoving to curses and crushing. I knew it was useless to look away from Nancy to find Bishop—I'm nobody's knight, I'm a lawyer, and even jousting paper, more often than not, I break my pencil lead on the futility of my conscience—I wasn't going to stop him and he would only appear when he wanted to be seen.

He was beside her. The brush pass accomplished with one hundred percent transparency. Bishop vanished, but Nancy stood like a high-school actor in the spot, lines and blocking forgotten from *Our Town*, not particularly realizing life as she lived it.

Then, as if at the whisper of some imagined teacher in the wings she could only hope for, she lurched away and separated from the crowd. Totally realized. Which means, in parlance: fucked. That gal *always* dies in the play—and no one's ever explained a good reason why.

They were wolves, the men who tracked her with their eyes. Three of them bound off in a surrounding pack. Nancy passes on my right within arm's reach without seeing me. In front and to my left, Bishop reappears, backing into two of the least vocal, least physically engaged of all the assembled antagonistic "press." (Everyone else, wilder than us, always uses press cover. That's why they slit our press's throats.) Except for the four Mossad types detailed to the Israeli ambassador at the rostrum, these two were double in height and weight of everyone else in the room.

Except for Bishop.

They only had a couple inches and maybe thirty pounds more muscle between the two of them. Each clamped one of Bishop's shoulders. Think of Bishop as I've described him. Then, think I did it badly. Give him two extra more of everything. It was some kind of Syrian-attempted Vulcan grip, but Bishop was more Jedi than Trekkie, and Darth Vader Jedi at that. Without discernable effort, he shucked the porterhouse paws, pulled the first from behind into the upward ramming fist of his free hand—plug under the jaw—driving out and letting momentum swing the guy backward in an arc into the second man on his left. Bishop folded his arm, adding momentum to his elbow, scything it into the right cheekbone and across the bridge of the second man's nose.

The crowd was drawing apart, away from the violence. For a moment, I thought Nancy—moving carefully, eyes front, into the passageway to the Conference Building exit—would be sucked back by its riptide.

She made the door. She went through. Three bad wolves loped after her, one speaking into his sleeve, engaging a vehicle team at street-level above. It would be a three-man team in the car and whether Nancy took to a vehicle or moved on foot, the six-pack would stalk her the entire way, awaiting determination—straw-sticks-bricks—surveil, detain, or dispatch? It depended on how their compatriots handled Bishop.

Our manual, theirs, and every service and terrorist group between, dictated that Bishop make fleet feet after having dropped his two opponents, but to their delight, his brief flurry of activity was all he had in him and they were back all over him as two officers of the United Nation's PD rushed toward them.

I would learn later, Bishop's two opponents were part of the External Branch of the Idarat al-Mukhabarat al-Amma, Syria's General Intelligence Directorate. Bad players. Excellent spies. Recovered, the first of them broadly tore Bishop's ID from his shirtfront, using this distraction and his body placement to facilitate his broken-nosed partner's expert picking of Bishop's back waistband to acquire the notebook. This player was hustled by friendly hands and protective bodies into the sympathetic crowd.

Poison pill delivered.

Bravo, Muir. Bravo, Bishop. Don't think about Nancy.

Both police officers approached. Guns drawn. The remaining Syrian agent tossed Bishop's phony ID at the cops' feet as Bishop raised his hands, surrendering. He shouted something in Hebrew that agitated both sides into a vocal and physically threatening response that covered the second Syrian's escape. Bishop didn't need him anymore.

Bishop was the cops' singular focus. One covered Bishop with his pistol as the other holstered his gun and came forward with handcuffs. Bishop offered no resistance. The first bracelet ratcheted his right wrist. They spun him for the second cuff. His gaze swept mine, lit for an instant—he already knew where I was—and that moment held in my mind for the rest of the day and into the night as I tried to put it into words and still can't.

Delight. Approval. Welcome.

Here's the difference between us and everyone else: even getting handcuffed is part of the plan. Control is best taken suddenly from a point of perceived weakness.

My ego tried to argue that I'd been playing under the table (perceived weakness), tying people's shoelaces together longer than he has, but my heart forced me to admit this was the first time I'd pulled up a chair with the grown-ups where you tie their shoes with your toes.

The UN cops frog-marched Bishop from the hall as more officers came into the basement to deal with the crowd, and the statements, and to see if they couldn't help get things back on rancorous track. I moved around its edge. I followed Bishop at a distance.

They took him around the corner to the elevators.

As Cop One hit the call button, the other got on his radio.

Bishop let the handcuffs drop to the floor. They made a ringing noise on the tile.

This never happens. Little training is given to this circumstance. Both cops did what I dumbly did. Looked at the floor.

Yup, those be handcuffs.

With two sharp blows in opposite directions, Bishop dropped both men. One was out before he piled up against the elevator door. The other got to hands and knees as if offering a pony ride. Bishop drove his toe into the man's solar plexus, lifted to collapse him. The elevator opened. The first cop fell inside to block the door from closing.

Bing. Bing. Bing.

Bishop was already halfway to the stairs moving behind a series of concrete pillars. A calm and steady pace.

He passed behind the last pillar. He broke his pace. For eight, maybe ten seconds he didn't emerge.

Four more cops rushed down the staircase.

Surely, they saw him.

Just as they were about to reach his pillar, Bishop stepped out. Two inches taller. Heels platformed his black oxfords into Chelsea boots. Long, curly black hair you'd call a few years later a Howard Stern 'do drooped like black seaweed beneath a sweat-salted ball cap. His dress pants somehow ripaway-gone, white jeans now, a skintight lips-and-tongue Rolling Stones T-shirt where jacket, shirt, and tie had been before. A camera bag across his chest and a camera aimed at the cops, Bishop backing up before them, clipping off action shots they ignored as they pushed past in annoyance.

Bishop made the stairs and without a backward glance was gone.

I was jubilant. Bishop wasn't going to say a word. I'd seen his eyes. He'd enjoyed my appreciative audience. Disguise kit had been the highlight, with maybe the Houdini cuffs a close second. I felt sorry for the cops—they got the worst of it—

Don't forget Nancy.

Nancy. I reasoned that out. The wolf pack wouldn't move against her until they'd assessed the notebook. They'd keep her under surveillance for now. Muir, I'm sure, would have warned her and, to be safe, be keeping counter surveillance on her. Once the

Syrians found they'd struck gold—fool's gold in this case—the team on Numbers Numbskull Nancy would fade away.

She'd be safe.

She was good as safe already.

Of course, I doubted she'd ever share so much as a look up her ledger with me again.

And yet, this proves wrong. She'd seen me in the crowd the moment I'd seen her. Thought I was part of the op.

Turned her on.

Muir, she admitted, told her I'd been there to pull her out—"throw the game board," as he'd put it to her and she to me—if I thought she couldn't handle it.

Embarrassed by this, made to feel a fool again by Muir, still, Nancy and I made love the entire summer while she helped me through the horrors of my recovery until it was time for her to marry Derrick in the fall.

More frisky than any lover, save for my fallen, fated Madeline.

And, by then, I didn't need her or Derrick's or anyone else's Bishop intel any longer because that evening, after we all walked from the headquarters of the United Nations, Israel invaded Lebanon. Two days later, Bishop hauled my ass from a puddle of blood and urine and my own diarrhea and self-destructive alcoholic suicidal vomit, giving birth to the most important friendship any man could have or ever want.

8

YESTERDAY MORNING, September 29, 1991. After Madeline and Dr. Beardy-Baldy, PhD, but before I'd left for Muir's: Seventh Floor Conference Room, DCI wing. No call yet from the Second District Metro PD homicide detectives. Harker had left me to my work three hours previous, taking his invisible golf clubs and invisible balls in hand, and now I was in Director Troy Folger's conference room. It sits off of both his private and outer office, a connecting door to each. The seventeen seals of every government intelligence agency, civilian and military, hang on the oak paneling above enough chairs to accommodate the heads of each agency those seals represent. The CIA seal, larger than the others, hangs behind the director's larger seat at table's head and is flanked by the American flag on one side, the CIA flag on the other. The expensive blue carpet is thick. Pocket trash and inconvenient agents have gotten lost in it.

Standing behind that largest of chairs, former federal prosecutor turned Shearson Lehman Brothers board member presidentially enthroned as CIA director, Troy Folger, of the ever fiddled-with Phi Beta Kappa key and chain on his waistcoat, wore an expression of smug self-satisfaction. He examined his copy of the briefing book I'd prepared, reading each page, tilting it up as he finished and languidly releasing it to fall as his eyes moved to the next. I listened to the air-conditioner cycle and waited, seated across from Harker, who'd made a point of burning through his copy of the pages, slapping his book closed, and pinning me in his hooked-bass frown.

"Well, he's certainly done this up right." Director Folger met Harker's stare.

"Why I selected him for this, Director," Harker said.

Speaking of me as if I weren't dumbly smiling there.

"Don't brown your nose on my ass, Harker." Director Folger looked at me. "From what I read of your history with this agency, Mr. Aiken, only Nathan Muir has ever had much of an opinion of you here."

"And Tom Bishop. Muir recruited us both."

A more veiled and, in that, more telling look passed between my two superiors.

Folger said, "Hong Kong Chief of Operations Bishop is no longer associated with Nathan Muir. He is not to enter into this op—well, it isn't an operation per se, is it?—this *program* in any manner whatsoever."

"Yes, Mr. Director. I'm sorry."

Folger shooed away my apology as if it were—*ergo*, me by association—a pesky fly.

"In going out to meet him," he said, "whether Muir has anything to do with the Charlie March flap, you've added your own wrinkle."

"Yes, Director, I have."

"Ambitious. I'd been told you weren't."

I pictured myself burying my hands in my pockets and scuffing a shoe.

"You propose to effect this Agency's larger goal of securing Muir's total disassociation with this agency? Is that correct?"

"Correct, sir."

Folger absently toyed with his school smarty-pants vest fob. "Do you think Nathan Muir murdered Charlie March?"

"Immaterial. As you can see, page two, the Intelligence Act of—"

"I'm a political appointee and from my perspective this move is political. Acts, executive orders, bills, legislations, and regulations: disinterested."

Sure need more like you at the top of government, Troy.

"Answer me," he added, impatient at my non-pocket hands, non-shoe scuffing vacuousness.

"On the surface, it seems outrageously impossible. Charlie March recruited Muir from the Marine Corps in Korea. He was father, brother, mentor, confessor—Muir's only friend in or outside the Agency."

"You're not telling me anything I haven't read."

"Statistically, 74.5 percent of murders fall into the category of acquaintance, friends, and family."

"You include family?"

"Muir married Charlie March's sister. They're related."

Folger sat. "That's new."

"That, along with March's final words: no other suspect need apply."

Harker, still smarting over the "brown nose" comment, piped up. "Muir's been married more times than I can count."

"But his heart stayed true to March," I said.

Folger pushed away the book on all of it. He looked me dead in the eye. "Bury his heart."

I closed my hand around my feline mug, my mind back from the director's conference room and pushing away another image. The image of a detective's rubber-gloved hand reaching into my vehicle's passenger footwell, finding Mom's .22 pistol. Gun lifted to a nose and sniffed. I poured myself another Macallan, my thoughts leading me to direct confrontation of the matter at hand.

"Did you kill him, Muir?"

"Having another, Russell?"

"Harker doesn't care. Nor the director. Nobody, really—"

"Not even you, Russell?"

"Except maybe the FBI, if they get close."

"Aren't you here to prevent that?"

"Indeed."

"And what about you? You don't care either, Russell? Huh?"

"Stop doing that."

"What?"

"You know what. My name."

"You said to call you 'Russell.'"

"I know what I said. People don't just keep using people's names to them when they're talking. You're mocking me. And I don't have to take it."

"There you go. Good."

I drank half of the next mug of scotch and I liked it. I chucked the burden of Muir's Rules of Thumb from my back. I looked at him straight. "I'm going to pin the murder on you regardless. So my opinion doesn't matter. But, yes, sir, I don't care because I know you did it. Somehow, for some awful and immoral reason, you murdered the hero who made you: you assassinated Charlie March."

"Jesus, Aiken." Smoking and faraway. "You never see it when you're being played."

"So you've always said. Kept me out of the field for it."

"One's salvation: easiest thing to ridicule."

He poured himself another, then me a third, as, seeing we were near the bottom of the bottle, I said, "There more?"

"Endless amounts. What's your plan after you falsify my confession?"

"Personal plan or the Seventh Floor's?"

"Think I give a damn what you plan to do with yourself? For me."

"I offer you an ironclad 'Get Out of Jail Free' card in the form of a document I have inside my briefcase." I nodded backward at the place he'd ordered me to drop it.

"Thought that was a bathing suit and jammies in your mailman bag." Then, knowing, "My pre-approved request for immediate retirement."

I nodded.

"You won't get a confession," said Muir.

"You won't sign one… but you know we can always do that for you."

"That's the iron fist. Touch me again with the velvet glove?"

"An Executive Order granting you immunity from prosecution in anything ever relating to the case of the murder of Charlie March."

"You can make it stick?"

"One thing you know I can."

Muir did. As Harker said, I was the one lawyer whom Muir trusted. We drank quietly apace and Muir smoked. In the time of our interview so far, it had become a light-fading time-wasted evening.

"Rain's not stopping," I said.

"Rain always stops. Ask Noah." He leaned forward, elbows on his knees, eyes intent on mine. "You knew, standing in it, I'd have no choice. So why did you bring your jammies?"

"I need to know why you did kill him."

"There is no 'why.' I didn't."

"Then tell me *how* you didn't."

I hardly recognized my voice. They were the first honest words I'd spoken since I'd told Madeline I'd be in the office overnight and followed her and Beardy-Baldy home. I'd dropped my pretense of a nobility I've never had; I'd thrown teeth from the bag of my own scrotum. Ballsy, eh?

"Fuck it. Open that cosmetics case you dragged up here. I'll sign your shit now. We got nothing to talk about."

"No."

I just sat there. Muir nodded a few times, slowly, then he unfolded himself from his chair, commented he was going in for a fresh bottle. It would take a minute. I told him I was made of time.

He said, "Precious commodity," and disappeared inside the house.

As Muir predicted, the rain did stop, a few minutes after he'd gone inside. Now, more than an hour and a half later, it was still stopped. Nothing to do as an employee not anxious to head back to headquarters, or go home, or get arrested. Made sense to wait.

I listened to the thousand splats of water dripping from canopied branches and twisting vines to broad flat leaves and crenellated fronds. *Splat, thwap, splat.* The creak of banana trees, the scrape and thrum of insect wing on belly and leg. Fog rose from the ground, giving texture to the dark. The buzz of my Motorola MicroTac startled me. Not so much the sound or vibration against my chest, but the sight of Madeline's number on the red LED readout. I declined the call, nervously powered off the phone. I slipped it back into my breast pocket as Muir came through the sliding-glass door with a fresh bottle.

"Twenty-five-year single malt. Same age as your wife."

He might have seen the phone. I don't think he did, but supposing he had? He couldn't have seen the number on the display. He wouldn't have recognized it anyway. And herein lies the difference between an ops officer and one who's not: instinct and when to lead with it.

"Been destroying evidence?"

"Took a nap. Pleased to see you haven't moved from your spot."

Another dog cut.

"I told you. Sofa's comfortable."

"Our pal Charlie March gave me this patio set on the occasion of my marrying his sister."

I puzzled that. It isn't what Muir said before. We both knew it. He handed me the bottle.

"Pour. We'll drink to marriage."

My back tightened. I did as ordered.

"We had a war in Korea. Called it a *police action* to nicey-nice it through the UN, so you might not have heard," he said.

In the intervening time, I'd taken a miniaturized DAT recorder from my briefcase. Muir acknowledged it with a dip of his chin. I activated it. The digital counter rolled, measuring past becoming present, a backward countdown, numerals ticking upward from 0:00 as Muir spoke onto the digital tape.

"At any given time in the month of June, 1950, there might have been a platoon's worth of US Marine advisers in Seoul liaising with the ROK Army—the South's armed forces—either at bases, in the field, or, like me, at our embassy, and the lucky spot of my big day, when seventy-five thousand politically misguided, and personally murderous, North Koreans overran the thirty-eighth parallel and crashed my wedding."

He raised his tumbler in a toast. I lifted my mug. He said, "To first wives," and then he took me back.

9

MUIR ASKED, "Ever see a Korean wedding dress?"

"Never been to a Korean wedding, so no."

"*Hanbok*, what they call it in the South—there's a Nork version called the *Joseon-ot*, difference in the needlework and that's only post-war thanks to Stalin's gift of deprivation in all things—*hanbok* is the traditional clothing of the Korean people. Three types. Children's—think airport souvenir dolls—cutesy, brightly colored. There's everyday dress, which back-when-and-a-hen, more than half the population, especially the women, still wore. Not much anymore. Then the third category: what you'd see at a wedding."

"This first wedding of yours," I said.

First wives mean not-anymore-wives. Cheers.

"Yes."

"Mr. Muir, the focus here needs to be on March. I don't suppose you married him?"

"As usual, you suppose wrong. He didn't wear the dress. I didn't even know Charlie March was there that night, and if you want to stop smart-mouthing, you'll listen to me tell my story my way because I'm going to tell you everything, and everything I'm going to tell you—including who was wearing what *hanbok* when—is vitally important to your mission."

Bury his heart.

My mission was to take Muir apart. If he wanted to do it in a *hanbok* or giving himself a handjob, who was I to stop him? I poured more to drink and did.

He continued, "*Hanbok* is all about graceful shape. Vibrant color. Rainbow-plenty of it, though, interesting: not gradated in shading. Instead, its bold primary statements are linked with the five elements of Chinese yin-yang theory. White for metal, red for fire. Blue: wood, black: water. And yellow is earth, where we all begin and to where we shall return. Right? You went to Christian school."

"As a child. But we don't go into that mumbo-jumbo magic color fortune cookie stuff," I said, smug behind my mug.

"My mistake, that Mary always in blue, violet for the sovereignty of Christ, white, black, red, green seasonal liturgical vestments just miraculous coincidence. Here's a Second Rule of Thumb for you: All is one, Russell."

He studied me as I fought to keep my memory of New York eight years ago, Nina, whom I would meet, and that one-thing truth I received from registering on my face.

Muir went on. "Embroidered onto the *hanbok*, delicate shades of the palate stand out to represent the wishes of the wearer. Peonies. Lotus flowers. You get three-legged crows. Bats—"

The scotch almost got me to quip, *Make a fine Halloween costume*, but Muir paused, ready for that, so I held back the trick and was treated to a bit on how the flowers symbolized honor and nobility, the bats a hope for children. Something about a pomegranate also for children—or bats for boys and pomegranates for girls. Whatever. Muir asked I picture the happiness these colorful patterns naturally evoked. And I did.

He asked me to picture the most beautiful girl in the world wearing them.

I did that too.

Madeline: white silk, and lace wrapping her throat.

Muir read my mind. "Think Madeline: exactly like my first and how much joy I felt. Me, all of twenty-one years. Grown up and old enough for serious in my Marine Corps, First

Lieutenant's First Marines, Fifth Regiment, G-2 Intelligence-attached best."

Nathan Muir has been married more times than there is possibly time to be married, so I tiptoed out a question. "Your first wife, I assume, Korean?"

Muir looked at the recorder. "Yes."

"She's not detailed in your personnel jacket. How'd you manage it? Military regulations about wedding a foreign national in a war zone during—"

"During a United Nations Police Action."

"Before. During. Since. Regulations do not allow for, nor have they ever allowed for, marriage between a junior American intel officer and foreign national tied by race, culture, and nationality to the enemy during active military operations. US Code—"

"More things in heaven and earth than are dreamt of in your US Code." Muir fished a wedding ring from his shirt pocket. He placed it on the table between us. "Read it and weep."

I examined the evidence. A line of unreadable Korean characters ran the inside of the golden band.

Ha-ha, Muir. Very funny.

"How'd you manage?" I said.

"Figure it out. It'll keep you engaged."

He took the ring and dropped it back into his pocket. "We married in the main ballroom of the US Embassy, Seoul."

"No American embassy has ever had a ballroom."

"God. You're like a kid here with the interruptions, Rusty."

Baiting the name hook again. I let it float past.

"From '48 to '62, American Embassy, Republic of Korea, located at the Bando Hotel. Entire fifth floor. Colonial. Old-world elegance. Built 1938. Survived the Japs and the Norks... Up in flames twenty years ago."

He fired the facts with machine-gun rapidity only to have the belt jam on the last round. He worked that one out careful and slow.

"Gas explosion. Year after you and I met. People got trapped on the roof. Lots of them died from smoke. Embers blown back down from the rotor-rescue killed the rest. It remains the deadliest hotel fire in world history. Lost friends who'd known us. Known her. Worked there all those years."

Bother creased his brow. He took a drink, wetting a smile to help him back to his embassy ballroom, twenty years burnt up like the cigarette he sucked.

"The ceremony was performed by a Korean priest, Anglican Church of Korea. Somewhat long service, he ran it a tad hastily as North Korean troops, driving Russian T-34 tanks, who'd spent the day overwhelming South Korean military positions, gained main highways and were barreling right into Seoul two days into their surprise attack. No one had thought they'd reach the capital city so damn fast.

"So… we hurry to exchange vows and rings. Our guests—limited to embassy and military staff, US and Korean. Some Aussies and Brits. And this major with the Turkish Brigade, Miraç Özdemir, whom I'd gotten to know blocking his clumsy but sweet passes at my bride—a delightful guy, he stood best man—all of 'em: constantly rushed by messengers. Sound of their voices overwhelmed the sound of the priest, who, to make sure I'd heard, made a kissy face at me as the go-ahead to 'kiss the bride.' My bride hadn't heard. All looking around and flustered. I said, 'Let me kiss you.'

"She met my eyes, fearful at what was happening. She looked at the priest all puckered up and thought he wanted one too.

"'Kiss me. You're my wife.'

"She smiled, clinging to the impossible. I smiled back 'cause I was head over heels and love makes everything possible.

"I said, 'I'm your husband,' and we kissed. And, along with everyone else—them on panicked feet, us skipping on clouds—we raced to the street."

Muir reflected, hitting deeply from his cigarette, then—signaling me to remain where I was—stood up. He stepped to the railing. He reached over and down the length of his arm. His arm reemerged, hand gripping an orange juice carafe filled with rain. As it turned out, this was one of a pair he'd put out before I'd arrived, already planning for the long run he'd make at March.

Noah prepared.

He made us fresh drinks. Rainwater sweet. Scotch whiskey better for it.

"The skyline burned. Fire everywhere, punctuated by the white flash of the invader's artillery. Y'know how you can get used to that?"

"No."

How would I?

"Right. Me either, then." And he flicked his hand a few times like a pitcher releases a baseball to punctuate the blasts just to rub it in.

"Personal cars. Military vehicles. Rushing past, swooping in to scoop up our guests, all headed south. A steady stream of South Korean Sixth Regiment—the only unit to stand fast and fight—rolled north to defend their capital. Smoke was swirling. Funneled down the high-rise street, dust devils touching down, spinning 'round, and running straight. Her hair was beautiful. The ash was flecking it. It was time for her to go. And, Russell, if you can't remember their hair when you marry them, don't kiss 'em on the altar."

"This is bullshit. Regulations be damned: this fairy tale—"

"You sure you can damn those? Damn regulations being of the law, and you my faithless attorney?"

"Stop it. Why would anyone attend this wedding, an invasion coming down on them?"

"Asked myself many a'time. More times as I get older—*and* more as I've continued to participate in matrimonies. Here's what I think, but take it for what it's worth, as I'm pretty much last man standing, hmm?"

I *hmm*-ed him back.

"Weddings are a way for society to solemnize a committed relationship. Weddings are a way to honor the people who stand in witness to support that community. Do it for you, do it for themselves. Human nature.

"This wedding. Those people. Allegiances and services weighed against invasion commitments. They came to witness more than the union of an American soldier and a South Korean angel. Their world on fire—? They came to witness a bonding before God of a greater national commitment binding one country to the other at the moment invaded: because they were being invaded.

"Shit like this happens all over history. Nero's Stradivarius doesn't get in his hand by whim or by accident. When you got jackshit cards and you've already played the sleeve, you *bet* you hit a wedding and try to discern God among the dung balls."

"Don't look at me," I said.

"Why do you think anyone bothered to come to yours?"

Yep. Case closed.

I didn't speak until he did. Meaning to say, speaking in my mind—

Madeline went out of her way for all our guests; so proud; so failed—

I answer my truth most only to myself.

"The symbolic transformed manifest," he said.

I laughed.

Madeline: poof.

"Your ego is incredible," I said.

"Not my ego, buddy boy. Me."

Muir finished his drink. He signaled me to do the same, half-hoping I'd chicken out—we were halfway into bottle two—but I didn't. He slammed down his tumbler. I gently replaced my kitty-cat mug. He went on.

"Y'know, in a Korean wedding—some say the very centerpiece—there's literal binding. *Sonsugeon*. You know *sonsugeon*? Translation: handfasting."

"Know all about it. And bullshit again. It's not Korean. It's Celtic."

"Jesus. You think I'm talking the pagan knotted-rope handcuffs you used at your marriage?"

"Though developed in pagan times," I countered with activist disinterest, "celtic handfasting is acknowledged and blessed by the Christian, Catholic, and Apostolic churches."

"Well, in Korea they don't do it with the thirteen-strand hemp reserved to hang people you tied the knot with. It's commitment. Not capture. Silk ribbons for the people in that ballroom losing their country to the gook hordes riding down hell upon them—"

I sneered. And when I did, I knew I was in my warm whiskey-blood-face place. Buzzed. "You do know the original usage of *gook* was for whores?"

Muir tapped my recorder. "You're sure giving the transcriber a hoot-and-a-half with all these comments. Not to mention, pissing off that bold Young Turk Harker by preventing me from getting to Charlie March."

"You're the one sidetracking this whole thing!"

"You made the easy-open-thigh comment about who marries whore wives. Subject here isn't wives' fidelity. Unless you want it to be." Muir cocked his head at me, then dropped a mock warning glance—big and bold and open—back to the recorder.

Shit.

Last thing I wanted was Madeline on this tape. My whole purpose to lock Muir's mouth on Charlie March from the FBI could be gutted by a smart Metro detective and a no-nonsense judge coming after me to serve no purpose but to point out I sucked at my job.

Muir poured. Lit a fresh cigarette. Said, "Handfasting," fully amused.

Buzzed equals drunk. I shut the hell up.

"Our ambassador, Mr. John Muccio, was a friend of Truman's. Old-country born and true. Cute Neapolitan accent, and always a white Italian suit with a bowtie. He'd given my wife her job with us. 'Bout a year before I took my first bounce off North America."

"She worked for the embassy?"

"That's right."

"For the record—which she is heretofore absent from—I need the full name. Spelled. Your first wife."

"You bet. Clerk-translator for our military command. We knew the Norks would overrun Seoul—not that night, that was unexpected—but we knew it was unavoidable once the balloon went up. Ambassador Muccio had promised when the time came, he'd take her, let her stay with Mrs. Muccio until we'd fought our way back. So: one more kiss.

"'For luck,' she whispered, and an 'I love you,' her lips warm against my ear, and I told her something like a 'That makes me luckier than you,' and then Mrs. Muccio gently removes her from my arms, and I'm hauled off by my CO into his car."

"Name of wife?"

"The last I saw her, our wedding night—what I picture right now talking to you, not the tape—eyes on me—is a profusion of blue and red and yellow Westinghouse Perfected Color TV real and full, bunching up in the skirt of her *hanbok*, and the ambassador closes her inside and gets into the front beside his driver, and they were gone."

"Wood, fire, and earth," I mumbled, matching the colors I pictured to their yin-yang values to prove to myself I was listening, and then I was back in *my* wedding limo. Mine and Madeline's.

For the first time since my wedding day, I recall her bouquet. Yellow rosebuds and white lilies of the valley. And her hair, it was perfect—thick and beautiful, dark, but always magnetic to light, drawing it in, shimmering with white, golden, and always. She loved me then.

Will I ever see it again all pulled back, up, and in place?

10

"I DIDN'T MEET Charlie March until after the Inchon Landing. After we'd pushed back into Seoul," Muir said over the rim of his tumbler before knocking back a swallow.

"Hold it. What happened to your wife—whom you must name? Did she stay with the ambassador and his wife? Did you and she reunify?"

"Reunify?"

"Reunify: legal term. Family law."

Muir wouldn't have spent so much time on her, their wedding, if she weren't somehow crucial... yep, to my mission today, like he said when I didn't believe him. In this instance, more about Muir for me than about March, I *needed* to know.

"There was a problem with her papers. The ambassador lost her. A leap from the car. She became trapped in Seoul."

A pensive sigh passed Muir's lips, the last breath of some sort of long and deep regret. He looked at me with a glimpse of that familiarity we'd had at the very beginning, caught himself and buried it.

"Once the North Koreans entered the city, they initiated mass killings. All anti-communists. Real or imagined. The more well-known political figures who hadn't escaped were tossed in jail. Hastily organized 'people's courts' carried out mock trials that had a zero percent survival rate, but mostly, resistors to the North Korean regime were shot on the spot.

"The official number of murdered citizens due to these round-ups comes in at three thousand. Unofficially, the honest number is closer to three times that.

"At the truce, when the official number was agreed upon, the Chosŏn'gŭ, the KPA—Korean People's Army—and their political batboys, insisted wording to the effect that they were 'careful, in the initial occupation, to avoid arbitrary and brutal dispensation of justice,' which—MacArthur already kicked out to argue it—the liar Truman agreed.

"I'm a kid, though. I mean, manned up enough to be married to a *gook*, as you say, but I'm twenty-one at the time. I didn't know any of this was going on. If I had, I'd've gone AWOL back for her. Thankfully, for my continued life—'cause they'da shot me—no one told me she ditched because having worked for the US Embassy, she'd've been one of the first to catch a bullet with the back of her head."

Muir tapped the back of his skull with two fingers to reinforce the point. Then, self-conscious, trying to hide the bullet, he rubbed his head as if that's what he'd intended.

"She never told me how she survived it, but the papers she'd stayed in Seoul to acquire—that was by her own choice. See, in Korea, the wedding ceremony isn't the legal marriage. Only legal way to get married is to file papers and change the family registry at the local government office. You don't need a ceremony of any kind. Most Koreans file first, then do the ceremony afterward as a purely social event. Me, straightjacketed in Western convention, I wouldn't hear of that. A married couple is joined in ceremony. The union happens before God and man. The government paperwork—far as I was concerned—was the equivalent of filing an after-action report: 'we lumped a whole shitload of HE FFE'—that's high-explosive fire for effect—"

"I know that, Muir—"

"—on the fill-in-the-blanks' battle already won or lost." He finished his sentence, hit his smoke, shot me with a smoke ring.

"But that wasn't the law, and my new wife wasn't my wife at all in her eyes, the eyes of her country, and in her heart."

"Registering a marriage to a US serviceman would have been asking to be shot," I said. "Now, her name. Please, Muir. Quit screwing around."

"Yes." Again, he ignored my request. "It carried pretty high odds that's what would happen, but those papers meant everything to her."

Fog surrounded the entire porch of Muir's vacation rental. Tendrils licked the edges of the sitting area where we drank and Muir smoked, stretched out in his chair.

"Her name was Kim Jin."

"Is that a first name? Or a first-last before marriage, or a—"

"Or a shut up. I've thought about this before: if you were an architect, you'd see all doors locking from both sides. You've always saved my ass—and Bishop's—by not letting us back up inside to get locked in, but I'm trying tonight for doors with no locks at all."

"What?! For the record, Mr. Muir: Kim what?"

"In Korean, the surname comes before the first name. Kim. Her first name, chosen by her parents, was Jin. Kim Jin Muir. She was a clerk in the embassy commo room when I arrived—"

"Kimono?"

"Don't be dense. Communications. We did spend some pocket change on you to learn that."

I flipped him off and he blew me a kiss. And he went on:

"Smitten the moment I met her. Just fell into her eyes. Amber, a russet kinda copper-hued. Unusual among Westerners for starters; eyes that color are extremely rare with Asians. She was named after them. Her own eyes. Once I'd seen her, those eyes, I quick made sure she became my secretary. Needed to hold her in place until I could get her to fall in love with me."

"Aren't you the gentleman."

Muir patronized me with a single shake of his head. "Russell, picture a double helix."

"Not interested."

"Doesn't matter. By saying it, I already made you picture it," he said. "In perfect love, every twist one partner thinks he's secretly wrapped the other around his finger with, she's made a covert twist of her own. Both man and woman end up believing they are the ones to have the other wrapped around their finger and like the double helix: that's the first building block of an entwined and living love."

Muir blew another smoke ring. This time he reached after it, snapped his fingers above it, and it formed a heart before dissipating.

How come I don't know any tricks? Like using a silencer on wifie and her lover. Like throwing away a gun.

"Waste of time," I said. "Sorry I asked. Just tell me what you called her."

"I called her Ginny because I wanted to be cute. By the time the Norks abandoned Seoul and I returned to her with a momentarily victorious army, I'd learned what Jin means. It means jewel. I've called her Jewel ever since."

As he told me her name, what it meant and what it meant to him—I knew, having never known of Jewel, I've never known Muir at all. It suddenly dawned on me where Charlie March fit in to this part of the story.

"Charlie March was at your wedding. You said that, right?"

Muir stubbed out his cigarette like he was killing it. Or killing something. He felt around inside the old pack before unzipping the cellophane strip from a fresh pack. "I don't remember seeing him there. I'm sure I didn't. He never told me. But you got it: Charlie March was there."

"And your being allowed that marriage was as unusual and unconventional as I've pointed out?" I ticked boxes in my head.

"Of course it was."

"And the only way it could have happened was if he'd pulled the strings to make that happen."

"Very good. This is why I like you. You never need to be told the things you need to hear."

I faked a smile. I wasn't going to let him get to me with double-edged compliments.

"When did you first notice—strike that, immaterial—when did you first become acquainted with Mr. March?"

"I first noticed Charlie March after my return to Seoul. He was in the country on a CIA fishing trip. We were back in business, our US Military Staff Headquarters set up at a high school adjacent and attached to a Republic of Korea Army base. They liked to funnel kids straight from classroom to officer's mess. I was up at the blackboard, briefing the US and ROK general staff on North Korean regiments, divisions, units in areas of operations.

"As I was the junior intelligence analyst, most of my military audience was bored, half—maybe more—conducting other business from their seats. Like my wedding, right? One guy in the audience, however, was riveted: kept encouraging me with his eyes."

"Charlie March?"

"One and only. He was in his thirties. Younger than you right now and so much more accomplished. More maturity, though—"

Why does he hate me?

"—than both you 'n' me right now. He'd seen a bunch of action in the war. OSS fighting the Nazis. You all know that, though." He glanced at the DAT as if he was saying words to make it seem small instead of me. "Square-jawed, with that hair. Lean and rangy like a lion. Full of promise… and promises. He was also the only civilian in the room. I couldn't help but watch him." Muir drank, smoked, quipped: "Having no idea why this confident, grinning rake was there, civilian at that, pissed the crap out of me—him and his expressions of knowing affirmation.

"As my briefing wound down, I opened the room to questions. But as usual, our officers set the tone. They rose to leave and the ROKs followed.

"'Tail feathers wagging like happy, stupid ducklings,' said Charlie March to the empty room and me.

"I had no idea who this man was. Would never have guessed the effect he would have on my war, the next, or the next."

"Or today?" I said.

"Or my entire life. I didn't know Charlie March. I collected my materials and he watched me all the way to the door.

"'You tell it like it is, Lieutenant,' he said.

"'If you say so, sir.' I attempted to move past him.

"Charlie March blocked me. Big grin. Oh, so sympathetically. 'I'm a stranger. I get it.'

"I attempted to hand him my stack of folders.

"'Since you do: feel free. Take all this back to Washington. Get a pass from State, or Commerce, or Development—wherever you're from—to Harry Truman, have him drive this over to the Pentagon. Have the generals consider what's here. Have them call MacArthur, have him call this staff. Have them clue in to what's happening on our front—*yesterday*—and maybe, stranger, you'll get us a list of the Marines to bury when they're overrun tonight.'

"Charlie March's encouraging expression didn't change. I hated him for it. I tucked my work under my arm and—'Gangway. Sir'—shouldered past.

"He trailed me. Didn't say a word. I pretended to ignore him."

"Pretended to ignore? Isn't that just ignore?" I spoke only to let Muir know I was engaged.

Not thinking Madeline.

I braced for his smackdown.

"It's not. To ignore is to actually not pay attention. My mind was fully active with Charlie March. By the time we reached the hall to my office, Jewel in her plain skirt and theater-usher-style fall jacket, embellished with her ID tag, waiting, eyes reading my 'help me out' SOS. Which she did. Allowing me to enter but blocking Charlie March and shutting our door in his ruddy face.

"I went into my office as Charlie March let himself inside Jewel's outer office guardhouse. He spoke to her in Korean, something charming to the effect that he could be my best friend if only she'd let him.

"She didn't let him play her with his Korean. In clear English she said, 'Lieutenant Muir is very busy. May I inquire who are you?'

"'Toldja, honey, his best friend: Charlie March. One of the good guys.'

"As both Jewel and I were still choking on his 'honey,' Charlie March marched into my office.

"'I thought I was rude enough,' I said from behind my desk, already entrenched behind new intercepts.

"'Naw.'

"He told me I was 'awright.' That I *was* right—for all that did my Marines—and I told him, 'Be glad it's not your problem.'

"'Overtly, no. Covertly… Here's a fresh idea. A real winner, I promise. Let me work for you.'

"'Yeah. That'll be the day.'

"I demanded ID. Better sleight of hand than a magician, Charlie March suddenly offered a CIA credential. I took it as casually as absolute curiosity allows.

"'Beg your pardon. Charles—

"'Do Charlie.'

"'Beg your pardon, Charlie March: Central Intelligence Agency.'

"He reclaimed it quicker than I could register. 'First Rule of Thumb: Never carry your Agency credential into your AO. Second Rule of Thumb: Never ever relinquish it to a stranger's hands.'

"I suggested I was the epitome of 'stranger.'

"He threw his first pitch. Easy lob across plate's center. 'Please, Nathan. I know everything about you, down to the lambies on your baby blanket. Down to the fact that what you aren't talking about in your briefings is that your LPs'—so much for the secrecy of my listening posts—'are hearing Chinese chop suey from across the Yalu River—'"

Muir paused mid-thought to change tempo. To draw me in.

"'Which your superiors don't want you to enter into the discussion. But which you and I know—sure as the Lord made commie-red apples—ain't gonna stop the Chicoms from entering this war and screwing the whole thing up the butt.'

"I felt like I was the one getting the goose. I said the conversation was over and he said—big shit-eating grin—'Let me work for you. Help you get this out.'

"With his eyes, Charlie March directed me to the intercepts on my desk between us. I attempted to conceal them, shuffling them with my hand.

"'Ever go to a magic show, Nathan?'

"'My tenth birthday. I guess you already know that.'

"His smile indicated he did. He said, 'The best tricks, hardest ones for smart guys like us to figure out, are when the magician uses his audience and the magic seems to happen in their hands without the magician's touch.'

"'I could be court-martialed sharing anything with you.'

"'The good magicians can do their trick in a *real* stranger's hands. I'll teach you that, if we ever get a chance, but for now, the easier way is for that random audience member to be the real trickster. For your next show, all you have to do is pick me from your audience.'

"I figured he had my number. Whether I permitted him, he'd be there and he'd ask anyway. 'What question you want?'

"And he said—his best big-brother voice—'The one that means most to you, Nathan. I want to see you shine brightly.'

"He indicated the intercept my hand covered mostly. 'That one got you most concerned?' he said, and I delivered it to him."

Muir's eyes went to my digital recorder's readout, watched the silent count. The fog wrapped us fully in Muir's secrecy. His smoke, blown in dreamlike currents through it, absorbed.

"Screw Charlie March," Muir said. "That was a court-martialing offense. If I'd been caught right then, neither he nor the Agency would've hauled my ass from the fire. I knew that, but at that moment, I only cared about two things: to haul ass to safety with my Jewel and to protect as many Marines as I could before the hammer fell."

He added the butt of his cigarette to his ashtray. Shook his pack. Lipped a fresh one. He struck his match and, offhand between lighting puffs, said, "What I didn't understand was those were the very two things Charlie March arrived with in Korea as bait."

Muir shook out the match. He added it to the pile.

"Morning briefing, next day. Least important and last. I stepped to my podium. Made my intel report to disinterested brass. Announced Q and A that they, as usual, took as the announcement to head for the doors, when Charlie March commanded everyone's attention thrusting high his hand in a most eager *Teacher, you forgot to give us homework* manner.

"'Sir? You. Yes?' No one noticed. I raised the volume. 'You are credentialed, I'm assuming, sir, since you are here?'

"An impromptu flash of clandestine officer instinct: transpose a false question of security upon your cohort to draw your targets to you as allies. The officers leaving the room stopped.

"A light bird colonel, in whose path Charlie March stood, demanded Charlie March's credentials. Charlie March presented a State Department passport and US military clearance credential entirely different from the identification he'd shown me. Once confirmed 'good guy,' everyone lingered in annoyed reluctance to listen.

"'Your question, sir?'

"'At State we've been made to understand that your Marine listening posts have intercepted Chinese cross-talk,' said Charlie March.

"That put the entire staff back in their seats.

"'Those Marines are relaying information back to you.' His voice was raised, practically shouting at me: 'You, Lieutenant!'—Muir pointed to himself and mouthed, *me*, as if reliving his surprise—'Cross-talk that Red Chinese military forces are building up an invasion force along the Yalu River.'

"The South Koreans were angry. The US staff officers: wickedly guilty. I was stunned. What an asshole. I hung like a marionette, with the tension released from my strings. He blasted me again.

"'And yet, Lieutenant, you peddle pabulum and bring up nothing of this pending threat.'

"Some kind of best friend; the son of a bitch was hollering at me. I collected a breath in preparation to defending myself, but Charlie March gave me a twitch of his cheek: *Don't speak.*

"So I didn't.

"The light colonel filled the void. 'Undersecretary Grigsly,' he addressed Charlie March. 'We are well aware of the Chinese military demonstrations along their border. We do not at this time—as the United States of America are not at war with the Red Chinese—believe it pertinent to this briefing on current combat conditions.'

"That drew in a little manly 'Merican bluster from our team, but our South Korean counterparts agitated. Their voices rose in the high-pitched snap-crackle glissandos of their language.

"Sounds somewhat whiny when aggressive. In that room: like a concerto for tile saw. I didn't move or change expression, but I was secretly damn-well pleased.

"The lieutenant colonel was on the spot now, so he angled his ire on me. 'That said, Lieutenant Muir has been collecting intelligence reports on these Chinese demonstrations. Why hasn't he presented them? I have no idea, but it will be looked into. If he would present that intel at this time—Lieutenant?'

"I accepted a file from Jewel, proud of her man's sudden ascendancy, no one bothering to wonder why she'd come prepared with it.

"Believe me: I spoke at length—my first briefing on the Chinese threat—to the alarm and embarrassment of my superiors."

Muir's eyes gleamed in the faraway light of memory and, with whiskey help, drew my inner eye to see to the other side of the misty curtain his words were drawing back. I pictured him young and handsome in the way his beautiful Jewel might have seen him. I saw him as someone I'd never known. It bothered me and made me sad—and that bothered me more.

"From actions taken based upon that briefing," Muir went on, "Charlie March secured the second part of his promise to me.

Marines were saved. But it was much too little, half again much too late. Chinese soldiers were crossing the Yalu into Korea. RF-80 converted Shooting Star fighters, flown by Charlie March's irregulars gang, showed photos of Chinese forces, thousands strong, extended as far as the eye could see stretched along a curving dirt road back into the barren, flat, snow-covered wastes of China."

Muir added another butt to his ashtray and stared at it a long time. "Our forward positions, far too undermanned to oppose the invaders in force, fell back with heavy casualties."

A mound of snow-white ash. Burned and broken matchsticks. The butts, brown-tarred filters with black crumpled ends. A heap of fallen dead.

11

"On November 14, 1950, a cold front swept down from Siberia through Manchuria, to descend upon Korea."

Smoke.

"Temperatures fell to thirty below."

Smoke.

"Men of the First Battalion, Seventh Marines, First Division—about fifteen thousand—dug into the frozen ground and fought the snow, ice, and wind of the most brutal Korean winter in fifty years."

Smoke.

"Frostbite chewed fingers and toes, bit off nose tips, blackened cheeks. Weapons malfunctioned as snow, dry as dirt, jammed mechanisms. Grease froze. Vehicles needed constant heating to keep drive shafts from locking and engines from seizing. Those guys had enough on their hands and were glad to be out of combat. But heavy combat was coming.

"Thanks to Charlie March, I'd made captain by then. I'd graduated from the schoolhouse all the way to a weekly briefing inside MacArthur's personal headquarters at the Dai Ichi Building in Tokyo. Instead of a chalkboard and my dingy files, I had an honest-to-God *Strangelove* Big Board replete—"

"Replete?"

"Adjective. Filled, fulled, well stocked—"

He poured me more to drink.

"Replete. Aerial photography. Weather and battle maps. All professionally produced by Marine Corps geographical staff. Hell, I had my own pointing stick." He mimed slapping it in his hand.

"Better than that, or so I thought, our American Caesar seemed interested in what I had to say. I reported that the Chinese People's Volunteer Army was assembling for an all-out thrust down the road between the Chosin Reservoir and Kot'o-ri, and I got Big Chief worried. Problem was? I was a lone voice of disaster and I was going up against MacArthur's own vanity-led, anti-CIA, 'Go Army!' G-2 in the form of the maybe-maybe not birthname-born Adolf Karl Tscheppe-Weidenbach 'Sir Charles' Willoughby."

"Who?"

"Yeah. He wasn't wearing his monocle the day I drew the target on my own back by contradicting what he'd been whispering in MacArthur's ear."

Muir shook his head at the memory. Drank.

"An extreme right, racist, anti-Semite whose proclaimed hero was Spain's fascist dictator Generalissimo Francisco Franco. Willoughby was not simply MacArthur's chief intelligence officer for the Korean conflict—"

"Police action."

"Stop interrupting—he was the *only* intelligence officer allowed voice. Mac was worried. Worried the truth about the Chicoms would get out. Willoughby's sole purpose was to keep the CIA out of Korea and that meant ignoring the Chinese coming in.

"Charlie March knew this. He'd sent me into MacArthur's Tokyo court of toadies not to warn but to goad. He knew that Willoughby would scrape me—a wet-behind-the-ears Marine town crier of a Chicom doom—off the bottom of his shoe and show his big daddy the excrement.

"In other words, I was the sacrificial fly for Willoughby to easily swat into a catastrophic failure on the whereabouts and intentions of China's armies. Only then—with a MacArthur boner—"

"His dick?"

"Means blunder, dick. Only then would the Agency finally be allowed en masse into the region. So, in spite of every bit of accurate intelligence my recon units and LPs were providing me, Willoughby sent me on my way, thanking me for my misanalyzed diligence, and proclaimed that what I'd reported was little more than a raiding force.

"On December first of '51, the Ninth Corp of the Chinese PVA—nominally one hundred fifty thousand strong, making the PVA the largest volunteer organization never to have seen a volunteer—surrounded the Marines dug into the bitter winter at the Chosin Reservoir. Finger-and-toes guys, remember?"

"DAT's got it—don't distract."

Muir flicked the long end of ash awaiting attention at the front of his cigarette and took a satisfied drag. He studied me a beat.

What is he waiting for, applause?

He let the smoke flue through his nose. "We Marines are such that we wear one of our most brutal, bitter defeats as a badge of honor. None of us who were there should have survived."

Us who were there?

"Muir, your hotel headquarters sheets-changed-daily double bed versus a hole in the frozen ground are a whole lotta different kind of 'there.'"

"What you know, Aiken, could be written on the head of a pin. In my office at Langley—gotta flag..."

I know his flag. Seen it. Many times before. Muir didn't know, but as recently as this morning. I'd finished writing my proposal for not only locking Muir's mouth as Harker had requested, but with my added recommendation and plan for making the lock permanent on the front door. Although my career along the sidelines gives me every personal reason for vindictiveness against the man who kept me from the only job with the Company I'd ever wanted—would have been excellent at—my decision to effect Muir's retirement from the Agency was nothing personal.

After the fall of communism, a new era dawns upon us. New leaders everywhere. Harker. Folger. Reagan's second—ex-CIA Director Bush—standing in at the duel. A different course. Dialogue better than dying. Kilobauds better than killing. Finesse better than Muir. My job as an attorney is to protect the Seventh Floor's vision. Build the foundation that secures the Young Turks a path to become the Old Turks. The computer age has arrived and dinosaurs are banned, too plodding and destructive for the information highway. We've all read Crichton: real dinosaurs cannot be contained by technology. I knew how they viewed Muir. He was the Young Turks' T-Rex. It was time for Muir to go.

THIS MORNING, back at Langley, I was inside Muir's office. Me, behind his lowest-government-standard, putty-painted, pressed and personality-free sheet-metal desk. He could have had any desk of his choice. His secretary, Gladys Jlassi—warm smile, hard eyes in the round, dark face of a woman as strong as her loyalty deep—she'd given up halfway through her twenty years with Muir to persuade him to change it. He insisted the desk was lucky.

I sat behind Muir's desk.

It was off center to the room, closer to the arrow-slit windows double-paned with anti-electronic eavesdropping white noise that fills the space between the glass. It faces three tight walls of mud-colored filing cabinets. The middle of each cabinet has a safe-style combination lock. With the two briefing books I'd prepared for Deputy Director Harker and Director Folger in front of me, I might as well have been Moses contemplating the tablets from God.

Mine: more airtight.

An officer from the Office of Security—a big, kindly, but no-nonsense bull named Palali, a Samoan guy, who works directly for the director—shoulder-braced the doorway as I took in the fourth wall. Fourth wall: only place in the office offering a glimpse into Muir's heart. A collection of maps from around the world. Antique parchment to sat-recon. They surround a tattered, partially burnt, forty-eight-starred American flag.

The forty-nine-star version became official Fourth of July 1959, followed by the fifty-star version ordered up by Eisenhower in August that same year to be adopted July 1960. Muir's wreck of a flag had been the model in service since 1912. It had only appeared on his wall in the past year. I'd asked him about it twice. The first time he'd blatantly ignored my question. The second, he'd told me, quite pointedly, that my business was to mind my own.

By counting stars, I was doing my math. Muir born 1929. Can't be a flag from the First World War. Enters the Marine Corps at eighteen. 1947. No service World War Two. Since he was staff and hadn't seen action in Korea and had left early in '51 to join the Agency, he wouldn't have hung someone else's credit as his own honor. Assume it's some covert Cold War hugger-mugger he'd pursued and choked on. After all: it is shredded and half-burned.

Palali exchanged words over his ear-mic'd radio. He met my eye. "Mr. Aiken, the director's ready for you in his conference room."

I gave him a nod and stood with a heavy sigh. I put my palm on the desk. A gesture equal parts drawing confidence and saying goodbye, a hand on a terminally fevered brow. I was jarred from the moment by the chirp of my mobile phone. Drew a scowl from my escort as a new and major rule few follow is that all cellular devices are to be deactivated upon entrance to headquarters.

"Forgot. Sorry."

I glanced at the number. Not one I recognized but definitely dreaded. I declined the call. I stared at the number.

"Mr. Aiken, deactivate your device or I will confiscate it. And do not keep the director waiting, sir."

I held up a *wait* finger and lifted the receiver of Muir's green—meaning secure and untraceable—desk telephone. I dialed the number that had just tried me. It was answered on the first ring.

"Homicide. Detective Georges here…"

Back on the porch, Muir repeated, "You've seen my American flag?"

"I heard you. You know I've seen it."

"That flag flew at Chosin. Marine Headquarters, Yudam-ni. I snatched it before we retreated. Before I was hit."

Muir reached in. I thought for his drink. Instead, he switched off my recorder.

"You can't do that."

"Then you forgot my First Rule of Thumb."

"You have twenty 'First Rules of Thumb.' Your 'Second' rules I can't even count."

His eyes laughed at me. Or, maybe—thinking about it now—with me. I don't know. I don't know why I should care. I gave it to him. "Give me the Rule."

"First Rule of Thumb: Always achieve the impossible."

"Well, in this case, your achievement makes me look stupid. And suspicious. There's a chip in that device. It timestamps when it goes on and off."

"There isn't."

"Yes. Muir. There is."

There isn't.

He refreshed his drink. I indicated mine so he did that too.

"You never could learn," he said. "Looking stupid is one of the most effective tools in this job."

"That's why you've made me look stupid so many times?"

"Got you here to me today. Dumbo."

We drank.

He said, "I'm not going to be able to take that flag out of headquarters with me when this is over."

"I will make sure you're given a big enough box for all your personal items."

"Listen to me. The flag isn't mine."

"Whose is it?"

"It belongs to Bishop."

"He wasn't even born in 1950."

"Trust me. It's his. It was Tom Bishop's *Strangelove* ticket."

After Vietnam, Muir had made the Bishop recruitment approach in West Berlin's Tierpark U-Bahn station. I have my own copy of Bishop's file and Muir's recruitment reports to verify that. They make no mention of a flag.

Same way they don't mention a first wife.

Goddamn with his keeping secrets—even from *us.*

Especially from us, Muir would say. And I know now how very dead-on right indeed—even though at that point he had no idea how I was going to fire my arrow through his heart.

I looked at the recorder.

Muir shrugged. "His loss. And yours."

We both grabbed the recorder at the same time, his thumb hitting Record, mine plunging Stop. I wrenched it away.

"Talk. Then I'll decide what I do with that mangy flag a'yours."

Muir measured me with his gaze. For a coffin. He assured validity with a sage nod: a move designed to make you feel worthy and indebt you to him. Seen it a thousand times.

Take your best shot, Muir.

"Christmas Eve. I was married to Sandy at the time."

"Your second wife. Longest marriage too."

"Don't earmark her. You don't know her."

MAYBE I'M TOO WASTED at this second as the stewardess—oh yeah, *flight attendant*—reluctantly gives me another Johnnie-boy I unscrew and shoot. Maybe I am and I'm wrong, but he wanted me hammered to join him at his level, and at his level I've distilled this: every time he's worded phrases to hit me below the belt, I think it's always been a decoy to protect his most vulnerable side.

The side that tells the truth.

12

"WE'D HAD A COCKTAIL PARTY. Our place. Embassy folk—Ambassador Cathcart and his lovely wife were there. I wanted to ply Bishop with as much back-home bonhomie as I could pack into a little Tierpark two-bedroom. Postcard American Christmas. The holiday food and the drink. *Mutzbraten* instead of ham, but what the hell? The music—a little of your favorite Sinatra *'World falls in love'* Kris Kringling *'time a'year'* on the hi-fi."

Asshole.

"To follow it up, we all caroled our inebriated way through fresh falling snow—that I didn't arrange but gave the proper thanks—to the midnight service at the American Church. I stopped him on the sidewalk at the bottom of the steps, asked him to wait while I finished my smoke and let everyone else get inside.

"'Something I got for you, Tom.' I reached into my overcoat and offered him a present wrapped poorly enough to seem earnest and homespun. He had snowflakes on his nose and eyelashes, pretty much a kid at heart. 'Go ahead. Open it.'

"He did. I'd folded it such a way it looked like a bundle of red and white rags. Then Bishop turned it over and revealed a star.

"'A flag, sir?' he asked, spreading it out, revealing it as you've seen.

"'From Marine headquarters at Yudam-ni.'

"Same way I said it to you, Aiken. How I snatched it before we retreated, before I was hit. I told him.

"'I want you to have it.'

"I could see I'd already choked him up. He didn't know what to say. He said: 'I don't know what to say, sir.' Then he said, 'Did you know my father served under this flag, Mr. Muir?"

Muir wasn't about to get me choked up. I'm not a fool for Muir as much as Bishop. I kneaded my tongue with my teeth to be sure.

"I told him; I knew his dad served. Sure. And Bishop laid it right in my lap.

"'He was Marine. Like us. KIA in Korea. Body never recovered, never returned.'

"He was taking it hard. Like a Marine: trying not to show it. Singing began inside." Muir blew a stream of smoke right at me and chased it with, "*'Hark the herald angels si-ing...'*

"I put an arm around Bishop's shoulder," said Muir. "'Semper Fi, Tom.'"

"'Back at you, sir.'"

Muir held his current cigarette straight up like a soldier at attention. He blew across the tip, staring at the red-hot cherry.

"There's nothing about this in his record," I said.

And fucking par for the course here.

"There's nothing about yours in yours either. Fathers are private. I avoid them at all costs."

I'm still puzzling why he said that. His entire *modus operandi* operates around fathers. He knew all about mine—I'd told him—so if it wasn't in my record, that was his doing. This father thing was all about him. I realized in all the years I'd known him, he'd never mentioned his own once.

I felt for Muir. Felt for Tom Bishop. Felt for all they'd had and all they'd lost. Muir hadn't gotten me to his level yet, but I suddenly felt a twinge of alcohol-lit charitability. Their relationship was so broken. I actually feared for both of them—Muir especially—if they ever were to meet again.

He reached to reactivate the recorder, but I waved him off.

"Why do you have the flag and not him?"

"If I don't get to that, will you still carry out this last request, as it were?"

"As it were, is, might be, or might have been—get this straight, *sir*," I mocked. I'll never show him an emotion. "I don't owe you anything."

"Jury's out?"

"And they don't like you." I snapped on the device. "Why were you at the front? Something to do with Charlie March?"

"No. He wasn't a Marine. I went on my own initiative."

"You Marines, all about initiative."

"Number Four out of the 'Fourteen Marine Corps Leadership Traits: Initiative is taking action even though you haven't been given orders. It means meeting new and unexpected situations with prompt action. It includes using resourcefulness to get something done without the normal material or methods being available to you.'"

My forehead furrowed. "How's that translate to you stealing a flag?"

"Somehow it does." He chuckled. "By the time I'd arrived, the Chinese had overrun our position, everyone fighting for their lives and falling back. Grabbing that flag was all I had time for.

"I'll be honest: I was scared to death. My sergeant and I pulled as many men as we could onto our jeep and joined the breakout. Small arms fire—both directions—then about a half-dozen mortar rounds that, unlike the movies, don't whistle in their arrival. Just sudden explosions of not-there, relentlessly-there. Next thing I know, jeep's flipped. Hit? I dunno. My back feels ripped open with fire, the ground slams up into my face. I watched a tank swerve to miss me and that's it.

"Some guys from the tank jumped down and grabbed me. Pulled me aboard. I'm told I two-fisted that flag so tightly, Corpsmen had to tear my parka up from behind. Couldn't get at my wound any other way."

He stopped to smoke, to let the moment resonate. Moments can't resonate on tape. Because tape doesn't measure emotion. Tape can't be played upon.

"The reason I'd taken the initiative and gone uninvited and unannounced was I had begun to feel in a corner of my heart I wouldn't consciously acknowledge that my intel was compromised. This had been going on inside me for a couple weeks. Had I seen Charlie March in any of that time, I'd have brought it up with him. But, having successfully launched me on my path of lifelong duplicity all those months earlier, he'd vanished. I'd gone to that Frozen Chosin because I knew it was going to be bad and—if it was all going to hell anyway—I wanted to go to hell with my brothers in the Corps." Muir sighed. "Almost did."

He lifted his glass to drink, then stopped halfway with it. He was there again, staring at that something his story was leading to, wanting and not wanting to get there. He was leaning forward, elbow on his knee, the glass of Gulf rainwater and liquor the color of Jewel's eyes level with his gaze.

"Jewel carried me through the worst of three operations they went in to mine the nuggets of shrapnel, and each time she brought me back. If I hadn't had her, it would have been easy to let go and take the permanent leave that presented itself every time I went under the knife.

"Strings pulled by Charlie March had me recovering in a private room in a Seoul hospital rather than aboard one of the hospital ships where the rest of the Marines went. Jewel would sit at my bedside cleaning my wounds, dressing them. She'd hand-feed me soup—something you want later in life, not when you're twenty-one."

I nodded—*Never going to have that*—to keep him talking.

"She'd admire my Purple Heart, well deserved, and my Bronze Star I'm sure was a mistake.

"I'd say, 'Jewel. Put 'em away, they embarrass me.'

"And this is something I noticed. And it stuck with me later." He sipped and put down his glass. "She didn't look at them all dreamy-eyed and girlie; she studied the medals as if trying to find the secret of me inside them. She said once about the Purple Heart, 'They should have cast it from the pieces they took out of you. That's how we'd do it.'

"'In the drawer, honey,' I said. 'Come on.'

"She put them away and I reached for her. 'Now kiss me. Let me know I'm still alive.'

"'I kissed you ten minutes ago for that,' and I'd tell her, 'Kiss me again,' and she would."

Muir picked up his glass again. "Jewel. Those eyes."

He drank some. "Charlie March never visited me all that time." Muir polished off the glass. "They didn't like each other."

Muir went on. "In recovery, those feelings that had brought me to the front had coalesced, moving from heart to mind. To belief. A belief that no matter what we were secretly picking up from enemy broadcasts, the Chinese knew that we had it and readjusted to thwart any countermove we attempted to make.

"I was convinced we had an enemy spy among us. I was desperate to contact Charlie March and urged Jewel to find him.

"At first she refused, but I pushed her and bit by bit, through her civilian connections, she put the puzzle of his whereabouts together."

I let myself imagine Jewel's refusal of Muir's request, the strain Charlie March put on their relationship, and her submission to Muir, the dutiful Asian wife. I was drunk with stereotypes to assail my own matrimonial misery.

"And then came Hill Six-two-six. I was back at MacArthur's headquarters and we were about to turn the tide against the Chicoms and the Norks with a counteroffensive that was anchored by my best, longest operating Marine recon team."

He described the briefing by *The General* himself, Muir one of many Marine and Allied officers vigorously taking notes. He had me picture his G-2 communications room, secure and guarded by armed Marines who had orders to shoot anyone unauthorized coming through the door. He painted himself into a room in a desperate panic.

"'They can't be gone,'" Muir said, reliving it.

"I was shouting to my operator, 'Just *gone?* They can't be. We just spoke!'

"But all my radioman kept repeating was, 'Captain Muir, Hill Six-two-six is off the air and the wire is dead.'

"Back at my office, Jewel watched from the doorway as I shoveled telex sheets, reports, files into my safe. In my eagerness for action, I almost blustered past her, but I stopped. We embraced—me angry, she sad, something inevitable about herself even then—but we didn't speak and I hurried out.

"She'd located his whereabouts. A weeklong bender at some geisha house. They call them *KiSaeng* in Korea, but they're identical to the Japanese equivalent. Still are. Anyway, I barged into a private salon, to the sight of dainty fingers with bright-red nails placing deep-fried, salted minnows on Charlie March's tongue. Another set of fingers—different nail polish distinguishing—following the fish with a slice of peeled orange before a third hand came in with whiskey and I said, 'You've gotta get me to the front. And I mean it. Now.'

"Charlie March pushed the whiskey away. He pushed away the KiSaeng girls. He put on his mask of embarrassment.

"'Nathan? What're you doing here? How did you find me? This looks awful. Who else knows—'

"'Shut up. I don't care.'

"Tellya, Russell, I was crazy.

"He said, 'Nathan, I guess I dropped the ball—what's happened?—I thought—' and by this time he's shouldering into his combat bush jacket conveniently at hand—'I thought you had everything under control.'

"Then he guilted me: 'No one knows you're *here*, I hope not.'

"'So what? Here? No!' I stammered. 'Listen to me! This is important!'

"'Of course. Ask. Anything you need.'

"By the time I'd finished he was already pushing me aboard an unmarked chopper. He signs off for it, and then he boards behind me, and that's how a good recruitment plays. Get your asset to think he's the control, then create the debt; when he takes the ticket, it was his idea all along.

"The moment I boarded his helicopter, I wasn't flying so much to Hill Six-two-six but to the waiting tit of Charlie March's CIA."

Muir gave me a perfunctory look. I knew exactly what he was talking about. It's how we work. How he worked Bishop with the flag.

"Charlie March knew what we'd find. I had an immature hope they'd been captured, read their Geneva Convention, marched to a camp for later exchange, but my men hadn't gone anywhere. We discovered the bodies of my entire recon squad, all nine of my men, face down in the icy mud, hands bound behind their backs with their own radio cables, each shot execution-style in the back of the head.

"I was devastated." He took a deep breath without smoke and dove back in.

"This job kills everyone it takes. Some bang-to-the-back-a'the-head quick. Others cut by cut, one piece carved at a time. The knives: that much sharper as the years grow long and leathery tough. Once we realize that and admit it—admitting it, Russell, that's the important thing—we work to minimize the collateral damage among those on the outside as we defend against all the ways it stalks us. Until we force it to take our unnatural lives by natural causes in the last and tightest corner we've backed ourselves and lured it into."

I've always hated how he throws his sick philosophies and stupid thumbs that are his alone and tries to make them stick in everyone else's eye.

I drank greedily. "This isn't your *Barbara Walters Special.* Stick to March."

"I stuck to him. He braced me with an arm across my back, the brother I never had, and kept me from the collapse I wanted to give into. He walked me away with three horrible words.

"I turned my face to Charlie March—pain, tears in my eyes—I pulled all I could from the phosphorescent rage I saw in his. He was furious. I pulled from that rage because those three words he'd said I knew beyond a shadow of a doubt were true."

I said, "What three words?"

"You've been penetrated."

13

"ALONG WITH MY CAPTAINCY and my marriage, Charlie March had acquired for me one of the twenty-seven private villas—mine really just a little one-bedroom garden house—that attached embassy staff rated if the under-the-table money was right. It would be the only home Jewel and I would ever know. Jewel, and I, and Charlie March. And Johnnie Walker, Charlie March's drink of choice.

"After Hill Six-two-six, Charlie March and I spent long afternoons deep into evening, shades drawn, photos spread across the kitchen table, going through the faces of all the men—US, Allied, Korean—whom I briefed and/or were privy to my intelligence through the distribution chain."

The heat, humidity, and the dew point had gotten back into cooperation. The fog was gone. Wet residue coated every surface to make the world of Muir's Captiva house look like the inside of a polywog's terrarium. I hadn't dried out and I was beginning to smell like I was metamorphosing into a frog. My clothes faintly bath-towel mildewy. Stale tobacco.

1.1 Did the police know where I was?
1.2 Would the Agency work to my favor as long as I worked over Muir to theirs?

Stale guilt.

2.1 Was that why I was letting Muir play his Scheherazade to emasculate the Young Turks at Langley?

2.2 Didn't he know the American version, by Poe, ends with Scheherazade's beheading?

Shit, best to let him keep at it.

Like he said:

3.1 The job's going to kill us all in the end.
3.2 According to Muir, the successful officer prolongs that inevitability as long as humanly possible.

Prolong, Russell. Prolong.

I checked my mind's whiskey ramble and ran it to catch up to Muir as he said, "We zeroed in on the most likely suspects and I began my first fieldwork. We'd separated nine individuals—four American, four South Korean, and my delightful Turk, Miraç Özdemir—from the others. I made clandestine searches of offices, homes, vehicles. None of them turned up shit.

"Meanwhile, Truman removed MacArthur and the US-led UN forces began clobbering the Chicoms and the Norks."

His slurs called up Tolkienesque foes under high-explosive earthquake and napalm downpour to my sotted mind.

"Armistice negotiations were making headway," said Muir. "I knew that once commemorative pens were put to paper, my betrayer, and the betrayer of my Marines, would walk. I got extreme. Some ill-advised break-ins where subjects slept—and woke. Conversations that became hostile interrogations. One night I broke cover completely and busted in on my Turkish major at barbecue. I'd pulled my affable friend out of his seat and my screaming in his face changed his mood straight into elbows."

"Elbows?"

"Miraç was always a bit precious about bruising his fists. Elbows knock heads, split lips, and crack molars better—didn't they teach you that at The Farm?"

"You know everything I was taught at The Farm. You designed my coursework."

"And you've resented me every day since." Muir smirked.

As if I'm in the wrong, wanting a different life than what you forced on me after you dug me from my grave?

"I'd have been back in the hospital had Charlie March not intervened," Muir continued. "He pulled me off and placated Miraç Özdemir, saving face—figuratively and mine literally—with a bottle of Johnnie Walker, a banker's bundle of American cash, and a horny gal from his ubiquitous KiSaeng crew.

"He hauled my ass home. He chewed me out good and I couldn't believe what he went onto next.

"'This is my job—what I do—and I'm giving it up,' said Charlie March.

"I was deranged. I wasn't about to give up.

"'You will. Listen. Truman's found a way out of this—trumps everything. The mole hunt has got to be over.'

"'What way out?' I demanded. 'The negotiations aren't going anywhere.'"

Muir teed me up with a pointed look. "US-Soviet nuclear parity pulled the teeth from the nuclear threat years ago, but back in the golden olden days when we had the only deliverable nuke on the block, dropping one was a real and potent threat. Charlie March says to me: 'President Truman has finally accepted the Company's advice and is threatening the bomb. Tonight. Tomorrow, Pyongyang will sign a treaty or we'll make Hiroshima seem like American compassion. Now sit down and listen.'

"His revelation dropped me into a kitchen chair. I didn't want to believe it, but I did. He went on.

"'What I'm here to ask you,' he said, "is if you're willing—for the good of your country and the betterment of your and Jin's lives—if you'll accept an official offer to come back with me to Washington and join up, permanently, in this work of mine you've taken to so well.'

"'So well? I failed.'

"'Not the way I keep score,' he soothed.

"Like a magician, Charlie March produced another bottle of Johnnie Walker he'd stashed in our place. He put it on the table between us. 'Let's celebrate that tonight, then get out of here—you two with me. It's all arranged.'

"I asked him did the spy get to just go free. Would we never know?"

Muir poured for us, telling me how March did the same for him that helpless night. As they'd raised their glasses, Muir raised his now as March and I became Muir as I touched it with my mug. He said both then and now, both Charlie March to Muir and Muir to me:

"To our future."

And it hurt a little inside.

Only after we drank did Muir say, "But I didn't pick up my glass. I couldn't leave Korea not knowing. I felt my twenty-one years that had made me so grown-up on the altar were kid years, me still at the kids' table. I swore to him I wouldn't give up.

"Charlie March slammed down his glass, hard. 'Don't dare do this. I am giving you exactly what you wanted: getting you and your wife out of the shit. Now, drink.'

"And that's when I saw it. Charlie March's desperation to cover the truth.

"'You know,' I said. 'You know the spy and you won't tell me…'

"Charlie March drained his drink down his throat. He stared me down. 'What I know, you don't want to know. Drink.'

As the power of Muir's story increased, his voice softened. I leaned in, slightly captive if only to capture him. I knew I didn't want to hear where this would go. I watched Muir as if there in that little foreign kitchen with him as he whispered, "I just kept repeating *you know, you know, you know,* and his shoulders slumped and Charlie March bowed his head.

"'What's done is done,' he said, and something about the justice we'd find, hardly worth the personal damage it would cause.

"'Cause whom?!' I flung words at him. 'Who the fuck else do I care about in shithole Seoul? Cause you?'

"But he didn't answer. He didn't have to. I told him what you'd tell him. What anyone in that position—anyone with a heart would tell anyone: 'You're lying.'

"It sucks, Russell, when you can put a count on the times you made love to the person you were supposed to make love to for the rest of your life. Love isn't supposed to be finite."

Muir as March. Me as Muir. And Madeline. And my *heart.*

"I ordered Charlie March out of our house.

"He stood his ground. 'Jin did what she had to do to keep her own family alive and to save you.'

"I beat the living shit out of him and he let me, saying between blows and blood, 'Jin's Soviet control—I killed the son-of-a-bitch. I'll take you to his body—he held your life over her. She had no choice.'

"I kept hitting him as he made for the door. 'She loves you, Nathan. Nothing she did changed any outcome at any time worse than it would have been anyway.'

"'Tell that to my Marines on Six-two-six."

Muir glared through the blue smoke clouding the porch. The rage was there. It had never left.

"Get the fuck out of my home!" Muir barked at March and at me together, and then he blinked. He looked at the Florida night. He smoked.

"I shoved Charlie March onto the gravel walkway." Muir was back to a whisper. "And Charlie March said, 'I'm the one with the authority to make the call here and I say be a man and drop it and grab the love you have.'

"But I grabbed my forty-five. I aimed it between his eyes.

"'If you're not out that gate in five seconds, I'm going to put a fucking bullet in your fucking head.'

"I stalked right up to him. Footstep after footstep, the gravel crunching beneath. Charlie March staggering back.

"'Three, four—' I counted.

"I thumbed back the hammer—'and five,' but he'd backed all the way into the night and was gone."

"You're full of shit, Nathan," I said.

Muir flinched. And then he faced me, his lips spread in a closed-mouth smile.

I said, "There was no Soviet spy in Seoul whom March or anyone else killed. And I know enough about him to know he would never have let a traitor go unexposed, unpunished."

Muir laughed at me. "You naive jackass. Every time you open your mouth with 'what you know,' you reconfirm my decision to never put you in the field."

That hurt deeply… as intended.

"I only regret I didn't listen to him," he said. "Not too long after he left, Jewel came home with the groceries. She called to me from the open front door. I didn't respond. She found me sitting in the dark of the kitchen. She turned on the light. Her pretty eyes went from the Johnnie Walker bottle, empty on its side, to me. Shit-faced and empty of… well, everything.

"I held two items in my lap. She saw them and then she saw my gun where I'd dropped it on the floor. She was duly and wholly frightened.

"I slurred out, 'You betrayed me.'

"Jewel was shaking as she put the groceries on the counter. Fear of exposure. Hiding her secret.

"'Why do you say that, Nathan?' she said. 'Why are you drunk and so angry with me? Why do you have my photos, my *hanbok*?'

"But it wasn't *hanbok*. It was *Joseon-ot*. North Korean. I waved the stitching under her nose. She recoiled.

"She bowed—Asian shame—'I'm alone. I couldn't afford proper *hanbok*.'

"Then she looked at me, excited, as if she suddenly had the answer that solved it all.

"'You asked for it. Remember, Nathan? I wanted to wear my uniform. Like you.'

"'I don't wear Nork dress up.'

"She recoiled as if struck. But I hadn't gotten there. Yet.

"I said, 'Why would you give my secrets to my enemy and allow the men I serve with to be killed? What kind of person are you?'

"Jewel went rigid. She was terrorized yet still so beautiful, and that just made it hurt so much more.

"She denied it, of course. She claimed not to know what I was talking about. She made herself look fragile like she could. Oh, yeah. She was good at that."

Muir smashed a cigarette. He didn't light another. "Fragile like she was. I leaped at her. I grabbed. I twisted her arm around her back. I pulled her into me. I bent into Jewel's ear and I screamed in it:

"'You're a fucking spy! And you fucking betrayed me!'

"I hurled her across the floor. And she smashed into the cabinets. Made the whole kitchen, whole house, rattle."

Muir made a gentle sweeping motion with his arm, nothing like his words described—a motion all given up and defeated—and ended with a cigarette. He struck the match with his thumb like the plunger on a detonator.

"I swayed over her. She tried to get up. I threw her back. 'Makes fucking sense how you survived in the city all alone without getting shot.'

"She insisted she was getting our papers, so I banged her head again. She was crying and covering her face.

"'Stop hiding!'

"'Why are you saying this to me? You love me!'

"'I hate you.'

"She dropped her hands to the floor, sobbing out her hope, but a little bravery was left to meet my gaze and say she loved me again.

"'You gave them our secrets.'

"'I did not.'

"Admit you did.'

Muir was rolling with it, his eyes dead and locked with mine, forcing me to be there with him.

"'I won't,' she said.

"'You will—' and I grabbed her thick hair all done up on her head and I bowled her into the table. 'Oh, you will.'

"That photo album I mentioned? I opened it and I beat her head with it. Photos of her childhood and her family—her whole life—violated, mixed up, scattered with her falling tears.

"'This is your family. I shoulda looked. Almost all in the North.'

"She bawled, 'They were executed—my father and my mother!— when I joined *this* government. You know that.'

"She'd only told me that. I didn't know it. I said prove all I was saying, all I was accusing her with, *wasn't* true.

"'No. Nathan…' she said. 'No. If you do this… then you do not believe I am your wife.'

"She reached out longing arms to save me, but Jewel could see past the rage, through my eyes and into my heart, that her words meant nothing to me.

"I told her I'd given her an order and she was to prove she wasn't a spy. Right then. Right there.

"She answered me in Korean. 'Our marriage is my proof. Kiss me. You love me.'

"I screamed back in my drunken Korean that that wasn't good enough and I lunged for her again, but I was hammered. I twisted and stumbled, and she'd already formulated a plan. She dodged me, moving to enact it.

"Before I could grab her from the snow of photographs, I fell on the floor. She had my pistol."

Muir paused to drink. When I didn't move, he said, "Bottoms up." And then he muttered something that sounded like *I can't* or maybe *I won't do this alone.* I couldn't swallow, I'd felt the weight of that same gun in my hand last night.

Muir sat back in the chair that was either part of the ugliest set belonging to the guy who owned this place or a wedding gift from Charlie March after Jewel. He collected himself.

"How horrible it is," Muir said, "to feel hatred for someone you love more than life itself."

I was terrified by that, but if Muir saw it in me, he didn't understand the whole of my present truth—my lost jewel, my Madeline—lying in wait for me.

"I could have found a way to forgive her… I tell myself every morning when I wake up. Before I open my eyes. That she is beside me. But it never comes to that. Jewel took my gun and our marriage on her lips—"

My mind flashed to my car. Fort Marcy Park. My own gun against my head, inside my mouth, behind my ear. Jewel possessed none of my hesitation. I hated Nathan Muir, at that moment more than now, because my heart was breaking for him and, thank you very much, I've broken it very easily all by myself.

"My Jewel put a bullet through her heart. Her secret died with her. Two days later, he came back."

"Charlie March," I said, for clarity on the DAT.

"Who the hell you think?"

"Come on, Muir. I'm sorry, it's for the"—I jerked my head at the recorder—"for the record."

"Two days later," Muir repeated, "he came back."

I flipped him off. He smirked. Cold bastard.

"He made his way through the mess of the kitchen to our bedroom. Jewel was dead and bloating—"I'd moved her onto the bed. Me, I was lost in a sea of alcohol and recrimination, broken and washed up on the floor at her feet. Bottles everywhere. My boozy, cried-out eyes flickered to the spook.

"Charlie March buried everything. Nowhere in any record is there evidence that my wife or anyone else on the intelligence staff spied against America in Korea.

"He pulled me up. My legs were Jell-O. He held me. Up to that point, I'd thought of him as a big brother. That day he replaced my father—who'd been absent in my life enough for me not to know him. I'm not sure how long I cried into Charlie March's chest, but the memory of him patting my back and soothing me, and the smell of his bay rum cologne he always wears—wore—comes back to me as hours just being held and comforted. Understood and loved.

"Charlie March took me under his wing. He became everything to me. Father, brother, priest. He got me out of Korea, out of the Corps as he'd originally come to Seoul to do. He took the broken pieces of my life and he put me back together in his image."

Muir lifted the bottle. "Two done. Keep it running," he said about the recorder as he came to his feet.

"I eventually healed, which is to say I came to a place where I could accept that I would never be whole again." He spoke these words as he walked to the doors, the condensation from the fog-drip ran snakes down the glass.

"Third bottle, Jeremy," he called, stepping through, mocking Harker through the tape. "If you're counting."

Muir came out with the fresh bottle, saying, "You asked when I married him?"

Charlie March. Yeah, I asked.

"April Fool's Day." He cracked the seal, pulled the cork, poured. "We always got a kick out of that—1951."

Muir resumed his seat. "Lobby of the Old Headquarters Building—only building then—and brand new. Standing over the seal, Charlie March behind me with some other Agency personnel in attendance, me and nine other newly minted officers welcomed to the Clandestine Service by Director Allen Dulles."

Muir relaxed back into his confession, into his obscuring smoke, his drowning drink.

"With March at my shoulder guiding my path, I officially became an officer of the Central Intelligence Agency, Clandestine Service."

PART TWO

CESSION

"Just as dogs love to chew bones, the mind loves to get its teeth into problems. That's why it does crossword puzzles and builds atom bombs."

—Eckhart Tolle, *Guardians of Being: Spiritual Teachings from our Dogs and Cats*

14

I'D NODDED OFF. Fuck it—strike that—I passed out. I passed out two swallows into the third bottle. I remember Muir opening it. He said something like, "Never delay killing a pretty girl or opening a bottle of whiskey," or maybe I'd substituted "killing" inside my head for the "kissing a pretty girl" he'd offered, or maybe it was the other way around, but they both amounted to the same: Madeline. It's a shame because at that tipping point of the kitty-cat cup, I remember loving the taste and the feeling, and declaring it to myself, and probably out loud but maybe not. So much I pretend I say out loud because in my mind I'm capable of anything. A whole life unstated as a different man—the past as well as the future—with a heart of darkness.

I was back on the drinking train. All the way to the end of the line.

"The Young Turks. They all know about Madeline," Muir said.

After last night, more than you, my good ol' dead-wifed pal.

He guided me to a back bedroom he'd made up. He waited in the doorway as I stumbled inside and took what bearings I couldn't quite navigate.

"If you're not careful, they'll use it to destroy you."

I didn't answer. Intelligible speech tweren't me strong suit at the moment. But Muir wasn't looking for my answer. He gave me a shove that propelled me to the bed, the edge of which I grabbed halfway to the floor.

"You used to do this better, Russell."

You remembering the last time? Remembering New York City?

"I'm getting 'Rusty,'" I sniggered.

"Do yourself a favor and take those four aspirin with that jug of water I've put out. Then do forty push-ups. You'll be fine to start again when you wake. Or have another drink. You'll find that in a decanter behind the water. Suit yourself."

I tilted until gravity sent me two-stepping to the dresser where those things were. I considered the aspirin, the water, or would I do the booze? Whatever the remedy, neither would include any push-ups.

I thought he'd gone but wasn't really surprised to hear from the doorway behind me as I swayed there, stupidly staring: "Aiken, I'm going to tell you something now and this *is* important. So listen, okay?"

The guy's favorite fucking phrase. I'm done listening, Mr. Muir, Nathan.

I refused to turn. Would have fallen anyway. I didn't feel like picking up my dignity in front of him. I handled that by butt-twisting down onto the bed, painfully hitting some kind of wooden board that extended from the frame much higher than I'd count on were I sober. I gripped it two-handed.

Muir said, "Honesty and morality when doubled up as a reason for being, or for doing, or for having your way of it—when each needs the other for reinforcement and validation—honesty and morality become a limited partnership in crime."

I cocked my head, indicating, or trying to indicate, that I was listening. I wasn't understanding.

"You a spiritual man, Aiken?"

"I go to church. Y'know Mad'lin and I go t'church."

"Shut up, Dumbo. I didn't say 'religious,' I said 'spiritual.'"

"They different?"

"Forget it. For now."

He left.

I skipped the aspirin and water—

I'm a drinkin' man again—

—and took a big pull of scotch before throwing up in the wastebasket and collapsing.

I'll be honest. Some time was spent on the floor. I don't know how much.

I was much better for the vomiting and climbed over the wooden side of the bed onto the mattress. The wood ran head, foot, and sides for a coffin-like sleep experience. Muir explained later that the bed had belonged to a nineteenth-century ship captain and had come from the sea. Washed up on the beach, or bought at auction by Muir, or by "the man who owned the house," he didn't bother to bullshit me, but the bed had the sides so in the pitch of a storm, a fellow wouldn't easily roll onto the deck.

Lying there, I steered my thoughts from coffins, and let it remind me of the top bunk of the bunk beds of my childhood. I loved those beds, even though the bottom bunk remained empty, my father killed before he and my mother got around to a brother I wanted that they'd no intention of conceiving. They hadn't bought the bunk beds. The beds were hand-me-down.

It was how those bunk beds became mine, I remembered now, waiting to pass into a drunk's dreamless unconsciousness.

Thirteen years sober. What am I doing? God, why have I done these things I've done?

For a moment, I despised myself more than usual.

Cirrhosis of the liver killed my uncle George at the age of fifty-eight—four years younger than Muir is now. It's the primary reason I promised myself I wouldn't be a drinker or an alcoholic like my dad's brother and, if honest, my own father, who'd have probably gone the same way if not for the love-drunk kid in the liquor-dry Kansas town of bloody Quinter.

I started learning about drinking on Saturdays when I was six or seven. My mother would allow me to go with them—Dad and Uncle George—on their Saturday-morning walks. These walks never strolled down any lane or set foot in any George Seurat park painting, though my mother may have thought it the point. These walks took me from one bar to another, then another, and another, where I would be left to peek into the perpetual cigarette smoke day-for-nights or the permanent Happy Hour fry kitchens framed in alley backdoors by the light of the living world that never creeps into a good bar if the devil can help it.

From my vantage point, I watched them flip back shots and beers while George worked his snitches and took protection payoffs from the prostitutes who didn't want pimps—their drugs and their beating—but because they had kids couldn't use their own apartment beds. In turn, George would kick back some of that to the local no-tell motels where they could safely trick.

Uncle George worked narcotics for the Los Angeles Sheriff's. He wasn't a white-hat good guy, but he wasn't a dirty cop. Since he was around more than my dad, he was my primary role model and, because I was there on the night I'm about to explain and know how George came by the bunk beds and what he did the morning after that, Uncle George was my hero.

I was nine years old and an unruly kid. My luck—there weren't any boys on my block near my age—and because I didn't take orders from my sisters, I chose to play alone in the Big Tujunga Creek runoff or among the vacant lots of the Crescenta Valley, scavenging junk I saw as treasures, wire, and string, breaking things, stirring up anthills, digging holes for nothing but that I thought like a terrier, and building forts to play army. Never one-sided in war, I'd build my defenses for a few days, then I'd attack and destroy them for the rest of the week. I'd really needed a brother.

Saturdays I'd always have to come in for soup or slimy canned macaroni and cheese. Sundays, church and chores. Then reading, or puppets—I liked making puppet shows no one watched, thinking out all the dialogue in long silent monologues—or watercoloring with a paint box from Wales, never able to capture what I thought, wild on the page, where the dazzling red monkeys—to riff on the Welsh poet—are still throwing blue coconuts in the rainbow-scribbly jungle. Always indoors.

The six days I wasn't indoors, I made and lived by my own rules. My first drink from a can of beer was in one of those lots around the time the "Big They" (only ever half seen, the "Big They" were the nameless grown-ups who infringed from the outside world they controlled) brought in construction equipment that appeared one morning in preparation for taking down the trees, busting up old foundations if there were any, and clearing the lots to make way for the apartments and condos that, once were all completed, paved over and walled off my childhood imaginary world. I found the Olympia beer can under the seat of a front loader. It was half full and warm from the sun. I took a big swallow.

Of urine.

I still can't get over why the hell the driver peed in the can when he had an entire lot as his toilet. The "Big They" had it out for kids.

I was nine. I'd hidden in Uncle George's car when, overhearing him tell Mom he was going out that night to bust some Mexicans growing opium up the Angeles Crest Mountains above La Cañada, I decided to go uninvited on a ride-along. First stop, a *taqueria* hole in the wall off Colorado Boulevard in Pasadena and the phony bust of a lanky Mexican doper under the red neon El Toreo Café sign.

Uncle George found me on the floor of the back seat where the doper was supposed to go.

"Shit, Rusty."

He and the Mexican spoke Spanish. Some cracks about me, I'm sure, then, I suppose, about their plan for the night. George had cuffed him, but that had been for show. He didn't seem too concerned now, having freed him in the back seat with me.

"I'm Rusty," I said. "What's your name?"

"You don't need to know his name," said Uncle George.

They were friendly, but this chico was definitely under my uncle's thumb.

Uncle George didn't say anything else to me. He wasn't happy, but he didn't seem particularly angry or sad. We drove from the foothills into the mountains. Off the main highway, we wended onto an older paved offshoot, then a long dirt road into a canyon. He parked. He took some flashbulb photos of a blossoming poppy field. He came around and let the Mexican out of the car. They marched into the starlit darkness and, over the next three hours, pulled the entire crop.

While this was going on and confusing me, the Mexican's wife came out of her shack. She lured me from the car to the single-step wooden porch where I sat and she fed me tamales and green beans that Uncle George would tell me later, "Those weren't beans. That was *nopales*—cactus, dodo-bird."

I hadn't remembered the cactus part until just now. Anyway, they finished with the opium poppies and the Mexican woman woke her nine-year-old twin daughters—phantom-eyed girls whose dark faces I'd already seen peering through the shack's single window at me, occasionally at their father and my uncle, but mostly at me.

When the poppies had all been pulled from the field, when the family's possessions had all been pulled from the shack, when the mother, the girls, and I loaded those belongings from that magical night—as only children can see such a night of secrets and crime (if Dad's Sinatra records were grown-up untouchable, an opium farm was out of this world, juicy fruit forbidden)—into the back of their truck, George and the Mexican transferred the uprooted fetal dope into and around the now empty shack. Uncle George and the Mexican siphoned off half of the gasoline from George's car. They poured some on the flowers outside, carried it into the shack and came out with it, just about empty, joking about Uncle George's lighter tossed back and forth between them. Neither man wanted to strike a flame with gasoline-doused fingers.

The Mexican threw the burning lighter through the door—sure enough, his hand flash-lit—and, as the shack and the drugs went up into fiery oblivion, the girls and I and even their mother grinned at the bonfire until Uncle George pulled his revolver, the Mexican cried, and the gunshot rang out.

Like I mentioned back when I was firing my gun: guns are louder than TV pretends. Even louder when you're a kid, and when you're a kid every bullet speaks its singular name as it does its killing work. The Mexican's workhorse collapsed. Uncle George doused it with the rest of the gas and jumped back as the fire leaped onto its hide.

That's how a story about not so innocent Saturday walks to La Crescenta and Tujunga bars becomes the story of my uncle-surrogate-dad shooting an innocent horse and my innocence being corrupted up in the mountains of Los Angeles. A little before sunrise, when the fire was just about over, Uncle George and the Mexican waded into the cinders and smashed up the skeleton. Big bones into little, then scattered. Uncle George gave a wad of money to the wife—money I recognized from his Saturday collection wallet—and transferred the bunk beds, broken down, to the car trunk and back seat. He pointed me into the front seat and then he drove me home.

I sat beside him where he drank from a jar of mescal the Mexican lady had given him and he gave me my first sip or three.

Didn't taste any better than piss, but the aftereffect was soothing and warm.

Two days after the incident with the Mexicans, when I couldn't get that dying-horse-carcass-burning-image out of my mind, my mother told Dad, home on a straight shot from Providence, Rhode Island, late the night before, "Daniel, Russell has been crying all day for no reason and I am sick of it."

"Rusty, kitchen. Front and center. Now.'

A whistle couldn't have brought a dog quicker.

Dad looked me in the eye. "You're crying for that horse and I want you to stop it."

He knew.

"Russell!" my mom called from the kitchen. "If getting a horse is what you—"

"Tami, you've had all day with this. Russ, mules look a lot like horses, especially in the dark. And part horse is exactly what they are. But here's the thing you need to learn right now. Mules have no life in them. Not the kind that God intends. Mules aren't real."

I didn't know what he meant yet, but the water I was treading had been getting colder inside me and the ring he'd tossed was the first one that didn't say *Titanic*.

"It was a mule?" I said in three sobbing attempts.

Yes, he nodded, loving me more than God; yes, he squeezed my shoulder, and Dad allowed the truth. "Even if that mule was a horse, a family like that needs bones to leave behind for the real bad guys."

My mother didn't get it but knew she wasn't supposed to and let herself be glad that whatever this meant, my father had comforted my tears.

"You don't believe me, ask Uncle George."

Uncle George told me never to ask him about that night. I never did. But I found out at fourteen, when Dad decided I should get a head start on driving, and we practiced in the Angeles Crest.

Between frantic "No! No! Stupid, I said clutch... There. No! Clutch! Clutch! Clutch!" my father told me that Uncle George and some deputies had gone up to the site of the burned-down shack the next day with enough handcuffs to shackle nine Mexican Cholos arguing over the kind of teeth the ashes had produced. Went down as the biggest bust of George's career.

As far as I know, the Mexican family survived, protected by the record of that night—both official and Cholo—as having been victims of a murder-suicide that left behind only their large teeth and Ezekiel broken prophecy bones.

Drifting into drunken sleep in the bunk Muir had provided me, I thought again of those two girls with the phantom eyes whose bunk beds my uncle had gotten in the deal that saved their lives. They were my first crush and I wondered if in some miraculous way, had I married one of them, would love have been revealed as something more than the figment of lust and too many lies told too many times that it has been revealed for me?

Of course, I never saw them again and know, as Muir's whiskey finally knocked me out like a bullet in my own skull, that my first loves haven't remembered me at all.

I steadily drank from that car ride in 1960 until I quit in 1978, fourteen years ago in a Manhattan safe house suite where I'd promised Tom Bishop, who'd come to scrape me up, that I'd never touch another single drop.

Here's to you, Bishop, from a mule to a thoroughbred.

15

SO A GUY walks into a Soho bar.

Me.

Place called The Ear Inn. A hole-in-the-wall with a cluttered, oar on the slat-ceiling, brass diver's helmet, forever inchoate but always striving nautical theme that goes back to its earliest days when it opened in 1817. For all the years I'd known it, the neon sign above the door read "BAR." Though its patrons called it The Green Door, it had no other advertised name beyond. Wandering in that afternoon of March 14, 1978, I noticed that new owners had taken some black paint and covered the curves of the gas tubes' first letter, changing it to read "EAR," which it has been known by—The Ear Inn—ever since and ever on as far as the future has come to pass beyond the green door.

It's a two-and-a-half-story, Federal-style townhouse, the James Brown (not that one) Building in an otherwise industrial neighborhood. Fifteen stools along the prominent bar and maybe ten small tables, enough to fill the main room, while a back room has larger tables and linens and napkins and laminated menus. The upstairs has seen its time as both a gaming house and a brothel. A TV high in the far corner, a kitchen with a grill: mostly burger fare, but sometimes crab cakes, sometimes shepherd's pie—once, I remember, spaghetti and meat sauce I ordered and didn't eat. I didn't much go there to eat.

A pre-war wooden and glass phone booth stands just inside the door where, when I entered, a florid-faced, stout fellow in a ratty cardigan and Irish cap was slouched, door closed, phone receiver on his shoulder to disguise, poorly I'd add, his afternoon boilermaker-made boiled-down snooze.

"He's on long distance to Farrah Fawcett on the coast," one of his pals said.

"*He's* Charlie?" I took a stool one removed from them.

I was high from my first field op, criminal as my involvement—well, not *involvement*, maybe *audience-ship*—was. I was bored with tequila, and as The Ear Inn had originally been built on the Hudson River shore and had erected its reputation as a lady-free public house for seafarers and dockworkers, I sailed from tequila to light rum grog. After a pair of those, I tried it with dark rum. After that, I settled on a light-dark combo by reducing the amount of demerara to make room—demerara, the brown-sugar simple syrup from Demerara, Guyana, where Jim Jones had recently located his Jonestown cult and where, in eight months, parishioners would be served a different kind of grog. I upped the lime. No scurvy or cyanide for me.

1978 was a hell of a year for drinking.

Around six o'clock, I tacked east and a bit north on my barstool to Long Island and pirated after their iced teas. I was three-quarters through my third tea; my favorite show, *The Paper Chase*, beginning on CBS up on the TV; and I was engaged in a sparring conversation with some wooden-nickel, woolen-headed immigration lawyer on what a big phony John Houseman was as a Harvard law professor since he didn't resemble any professors this Fernando D. Something-or-esquire had encountered in the heady days of Brooklyn Law night school 1958.

I told him I ran a pipefitting company.

I suggested the networks drop lawyers from all schedules and create a hit show about a refinery. My "you could do a whole season on the plant's HVAC system alone" was enough to get his teeth off my ear, but I didn't get a chance to watch crusty Houseman grumble and kneecap his earnest and angsty TV-pretty students, as programming was interrupted by a *Morton Dean Newsbreak*.

Israeli forces of the IDF had commenced Operation Litani. The Dalal Mughrabi Fatah "Coastal Road Massacre" demonstrated a clear desire by the PLO to sabotage the peace process between Israel and Egypt. The objective of the operation, Morton assured America, was limited to the destruction of PLO bases south of the Litani River in order to restore security in northern Israel.

The Ear shut down at four in the morning. By that time, I think, I'd ordered the spaghetti and meat sauce once again and settled for the burger they actually offered.

I'd made two or three sets of bright-eyed best friends, come and gone and good-riddance that idiot lawyer-loudmouth. I'd made out with a barmaid from up (or was it down?) the road (down the block upstairs—I think, maybe), who had salmon-aspic arms, all pink and covered with tiny red and hard-tipped permanent gooseflesh. I'd personally finished entire bottles of tequila, gin, and Bacardi, and the bartender tending me asked if I needed a cab, but I told him, "I'm good. I'm taking a hotel," while my mind kept swimming back to the television.

The Israelis taking tanks into Lebanon. Palestinian settlements overrun. Bulldozed from God's planet, and Muir, having flapped butterfly wings in New York, had I become party to this killing?

How could that be? How could Muir have anything to do with this Middle Eastern war?

Muir was Berlin. Europe. Bishop: new posting to Moscow.

I hitched up with a group of twenty-somethings. Max, Maria, Punk One and Thing Two, pin-cushioned faces and wild green hair, and a black Cuban named Nina, who with Maria doing the shots I'd met them with, dubbed me Pinta, to which I masculinely conjugated to "Pintao."

We chose to set sail for the New World of an after-hours bar the punks knew in the Village, and all of them clapped and drew me into closer company when I'd gotten off my stool, paid all our tabs, and nicely mimicked the act of ambulation.

But the after-hours was after hours. We wound up in a little nook of a cranny dog-piddle park. They still itched to keep the party alive.

"My room's got a minibar," I said. "Definitely restocked since this—yesterday morning. Imminently so."

None of them had ever seen a minibar, that boon companion of travelers having only made its way from Hong Kong across the globe in the past year. My hotel was above the Village on 21st near 7th. Max suggested that since it was a bit of a trip, we make it worth the trip by tripping.

"It's Green Dragon with Red Dragon overlay," he said, unfolding a piece of soft paper from a tinfoil packet in his wallet. "Not a bad trip on the blotter."

Punk One leaned into him. "Must know, dude. You guys already blazing?"

Maria said, "Pretty much rode it down in the Ear."

Max was tearing off little perforated squares from the sheet and passing them out. Thing Two laughed nervously that the green dragon stamp was Walt Disney's jolly serpent of the recent cartoon.

Max looked Nina in the eye.

She gave him a shy little nod.

He gave her two tabs. She put one on the white frost coating the pink of her tongue. I watched her close her mouth. I could see her rubbing it around the hard palate, sucking and moistening it with saliva. She held the second tab over my waiting hand.

"You ever drop acid, Pintao?"

"I don't think so."

Punk One and Thing Two chuckled to each other. Happy, not mean or menacing. I didn't sense any negativity.

Max said, "You're not a pipefitter, are you?"

"Uh, no."

Nina said, "You have a job, though. What do you do?"

She was sweet. Her hand kneaded my shoulder blades.

Certainly not allowed to, I didn't want to tell them; my mind said *Don't*, but my mouth violated the law to say for me, "I work for the CIA."

Punk One and Thing Two's chuckles became laughter. Nina smiled tenderly. I could see that I delighted her.

Max said, "Well, this won't be speedy at all. Grade stuff like your folks used on the dude who tried to fly out the Statler window."

My stomach clenched. I looked at my shoes. I muttered, "I think we threw him." I looked up for forgiveness. "I'm sorry."

Max gave me a chuck on the shoulder like we were old army buddies. "You don't come off to me like the kind of guy that they'd give *anything* to do..." then tacked on: "with anything like that."

"This will be good for you," Nina said. "Open wide."

And I saw myself as a kid in the dentist chair at the Bar DK children's dentistry, and I tilted back my head and opened my mouth. I felt the edge of her fingernails, smelled my dentist's persimmon Reed's candy breath in my imagination, tongue-touched the warm tips of her fingers as she placed the square of blotter paper tiny green Pete's Dragon red dragon overlay on my tongue.

"How will I know if it works?"

"You'll know, dude," giggled Thing Two.

Nina stroked my cheek. "You're going to stick with me the whole trip and I'm not going to leave you. I'll be your guide. And if you get all thinky—usually not like that anyone's first time—but if the camera turns inside, you're not to talk inside your head. You say everything out loud. To me."

She got excited and joyful. "I'm gonna be the best friend you ever had in the whole wide world, baby. This'll be your bestest Christmas, Easter, and birthday roll't all into one."

And she kissed me. She told me to tell her when I started feeling strange in my stomach.

"Like getting sick?"

"Nope, just strange. Kinda electric. Kind of wiggly. More like an idea of something happening in your tummy than anything actually happening."

We lingered in the park. Maria came on first. She waved her hand in front of her face and secretly smiled. Punk One and Thing Two huddled together, whispering, giggling more. Max looked like the other dog-person-thing in the Goofy cartoons. Goofy's big, rotund neighbor, which I found amusing in its obviousness.

Nina leaned her head on my shoulder. "You feeling it now, baby?"

"I don't think so," I said, distracted by the pattern of weathered paint flaking on the wire bin of the trash stand.

And USSR subs in Bengal Bay, Mandrake.

It was the prettiest green I'd ever seen. It seemed to me the green felt sad. Or the painter had brushed his own sadness into the paint with every stroke. He'd left behind some horsehair bristles. Trapped dry.

Fire leaps from the opium flowers to the mule that wasn't a horse's hide and I'm flying like a Disney-impossible creature.

"Do you see how the lights make the colors look like they're breathing?" I noticed the streetlamps that had been thundering in patient silence for me to notice them.

"Pintao's comin' on to it," Nina said.

Max waved his hand slowly before me. "Any trails?"

"No," I said. "Yes," I said. I saw his hand move in a wash of hand and arm, following it and catching up with a silent sound of *whoosh* I heard-felt-heard.

Like a train into a tunnel.

Sex.

We were walking. Nina was holding my hand. Her hand was warm and dry and a thousand textures. We were all speaking at once and no one was speaking to anyone else or about the same thing and it all made the most beautiful sense spoken word can make.

Although I've never seen, or at least paid attention to any woodchucks I might have seen, Punk One and Thing Two were what woodchucks would be as people. I liked woodchucks as the best animals because of the expressiveness of what woodchuck faces are when in a human form and the chucking noise like wooden clocks their voices made.

As we neared my hotel, I started to understand the meaning within the meaning of what everyone and everything was telling me.

It was a definitive answer, but I struggled to grasp the question. My ears and my hand in Nina's were hearing it exactly-same.

The heartbeat.

The in-out.

I've just met her. Because I've known her forever.

"Nina, are we from an in-out parallel universe?"

"Maybe, Pintao," she purred. "Go with it. If we are, we'll find a photo of us together one day in an empty frame from the sea and then we'll know."

She makes perfect sense.

In-out. Everything from pumping blood that makes us live, to the energy that powers streetlights—in as electricity, out as light: textured, physical—the gas the cab driver puts in his taxi goes "in" the combustion engines and comes "out" as power.

Like blood.

Like sensation/experience "in" as thought, "out" as ideas/action. Like food. (I'm not hungry at all and don't need to poop.) Like booze—drunk not because I'm thirsty. "In" because I want the "out" it releases.

"INFORMATION!" a silent Muir-unlike voice booms.

Alcohol releases me.

The "In-Out" trays on my desk. The in-out of my job. Plan in, ink out; CONPLAN in, war out? Lifeforce in, deathforce out.

This war was already planned before I sat down with Muir.

Before Dalal Mughrabi took her holiday on the Israeli shore.

Someone else's in-out.

"You quiet, baby. You tripping out?"

"In Out."

"Everything. Yeah. We're here. Isn't this your place?"

I peered through the steamy moist glass. I could see the woman at reception. The night manager and the day manager behind, discussing the matters of their shift change. The night manager feels superior to the day manager. He's mocking him, blatantly shifting and posturing like some kind of red rooster. The day manager knows, allows, tests poses like a frightened boy. Their lips are pulled and bouncing rubber bands.

The young woman at reception is beautiful. Her makeup is clownish. Why?

She's self-conscious.

You'd look so good, honey, without that painted face.

Life Rule: Juggling is for clowns.

Am I in love?

It's sweet, I realize I thought this before but didn't recognize the thought—LSD makes you expert at recognizing thoughts—and I feel her warmth inside my heart. She's snickering at the conversation behind her.

"They're going to know I'm high."

Max said, "Every time you've dealt with them you've been drunk, right?"

"Uh-huh."

"If they're surprised at all, it's because you're going to come off sober."

And he opened the door.

And I'm on a conveyor belt. An in-out part carried by the universal machine, I can't stop progress anyway, but Max is radiating cool confidence only we can feel. It envelops us all in his careful, caring cocoon.

There are good wolves and bad wolves, Dorothy.

I laugh inside: the flying monkeys in *Wizard of Oz* are actually flying wolves sent to fight the scarecrow-wolf.

I'm already at the desk and have given her my alias.

"I know you, Mr. Camden," she says and hands me the key on its anchor-heavy fob. "You know, you don't have to leave it with us every time you come and go."

Three thoughts while I stare: she's attracted to me; I can't feel my dick; and a Muir Second Rule of Thumb: Never take any item that can provide access to your life away from your person into an operational zone.

I'm humiliated.

I'm horrified.

I've thought about my dick because I left it hanging out after the last piss I took and everyone can see it but are pretending they don't to save me embarrassment. I glance down.

No dick out. *Phew.*

One response reduces four things to one, the mind always combining, smoothing, moving toward the concept of oneness. "Gives me an excuse to chat with you—"

Beside me, riding up against my shoulder, Nina coyly smiled at her.

"Rebecca," I remembered. "We won't be too loud."

"I'm sure you'll be just fine, sir."

16

I LEANED BACK against the room side of my door as if I'd popped forward in time and space with no idea how I'd gotten there, but inside Max's wolf-gamboling field we all were laughing heartily over the adventure through the lobby.

We raided the minibar.

We got into a long discussion on language and how it builds walls between people. Nations. But we are all trying to say the same thing. Everyone tries to say the same thing.

All the time, at all times.

We'd moved to the Beefeater bottles with their white-whiskered Tower of London guard, his smile growing as I studied him, his eyes scanning us all—chop our heads or give us a bloody ticket to the show, he Anne-Boleyns—and we decided to conduct an experiment.

Max spoke Polish from his parents. Maria, Spanish. I had Latin, which I'd studied from elementary school through a minor at George Washington—and if you want a real sense of anything, we all should speak it. At all times. *Prima et sola lingua.*

Nina had majored in French. At the Universidad de la Habana. Before escaping during a student exchange semester in Paris in 1970. Punk One and Thing Two only had English and that wouldn't work, but it didn't matter as they went into the bathroom playing with each other's face and metal buttons and sticks in the mirror. The last we heard from them for a while was Thing Two's thoughtful inquiry into what one might see were they to look into a full can of mirror paint—a 3D reflection?

We began to converse in our languages. We tried stringently not to translate each other—deciphering what we heard—but instead spoke only what we felt. Babble at first and for what might have been hours, then our minds opened.

It all made perfect sense. I don't remember a bit of it.

Love.

The meaning of everything.

Sublime and remarkable. We laughed and conversed. We sang *Sgt. Pepper's* all the way through. Perfect harmonies. Four tongues melted into a rainbow puddle of one.

Punk One and Thing Two made love with the door open. Alive and in person. In the mirror in front of them. The mirror on the back of the door. Six versions of them impossible-existing-possible doing simultaneous different things in each display with their young, gymnastic bodies.

Dressing, they came out. Time to go.

Maria and Nina spoke quietly and apart in Spanish. I asked Max if I could pay him.

"No, man. You've paid both of us."

He squeezed my shoulder excitedly, squeezed it the exact same way my father squeezed it. I felt both their hands. His eyes blazed.

"You did the impossible, CIA man. You are the impossible."

I was, wasn't I? Couldn't I be? Wouldn't Muir ever see that?

Had Bishop—delight, approval, welcome in his eyes—seen it?

I gave Max fifteen bucks, arguing that I'd dragged them all out of their way and they could use it now to get home.

He took it, and Maria, and he told me, "Enough with the booze, huh? You gotta quit drinking."

And they were gone.

I laughed at his joke, finished the brandy in my fist, and turned to find Nina nude, God's glowing perfection, before me.

In. Out. But it was so much more than the sex about to be. Being with Nina was already the meaning of it all.

I've never made love to a friend before. I mean, they're all friends *per se*—it could be well argued that consensually performed, it's the friendliest act there is. What I mean is that all who came before in my nine years of sexual activity, those friendships had all been established on a *quid pro quo* sexual-need basis.

I had no sexual designs on Nina when I'd made her acquaintance at the Ear, nor at any point during our trip thus far. I just thought she was really cool and fun, and just a little bent in a fascinating, foreign way. What was happening now—she before me, deer in the glade—looking up suddenly—frozen, inquisitive still, and I outside my body watching myself unclothe—what was happening now was human connectivity over horniness. Friendship over fuck. And it is, still to this sad day, the most remarkable human experience—an experience of being and why-being, not of emotion or why-thinking, I've ever been blessed with by God as man.

My lips on her warm skin. Her lips on my eyelids when she said, "Russell, shut your eyes for once."

As we came together in perfect embrace I asked, "But why me?"

"Soy Cubana. When I escaped my group in Paris, I went to the American Embassy. The CIA made it possible for me to stay. To emigrate."

"You helped us, I'm sure."

"They helped me. They got my mother out."

"Your father?"

"He was murdered for it."

I awkwardly changed the subject. "To be allowed to go to Paris, you must have been a Communist."

"Was that a capital *C*?"

"You tell me."

"I just told you everything about me without language. My whole family was. Pretended to be. The 'how' everyone lives in Cuba. Havana is like—living anywhere under socialist rule, I think—is like living in a puppet show. I couldn't believe my parents when they took me into a closet before I left and whispered what they wanted me to do. I'd been a believer. A puppet since I was a baby."

"But you did it."

"I wasn't going to, but as soon as I got off the airplane and saw what the real world was, my strings were cut, and I was free." She caressed my face. "Your people are the only people who tried to fight for any of us."

She kissed my nose.

We made love again, warm and close. Primal and raw. In chorus with the only right, important, perfect thing of living that two humans, their strings all cut, can do.

Later, we found the *Gideon's International Bible*.

We talked about how it's the one book in which everything is said. Every idea known to man and the soul of man, expressed. But the Bible is finite and God is infinite, so what if we read it and find the one thing that isn't in it?

That would be the meaning of life.

We did and, excited, had the answer in our grasp, each fishing the other's thoughts, but we were coming down and as the One Answer was hooked on our tongues, the telephone rang. Jarring. It snapped—*pang*—our fishing line of thought. We were chilled and we laughed at the hair standing sea grass on end along Nina's forearm.

"God doesn't want us to have the answer," I said.

"Yet."

We stared at the ringing phone. I didn't answer. The conveyor *chunked* to a stop. The trip ended.

After we made love again, after Nina dressed and we kissed and cried and said goodbye with smiles filled with the marvel of it all, she said, "Welcome to the New World, Pintao," and she slipped through the door—said one more thing I can't remember, about the picture frame from the parallel past-future maybe?—and I see her in her dress. A one-piece square-neck and sleeveless number, bright yellow against the blue-black glow of her skin. Yellow, in Muir's yin-yang lexicon, meaning earth; black meaning water. In mine: joy and confidence and self-worth. I held on to those a few seconds until she skipped to the elevator and left me.

17

I DRESSED IN LEVI'S. In an old button-down beneath an Yves St. Laurent tennis sweater, and Stan Smith Adidas I'd never worn for tennis because I'd never played.

Tennis = Fad.

It was 7 p.m., March 15, 1978. As I wasn't expected until tomorrow, I didn't call headquarters. I left all my other possessions, stepping over the pieces of my three-piece suit and tie, the snake-like LSD ecdysis of my previous life, and went to the desk to check out.

I asked if they had called me about my late checkout. They hadn't. Rebecca ignoring me as anything other than customer-hardly-a-person—*I saw that girl you fucked skip out of here*—her words unwelcoming as she said they'd already billed me for tonight and I could stay.

Not welcome to stay. Could *stay.*

I asked for any messages. There were none.

Weird. I know the phone rang.

I paid. Took a *New York Times*. Left, saying:

"Give my belongings in my room to Goodwill, please."

"You need to take your belongings with you, sir," Rebecca's voice chastened.

"And having chosen not to?"

Only one answer to that. I'd already given it.

Fully disappointed, she watched me leave.

It was a chilly bit of winter returning on the night. People bustling along both sidewalks revealed their daytime hopes for spring brightly peeking from beneath solemn coats, jackets, and scarves still sensible. The effects of the LSD were gone. My mind and being, my soul, chemically deconstructed and rebuilt *in toto.* My mouth was dry, my tongue like corrugated cardboard.

The last flight available to me was the Eastern Shuttle: La Guardia to Washington National at ten. That gave me time for a leisurely drink-and-dine, where I could catch back up with the world.

I could also puzzle who called.

If I was in any kind of trouble, the Office of Security would have retrieved me by now. I'd think more on it at dinner.

J.G. Melon's is a great saloon already grown famous in the handful of years since opening in '72 for its dynamite burger served on a tea plate—a larger plate would waste drinking space on the bar—and I grabbed a cab to the Upper East Side.

The skate-key-shaped sign came into view, neon abuzz and aglow. The cab stopped. I paid with a five and tipped the driver the change.

Rule of Inheritance: You'll always have cash on hand.

I entered. It was full—it was always full—but it wasn't packed. I took the last stool on the corner of the bar, my back facing the door getting a cold draft with each opening and closing. Also known for their Bloody Marys, I ordered a double and a cheeseburger.

I turned my mind back to the telephone call. Headquarters would have left an innocuous "have Mr. Camden call the office" message. Headquarters hadn't called. Muir knew where I was, but having used me, he wouldn't call just to check in or chat.

Muir is not chatty.

My gut told me Bishop wouldn't have reported seeing me to Muir, so Muir wouldn't know where I was. Would he?

Most likely, Max or one of the others, possibly-probably Maria, had noted the number and called out of curiosity to check on Nina. I lingered on Nina for a moment—I've never really stopped—then flipped open my newspaper. Above the fold ran the headline:

> **Israeli Retaliation: Troops Move into South Lebanon**
> *The Israeli military command announced early today:*
>
> *"Israeli defense forces began a mopping-up operation along the Lebanese border a short while ago. The goal of the operation is to root out the terrorist bases near the border and to strike at the special bases from which the terrorists set out for operations deep inside the territory of Israel.*
>
> *"It is not the Israeli Defense Forces' intention to harm the population. The Lebanese Army or the inter-Arab force, but only the terrorists and their helpers, in order to safeguard the life and security of the population of Israel.*
>
> *"The object of the operation is not retaliation for the terrorists' crimes, for there can be no retaliation for the murder of innocent men, women and children.*
>
> *On Monday, Prime Minister Menachem Begin vowed that Israel would "cut off the evil arm" of the Palestinian guerrilla group responsible for the attack.*

It was everything I already knew from yesterday's TV news. The *NBC Nightly News* playing on Melon's RCA was reporting that the main fighting was already over. A hoped-for Syria cavalry charge wasn't coming to PLO rescue. In Tel Aviv, Prime Minister Begin announced that Israeli forces would remain in the belt of

Lebanese territory until an agreement was reached to prevent the Palestinians from returning to the area. And in Washington, Jimmy Carter—a strong proponent of Lebanon's sovereignty—wrung his hands and hoped the upcoming meeting with Sadat would carve a path to lasting peace. He and the rest of the country, ignorant to Carter's drunkard brother Billy buddying up to Muammar Gaddafi that same day to see if he and his Georgia cronies could make a buck off Libya to spite the Jews in the current anti-Israel moment sellin' beer and "good, honest, 'nuts."

What's it my dad used to say? "Pigs get fat, hogs get slaughtered."

There was no Muir in any of it I could see.

I ate my burger. Ordered a second Bloody.

Turned newspaper pages for European reaction, response, or any other event on the Continent closer in context to his and Bishop's turf.

Three things happened at once:

1. *My drink arrived.*
2. *The TV was showing Israeli aircraft bombing Lebanon with munitions I recognized—and was pretty sure the rest of the world that paid attention to that sort of thing was recognizing as same: CBU-58s.*
3. *And an article on page twelve reported the execution-murder of an Italian terrorist, Silvio Lombardi, fished from the Tiber River in Rome, identified as a member of the Red Brigades involved in a number of bombings and linked to the murder of two Carabinieri, and an Italian magistrate.*

The connection between the second two leaped out with LSD-portentous clarity. The CBU-58s were US-produced cluster bombs.

Each bomb, optimized for soft targets, contain 650 baseball-sized bomblets, each bomblet contained 5-gram titanium pellets, making them incendiary and useful against flammable targets, that is, personnel and light-skinned military and—more importantly for anti-terrorist conflict—non-military vehicles. Arming Israel with these bombs had been internationally inflammatory and much had been made and promised and signed-for that such weapons would only be used defensively. This was sure to blow back at the United States. Israel would not be using them against the PLO had they not received secret—read CIA—permission for use, especially on the eve of our president hosting the Israeli premier and Egyptian president for peace talks and peanuts.

The Red Brigades in Rome were backed by the Czechoslovak StB and the Palestine Liberation Organization.

By his execution, it was safe to assume Lombardi had run afoul of his Red Brigades comrades. It was also an easy leap that, had it been insider politics, his body would have been hidden, never to be found. Any projection of Red Brigades inner dissent: bad publicity. The public dumping of the victim was meant to send a message. The obvious message here is that Lombardi had been uncovered as an infiltrator.

Muir's UN operation had allowed, with Bishop's loss of the notebook, the PLO to ferret out an Israeli agent planted within the Italian Red Brigades and murder him. Israel was paying it back by using our debatable human-rights-violating munitions on Lebanese, predominately civilian, terrorist targets.

I polished off my drink and told the bartender to forgo the bloody portion and bring my next lime with just the "merry" on the rocks. My immediate rush of cockiness at having figured out the op I'd witnessed turned to ash in my mouth before the fresh drink arrived. The television was reporting over one hundred Arab casualties and counting. Plus one, as only I knew: an Israeli of the Mossad, in Italy of all places. I'd made legal the illegal op that gave the "go" to both.

I silently toasted the television.

Downing the drink in one open-throat bolt, I signaled another, handing over a fifty-dollar bill to keep 'em coming.

I didn't doubt I was right. The pieces fit together. Muir had exposed an undercover Israeli agent to a communist terrorist group in Italy in order to effect that man's death.

Why? Since when did Muir help communists?

The Red Brigades and other far-left terror groups, operating unchecked in Italy, were driving that nation closer and closer to civil war.

Already the former Prime Minister Aldo Moro, leader of the Christian Democracy Party, one of Italy's greatest and most popular statesmen in its history, was on the verge of signing the Compromesso Storico, the Historic Compromise, formalizing an alliance between the Christian Democrats and the Italian Communist Party. It would bring the communists official recognition in the Italian government. Official recognition was no big deal to the West, as Italian communists had been clownishly involving themselves in Italian politics since long before the Second World War. While the benefit would be the end of activities of left-wing terror groups who would now have a voice more articulate than a bomb, uniting two sides of the government against the smaller though no less dangerous terror groups of the far right, the Red Brigades and other opponents of all that would be out of the game.

Maybe that was my answer. Israel wanted the Red Brigades to persist. The more unrest in Italy, the more the United States would rely on the Israeli state for security in the Mediterranean.

I guess I could drink to that.
And, skipping my flight, I did.
All night.

18

I MADE MY WAY back down to my hotel. Thankfully, Rebecca was not on duty. I presented my Camden cover identification and credit card and asked for the room I'd already paid for the night.

"I'm sorry, Mr. Camden, but that room is unavailable as it hasn't yet been cleaned."

I remarked that the cleaning-up was after me and I hold no fault to my own mess, no superstition of my own germs.

Didn't make the room less unavailable.

I asked to book another room. I offered cash.

The clerk went back to consult with the night manager. I could see the room racks, the reservation cards, and the computer lights showing occupied rooms, rooms needing cleaning, rooms expecting checkout, and vacancies, of which there were plenty.

"I'm sorry, Mr. Camden." The clerk returned from the back office. "We're fully booked, all rooms, for the rest of the week, sir."

I argued.

I was escorted from the premises.

I had nowhere to go.

I needed a drink and I knew plenty of bars that went until four. Just stay the night up. I wasn't all that tired. Something near the Triborough Bridge for a few pops, then a quick shot over and out to La Guardia at dawn. I could make that plan work and I did.

To a point.

Made it all the way to outside the terminal building. No drunker then than I am now writing this up, this flight home from Muir and Florida tonight. Fully loaded.

I'd opened the door to get out when the cab driver switched the radio from music to the news.

International headlines.

Former Italian Prime Minister Aldo Moro kidnapped in Rome. Details sketchy. What's known: a group identified as Red Brigades terrorists attacked Moro's car with automatic weapons in the Via Fani in Rome as he headed for the Italian Parliament. Moro's bodyguard of two state police Carabinieri were killed in his car, along with three police officers in a following car. Unharmed, Moro, beloved of the people: seized and driven off in a car bearing false diplomatic plates.

Sickened. Shaken to my depths. I ordered my driver back to the city. He mentioned something about double the airport surtax. I shoved two twenty-dollar bills through the slot and told him to get me to Grand Central Station and shut the fuck up.

You can walk back everything but your words. And the souls of the people your words have killed.

I found the tunnel entrance to the Roosevelt without too much stumbling. Padlocked, rusty, old accordion gate. Some attempts by the homeless, the taggers, and other vandals to pry a crawl-hole at bottom and top, made and abandoned. The gate built of steel rather than iron, the rust painted on, would bend only to Superman. A purposely manufactured, unsettling white noise issuing from within worked to dissuade further and concerted efforts. A slot in the grout between wall tiles fit the key card Muir had given me.

I removed the key from my wallet. A plastic punch card with thirty-two holes covering a magnetic center allowed for 4.2-billion key combinations. The lock-code could be changed remotely and the key would be useless until re-magnetized and paired at a base unit. But if the key worked here, it would work the elevator, as Muir had used it for both. More importantly, if it worked at all, it would mean that the courier had yet to come and both CONPLAN and OPLAN would still be available to me inside the safe.

I inserted the key. A satisfying clunk of the bolt. I slid the gate open at the side. I passed through.

My plan was simple. My plan was final. I would destroy the original CONPLAN and in a new version write in a silver bullet that would condemn us all—Muir, myself, and, sorry, new pal Bishop. By not matching the OPLAN, it would indicate duplicity and cover-up by the three of us.

I'll read The Shining *on my prison cot.*

What I planned couldn't put the genie back in the bottle, but it would make sure that I would never be allowed to uncork another, Muir be allowed to rub it, and Bishop allowed to pop out. I secured the gate behind me and marched down the dark, humming tunnel toward the elevator, feet fueled by the anger of my betrayal and the Jacob Marley chain of violence and death my paper had set in motion.

Once inside the suite, once I had opened the cabinet and pulled a bottle of Jameson's and ate a French fry bit-a-potato or two left over on the counter, I organized material I would need at the typewriter. I would rewrite the plan, attaching Muir's signature page—*teach you to sign things without reading*—return it to the safe and leave.

Oh, yeah, Muir, I'll make sure to buy scissors before I hit the airport.

I fortified myself with three fingers of Irish courage. Ah. I went to the safe. I turned the dial. Right 57, left 08, right 22, right 72. I gripped the handle, gave it a yank.

It didn't budge.

A stab of annoyance. I realized I'd forgotten to clear zero between 22 and 72.

I did it again, correctly.

The handle didn't budge.

The key card had worked, so I was doing something wrong. I had another drink and figured it out. Not right. *Left* 22. Clear 0. *Left* 72.

That didn't work either.

More whiskey to think. Ah, it wasn't 8. (Maybe.) It was 5?

It wasn't.

More, ah, whiskey. I thunk.

They wouldn't have changed the safe combo, and not the room lock. That wouldn't happen. Why let me back inside if I couldn't get into the safe? I drank more and played with the numbers and my memory of Muir's instructions.

Ever since my senior year at law school in '75, I've had this recurring dream. I still have it to this day. I am my current age, and I'm visiting my elementary school for some simple and unnecessary purpose. An administrator I don't recognize—I just make up, always different, always nobody I know—waylays me in the sixth-grade corridor. He tells me to, quick, get my books, that I'm late for a test.

A polite chuckle and I tell him that I am a visitor, not a student. I'm grown-up. I'm graduating law school first in my class. (Dream lie: I was second.)

Writing lie: third.

At this point, other adults have joined him. A woman with a macramé home-crocheted vest and hideous red curly perm informs me that while what I say might be true, I owe this test from when I was in sixth grade and if I don't take it, everything I've done with my life since will be invalidated.

How hard can a sixth-grade test be?

Playing along, I ask them what class it's for and I'm told it is science.

I freeze.

It comes to mind that all those years ago, I'd forgotten to attend science. It had been on my schedule, but I'd skipped it the first few days, forgot it the rest of the week, then had forgotten it completely for the rest of my life. I'm terrified now that I will lose everything—the dream more terrifying with each year of accomplishment I'm poised to lose, I might add.

I don't know the work. I don't know where the classroom is. The administrators are gone, the bell rings, and kids are laughing and racing all around to get to class.

I find my locker. A girl that my dream says I remember, but I don't really remember, tells me she hasn't seen me all semester, but that today is the big test that means everything for the rest of our lives.

Nina.

Madeline.

Pull trigger, pass "Go."

I can't unlock my locker. The crowd of children thins. I'm all alone, spinning the dial and trying numbers. Once I finally remember them, the numbers on the dial disappear. The whole thing is rigged against me. I'm going to lose everything. Even though I don't like most of it—most of everything—it is mine. I'd rather have that than strive and fail all over again with new shit.

I'm living the dream in New York City. Twin Towers out the window: young, strong, hard, tall and both, bold in sight.

Look on my Works, ye Mighty, and despair!

I'm drinking and I'm throwing up on the carpet, and I'm drinking again, chasing straight liquor with tap water I let, opened, keep running in the sink, leaning in after I drink from the bottleneck to wash down the vomit and burning bile that keeps coming up anyway and thinking that even if I'm throwing up, the liquor stuck its proof.

Things are indistinct. I lurch for more to drink. Grab another bottle. A different flavor. Think, *Go back to the safe*, but instead throw myself crashing over the coffee table onto the sofa.

I've not recalled this with so much effort since that day, I'm thinking now as I hammer it out on my laptop for all of you judges, that maybe the locker dream might have started after the Roosevelt safe house because how could I have dreamt my own future?

I remember lying on the sofa, weeping and wailing at the lives I'd destroyed. Not only the dead of Lebanon and Italy, but the living. The hearts broken. Souls rent. Wives, husbands, children, parents left behind with my sentence of irreparable tragedy.

Sentence?

Sentences. CONPLANS and OPLANS—

and have you any wool? Yessir, yessir, just following orders, to pull it over your eyes, socks for Civil War soldiers to die in—Mary actually did have a little lamb but I lead myself to slaughter.

How many operations had I legalized and indemnified?

Twenty? Thirty? Personally, about that many. Six hundred and forty-three with just my *Yeah, that's fine* stamp. It's what I do for a living. A sheep in wolf's clothing. And what had any of them achieved that I'd willfully not witnessed or bothered to investigate?

All that was left for me was to drink myself away.

I'll have it known in writing that I did succeed in this.

The away.

I am only alive—a second life today—because when I was dead, Tom Bishop came through the door like he owned the place.

19

THE NEXT FORTY-EIGHT HOURS of my memory are fractured. I have only random pieces. A strange dream about my father coming home from the Army—in it I'm three, maybe four, but he was never in any army—dropped at the curb at our house by Muir. That's vivid and I have no idea what it means, but I kind of do and hate that about my mind. Of conscious events, I'm not certain of their chronology. I'm only certain of the gaps. It's mostly just bloody bile spewed in different places and upon different rugs.

I'll piece what I know in logical order. Dream over, nighttime again, and Tom Bishop is beating on my chest and resuscitating me. "C'mon, baby, breathe!"

Baby?

I breathe, but I choke, and then I'm rag-dolled up in his arms, Bishop giving me the Heimlich. I explode with vomit, burning yellow goo infused with thin but distinct curlicues of blood and orange stomach acid.

There's a bathroom converted to a medical suite—without looking back, I think I've mentioned that—anyway, he's got me in there. I'm stripped to my jockey shorts. I'm blubbering, "Why are you doing this? Let me die," or at least I think I am, though Bishop insists I never said anything coherent or even tried to speak for the first twenty-four hours.

He has refused to ever speak about any of it in detail. All he says is, "You needed to get sober and I was lucky to be there for you."

Putting me on an exam bed, he took my blood pressure and heart rate. I rolled off and collapsed to the floor while he prepared a syringe: 100mm of thiamine shot into my arm. He wrestled me back onto the bed and ran glucose through an IV into the back of my hand.

I was laughing. I made nurse jokes through burning alcohol tears.

After Bishop strapped me down, he put an oxygen mask over my face.

He talked to me the whole time, and I wish I knew the details of what he'd told me, the feelings he was trying to express, how he expressed his wants and needs and dreams, because not knowing Russell Aiken, he told me all about Thomas Bishop.

The child who fathered this man to save me.

I missed it all. To this day, I have no idea what he told me, who he grew himself from, and every idea that his life gave me mine.

Nina's face: in tears. In the hotel room safe house.

Don't cry. I'll live if you love me forever.

Nina's voice: "I didn't mean anything by it!" Tom saying: "Get the fuck out!"

My vitals stabilized after twenty-four hours. He took me off oxygen but kept the glucose drip, which he racked up on a stand that allowed me—after he'd paid for the carpet to be cleaned, a new coffee table and the sofa switched out from my wallet—to move with it to the living room.

Bile continued to flow, but the internal bleeding had stopped. That's a plus, huh?

"You think you've put it all together, don't you?" he said.

"I know I have."

"You've gone way beyond the restrictions of your employment contract. Not to mention the law I thought someone like you held precious."

Someone like me?

"What about you?" I said.

"My conscience is clear. I trust and have faith in those whose orders I'm given and follow."

"Including Muir?"

"Especially Muir."

After that exchange, we didn't talk for a while. I slept, waking only to heave bile and dry my sleeping tears, salt-crumblies in the corners of my eyes, with the back of my free hand.

It was morning again. And the dry mouth.

"How'd you find me?"

Framed in fresh light through a window, he was engrossed in a *People* magazine article—*Mackenzie Phillips: 18 Going On 30*—and didn't look up.

"You're not going to tell me?"

Sunlight richer. *A Psychology Today* in his lap: "You're not cleared for it," Bishop said, his voice level and serious.

I gaped.

"Joking," he said—only now his reading material was a ragged Marantz catalog for stereo equipment nowhere to be found in the suite. His voice was cool like the late-afternoon shadows bathing him. "I like you. I look after the people I like."

Tom Bishop didn't tell me how he came to save my life. Never has. Maybe he'd followed me the whole time? Maybe the key sent off a signal? That would involve Muir, and I refused it out of hand. Didn't allow it then. Won't allow it now. But someone had kept tabs. Muir couldn't care less about me.

Wouldn't matter to me now, even after what I've done to him.

Goodbye, Mr. Muir. Chip-chip-churray.

THAT NIGHT we went down past Little Italy.

Forlini's on Baxter Street.

The lone purveyor of red sauce and pasta in the soy sauce China Sea noodle bowl-below-Canal. For my money, Forlini's is as good—if not better—than the absolute best Italian eats on Mulberry. It caters mainly to a lunch crowd of judges, attorneys, and the various others of the law trade from the Manhattan Criminal Courts Building farther down across the street.

There are two sides to the restaurant. The Bar side with smaller tables, and the Other Side with the larger tables and booths. Big Joe, the ready-smiled, garrulous proprietor whose father and uncle founded the place in 1956, led us to the other side, where we joined a family of three generations celebrating a teenage rite of passage. A married couple sharing food. Two maiden aunt tourists from Ohio, biting and forbidding, eating their garlic bread like excited little animals. A man I dubbed the Food Vortex: the most obese human I've ever beheld and one of the tallest. He enveloped two tables pushed together that had no less than seven entrées across them.

I'm in the field trying to shoot for recovery; he beat my chest to give me life. Muir likes him and he likes me and maybe I should do something about my drinking.

How could Nina have possibly shown up?

Over the course of our evening, fatty would devour all the plates—food, not physical plates and the aunts, deciphered as schoolteachers, would talk about their students back in their very own Winesberg over a bottle of dry Cellini red. Muir had taken me here the first time I came, and I assumed that's how Bishop knew it—and recently, the way Big Joe greeted him—but I didn't ask. Quiet, softly lit, not dark. We tucked into our salmon-upholstered booth.

Bishop asked for Chianti and, before I could choose, requested water for me. I didn't think I could eat, but pasta comes up as soft and easy as it goes down. It's not on the menu, but I ordered the house special spaghetti and meatballs.

Bishop leaned in close and comfortable. "I have answers for you. I don't know whether you'll like them, but they're the answers and I know you want them. Once I tell you, I'll be as far up shit creek as you already are. We'll both have that on each other—that we've violated everything we've sworn to—and we'll have it until the day we die."

I thought I'd seen Bishop serious before. If not in the hotel room, then certainly on the job in action. I hadn't. Because the side of his personality he was offering and allowing me now was the real man behind the mask. The real Bishop. And the real Bishop is deadly serious, firmly rooted in all he feels and believes as confident and able as a palm tree in a hurricane.

"The rate I'm going," I said. "I'm almost there."

"Don't fool yourself. You were already there when I found you. That's why this is a trade. I let you in on what's going on and I always will from now on, and you, Russell, you promise me, right now—you promise me, you will never touch a drop of liquor again."

I gave an embarrassed laugh I coupled with my signature sheepish, up-from-under look. *Baa.*

"I'm dead serious, Aiken."

He'd dropped the "mister." This was as real respect in as real a situation as I'd ever felt. He'd saved my life. Brought me back from the dead.

"If I can't?"

"It would mean you're ambivalent to it."

"I can try."

"It's not something you try at, it's something you do or you don't do. If it takes a clinic, if it takes AA once a week, or twice a day, or just your honest word to yourself that you want to live life alive, you do that. Otherwise, we're wasting your time."

The bread and our drinks were delivered. I chose not to envy his wine. I chose not to want wine. I chose my water. "Why do you care?"

Bishop grabbed some bread, knifed some butter. Spread it like slitting throats.

"I need to know if *The Shining* is as good as I think it is."

He grinned and his eyes twinkled. When he looked up to me: end of my heart.

He extended the bread toward my mouth. "Eat."

"I lied to you."

"How?"

"I've never read Stephen King."

Bishop swallowed some wine.

"Not all lying is bad," he said, thinking about more than me and King, I'm sure.

I took a deep breath. "Okay," I said, diving into a commitment I didn't want. "I'll read it."

Bishop nodded because he knew I'd given my entire promise to him, as he'd known all along I would and he had counted on it.

I was sober without an honest thought of liquor for thirteen years until yesterday with Muir and, for all intents *and* intensive purposes, I was walking dead already.

Oh. what Bishop told me—my secret sharer? That boils down to this: the most secret of CIA secrets.

Don't bother, Harker, you and your Young Turks don't know it. I'm not sure Director Folger knows—maybe some, I suppose he'd have to, but not all—and I'm certain he knows *that* and is acknowledging it as he reads this or is being briefed on its contents and will lie to you when you ask.

There is nothing more graily than this holy grail. If you were afraid of Muir over Charlie March, this you need to be more afraid of. It isn't my job to seal his lips on this one. While we all know he can keep a secret and are safe in that, I'd suggest you treat him right in leaving and just let him go.

Don't fuck with the door to Doomsday. Muir has all the keys.

BISHOP HAD STUMBLED upon the secret in Berlin. Didn't know that he had, but Muir realized that if Bishop were captured the enemy would.

It's why Muir created this New York op outside channels.

It's why a good Israeli operative had to be sacrificed.

It is why Muir gave the Israelis a *quid pro quo* go-ahead for our cluster munitions to be used on Palestinian civilians—because, face it: for every one PLO terrorist, there were five to ten innocent (but-in-thought) human shields.

It's that important to protect.

This secret is the very heart of why Aldo Moro had to be uncovered in the trunk of a car in the center of Rome, fifty-five days later, his body riddled with bullets. I've kept a copy of his last letter to his wife, Eleonora. I read it when the job becomes confused. Or when my legal letter writing—IBM Selectric tap, tap, raven tapping—becomes too rough for me. I've read it when I've thought to have a drink.

I've read it so many times I know it by heart. It makes me want to drink because it begins:

> *"Sweetest Lenore,*
>
> *"They have told me that they are going to kill me in a little while. I kiss you for the last time. I would like*

> *to understand, with my little mortal eyes, how we will see afterward. If there were light, that would be beautiful. The Government could have done something if it had wanted to. I die in the fullness of my Christian faith and in the immense love of an exemplary family that I worship and over whom I hope to watch from on high in heaven. If all is decided, let the will of God 'be done.'"*

Moro didn't know the secret.

I do.

Muir does.

Bishop knows.

Bishop's knowledge of this secret-of-secrets, named GLADIO and hidden by us and our British cousins in Italy and Belgium since World War Two, is also why Muir moved Bishop as far from the Stasi and Soviet AOs as possible.

There was never going to be a Moscow post.

Muir is mean enough to love us. GLADIO is indifferent enough to murder us all.

And GLADIO is why Bishop found himself posing as an arms dealer in Lebanon, welcoming committee and guardian angel for his and Muir's precious US Marines, who Bishop would never be able to save and has been trying to with everything he's done ever since they all died on his clean hands. Everything after that—even his finding love—would be a painful downhill fall for the best man and the better friend that I have ever known.

Thank Russell for me... Lie to him, he never murdered a soul.

20

EIGHT MINUTES past one in the morning, I made my way back out to Muir's porch. He was in his chair. My recorder was where I left it. I doubted that he messed with it, didn't care if he had, and don't care all that much now either. It had been around nine o'clock when I'd gone for my break, so I wasn't sober yet, but I was ready to continue.

He'd killed most of his cigarettes by then and either the whole of the third bottle and a quarter of the fourth, or he'd just waited on me, the third bottle exactly as we'd left it when it knocked me out.

Bottle math: a drunk's penultimate obsession.

Whatever the case with the booze, he seemed as sober as he'd been all afternoon and evening and where we were headed I don't see how it matters.

"Nice to see you back among the living," he said.

He moved a fresh glass in front of me. Yep, a big-boy glass, the kitty-cats retired from the field of catnip. Ready but empty.

"We'd left off at my induction into the Agency." Muir indicated the recorder.

His mood had changed, Jewel's presence gone from the porch as if she'd never been with us. With him. Muir was ready to get on with real life.

I activated the DAT and the counter marked time. Second after second of no return.

"I wouldn't see Charlie March for three more years," Muir started, "wrapped up as I was in training-wheel assignments in Asia. Happy to give you the cook's tour of those, but none involved Charlie March, so you won't find it pertinent to your purposes."

Goodness. He'd grown businesslike in the interim and I gave him a look that, quizzical enough, said as much. It asked him *Why?*, which he read in my face but pretended illiteracy.

He knows about Madeline. Maybe that detective called him. Maybe he thinks I've still got the gun.

"We didn't meet again"—he swatted a mosquito behind his ear—"Charlie March and me, until my wedding to his sister... And let's get one thing straight with Sandy: there's no secret with her; she doesn't figure into the story in any Agency way, and her life is private so, Mister Director, Harker, you—Rusty—and the rest of you Young Turks who take this and me apart: leave her alone. Anything else would be a fatal mistake I'm happy to make and walk away from afterward."

I didn't like that. Didn't like the reaction it might provoke. I quickly interjected, "A fatal accident like you perpetrated on Charlie March?"

I was both refusing complicity in and collusion with his threat while trying to remind everyone the only fatality in this whole business is Charlie March.

Muir frowned, gave me an ease-it-up motion with his open hand.

"I'm sure, Mr. Muir, if there is no relevance, there's no reason to contact her."

Muir narrowed his eyes and shook his head, his mouth stretched in his best *You don't know shit* shit-eater smirk.

"We held the reception at the Hotel Washington. One of those top-floor rooms that feed onto the roof patio overlooking Lafayette Park."

He poured for himself. I tipped my head at my glass, but he didn't oblige. He hummed some song.

"That's Mr. Muir being musical," I spoke to the DAT tape. "Humming," I added for clarity.

"'Memories Are Made of This'—Dean Martin's big hit that year. Sandy Muir-nee-March, age twenty-seven and three years older than me, the grace of a sexy cat—like the one the skunk chases in the cartoons and never gets, but I got her. It was our first dance."

Muir sang a few bars. I half smiled. He could do Dean Martin—sound just like him. I sat back as he worked to reel me in, singing about tender kisses and stolen blisses, and his own laughter cut in and he inhaled from his cigarette, sitting back as well.

This was "host Muir," "bosom buddy Muir," "cocktails and reminiscences on the patio" poison-toothpaste boat-bomb assassin Muir.

"As tradition dictates," he said, giving me a wink, "Charlie March—Sandy's only family—cut in and danced with my bride. As I danced with my mother, Charlie March said to his sis: 'He's a real winner, Sandy. I'm so happy for you.' And she let him know right back: 'You always bring me nice things from your trips.'

"Then she asked him what happened to me in Korea. Charlie March said I was wounded.

"She asked him, 'What else?'

"'Could you be a little more vague?' he said.

"'I don't know what to be direct about,' she answered.

He covered for me, letting on how war is hard, how it's bad, and how it sickens men's souls. 'Warriors need wives to get them over all that.'

"She asked if I'd been married before.

"That was a little sticky for him. I hadn't briefed him on if I'd told her yet. So Charlie said, 'No. I don't believe he was,' and she said it didn't matter. I was hers now and she loved me.

"My mother, foxtrotting in my arms, let me know: 'She's outstanding, Nathan. Thank you.'

"'Thank Sandy for saying *yes*.'

"Mother said, 'Your aunt and I are excited at the prospect of a grandchild to spoil.' My dad was long out of the picture by then.

"I took a moment with that.

"'Mother, you need to be happy without.'

"'Oh, things happen. You'll see.'

"That wasn't going to happen. 'I'm sorry. Sandy is with me on this'—she was—but my mother pressed it.

"'Last time you'd written us how you and your Korean wife were eager to have a family.'

"I stopped dancing. 'I asked you never to bring that up. If you do, or Aunt Linda, or anyone, not only will you not have a grandchild, you'll no longer have a son.' I was dead serious."

Muir still hadn't poured me a fresh drink.

"Is there a point to all this?" I covered my annoyance at his sudden lack of hospitality by feigning boredom.

"Yeah. If I'd had kids, Charlie March might still be dead, but you and I wouldn't be sitting here doing this."

And then he poured me a small one… and put it on the windowsill behind his shoulder.

"The dance ended. Sandy drifted off to be with her bridesmaids, and I went out on the balcony for a smoke. The park's below, like I said, the White House directly beyond. The Washington Monument beautifully lit behind that. To the right, farther out, is the Potomac and the Jefferson Memorial. Charlie March joined me at the view.

"He said, 'A kingdom worthy of our protection' and handed me a fresh champagne, lighting his own cigarette.

"'Sandy's all I have in this world. Only woman in my life—dopey-looking guy I am—only one there'll ever be. Take care of my sister.'

"I promised I would—he knew I would—I always have—"

"Except for divorcing her," I said.

"Naw, even in that, Aiken. And we smoke some, and we drink some, and then he says, 'I heard the word you brought back from Southeast Asia,' comfortable to be talking shop...

"'If the French keep it up,' I said, 'we're going to see a lot of Vietnam when it cooks off.'

"'Tired of the Orient?' he asked, and I told him, 'To the bone.' I was suddenly concerned. 'I hope my disagreement to what's in motion in Vietnam hasn't forced the Seventh Floor to sic you on me... Maybe I shouldn't have said some things in my last debrief.'

"Charlie March laughed. 'Haven't you learned by now, Nathan? When the Seventh Floor sends me to a fella, it's with an invite to the next big party. Not handcuffs.'

"He was offering a new posting. My first posting with Charlie March.

"He put an arm across my shoulder. 'Island palm trees, good girls—better booze—Mediterranean sun and surf. It's gonna be a doozy, brother.'

"'Always wanted to see the Greek Isles.'

"I was joking, but he said, 'And if the Greeks have their way, Cyprus will be the next in their island chain."

Muir nodded to himself at the memory. He swatted more mosquitos. "Guess they like whiskey. They aren't eating you up?"

I shook my head. Muir leaned in, over the recorder. "Mr. Aiken shakes his head no."

He unwrapped his second-to-last pack of cigarettes. "Charlie March told me to go kiss his sister, make a baby, and be ready to fly in ten.

"'Minutes or days?' I said and he laughed.

"'Hours. Go. Do your wedding night right.'

"And we did."

I said, "The two of you posted Cyprus."

Muir spread wide his arms, smiling again, as if welcoming me to the island country like every country I've never been allowed travel to. He broke back into song. This time, Sinatra *Baubles, Bangles And Beads, jinga-linga-ing* his way into:

"The architecture is half Muslim, half Greek; half ancient, half post-World War Two modern. Cars and buses belch smog; donkeys pull carts. Cypriots shop, others beg, and sprinkled among them: rich, gloved, and pearl-throated British citizens, and soldiers and officers of the newly crowned Queen Elizabeth's Royal Armed Forces.

"'Member it like yesterday. That was the song on the radio—me and Charlie March in the back of some Turkish bloke's cab—you've never been in the field, Aiken, but at certain times it feels just like a movie—"

And you always do your best to make me feel like shit. Yeah. Thanks. Never in the field.

I reached across him for my tumbler on the windowsill. He intercepted it.

"Rained again while you took your sleepy-time." He topped it off with fresh rainwater. But he didn't return it.

"I was thinking, this was the best cab ride of my life. I sucked it all up—the strange new smells, the heat of the sun coming through the windows, the colors, the colorful sounds… Charlie March was more professionally focused in his attention. He's the one who noticed the boy on the bicycle, pedaling fast past his window. Noticed the foot-long length of lead pipe—capped at both ends—in the kid's wire basket. I didn't see that. I did notice the bandana scarf he wore like a Greek farmer around his neck.

Thought that travelogue quaint. Charlie March tapped the driver's shoulder.

"The Turk had a heavy accent, slightly British. The guy says, 'Almost there, good sir. Soon, soon.'

"And Charlie March tells him, 'Change of plans: turn now.' He points at a cross-street. 'Right here.'

"'One way! One way!'

"I give Charlie March a dumbass look and Ol' Blue Eyes is bauble-bangling, glitter-gleaming, and Charlie March, he lunges over the back of the front seat, grabs the steering wheel.

"He's so in control of the moment, he's able to simultaneously nod my attention back to Bicycle Boy twenty yards up who's pulling that bandana over his mouth and nose before lighting the fuse sticking out the end of his pipe bomb.

"I throw for cover across the seat. My head's where Charlie March's ass should be. I yell, 'SHIT!' And Charlie March yanks the wheel hard right."

Half acting it out, Muir twisted and did the look for me as he said in March's voice, "'Welcome to the E-OKA!' right as the pipe bomb shatters a British By-Appointment-to-HRM-the-Queen haberdashery window as oncoming traffic on the one-way street Charlie March has forced us onto blares horns and bends fenders"—Muir's arms gesturing the action—"KA-BOOM!

"The civilians on the sidewalk blast to pieces. Store dummies and customers rocketing in parts into the sky, and your favorite, Frank Sinatra, belts out his sparklers and spangles and singing hearts all to cheery hell."

Muir sucked his cigarette. Blew smoke big.

"Cyprus: a Mediterranean island, a British colony, its population eighty percent Greeks, twenty percent Turkish Muslems, all of them divided against each other in every possible way. For

Britain, recently thrown out of their Egyptian bases, Cyprus stood as the last Western bastion against Soviet expansion into the Mediterranean and Middle East. A loss of Cyprus would potentially allow Soviets to turn the right flank of NATO and seize control of Mideast oil fields, an act that would spark World War Four."

"What happened to Three?"

Muir nodded, like saying, *Figures*. "The Cold War we're talking about. Russell. Just ended last year. Or maybe you've not read the paper yet."

"Oh, that. Look who's talking. Berlin Wall comes down, but somehow you and the ops boys missed the announcement and were late to the show."

Muir met my gibe like a car driven full speed into the wall of his disdain.

"Our cab driver—grateful to be alive once Charlie March relinquished the wheel—dropped us off at the Nicosia Country Club, main entrance. Our bags were taken by non-terrorist bell-boys, and our Turk roared out of there without waiting for Charlie March to pay. We shared a laugh at that and headed inside.

"For the Greek Cypriots it is the time of enosis: a cry for unity with Greece. Fueled by the EOKA—an anti-British terrorist campaign led by the World War Two Greek war hero Colonel Grivas—bombs began going off daily, destroying British property and killing British subjects.

"We walked through the London-transported lobby of tinkling teacup spoons, straight out the rear entrance, where an unmarked sedan idled ready for us.

"The driver and our escort were both US Army. Both wore civilian dress, casual in Ray-Bans and short sleeves, chinos, chukka boots—although the stubby submachine guns our escort wore strapped diagonally over his shoulder was as anti-casual as guns tend to be—and with eyes alert to dangers perceived or imagined, he hustled us into the vehicle.

"Charlie March stripped his tie, so I stripped mine. He shed his suit jacket and I mine. We signed for our sidearms—tropical vacation over before it started—and off we went to grab the fuse already burning on the barrel of dynamite where we'd just sat our asses."

21

THE IN ONE DOOR, Batman out the back wasn't real—I'm sure they caught a shower and downed a drink, mapped out basic tradecraft constructs in between rides—but it was better than one of Muir's pointless digressions. I displayed some good humor I felt expected of me, letting him jump in and motor his unmarked, unarmored, but comfortably armed sedan straight to a World War Two steel-reinforced concrete bunker built into a hillside by Royal Engineers that housed CIA Intercept & Relay Station, Cyprus. It bristled with antennae and connected to a giant mushroom field of NSA-installed satellite dishes and the geodesic radar pods that control them. More of Muir's desert-boot, bowling-shirt paramilitaries seconded from the Army patrolled the double-razor-wire fence with automatic weapons and razor-mouthed dogs.

"We were cleared—outer guardhouse, inner gate—exited our ride, and ushered inside. Ever been to NORAD?"

"No," I said. "You've seen to it I've been nowhere."

"Not true. Sent you a bottle of champagne to the Hilton Hawaiian Village a few years back for your honeymoon. Most people remember their honeymoon."

"Sent, knowing that I don't drink."

I looked at the glass he'd moved from reach. My mouth tasted empty without it.

"Whatever. Seen that kids' movie *WarGames*? They got to film outside NORAD."

Wait him out… wait him out…

"Same kinda blast door. Just itty-bitty in Cyprus—like Chief of Station Burt Wilton, who welcomed us with warm and pompous Napoleon-complexioned arrogance.

"'I'm glad Langley came to its senses and sent me some field hands,' he said.

"Charlie March gave me a broad smile and I smiled back a perfect copy, indicating to my mentor unified displeasure with the comment. Field hands—I mean, are you fricking serious?

"Wilton interpreted our grinning as calculated. He required subservience to his personal superiority and professional authority. If he'd been a firefly, his little butt would've been glowing. But poor Burtie Wilton. He was about to splat in a luminescent smear on the windshield of Charlie March's mean disregard.

"Wilton continued, sternly now, 'What I am *not* glad about is to be meeting the two of you at this location. Not glad at all.'

"The room he led us to was filled with all kinds of high-tech listening and recording devices, covering the entire spectrum of cutting-edge electronic intelligence gathering."

Muir pistol-pointed at my recorder, drilling it with a single invisible bullet.

"CIA listeners and SIGINT analysts manned the equipment banks like a bunch of gals at Bloomingdale's switchboard.

"Charlie March said, 'Just like to know who and what I'm working for before I go out and get foreigners to betray their countries over it.'

"'He's old-fashioned that way,' I chirped.

"'Well, I don't like it. You two are supposed to be undercover. Coming out here was an entirely unnecessary risk.'

"Charlie March startled both of us with a 'wrong answer' buzzer noise.

"'What letter you put after your name on the roster, COS?' I asked—COS, for Chief of Station.

"'I have a PhD from MIT, if that's what you are asking.'

"I told him, 'Save the alphabet soup for lunch. Intelligence or Operations: your directorate?'

"COS Wilton made it obvious he was shocked by my—'junior's'—attitude. He gave Charlie March a censorious look. Got nothing in return, Charlie March being the Muir-attitude architect—and Charlie March said to me: 'Lemme answer for him, pardner. He's *Intelligence*. We're Operations. Now, Nathan, watch this...'

"And his magician hands suddenly appeared working on the controls of one of the sophisticated pieces of clunky equipment. Burt Wilton gave a holler, 'Don't touch that!' and Charlie March said, 'Why not?' and COS, chief-of-scolding, Wilton said, 'You don't know a damn thing about it.'

"Charlie March leaned into his face and appeared to snap teeth at his nose with: 'You know jackshit about *field-hand* work.'

"Burtie Wilton scuttled back from Charlie March's fangs. 'I didn't mean *field hand* like coloreds. I meant like an *old* hand: good at your work. Please.'

"'Get this straight,' said Charlie March. 'While my partner and I are on this island, we'll have final—make that *only*—say about what risks we take. Now'—he hooked a foot on a rolling chair and scooted it to me; he found one for himself—'what's all this ruckus about here?'

"'Surely the two of you have read in,' Wilton said.

"I said, 'Okay. If you want to talk about something else... Play any sports at MIT?'

"Wilton snorted. 'I know about *your* abilities, Mr. March. This one'—meaning me—

"Charlie March swooped in: 'Is teaching me new things every day. This is the only time we'll give you your say, so talk.'

"Burt Wilton was very smart. Smart enough to know he was verbally overmatched. He spread his empty hands to say as much, then laced the fingers oh-so-professorially to say, on top of that, he was not intellectually overmatched. Steepled fingers, he thought, proved he never could be.

"He said, 'The minority Turks here live in fear that if union with Greece occurs, ethnic Turks will be persecuted and slaughtered by their Greek neighbors.'

"'Will they?' I said.

"'Yes. Causing the nation of Turkey to invade to fight the Greeks, which the Brits will have to stop. Militarily. And the US—'

"'Us,' Charlie March chimed in and got one of my all-time favorite responses.

"'Punny,' said Wilton, then went on, 'And the *US* look on in horror as three bedrock members of NATO go to war. What I need from you is to make sure that whatever happens between the island's three belligerents, our electronic spy capabilities in the form of this station remain permanently in US hands.'"

Muir burned one cigarette to the next. It was getting tiresome.

"You ever breathe air?" I said.

He exhaled an extra-large cloud that hung like an unreadable thought-bubble over both of us.

"Play golf, Aiken?"

"I don't participate in fads."

"What possible terms can you set for yourself to reasonably judge a game played continuously for five hundred and almost fifty years a fad?"

"Too many people play it these days."

"Ah, an elitist. No golf for the unwashed masses? What about tennis?"

"Became a fad during the Chrissie Evert phase. Don't see it turning back."

Muir was enjoying this. He puffed, he drank, puffed again. I was getting smoke under the collar.

"Bicycling? Old-time sport or fad?"

"These days, fad absolutely." Then I took a bluff shot: "Golf, tennis, *racquetball*, bicycling—once the accoutrements become predominant..." I spread my hands, showing I wasn't holding the head basket.

If you could give a cigarette a rueful look, Muir's cigarette got one. "Batter up." He swung it like a little baseball bat, amusing only himself.

He did an inner rewind. "About the breathing. Let's just say, I'm uncomfortable with the 'last cigarette' concept."

This is your Last Supper. Smoke 'em while you got 'em.

"Let's move past golf and cigarettes and get back to Cyprus."

Muir agreed with a decisive nod and went on to do the exact opposite.

"In 1956, the Nicosia Country Club sported the sole golf course on the island. Nine holes laid out by those busy-beaver W-W-I-I Royal Engineers. The only playable links in the whole Mediterranean Theater where the Johnnies wouldn't come under fire—though playing under fire is not impossible, as Charlie March and I would later find out in the Congo. Courtesy of American Express.

"The Nicosia course got wiped out in '58, but we'd already played enough there. Hear they've broken ground on a Donald Steel course at the old Minthis Hills monastery."

Muir ashed his stick, took a drink, then sat back and looked me over a long time.

He spoke. "Okay, the pink's back in your cheeks."

He offered me my drink. I took it. Our eyes locked. He was challenging me, but was he challenging me to shoot it back? Sip it? Deny it?

"That's gonna be twenty-six-year-old scotch by the time you can't figure me out."

I'm a lawyer. I drank half of it. With a slow start, fast finish. I put the glass down.

"Back among the living," I said.

I thought maybe he was disappointed, but then why force it on me?

Maybe I was.

"Charlie March and I got back in time to play a fast sunset round. On the fourth hole, I stepped into the tee box. Gave it a whack. Said, 'Sure liked him. Liked our COS.'

"My ball landed far short of the green.

"Charlie March placed his. 'Yeah. Guy's a real confidence-builder,' he said. 'Closest to the hole gets the Brits.'

"'Aren't you supposed to put the challenge before I drive?'

"'And take the guaranteed win out of it for me? Never follow foolish with a foolish question, Nathan.'

"'How was my question foolish?'

"'Because I was talking about my following question.'" Muir added, "There's a lesson in that for you, Russell."

"Goodbye, Mr. Chips," I said.

"No chips. Getcha some snacks in a minute," he volleyed back my dud grenade. "So Charlie March got the Brits. His days spent pretty much doing what we were doing that moment. Or at tea. Or in one of the London-teleported clubs in Nicosia, convincing the British island rulers to fold their tents and clear out before they got into a war that Eisenhower—who'd made sure bluebirds instead of swastikas flew over the White Cliffs of Dover—would rather they didn't. Me, I got the Greeks. And the Turks. And the bombs."

Government buildings, restaurants, marketplaces pipe-bombed; Turks hanged with piano wire from telephone lines; Cypriot police patrols ambushed by Turkish "freedom fighters." Muir witnessed it all and sketched it out for the record. He immersed us in the violence.

"Within a month," he said, "I had in place the best network this agency ever had anywhere.

"I had a Cypriot Army Turkish conscript conflicted on which side to serve: the army he belonged to, or the Turkish freedom movement. He settled by serving me. Every day, they'd make their same patrol, take their same break. Canteens and cigarettes for the rest of the squad—Greeks—and he'd use the time to roll out his rug and kneel to Mecca for afternoon prayer. The others would joke and flick butts at him. His British sergeant would some days smack them with his swagger stick, or him—he was democratic that way—but it would always be beside a particular lamppost.

"I roll by at night. If there's a chalk mark on the lamppost, I know to go back down the block they'd come off of, third doorway, west side of the little cobbled lane. A doorway deeper and darker than the others. The standard thing. I pull down the empty socket of a broken light fixture. From the hole, collect the intel he's left me.

"He was my first, and he was good, but they got better.

"In Pano Lefkara, there was a Greek colonel of the Secret Police. He'd rage at his wife about all that was wrong with the Turks and their Muslim faith. This was a tiny mouse hole of a third-story walkup at the top of a short hill. His wife ran her father's lock and key and knife shop all day downstairs—whole population big on toad stickers."

"I'm sorry—'toad' what?" I said.

"Toad sticker. Didn't you play with knives as a kid?"

I hadn't. "Well, I didn't kill toads with them." I covered my inadequacy.

Muir stretched the corners of his mouth, narrowing his eyes to his *You're lying* smirk.

"I never killed a toad. Or a frog," I insisted—whitewashing my lack of childhood bladework.

No one wanted me having a knife as a kid. I'd asked for a pocketknife many times for Christmas, one that really cut. Never got one. Then—because this is the mixed messaging that screws kids up—one year I asked for a gasoline-powered Cox P-51 Mustang, whipline model aircraft. You powered it up then took it off from the ground, spinning its tether in a circle, flying the airplane round and round above your head. They could get up to thirty miles per hour. But because you had to engage the gas-motor prop with your finger, it was deemed dangerous. "You'll cut off your finger," my mom complained.

I received a six-inch hunting knife in a fur-ornamented sheath from Santa.

"That's Malaysian macaque monkey fur," my dad said, and set my sisters and me howling as we repeated that. Mom, I remember, took Dad for "a look at something in the kitchen." The knife was replaced before New Year's with a stupid stapler made to look like a grasshopper, with which I promptly stapled my forefinger.

I rejoined Muir's Cyprus, returning to his Greek colonel's wife. "She'd still find time to cook three meals a day for the son of a bitch. Nevertheless, twice a week he'd pick a fight with her, beat her up, storm out, and head into the hills, where he'd help convince Greek boys to carry out terrorist bombings in his own city. He didn't do it so much for the politics as for the comfort of working closely and gently with the boys themselves.

"Her father had warned her of the rumors. Who-and-how he liked to touch and be touched by, but she'd been dazzled by his mustache and his uniform, and his perfect teeth. Yet now her father was dead, and her husband didn't even pretend to desire her, which was a shame because she was heaven and hellfire all at once in bed.

"After we came to our place of mutual satisfaction, she'd tell me everything he'd spill to her. She'd back it all up with the reports he made her type up for him."

"Muir, if you're trying to get a rise out of me with superfluous salacious details it isn't working."

He shrugged. "Denial is the sincerest form of flattery."

I snatched my glass and shot it like I'd shot the first one. I was way past sputtering.

"Now, it's a hairy bunch on that island. So there were plenty of good barbers. The best on my payroll. A half-breed Muslim—Greek-Italian father and Turkish mother who'd been something of a singing celebrity at weddings a generation earlier. He and his two sons serviced the heads of Cypriot Greek government clerks who came in to read and discuss the newspapers, one-up each other with insider tidbits and tips, and air their gripes against the Turks 'something finally being done about them,' but whom the three barbers secretly favored.

"Then there was my Bordello Busboy. This was at one of only two non-British sex establishments. Dark, red lights, velvet walls, booze, bowls of dates and almonds, and chubby, veil-only dancing whores. He was a Greek kid whose guilty conscience at having bombed a British school was as great as his lust for Turkish sluts.

"Charlie March and I would meet three times a week to debrief on the golf course. He'd encourage me. Tell me my pan was coming up with gold. More and more every day. He had me brimming with confidence. We made a good team. But he cautioned me from being blinded by hubris.

"'Seems like we're getting a handle on things,' Charlie March said one day. Then he tossed off one of his, now mine—and yours, if you'd only give in—First Rules of Thumb: 'Half of what we do is pointless—'"

Muir paused. He was feeding me the line.

"And the half that isn't shouldn't feel any better," I gave in response. "Never figured out what that means."

"Yes, you did."

I'll be damned if Muir didn't try to make me think he was holding me in some sort of equality.

"Why you quit drinking that night—should I say *dawn*—in Manhattan. And why you're raising your glass with me right now."

Muir raised his. He wasn't going to go on or drink until I joined him. What he didn't know was I was drinking to last night. Or maybe tomorrow night.

One more bullet left to be fired. One more bullet to kill.

"Back to the Nicosia pitch 'n' putt. Charlie March gives me the 'Thumb,' picked up his golf ball without bothering to putt it into the hole—which he'd do constantly, and always to annoy me. Terrible putter. He tossed it in his hand. I'm ready for another magic trick, or the hypnotist's watch. I don't know.

"'Don't see what's missing yet?'

"I didn't. I sank my putt to feel useful.

"'We came with the opening gambit without knowing the endgame.'

"'To protect our eavesdropping station.'

"'For Chief of Station Burt Punny? Nuh-uh. I mean for us,' said Charlie March.

"I snatched the obnoxious hypno-ball out of the air. I wanted to know. I addressed him in his language. 'Would you please be more vague?'

"'The British diplomat and civilian departures already created the vacuum. Last night, a little Turkish village out by the coast… Every man, woman, and child was murdered.'

"'By Greek-Cypriot soldiers off their British leashes. They'll be rounded up. Tried. Hanged.'

"Charlie March disagreed.

"I asked him why not, and this is why. 'Because it wasn't soldiers. It was Greek Communists sent to create a flashpoint for Moscow.'

"'How do you know that? What information are you getting that I'm not?'

"'Nathan, I'm not getting information, I'm using my eyes. C'mon, I'll buy you dinner. Show you.'

Muir leaned toward me. "See, Russell. He'd gotten me a long way—like I said, one of the best intelligence-gathering networks we've ever had. But lots of officers build networks just as capable and just as bountiful. Problem is—and the mistake Charlie March was pointing out, teaching me not to make before I made it—was not to let the network's bounty be its blinding success. The number one mistake in the field with a network so strong is to let the network drive the cart. Put you in the traces in blinkers.

"The Farm teaches, 'If the network's making product, back off. Let it do its work.' While that's correct, what it doesn't teach is that while the enemy ship has a steady leak it doesn't know about, it's still steaming ahead. Every other one of its systems functions, and those functioning systems are running independent, compartmented by watertight bulkheads from your leak. They very well may be your enemy's primary mission you know nothing about until your network walks your happy, feedbagged horse right into an iceberg."

22

"CHARLIE MARCH took me to dinner. An Italian-themed joint that served a lively international crowd. Wealthy locals—Greek and Turkish—foreign businessmen, international press, some remaining Brits, some North Africans... One of those exceptional places where the food and service are so good that political, religious, and geographical differences are left at the door."

"The jungle watering hole," I said.

"That's right, and just as dangerous—"

"I thought the watering hole metaphor meant *peaceful* coexistence?"

"I'm sure you do," said Muir. "But the watering hole is where predators take the savannah census. Get inventory on the pantry without a lot of running around. At the risk of flipping your anti-nihilism switch again, 'Ever hear of Bethlehem?'"

"Get back to the little town of Nicosia, please. What happened with Charlie March at the Italian restaurant?"

"As with everywhere, Charlie March knew everyone. The hearty owner led him to the best and only free table—specially reserved, with one of those little signs whisked away while big red napkins billow and snap.

"I said, 'So this is how you've been spending your time.'

"He wanted me to pick my poison.

"'I don't know,' I said. 'Italian wine, Chianti, that local ouzo we like? How 'bout British gin before it's gone?'

"Charlie March didn't say anything. Making a point, I thought, that I actually hadn't picked anything. But that wasn't the point—

I didn't know it, kinda getting annoyed—'Bottle of whiskey, if we're going deep.'

"'That remains to be seen. But good. You got the list: our drink and everyone else's matched to their toothpick flags for the cherries, limes, and olives.'

"I scan the dining room. What I could of the bar. Everyone else is drinking one of the beverages I'd suggested true to culture—regardless of who they posed as—including two European businessmen drinking vodka.

"'Them.'

"'Just like we reveal ourselves with our whiskey and these.' Charlie March put his pack of Lucky Strikes on our table. 'KGB officers world over can't go more than a few hours without potato juice.'

Muir gave me a pointed look. "That was big game. My first time to see the bull elephant in the bush. And I stared at the KGB a tick longer than I should. They already knew who I was, but it marked me as the amateur in the room. That's always embarrassing. Right?" His eyes twinkled behind a cloud of blue smoke.

Watering-hole safe. Wait for Muir to continue.

"I guess I was gaping 'cause Charlie March was plenty amused. He was right. Our gambit had been good, but my endgame was for shit. And those two KGB proved what they say about roaches and guns: When you see one, consider you're fully loaded."

"What—? Houses? Cyprus? Guns? KGB roaches?"

"Exactly. Which is why that night we drank whiskey. Charlie March's Johnnie Walker. As usual. And while it doesn't go perfectly with pasta, it did cut the sweatsock-bitter taste in our mouths—the KGB agents toasting us with their vodka and their deadly smiles.

"The next morning, my barber opened the door of his store and blew himself, his sons, and his three chairs to high holy hell.

"Two days after that, my Turkish conscript never finished stuffing his notes into the light socket. Dark doorway, two steps up behind him, single shot to the base of the head.

"You know, it's funny, Russell. Spy stories, movies—mostly movies—guys and gals always getting iced with the preposterous perforation to the center of the forehead. That's a job poorly done. Only idiots don't sneak up from behind. Snipers, sometimes when they go off the center-mass heart-stopping gospel—when they've got the itch—they do the forehead to see the target jig around."

"Does it?"

"What?" he says.

"Jig around?"

"Yes. Don't see that in the movies, but every single time. It's unsettling. And you're unsettling me by getting me off course."

Muir smoked. Continued, "By day six, my strip-club busboy hadn't been seen once. By week's end, I let myself into the little flat where I'd bed the wife of the Greek colonel of Secret Police. My heart leaped. Relief. I could see her in the sheets. Waiting."

Muir noticed a mosquito lancing his arm. He let it start on a big draw of blood.

"I was only halfway across the room when I noticed all the blood."

He popped the engorged mosquito with the tip of his cigarette. Hit the smoke. "Can't hardly taste it.

"I'm reaching down for her"—back to his story—"there's a rush behind me. Some fucking Turkish knife.

"If he'd come in overhand, it'd have been a little tougher, but he was going for the kebab—instinctively feels safe, doesn't open you up as much, and maybe he wanted to incapacitate me with the skewer, get me around, and carve my throat like he did the girl."

Muir lowered his cigarette half-smoked to the ashtray. I thought to crush it—fried mosquito and your own blood maybe bad-tasting after all—but he put it aside only to free his hands to demonstrate.

"You half pivot, step in, grabbing, pulling. Once you feel his balance go—gravity works with you, there's two of you; 'gravity' is its own Rule of Thumb—you help him down to the floor, pinning him with your knee, and help him continue his knife's momentum between his clavicle and shoulder blade, severing the pulmonary artery, and sliding it up into the carotid artery."

He went back to his cigarette. Speaking around it, "He was dying already—no way to stop it—but I didn't like what he'd done to the girl. Drew my pistol. Put a slug into the skull because it beats kneeling and cutting again. Smell's the worst part in a knife kill, so the cordite helps the nostrils.

"I leaned up to the edge of the window. The street below: two other KGB, flop-eared, bent-nosed farmboys in cheap suits, leaning against a car up the block and in the shadows. Alarmed by the gunshot—as intended—they bolt for the building. I give it a wait—one to the front door, one splitting off for the back. Now my coast is clear. It's out the window, a hang drop, and away."

"How very Bond of you."

"No. Bond's cool 'cause he's fake. You do something like that—especially the first time—you're scared shitless. Literally. Fear and anxiety equal acute constipation."

So that's why I can't shit.

"KGB dismantled my network as though I'd built it with dominoes. Just had to give the first one a push. I'd also become a target.

"Charlie March raged against this, back in his rooms at the country club. He was drinking out of the Johnnie bottle. Pacing. Raging. I'm sitting on the foot of the bed, downcast like a kid.

"'This isn't how the game is played!'" Muir was back, growling his leonine March impression. "'There's a rule—unwritten, but a rule—we ice each other's assets. Fair game. We don't ice each other! How fast'd the world go down the toilet we did that?!'

"He went for an hour that way. Could've gone longer. Thankfully, a bellboy messenger interrupted his tirade. Charlie March took the note. It was for me. And I should go back here. That Italian joint that night? I had an encounter there. On my own. I'd made a trip to the head. Reaching for the door it opened by itself into my hands. Who do I find myself face to face with?" Muir refreshed his drink.

Third bottle was almost gone. He poured for me and it was.

"Our old friend, Miraç Özdemir. I was faster than the guy with the Turkish knife, but Miraç was faster than me. Was in a stance, arm cocked, fist fired. Came right in to pat me on the cheek. Big gag, big smile."

"'No hard feelings from Korea?' I said.

"'No,' said Miraç.

"Coincidence?" I asked Muir.

"Not really. We're in the same business. I was on his turf. He said I had a serious problem."

"Back in Seoul?" I offered.

Muir cocked an eye at me. "Sure. What I thought too. Because he didn't go further with it. He came back to our table. We shared some whiskey. Charlie March liked him. They joked around. They'd done more business back in Korea than I was aware of. It was eye-opening. It was comfortable."

Muir paused. Smoked. I checked the recorder—plenty of digital tape. I checked my watch—almost 2 a.m.

"The message was from him. He was heading back to Istanbul. Wanted to sit down for a coffee. I didn't know what to make of it. Was he trying to recruit me?

"Charlie March laughed. At least that changed his mood. 'You don't recruit through bellboys. He was best man at your wedding. I wouldn't be worried about this. Purely social. Guarantee it.'

"We met the next morning. Charlie March was right. Miraç wanted to express his genuine sorrow for Jewel. I didn't want to talk about it, so that fizzled out. But Charlie March was also wrong.

"'Rough patch we're going through here,' I said.

"'Rougher for you. I'm glad to be going home.' Miraç's eyes were serious, penetrating. 'I have something for you, Nathan.'

"'What've you got for me?'

"'Bad news. Worst sort in our business, I'm afraid. Do you remember Tcha Sungho? Korean hotel staff working for your embassy?'

"I could hear it in Miraç's voice, he didn't like what he was about to share, but my attention had drifted across the street. There my busboy stood."

"Kid from the whorehouse?" I said.

"I'd written him off to the Soviets, but he was coming right over. I'd stopped listening to Miraç. Was half to my feet when this kid's pulling a bandana up over his mouth and nose. Lighting two pipe bombs and rushing with them right at us.

"I flipped the table. Ducked behind it as the boy tosses his bombs, makes his getaway. Double blasts of glass and nails and bearings. The smoke starts to clear. I pull myself up. There were seven of us at tables. A waiter. I'm the only one who survived."

Then he non-sequitur-ed it—if that's a word (is now)—"I mention Grivas yet?"

Muir knew he had. I could see it in his eyes. What he was doing was trying to decide whether or not to hold something back.

"If you're planning to walk from March's boat ride yesterday morning, I need everything. Who was Tcha Sungho?"

"We'll get to him in time." Then he added, "Look, if you forget about him, just mention his name to remind me."

I sneered. I wasn't going to make another stupid comment.

"Right now, you need to remember Grivas, whom I've mentioned."

"EOKA. World War Two Greek war hero. Alphabet soup, as you'd say, terrorist."

"Yep. And one-time friend of Charlie March, who said to him when we got there, 'This is reckless even for you, Charlie.'"

"Where was there?"

"The E-OKA camp. Boulders. Tents. Windy pines. The mountains. Grivas was about sixty at that time. Wore a beret and a French-style mustache twirled at the ends.

"Like us—Charlie March insisted before we got in the car—Grivas was unarmed. Unlike us, he was standing.

"We were on our knees.

"We were surrounded by his army of young men and teenage boys and they were armed. All their guns pointed at our heads.

"'Great idea, Charlie,' I said, of coming up there.

"'They all are, Nathan. They are.'

"Charlie March stood. Gun bolts clacked.

"'George,' he said. 'You know me. You taught me how to slit German throats without sauerkraut getting on my sleeve.'

"Grivas laughed. 'I think you were better at killing Germans than you are at all this you're doing here.'

"'I think you're wrong,' said Charlie March. 'But we'll have a drink to that later.'

"'Why should there be a later?' He shook out a stick from Charlie March's pack of Luckys. 'Smoke or a blindfold?'

"I didn't like the sound of that.

"'C'mon, George, you're scaring the kid—' but I could see Charlie March was just as scared.

"This wasn't good. And I liked that even less.

"I got up—almost got shot.

"'Colonel Grivas,' I said.

"Charlie March growled, 'Let me handle this.'

"But I'd already stepped into the cage. I said we'd found him without a map. 'You think if the US really marked you as an enemy target, it'd be us driving up here like we're on a picnic, instead of a bunch of bombs falling on your fucking beanie?'

"Charlie March shouted my name. 'Muir!' He wasn't scared anymore, he was furious.

"Grivas laughed. 'He's you.' He was amused, but not for me. For me, he said, 'If I kill you today—you CIA—your name will be buried by your country and no one allowed to speak it.'

"'He's right,' Charlie March said.

"Grivas pockets the cigarettes, says, 'No last cigarettes. Fine. Thank you.'

"In Greek he tells his Lost Boys, 'Put them over there,' and points out a large, wall-faced boulder. He gave his head an ain't-it-a-pity shake. "Charlie March… Forward march, Charlie."

"They march me and Charlie March up to and against the massive execution stone. Close in, I could see its face was covered with bullet pockmarks and dried blood. While they determined a firing squad by the Greek version of eeny, meeny, miny, moe,

Grivas says, 'I always liked you, Charlie, but this I cannot have. Too much work to move to a new camp.'

"'No,' Charlie March says. 'I see how nice you got it here. I understand…' and then he began to speak to Grivas in French, which I don't know a word of. Never bothered with it. Never will."

"You married a French woman. With the Airedales."

"French wasn't our problem.

"As a young man," Muir continued, touched up his scotch with rainwater, sipped, liked it. "As a young man, Grivas received his training à l'École Militaire à Paris. Whatever Charlie March was saying clearly upset the rebel colonel, who began to question him back in French. As the saying goes, it was all Greek to me. But it worked out okay, for suddenly on Grivas's orders, the young terrorist crowd parts, leaving in the circle of their absence"—Muir clicked his tongue—"my Greek busboy. Terrified.

"Grivas switches back to Greek. Orders given. Me and Charlie March are pulled from the execution spot and the boy—couldn't've been fifteen years old—he's hurled into our just-a-minute-ago spot.

"They machine-gunned him.

"Turned out what Charlie March knew and was counting on: Grivas and his rebels hated communists and the KGB—who the kid was really working for—hated 'em even worse than Turks and Americans.

"Colonel Grivas threw us a banquet. Now that *was* like Bond. That scene in—"

"From Russia with Love?"

"In this case, *With Hate*, but mm-hmm. Friendship prevailed. Charlie March and George Grivas hugging all night. Girls were brought in and we took it a lot further than fade-to-billowy-curtains black.

“Didn’t enjoy myself,” Muir said, directing his words straight into my DAT, the judge that the recorder had become for him. He looked at me. Jury or jester? “Keeping you safe on the salacity.

“It was up there, among those windy pines, I learned a terrible truth. That the horrible, gut-wrenching feeling of being first-hand party to the taking of a life—particularly a child’s—isn’t the worst of it in this business. The worst is when you watch as I did that day, and you find you have no feeling about the murdered kid at all.”

Muir was far away, not feeling it all over again. I didn’t know what to say.

“Wish I’d remembered that in Beirut,” he muttered. “Everything’d be different.”

My phone lit up and vibrated in my shirt pocket.

“Go ahead. Answer it. Might be Madeline. Have you even spoken to her since last night?”

My hand flew to the recorder. Shut it off. Shut off my phone. “You just had to do that.”

“Do what?”

“Get her name on this record.”

Muir gave me a careful look. “Isn’t the purpose here for everything said on that tape—”

“It’s *digital.*”

“Digital tape is nifty tape, Russell,” he mocked. “This *recording*—isn’t the purpose for it to be sealed up forever? An untouchable secret?”

“This record is supposed to be about how you killed Charlie March—none of that, by the way, in anything I’ve heard.”

“I didn’t kill Charlie March. I thought this exercise was about how I didn’t.”

I had said that. Didn’t know what to say now. I scowled.

He said, "You didn't think Madeline wouldn't cheat on you, did you? The way you treat her?"

"What you know about treating a woman…"

Muir lit a fresh cigarette.

"Could be written on the head of a pin. Yeah. Why don't we take a break?" Muir motioned me off the sofa. "Go call your wife."

23

On September 30, 1986, thirty-five years old and ten days into the two weeks' forced vacation every CIA attorney who prepared briefs and wrote opinions for Director Casey's legal team during the heady Alzheimer's days of Iran–Contra had been ordered to take, I met Madeline over a Rohypnol, four broken knuckles, and a missed opportunity to meet Senators Ted Kennedy and Chris Dodd. The senators, recently bored of munching waitress sandwiches at La Brasserie—the poor-sport screamer, waitress Carla Gaviglio, they had tried to bread between them in the private dining room, dishes and cutlery scattering (cocktails saved) as Teddy pushed Carla onto her back atop the table—had staled to that sex game back in July. So, a month later they booked a table at a different restaurant and tried their very best to Jabba Princess Leia, Kennedy anxious to get her to fuck Dodd.

"So," said Teddy, intoning the boyishly amused aristocrat, "do you think you'll be having sex with Chris at the end of your date?"

"Funnily enough," Carrie Fisher claims to have replied, "I won't be having sex with Chris tonight. Thanks for asking, though."

Kennedy dropped the boyish. He folded his glasses in his fist, pointed a finger, and went Committee Chair on her. "Would you have sex with Chris in a hot tub? Perhaps as a way to say goodnight?"

Carrie allowed she was "no good in water." A comment like that to a senator like Kennedy who'd had his own water problem just goes to show you Ms. Fisher was going easy all those years wisecracking on Han and Chewie.

The night I met Madeline, two weeks after Ms. Fisher made the jump to lightspeed back to Hollywood, Ted Kennedy—a new game in mind—would arrive at Nathan's one hour after me and leave fifteen minutes after that for a pussy party at the Mayflower. Five minutes into this seventy-five-minute block, I would see Madeline for the first time in my life. Without a word or she having even seen me, I would instantly fall hopelessly and most completely, exuberantly joyfully in love with her. If anyone had told me it would all end in gunfire exactly five years to the moment we met, I'd have done more than fool a son of a bitch into breaking his own knuckles. I'd have allowed the man I've spent my life becoming—the outside man, the rarely speaking up for himself, not-doing doing man whom Russell Aiken, legal counsel to the Central Intelligence Agency, United States of America, has distilled into—I'd've allowed him to turn around and walk out the door and congratulate himself for not having fallen for the false positive of the physiological chemical reactions that were exactly the same had I been OCD and smoked rock cocaine before hopping onto the wooliest rollercoaster in the park. Harvard doctors direct our understanding that testosterone drives lust; dopamine, norepinephrine, and serotonin create attraction; and oxytocin and vasopressin mediate attachment. That's all it is between guys and dolls—chemical? Yeah, chemical. I would have tucked tail and left, and the hidden man inside me—still actively interested in saving me at the time—would only have loathed Russell Aiken just a little bit more.

But Madeline wasn't wearing Dolce & Gabbana. She wasn't a danger to me or herself. She wore a United Colors of Benetton mohair pastel-yellow and aqua belted sweater dress, hair a slightly punk Madonna wrap up, and her feet dangled from her stool, crossed in perfect-in-pink sparkling jellies. Standing there in that chemistry lesson I was learning, my two identities switched. The Russell I wish I was, the me I like better and hide away in fear, became the outside me.

I tried to fight him. "We gotta go," public me said to me in public.

Madeline turned on her stool. "Excuse me?" She gave me an up-down look. "You need the bathroom? Out loud? To yourself?"

Empty stools stood on either side of her, her body canted to the one that had a vodka soda waiting on the bar above it for its occupant's return.

I heard myself lie, "I'm sorry. Never been here before."

"Just past the dance floor—where they usually are. Inside places."

Her expression held the half-drawn bow of a smile. Depending on what I said next, it was either Cupid's arrow she'd strung or Derision's.

I pointed at the other empty stool. "I'm counting on you to hold that for me and I'll be right back."

She dropped the arrow and spread her hands one at each stool. "Lose all my men to the little boys' room. I'll do what I can."

I needed to be fast. The urinals were both taken. A pair of biker types. I gave the stall door a push. It swung open.

"Hey! Occupied!"

That would be her date. He wasn't using the toilet. I caught a glimpse of a plastic pill package, his thumb pushing one through the foil onto the metal box that held the paper roll. Too small for a Quaalude, I thought, wondering what it was.

"Sorry." I retreated.

He slapped the lock shut. Urinals were free, but I'd never had to go in the first place. I'd just come in, A: to not have to explain to Madeline who I was talking to, and B: to see the competition.

Which I now had and could hear grinding up the drug. Super. He'll snort it, get high, lose out.

I went back, took the free seat beside Madeline.

Now that I've gotten your attention, let's get a few things straight for clarity's sake:

1. *The abovementioned "Nathan's" in no way refers to Nathan Muir ("Muir") or locates us in any place or time associated with Muir.*
2. *Nathan's (the "Establishment") is a well-known American bar & grill at 3150 M Street, NW, the most prominent corner of Georgetown at Wisconsin Avenue, Washington, District of Columbia.*
3. *The Establishment is named after Nathan Detroit ("Owner 1") and Howard Joynt ("Owner 2").*
4. *Owner 1 is in no way associated with the character Nathan Detroit created by short-story writer Damon Runyon, developed as a character of the same name for the Broadway production* Guys and Dolls, *portrayed on film by... Frank Sinatra.*

Were the usual Russell in charge here, these are the items I would be unraveling the crossword coincidences of, extolling the symmetry between idea and language, music and circumstance out loud to Madeline, hungrily shoving my Hush Puppies, her jellies, and everyone else's feet into my mouth.

Instead, I said, "You're killing it over every other woman in this place."

"You're an age-after-beauty guy?" She smirked.

"How old do you think I am?"

"How old do you think *I* am?"

"Isn't the law twenty-one?"

"I'm Madeline and the legal age doesn't change until midnight. Harruh-hurrah."

An *accidental* palindrome? My love tsunami-swept me away.

"But don't worry," she added. "I'll be twenty-one in six weeks. I've always been too big for my britches."

I introduced myself and positioned my offered handshake such that she had to turn away from Toilet Boy's stool. Glad he was taking a long time. Maybe the old "bump and dump," as they say. Falco came on overhead, imploring Mozart to rock him, and Madeline explained that she wouldn't typically come here, disinterested in the older crowd of pols, press, accountants, lawyers, dentists—said through tight, perfect teeth. "Are you feeling ancient yet, Rusty?"

I asked if she was on a date. She was. She didn't know him well, which is why she'd made him take her here.

"You don't trust him?" I said.

"He's a god to look at," she tossed winsomely my way, easy like a Sunday-afternoon shuttlecock. I clapped shut my mouth so as not to catch feathers.

"But Nathan Detroit—who owns this place?" she continued. "He's my godfather. My dad works for him."

"Your father's a *restaurateur*?"

Madeline laughed. "No, my dad's whatever's French for 'bookie.'"

I narrowed my eyes—secret-agent look. "I'm guessing 'Detroit' is an alias."

"I'm guessing you're right." And her smile clarified she was warming to me and, I imagined, clarified all the butter in Georgetown.

Falco got about as far as he could with Amadeus, then Phil Collins led Genesis in letting us know that *Tonight, Tonight, Tonight*, something was going to happen with a monkey. Speaking of which, Madeline's date ambled up.

He didn't like me before. Liked me much less now. "Dude, you're crowding me tonight." A mean laugh, threatening smile to go with it.

Toilet Boy put his hand on Madeline's crossed legs and rotated her stool back to face him. He was double-breasted, three-pleat Armani three-piece and I'm pretty sure Standard Oil owned rights to his SAE30 classic quiff hairstyle. Substituting for a handkerchief, on its lanyard and sticking out above his front breast pocket so everyone could casually see it for sure, was his green Senate staffer ID badge: 24/7 access.

"Sorry I took so long," he said. "Hope I didn't lose my place." His hand remained on her knee. To my disappointment, she didn't remove it.

"No, no," she said, pleasant and attentive. "Just glad you didn't fall in."

He smiled, but it was just as mean, and we all three knew she'd made the crack for me.

"No, I received a page." He showed her his pager. "Was on the phone."

Yeah, bullshit. Except I *sotto voce*'d it. Madeline dabbed her lips with a napkin to hide her mischievous grin. Toilet Boy played deaf.

"I told you I worked on the Hill," he said.

Madeline nodded. Finished her margarita rocks. He signaled for another.

"My call was actually spectacular news."

"I'm glad for you," Madeline said.

"It's for you too," he said. "I better tell you now. The senator I work for, he's having a cocktail party, suite at the Mayflower. I was really surprised. He invited us to come—both of us. He's never done that before. It's really an honor."

I sipped my bitters. He was earnest and he was drawing her in. He indicated a photo way down the bar. Nathan's is filled with photos of politicians. Photos and lacrosse paraphernalia. Madeline craned her neck past me—a whispered, "Sorry to lean" to me, and a "Which one?"

I pretended to also look, but my radar was pinging. I peripherally kept an eye on Toilet Boy. Whatever he'd crushed he poured it into Madeline's drink from a little triangle of paper.

"That one." He stirred her drink. "Whose brother was president?"

"Next to those sports sticks," I offered my help, then faced Toilet Boy. "You impress me as a field hockey guy," I said to him as he balled and dropped the empty bindle.

"Girls play field hockey. That's lacrosse, and yes, I played."

Madeline swiveled back on her seat. "Kennedy? You work for Senator Kennedy?"

Before I could prevent it, Toilet Bowl handed Madeline her drink, cheers-ed her with his. She took a swallow.

The natural impulse of Russell Aiken before that night (and, sadly, since) would be to stand and call him out for all to hear. I thank God I was not my natural self, as he would have clobbered me.

I thrust my hand in Toilet Bowl's direction, faking a how-do-ya-do handshake as an excuse to knock over her glass, but Madeline was quick. She moved her tumbler to safety.

I fawned at him. "I'm sorry to interrupt, but Senator Kennedy is a personal hero of mine. I gotta shake your hand. I'm Russell Aiken. Pipefitter."

Toilet Boy plumbed his gaze down his nose, his mouth a downturned parabola, gritted teeth the latus rectum, that is, a puckered butthole of disgust at me.

I gave him my "crookedest" smile, but he didn't move until Madeline said, "Gary?"

"Gary Moran. Thank you." We shook, his smile returning as he snarled, "You go by Rusty?"

"Yes. Girl's call me that." I turned back to my drink. "Nice hair, by the way. Very Rock Hudson."

"What the—? You calling me gay?" And he was off his stool where I wanted him.

Madeline gave me a funny look. She was coming on to whatever amount of the drug she'd ingested. Her eyes were glassy, but enough sense still shined behind them when our gaze met that I could tell she knew I was up to something, and that between me and Toilet Boy Gary, I was the one for her faith. I huddled into myself, looking stupid and small.

"Lookit," I said. "Gary. I didn't mean anything by that. I mean, he's a movie star. I got nothing but respect for you."

"You better."

"I do. That's why, full disclosure, when I leave here—"

"Make it soon," said Gary, puffing his already muscularly inflated chest.

"It will be. Madeline's coming with me."

Gary braced. "How do you plan to manage that?"

"Well"—I allowed my smile to droop extra-bent—"I'm tougher than you."

Gary snorted. "Prove it."

I turned and folded my fingers. Raised my hand above my shoulder and brought it down as fast as I could to the edge of the bar only to pull back at the last second to lightly graze the middle phalange of my four fingers across the hard, polished wood.

"Loser." He tried to get Madeline to drink her cocktail.

She pushed away her glass and caught me in a flirty gaze. "If you slam your knuckles for real, I *will* leave with you."

"Madeline, finish your drink." He checked his Rolex. "Senator Kennedy's car'll be here any minute. We're going to that party."

"Wait a minute," Madeline teased. "Don't you want me, Rusty?"

"I'll do it," I said, full geek, and, *crack!*, I did.

Gary was gobsmacked. "Bullshit."

"What do you mean, 'bullshit?'" I rubbed my knuckles, pretending they hurt.

"You hit the underside of the bar with your other hand." He came closer. "Do it again."

I did it again. Even harder. His eyes bugged out. I hadn't hit the bar with anything other than my striking hand. I winced for show, more knuckle rubbing, and through gritted teeth I hissed, "Tough enough, Gare?"

Gary reached across Madeline, grabbed his vodka, and finished it.

Madeline slid off her stool. She swayed a bit. She knew something was wrong. She folded her fingers. "If you won't do it, Gary, I will."

There is a moment "it" happens. The instant between a man and a woman where reciprocal love explodes between you. Rarely is it in an embrace after a kiss like the movies, or in the physical act of intercourse, which is only sex before the "it" and lovemaking ever after. It's always another moment. Out of romantic place and totally unexpected. It happens crossing the street, on the Metro, or at the gas pump. It happens cutting carrots, and walking dogs, and in movie lines.

WHAM! Madeline slammed her knuckles hard across the edge of the bar. People around us stared. Took interest.

"Jesus! Doesn't that hurt?!" said Gary.

"Hurts like hell!" Madeline said.

Madeline slipped me a grin. The moment "it" happened for us.

We gotcha, sucker.

"You're so tough, Gary," she said. "Do it and I'm yours."

His eyes darted furtively between us. "You'll finish your drink, go with me to the senator's limo, right? I mean it."

"All I want to do. I *love* limos."

The people around us *woo-ed* and chanted, "Gar-y! Gar-y! Gar-y!"

"Okay."

The sound of four knuckles shattering against unyielding oak is quite different from a slight bend of the wrist at the final instant that allow the fingertips to make the only contact, twitched opened and closed in a blur. Toilet Boy Gary screamed. This time everyone turned. He doubled over, moaning and cursing, expression twisted in butt-faced agony.

The bartender rushed over. "What the hell? What did he do? Should I call an ambulance?"

I reached into the inner breast pocket of my gray suit jacket and whipped out my Agency credential. I opened it three inches in front of the bartender's nose as Muir had taught me to be scary.

"You're calling no one," I heard myself say. "But we're going to use your office. Get us some towels and ice."

"Yes, sir," he said and hustled.

Madeline was bleary, still swaying, but impressed. I closed my hand around her drink. I offered it to Gary, writhing on the floor. He met my hard look with frightened eyes.

I said, "We both know this will help if you drink it." And he did.

I interrogated Gary in the office and Madeline sat through it, sobering up. He told us how Madeline hadn't been selected for him. He gave up the rest of the pill packet. Something called Rohypnol. It's getting known as the date-rape drug. "Roofies." We watched the limo pull into the lot. Got a glimpse of Ted Kennedy's mug when he rolled down his window, angry that Gary and his Madeline-turned-zombie weren't there before he and his driver rolled out.

Gary took another roofie for the pain and soon told us how one of his duties for the senator was cruising Georgetown and secretly photographing pretty girls. He'd snapped Madeline at the bank where she worked—

"When I'm not in class. I'm studying statistics at American University. I plan on getting my masters, in"—she dropped her gaze, thinking she was coming on too eager with me. Her gaze popped back up, buoyed by an exact forgery of my crooked grin—"in pipefitting, which I'm looking forward to."

"That would fit you," I said, causing her to blush as she realized she'd walked with me right into a double entendre.

Gary said Madeline ought to be flattered that Senator Kennedy chose her photograph. While Madeline punched his face, cursed, and then slapped his mouth shut when he attempted to complain, I located the restaurant's Instamatic Camera—they all have them for insurance—and photographed Gary. I pocketed the film cartridge—later, developed it—and for the next few months, wherever I went, I'd hand out a copy of the photo and let people know what Gary liked to do to ladies' drinks.

Gary passed out. He had been Madeline's ride, so I drove her across the river home to Alexandria. She invited me inside, but I loved her too much and wanted to wait until we got together on our own terms.

"You never know who you're going to possibly meet in this town." She peered out the door.

"No, you never do."

She shrugged. "It's all downhill from here for me."

"I hope not."

"Oh. I thought superheroes only showed up once. My mistake. I'll be ready tomorrow at seven."

She was, and "ready" was a silk kimono robe, hand-painted in a profusion of blue and red and yellow, or something like that, and when I brought her to climax, she shuddered and cooed like an infant sending out its first cry to God.

24

GO CALL your wife.

I went off the porch to pee in Muir's bushes. As if not using his bathroom made some kind of point, I drew a wet line in the sand and got a pair of piss-splattered shoes for all the good it did me.

I activated my cellphone. Four incoming calls. The one from Madeline's phone that I assumed was the cops from the house; standard operating procedure for them would be to check the last outbound call she made. I'd taken that call to tell her I'd be at the office until after midnight. Allowed Madeline her cover story that hadn't covered so well—didn't guess what I'd come and do—and neither of us had said much because that's where it had gotten to in the end.

After I'd shut off my phone, I'd had three more calls. Two different numbers. The first number, guessing from the area code, was Detective Georges from Second District Metro PD. The other I recognized as the CIA Office of Security. They needed me in Florida more than the cops needed me back in Tenleytown.

Langley wouldn't budge with the cops until I delivered Muir.

I trudged back up the steps.

"You didn't call her. Chickenshit."

If only you knew how disappointed you should be.

I said, "I'd like to get this wrapped up before sunrise."

Back at the sitting area, Muir had put out some crackers, pepperoni slices, and aerosol Snack Mate cheese. A bowl of dry-roasted Planters peanuts. The kind of food that's good only with booze.

I reached to switch on the recorder. Muir stayed my hand.

"I was serious when I said I'd help you with Madeline."

"How 'bout you shut up about that and let me finish assassinating you?"

Muir nodded, retreating to his seat. He gestured at the sofa. I curled my tail around me and obediently sat.

"I tell you the story about this furniture set?"

We both knew he had. Twice now. I played along, thinking I'd let him get to the bottom of the big "I don't care."

"No. I don't believe so..."

"They're a trophy the owner of the house brought home from the Second World War. Furniture Admiral Yamamoto had in his headquarters."

He pointed at the cushion where I perched.

"Yamamoto'd been sitting on that cushion, right like you are now, just before the car came to deliver him to his transport plane where, twenty minutes later, American fighter pilots—jockeying P-38s, most beautiful American fighters made—dropped out of the clouds and assassinated him. 'Course that's back in the day, when assassinating the architect of the sneak attack on Pearl Harbor was something every American looked forward to and, once done, applauded because good assassinations make decent Americans happy. Beauty is beauty."

"Ugliest furniture I've ever seen," I said.

Muir liked that. He nodded in a way I remembered him as my college professor.

"I tell you that because, Rusty, you've never learned: things have no intrinsic truth to themselves. It's the words we choose to put on things that are real and lasting."

"Even lies?"

New York, the UN, Lebanon, Italy. Israel. Killing myself.

"Lies even more than truth because we commit so much more of what we can lose with lies."

I switched on the DAT, making the click sound a "Fuck You" in my mind.

"Go: assuming this has bearing on our salient point, did you or Charlie March ever learn what Miraç Özdemir with the Turkish MİT was going to reveal to you?"

Muir munched some peanuts, pleased to lay crunching sound effects onto the recording. And then he spoke.

"Charlie March knew from the start. Me? Not for sixteen years. Then, in 1974, working with him at Langley on the CIA-conceived conspiracy that would permanently partition Cyprus down the middle—as split as Berlin with the Wall but more permanent—I proved to myself that Charlie March was a Soviet spy."

My eyes leapt to Muir's. He locked with mine, penetrable as a door slammed in the face. Not shutting me out but preventing my escape.

"You're a liar. You're lying right now."

"If I was, you wouldn't be here… I proved it to myself in '74. But I came onto it in the Congo."

"Your stupid witch doctor told you?"

"Diner's Club started it. By 1960, credit cards and that system of banking were the big must-have worldwide. Our cover was American Express. We were the ground guys setting up the deals with the foreign banks. We wanted that card accepted around the globe."

"Why?"

"Live now, pay later. Sell a whole lot more freedom and bullets on that. In a place like the Congo, where the Belgians had just been thrown out and Lumumba was facing a count-the-tribes-that-many-ways civil war, everybody wanted to buy their hand grenades with plastic.

"Picture the pair of us, me and Charlie March playing the King's Sport—"

"Horse racing?"

"No. That other fad with the sticks and the balls you bury like a guy in a hole," he snapped. "Golf. Picture us on a Léopoldville course, playing a round with our frightened African caddies, and a pair of Congolese bankers as a machine-gun-crackling civil war rages just beyond sight."

I did. And I pictured General Ripper pulling his .50 cal out of his golf bag in *Strangelove.*

"I bet American Express was pleased with us after that," I muled.

Muir dug out his wallet. He threw down his Platinum Card. I picked it up. *Member Since 1960.*

"We'd be chatting up the bankers like good execs, weaving a blue-sky dream of credit as the sunshine cure to all mankind's problems (as we'd been briefed by AmEx) and, literally, we would be making our way down the fairway only to come between two warring factions, guns blazing across the golf course. There'd be a tense moment. Shouting back and forth as both sides recognized the American Express guys—Leroy, they called Charlie March—"

"Leroy?"

"Yes. As in the French: *king*. His mane. King of beasts: shit he fed into. They'd stop shooting each other and politely let us play through. People—don't matter what side—are always dying to get their first credit card."

I didn't laugh.

"So anyway, we finally get a meeting with Prime Minister Patrice Lumumba. Handsome guy. Thirty-five years old. Horn-rimmed glasses, Western-style clothes with a cheetah-fur Jackie O pillbox hat. He's sitting up on his elephant-tusk throne. Charismatic definitely. Overeducated and articulate.

"He says, 'I well imagine the American Express Company is pleased you have used them as a cover.' Went right for the throat with the socialist grip.

"In response, Charlie March and I do what I just did. We find our wallets. Show him our AmEx green cards. The early version. Printed on paper.

"Charlie March said, 'Don't even care if we pay the bill.'

"Was news to me.

"Lumumba took my card. Admired it, turning it in his hand, purest capitalism at his fingertips.

"'Keep it.'

"Which Lumumba did and began racking up quite a bill. Never had to pay it either."

"Assassination does alleviate the strain of creditors," I said.

"Bet your boots, Russell. Of course, we wanted him to know who we were off the bat, so we could get down to political discourse."

Muir grabbed a cigarette and struck a match, leaning back to smoke. Lecture time, I thought.

"From King Leopold on, the Belgians had been brutal assholes to the Congolese. If the quotient wasn't made on the rubber plantations, empty baskets would be filled instead with—"

"Heads?" I blurted.

"No, Dumbo. Cutting off their heads doesn't get them back to work the next day. They'd cut off a hand. We were as happy to see the Flems go as Lumumba was. We told it to him like it was: we were there to throw America's support behind his recent election to prime minister... and to make sure access to the Congo's vast mineral deposits remained available to our military-industrial complex and was denied to the Soviets."

Muir paused to make a Triscuit, pepperoni, spray-cheese sandwich. He gobbled it in one bite, then described his starry-eyed postal-clerk poet turned African nationalist princeling's prized treasure: the Palace Projects Room. At no expense spared, he'd had Hollywood's top modelmakers build him a scale diorama—to rival any Albert Speer Nazi wet dream—of his capital, Léopoldville, reimagined as colorful, clean, and glowing. Had little lights, little trees and little figures, and an H-O monorail on a track: everything. Tomorrowland.

"It would certainly be a nice change. For everything off the Boulevard Albert the First, with its whitewashed buildings and white-gloved traffic cops; its European pastisseries, European boutiques, European banks, European sedans, and its American sports cars; its modern wonder of a brand-new seven-story "skyrise" apartment building—all of that: Lumumba's Potemkin Village front. A movie set facade to hide blocks of unpaved streets of crumbling buildings and crude shacks, where any car left unattended longer than eight minutes is completely stripped. Where bundles of fly-infested, rat-nested rags that litter the gutters by day, stir to life at nightfall, undead rising to beg at the patio beer bars or to raid the trash piles of the day's accumulated fresh refuse before it's burned in bonfires that do the job of the miles of non-functioning streetlights. Where enterprising lepers use those urchin children who still possess fingers to pick pockets, purse and food snatch. Where tribal canoes of primitive men bring in fish and unidentifiable meat from the interior to the market buyers, and trade ivory and trade ore for counterfeit medicines, sunglasses, and anything plastic with the squatters who rot and drink gin on the rotting European steamers enshrined and mossy along the riverbank they share with a hundred years of garbage and the daily drifts of carcasses—human and animal—devoured by turtles, fish, freshwater crab and shrimp, which are morning caught from stilted fishermen shacks and pot traps of reed and sold the same afternoon for human consumption. A Disney World Adventureland where beyond, always audible with animal jibber and avian jabber, awaits the brutal, fetid, disease-burgeoning jungle, the mines of shuffling broken figures living without day or night, their torment ascending forever, souls sacrificed for the mineral deposits of such stuff that hydrogen bomb dreams are made."

"Just your kind of place, Muir," I said, taking some peanuts.

"You know how it is," he taunted. "We'd go where the Cold War blows. The Congo provides sixty percent of the world's richest uranium. The arms race with the Soviets was galloping full tilt. We needed it badly and we'd do anything for our new best friend Patrice L.

"'You want that city,' Charlie March told him. 'We'll build it for you. And I am not shitting you.'

"And he wasn't. We would have," Muir insisted, doing me up a cracker hoagie.

I don't like pepperoni and tried to slip it from the middle of the processed mess.

"I know. I believe you. Did he?"

The cheese glob plopped onto my knee.

"No. And although he kept and used my AmEx like a drunken sailor, he didn't have us killed or anything, which was kind—"

I used the edge of the pepperoni to scoop the cheese up and to the ashtray.

"I don't want to look at that all covered with ash. That's what your mouth's for," Muir said.

I complied. He continued.

"Lumumba didn't stick with his metropolis plan anyway and, instead, decided to take Commie-credit on Russian and Chinese military hardware. I guess you can take the man out of the jungle, but—"

"Don't even stoop to that." I swirled whiskey around my mouth to wash away the ash.

He switched gears to a *National Geographic* description of a Baluba village, replete in my imagination with dangling-boobed native women clutching chubby-cheeked babies while balancing baskets on their heads, a single-lane collection of thatched-roof, reed and wood, high-end hut homes occupied on a broad but connected family lineage. The particular village he described was in a clearing with forest surrounding, but only as a kind of curtains connecting, by pathway, to similar clans' one-street setups, each village grouping gathered together for communal work, and commerce with the outer world, while providing within the social structure specialized artistic or cultural aspects of the people. It was to one of these that Muir and March brought their ill-fated poisoner Dr. Ezra, codenamed "Solomon"; they called him Fred just for kicks.

"Mostly just hot and dull and violent otherwise," he said. "Fred considered himself some kind of amateur Margaret Mitchell—"

"The *Gone with the Wind* author? Don't you mean Margaret Mead?"

"Yes. That's what the juju-man homebrewed. And that's what we were squatting there drinking: *mead* fermented from tribal honeybees."

"The honey?"

"The bees. Let me get back to my point," Muir said, as if I'd wandered off the conversational trail. "I'll just say this: Lumumba's tribal affiliation—his and its ancient grudges with all the other tribes—were scores he felt more important to settle before getting to his election promises of actually helping the people of his sad country.

"The juju-man threw his bones; he threw his teeth and his dung balls from the bag made from his dead rival's scrotum: he foretold Charlie March's death.

"'Hear that, Nathan? My death will be nothing more than the returning echo of my infant cry.'

"We listened to the fortune-teller's lounge act, then made our pitch. Lumumba had to go. We were getting our ducks in a row with the tribal leaders. Our buddy Fred was going to impregnate Lumumba's toothbrush with a deadly and instantaneous toxin. Our hotel room became poisoner Fred's tiny lab, with him literally putting the toothpaste back into the tube.

"I commandoed up all in black. Camo-sticked my face, and surreptitiously made entry into the Lumumba Palace. Gained access to the prime minister's chambers. His private bathroom. I switched toothpaste tubes. Didn't go in for fluoride—like you—I recall."

I screamed at Muir: Why do you keep saying that? I've used fluoride my whole life! Loud and clear. Inside my head.

"Yet, in the same way in the past we'd been plagued, our plan was betrayed. Lumumba went into hiding. This time, however, I had secretly prepared a contingency. Orders were 'Kill him.' So he was going to die and I was going to get it done. And without Charlie March's knowledge."

Muir played for suspense, pouring each of us a drink from the latest bottle. He eyeball-measured the remainder. It was past halfway. He nodded as if that meant something. We both drank a small amount.

"I went back to visit the juju-man. The Baluba's grievances with Lumumba were more strongly felt than those of his other rivals. His ball-sack dice bag had told him the toothpaste wouldn't get the tooth pulled. I thought an AmEx account for the village wouldn't be too much in exchange for the drilling done right.

"They got to Lumumba at the apartment safe house he was hiding in. Pulled him from his bed. There was a fight with his bodyguard. Some heads were knocked, others looked the other way—at the writing on the wall, so to speak.

"Seven months after he'd been elected in the first free election that country had ever seen, Patrice Lumumba was taken at gunpoint to an Impala—Chevrolet, not animal, which I also let 'em keep—and a rendezvous with his most powerful enemy leaders: suit-and-tie Africans backed by a Belgian execution squad. They took turns torturing until Lumumba was dead.

"They teach you at The Farm how everyone breaks?" Muir asked.

I crooked a smirk. We've already established Muir knew what they'd taught me.

"Lumumba didn't break. He couldn't because they never asked him a single question. In the end, free election or not, the Congolese didn't want to trade the yoke of Belgium for the yoke of Moscow. And CIA didn't want on-site control—just the uranium, thank you very much—break enough omelets you'll make an egg—so we cut a deal with Brussels: kept them in the background; made sure the tribal instability was maintained at perfect pitch where no one—except those who controlled the mines—would ever get a damn thing done.

"The evening ended for Lumumba in a traditional tribal *ratissage*. His body was hacked to pieces. Most of it was dissolved. Sulfuric acid. But the teeth, I hear, were kept as souvenirs by the Belgian police officers involved—"

The lie, the mule that was a true horse, eternally falling onto the pyre of my childhood.

"—and the best cuts of the man were roasted and eaten by the tribesmen."

I marveled at Muir. He could tell this sickening and shameful story without an ounce of sympathy in his voice. Worse, he wore a bit of ironic sneer.

He blew smoke at my disgusted face before I could properly set it with condemning disappointment. He'd led me laughing. Burning tear-corners: at African gypsies, at images of sexually liberated anthropologists done up as Scarlett O'Hara, at *Nat Geo* racism, at goofy toothpaste tricks, and he led me to the black center of CIA abattoir horror. And paternal betrayal. A feeling came over me that I was an imposter. I didn't want to go any further into the field.

Thank you, Daddy, for you have sinned. My mother, my sisters, and I take that to the bank. Daily.

"Charlie March and I fell out. Over that. The pupil had outdone the master. I'd prevented a communist dictatorship with murder, but for Charlie March, my success weighed nothing in the face of my disloyalty. We fought a pitched battle out on the airfield. Just words, but more damning than anything said on the path outside Jewel's and my Korean garden. He ordered me onto the plane—he was staying. Salvaging. And he sentenced me to headquarters."

"Suck sentence. Don't I know it," I said.

"All you ever had to do is rip the 'Hello, My Name Is: Sad Sack' sticker off your tit and you'd have recognized the happiness of your life I protected for you."

"I wasn't your fucking son!"

"No, you were my brilliant fucking lawyer who hid your light under a Bushmills basket."

We stared at each other. Was I seeing him? Was Muir seeing me? Did he say bushel or Bushmills?

We'd never drank like this together. Not to the point of truth. To that strange green flash of pure-truth return-sobriety before sunset total collapse. I'd never known Muir to get drunk enough to collapse. But Muir would have to collapse. Sitting there on dead Admiral Yamamoto's sofa set, I didn't believe I could ever get him there.

But I have.

Muir lifted his glass. "I knew we'd do this tonight. I stocked up this morning because I knew. You have no idea how proud I was with both of you. You and Bishop. After New York. That's how I got through all that went down—"

Muir cut himself off, glancing suddenly hunted eyes at the recorder at something he didn't want revealed.

Our secret unclean hands? Our Duncan's blood GLADIO?

"Then why did you trick me into drinking?"

I gave him a look across the machine—*I can say that, can't I?*

He slowly nodded, *Yes, Russell.*

The hunted look became relief. His expression, following, was gentle.

"Because you wouldn't be able to get where you're going to have to be to finish what's happened here the way it needs to be finished."

Muir wanted to talk to me. He had something to reveal. Something private. Something only for me. Not for the DAT.

He knew I knew. He smoked and gestured with his cigarette at the recorder: "So where were we on Charlie March?"

"1961. He banished you to headquarters."

"Right. I moved into that office I still have."

"Where your flag hangs to this day," I added for a little red, white, and blue color, to which he jabbed his finger at my device and viciously shook his head.

"Where my secretary, Veronique, would soon become my third wife."

"Your French wife was your secretary?"

Muir mouthed, *Good*, at me.

He said, "That wasn't the problem between us. From then on I was on my own in the Agency—where I would uncover that it was March who tipped off Lumumba to the poisoning plot on direct orders from his Moscow handler."

With those words, we were suddenly somewhere real, real Aldrich Ames fast.

18 U.S. Code § 794. Gathering or delivering defense information to aid foreign government.

18 U.S. Code § 2381. Treason. Whoever, owing allegiance to the United States, levies war against them or adheres to their enemies, giving them aid and comfort within the United States or elsewhere, is guilty of treason and shall suffer death.

Shit, I could *make* that stick. I could Hank Aaron Charlie March treason out of the fucking park. But, sitting there, watching Muir, reading him, I chose not to believe it real for one precedential reason. "Bullshit. If you'd uncovered March a Soviet spy, you'd have reported it."

"Why?"

"Why-why, 'why?'" Still stunned by the accusation, I wasn't terribly quick.

Muir said, "You think I cared? After Korea, after Jewel, this was just a game to me."

"You're saying, you are disloyal?" My voice echoed the hollow sound of the waves collapsing onto mangrove roots gripped to his wild shore as the tide reached its high-water mark.

"C'mon. I'm anything but disloyal. But I'd given my first loyalty—before God the Redeemer—to Jewel and she was dead, and now I wondered why. 'Why?' That's *why*. 'I'm loyal to the nightmare of my choice.' I oversaw plenty of ops the next couple years, but none intersected Charlie March.

"By '64, I knew he'd gone bad, I just didn't know the how of it. And I wasn't about to turn this over to Counterintelligence. Silas Kingston had just come in under Angleton and I wasn't about to give him his first scalp."

I shuddered at the mention of the one Agency scalphunter whose eyes bore inward on our institution. Whose way is pain. Whose teeth gnaw at the ends of all our plots.

"I worked on elevating my Top Secret clearance two additional levels. SCI, Sensitive Compartmentalized Information, and SSBI, Single Scope Background Investigation. With those under my belt, I could pretty much access his operational returns—current and past, before Charlie March met me—from the old Clandestine Services library.

"Your satisfaction came yesterday. The bomb?" I drank. I studied him. Had we already arrived?

"I didn't blow up Charlie March."

Muir wagged his head, disappointed in me. He burned his way, cigarette to cigarette, into the next link of his suicide chain.

"Vietnam got in the way of the whole thing anyway and I went there. And I did what Charlie March had taught me: what I do best—off and on—for eleven years. When you got a job, you do it; it pays the bills."

"Tom Bishop. You went and 'poisoned' him. What bill does that pay?"

Like a string pulled at the side of Muir's mouth, his lips pursed tightly as if he was having trouble holding back a whole lot he longed to get off his chest. I watched the yearning wash over him until he felt he could keep his real words, real-world locked tight.

"Yep... Just like with you a few years before. But by then I had all the answers and, lucky you, I didn't like the spy game anymore."

I felt everything I was, had hoped for myself, wrestler-smack-down-slammed to the mat. "I've hated you for it."

Muir shrugged, *maybe so, maybe not,* and we both spent a long, soft moment of the thinking about what-might-have-been.

"I know you, Muir. You don't run away. You didn't just run away to Vietnam for a decade. You must have found something in those files that held you from nailing him."

"No, you're right. I had. I'd traced Charlie March back to when they turned him."

"Cyprus?"

"Long before that. Before Korea."

It was horrible—I didn't want to say it, but I was here, Captiva, to finish off Muir for the good of the Agency. So, I did... "But if March was working for Moscow back then, Hill Six-two-six..."

"Six-two-six was Charlie March. It was all him."

Sick silence. I heard his voice in my head:

Your problem, Russell, is you believe things... You know, try never to believe anything I say, by the way...

"And Jewel?" My inner-voice rodent crept out from my thoughts, whiskers aquiver, eyes beady black with fright.

Muir finished the rest of his glass. He poured another. Didn't bother with the water carafe, just threw it straight into himself. Mud in your heart: makes it beat faster, makes it stronger, makes it stop.

There was a tiny bit left in the bottle so he took that too, took it from the neck. He looked at me like a stranger. Muir seemed weak, getting old before my eyes.

"Did I tell you about this sofa set?" He smacked his lips.

Taking a deep drag, Muir blew the smoke across the cigarette tip, glowing it red, staring at the ember. Speaking to the vanishing sparks. "That day, when Jewel came home from the pharmacy—"

"You said 'grocery—'"

"I remember the bag. I found it when I got home. A pharmacy bag."

"You weren't there?"

"I came in—so I was there at that point. I called to her: 'Jewel? Honey? Jewel, I'm home.'

"When she didn't respond—thinking nothing of this—I entered the kitchen and switched on the light. "She was seated at the table. She hadn't answered me because a bullet had made a neat third eye above the bridge of her nose. It wasn't photo memories all over the table. It was just her dead memories blown gray and bloody out the back of her head.

"I tried to revive her. It was absolutely hopeless, but I tried to resuscitate her. I pounded her chest. I shook her. I pretended I didn't see what I saw."

The hair on my neck bristled under my collar. My scalp tingled.

"Did Charlie March kill your wife?"

Muir nodded, the horror of the moment possessing his whole being, reliving it.

"You're nodding yes. Don't nod. Say it. You have to, sir."

I hated that I had to prompt him for the record.

Muir swallowed. "Yes, Charlie March killed Jewel, Kim Jin Muir." His voice was dry and lifeless. Dead butterfly wings.

"To protect himself? Why?"

Muir shrugged. He wouldn't speak.

"Was she a spy? March's spy? Had the two of them set you up even before the marriage? Nathan, was she a victim? March's smokescreen?"

"The answer to that is…" Muir looked at his hands. He sneered as if their age offended him. The spots. The tiny wrinkles coming in. He wiggled the fingers like a pianist or a death spasm. " …the record of my life."

He lifted a final unopened bottle from below the table.

"Last bottle?" I said.

"Very last."

He gave it to me, watching my every move. I realized: what he'd just told me he'd never told a soul. He studied me, looking for judgment, hoping for… Redemption? Compassion? In-Out?

"We're drinking this," I said.

"I know we are. Pour."

"You had every right to murder him. I'm going to protect you. Why keep telling me you didn't?"

Muir took his liquor, weary. "Because while I've killed for my country and never thought twice about it, murder is an unlivable thing."

My beautiful Madeline fucking that douchebag professor on our sofa.

My memory flashed to the two of us at Slagermann's Home Furnishings picking out the sofa, Madeline tipsy from lunch, bouncing on it, then reclining across the rich tan leather. The come-hither look, and all my deepest feelings of love burning in sorrow as I beheld Muir in his still agony.

I'd had Mr. Professor's head framed in my sights. I'd tried to bring myself to kill that man inside my wife. I couldn't. It wasn't his fault. It was hers. I turned my sights on Madeline. And then I pulled the trigger.

Bang. Bitch.

PART THREE

CONFESSION

"Guilt is the most merciless disease of man. It stains all other areas of living. It darkens all skies."

— John D. MacDonald, *The Dreadful Lemon Sky*

25

Muir's Floridian jungle whispered in vegetational creak and rainfall dribble while the early birds boasted—the cuckoo's croak, the turnstone's rattle, the woodpecker's rolling *kwirr*—of the worms and mates and territories over which they'd struggle and turd their coming day. Still dark, just after 4 a.m., Muir leads me down a sole-sucking mud path to introduce me to some girlfriend, Björk.

I've never heard of this Björk. Muir said she's been on *Saturday Night Live*. Excuse me, but I'm an *SNL* expert. If she's not Victoria Jackson, "It's Pat," or Ellen Cleghorne, Muir is mistaken. Obviously, one of Muir's stupid jokes. Maybe Björk's one of these obnoxious birds—some kind of marsh heron or something gawk-legged he wants to show me—what the fuck? I don't know.

We're off the porch though. Muir has affected our escape with a sudden announcement he needs a break. He'd pointed at the bottle and pointed at himself a few times until I understood to say into the DAT: "This is Aiken. Muir's been drinking throughout the interview, and I believe it prudent we break here so he may rest. And recoup. He's old," I added, for spite.

I reached for the Stop button. "Signing off. Russell Aiken, legal counsel to the Central Intelligence Agency, United States of America, uh, for now," and deactivated the recorder.

Muir had something to tell me. I wasn't going to ignore him. Even though I'm much more at ease on a patio porch than a jungle—be it cannibal Congo or cabin cruiser Captiva—I followed when he said:

"C'mon, let's go in the forest. I'll introduce you to my new girlfriend, Björk."

He led me onto a path into the foliage. Within moments, I could not see the house. I jumped. Was it a rat I saw? Then a family—or whatever it is you call a bunch of rats—scurry, scuttle—again, *whatever* they do in groups—into the trees.

It amused Muir to see me startle. "It'd be rats when we'd head out on lurps."

"Lurps?"

"LRPs, Long Range Patrols."

Vietnam. The field. Thanks, my wounds love the salt.

I said, "Those *were* rats."

"That was a scurry of squirrels. I feed them sometimes, so they hang close to the house. Don't want to feed them too much, though."

"They become dependent?"

"Squirrels are just fine being dependent. No. You overfeed them, they overbreed. You end up having to poison them or shoot 'em to get the balance back with the other idiot animals."

"Story of your life." I felt it the proper segue. "If what you just revealed back there is true, you killing March makes you a hero."

He pushed aside some branches. He didn't let them snap back at my face.

"It's true, but would you get off it? Do you actually think I put a bomb on that life-wrecked old man's ship?"

"Boat."

"Wreck."

I nodded, but he wasn't looking back at me.

"I absolutely do," I said at his back.

"Then, as usual, you're absolutely wrong."

He stopped to listen. Both sides of the trail were dense with mangroves. The slap of water close.

"Let's pop off the trail here. Björk especially likes the hyacinth. Grows among the roots. Along this part."

Björk isn't a person, as I'm sure you've figured out.

I patterned my movements after Muir, creeping between mangrove and swamp oak, sticker-bush and elephant grass. Mosquitoes had finally taken a liking to me. Bufo cane toads scattered but kept up their deep-throat bitching.

"Stop with the noise already," Muir said of my bug slapping.

It was annoying that they weren't bothering him now. They'd probably heard the death shriek of the one he'd immolated.

I stumbled on.

"I'd put the Charlie March puzzle together to my satisfaction and would've turned it over to Counterintel if I'd gotten what Tcha Sungho had planned to give me."

I halted. Tcha Sungho: the Korean from the Bando Hotel in Seoul. The name on Miraç Özdemir's dying lips, taken from him, presumably, by Charlie March in a pipe-bomb kiss.

"Our plan was to meet the day after Christmas, 1971, but Sungho died in the gas explosion on Christmas Day. It's most likely he turned the valve that had been tampered with. One of his daily tasks for over a decade was checking the gas flow into the building. Habits kill best in our business."

"Charlie March?"

Muir didn't need to confirm the obvious. He directed my attention to the water. A series of perfect swirls made their way along the surface toward us. They drew closer and I could see that a wide paddle tail created them. A whiskered nose broke the waterline. The wet nostrils, flat in a face like a Shar Pei puppy.

"A seal," I whispered, excited.

I'd brought the Macallan. I took a pull from the bottle and offered it to Muir, who *no thank you*-ed it with an almost imperceptible shake of his head.

"She's a manatee, Dumbo. Björk's originally from Iceland."

The manatee noticed Muir and rose vertical to hang in the water, huge, fat, and curious. More Chris Farley—shape-wise—than anyone else on *SNL* or in Iceland where there can be no manatees, Björk-wise or otherwise-wise.

"I don't get it. With the name."

Muir gave me a bemused look. "How is it you're twenty years younger than me and I've heard of Björk and you haven't?"

I sighed. He constantly fills me with defeat.

"Just get on with what we're doing here, 'kay?"

Muir was enjoying playing Marlin Perkins, taking pleasure from watching the beast munch the green leaves and purple blooms of the water flowers.

"It's all appearance versus reality."

Here we go, back to your 400-level Philosophy of Mythology class.

"You know, sailors under French explorer René de Laudonnière, who built Fort Caroline—over near where Jacksonville is—they thought manatees were mermaids."

"I thought that was Columbus."

"Why would French sailors think manatees were Columbus?"

I chuckled.

He took the bottle and drank.

I could see that the sadness he'd been dodging from his soul was quite dodged out in him. I realized I didn't want to hear anything personal. If it wasn't for the record, I chose now not to be interested.

"Everything you do is deliberate, isn't it?" I said.

"Isn't that circular? Answers itself," said Muir.

I shrugged, disappointed I couldn't get an answer for a stupidly phrased question I thought important.

"Since Korea. Didn't notice before. Notice everything in stark relief since. Curse. Don't get one—they suck."

"If what we're out here for has bearing on March—like the Sungho murder—"

"And a hundred sixty-two others that day."

I nodded, he was making my argument.

Final count: 268 Lebanon. Who's counting?

"It needs to go on the record. To protect you, Nathan."

He looked askance and patronizing. "Why is it we call out first names when we're talking, to indicate—road sign ahead—'Liar'?" Muir answered himself. "Don't get nervous. I do not have any secrets about you. My point about appearances and reality—the manatee and the mermaid: fundamental of everything we do."

"As spies."

"As humans. Why we need and use spies. And why spies succeed, and why people like Disney World and magicians—something about it. We thrive, our souls thrive, on things not being what they are and creating a seeming for them that isn't. Power is more times than not derived, assumed, and taken, by hiding our true intentions in seeming. Your pal Columbus, just now. Or, what-the-other thing—? Love."

I rolled my eyes.

"Did Columbus really believe he'd found India?" Muir professored.

"Yes."

"No. He knew after Cuba he hadn't. He also knew that were he to report that to Madrid's 'Seventh Floor,' he'd not be allowed back to the New World he had his own designs on. He had no fucking idea when he set sail—beyond the hypothesis of the law of averages he'd run into something—where India was.

"His pitch to Isabelle and Ferdie was a deception operation. And that's why at Cuba, which he knew *was not* India, he had his crew sign a sworn statement that it was the edge of China or be fined fifteen thousand ducats—or whatever they called them—and have their tongues cut out. Every crew member signed or made their check mark in the 'Yep, India' column."

He could see I wasn't following him. I could see he was taking me on a *Niña*, *Pinta*, and the *Santa María* cruise of misdirection because he was waiting my permission to talk about what he really wanted to tell me.

"This is all about Bishop—what you want to talk about, isn't it?"

People commonly phrase declarations as questions.

"It's about his flag. I'm going to rely on you to take it from my office tomorrow. Get it back in his hands."

He's always so sure of himself. He walks too fast.

"It's why I sent him to Beirut instead of Moscow."

He scooped up a handful of Captiva swamp-oak acorns and threw them out onto the water. Later, when Björk finished with the hyacinth, she puppied after the nuts.

"Bishop had his heart set on going up against the Russian Bear directly, but I quick put a stop to that. Contrary to all the spy novels coming out these days, Russia at the height of the Cold War was the worst posting in the field. Stupid-boring. We'd been cooking our books for years to reflect a Russia that didn't exist in order to support a US military-industrial complex that was way, way out of control."

"Easy for you to say in hindsight." I threw an acorn of my own accord. It hit a mangrove and bounced back into my knee. My next one made a splash.

"I said it back then. Whether Bishop liked it or not, the Middle East was where the action was. Between balancing our commitments to Israel with our need for Arab oil; the alphabet-soup terrorist groups threatening to bomb Americans at home and abroad; and, just for kicks, the Soviets arming Syria... Was gonna be work there for guys like us a long time coming.

"I put him in as a public works engineer—a front we used to spoon-feed his actual cover—"

"An American arms dealer out of Cyprus." I knew that part of the story.

"Good. Right. And guns, like fresh water, were indispensable in Beirut in 1981. Between the boutiques and the rubble, you'd have young Arabs in Gucci slippers and designer jeans thinking nothing of the pistols in their belts bulging bigger than the dicks they typically end up without."

"How would you know?"

"Artillery, tank rounds, high-velocity .50 caliber blast path: tear off clothes, even loose appendages when they miss too close. Shit *you're* not made to see."

He got back on track. "Or the AK-47s propped lazily against their knees, as they drank espresso at the cafés, wearing their titanium Paul Newman Porsche sunglasses."

"Appearance v. reality," I interjected.

"Nice, Russell. Yes," Muir returned, then, "I set him up at the Commodore in the Al Hamra district. Location didn't matter to Bishop, but I'd be flying in from Rome to debrief, and the Commodore had one of the few remaining watering holes the Shi'ite 'Temperance Society' hadn't shot to pieces. A good bar filled with Arab expats of all stripes, foreign journalists, diplomats, spooks, Lebanese officers, gold dealers"—a grin—"hookers and hookahs, huh?"

Muir had brought his cigarettes. He took one out and played with it, but this was interesting. He didn't light it until later when Björk swam off. Manners, I guess.

"Meanwhile, you got Israeli aircraft bombing the Beqaa Valley. Street fighting all over East Beirut. Building-dust rainstorms every day as artillery shells exploded into downtown structures for no particular reason at all—most of it kids just playing army with grown-up toys and busting things up for the fun of it. So if ever there was a place where a drink was required for breakfast, it was that bar at the Hotel Commodore.

"Within six months, Bishop had in place the second-best network this agency ever had anywhere."

"Your Cyprus network being the best. Did his end up like yours?"

"No, and don't get ahead of me. Six months turned to two years. This was his heyday, but it was eating him up and I didn't know." Muir gave me a discerning look.

I knew what he was trying to do. He was offering his defense to the only attorney who would take his case. "Go on," I said, as if I'd taken it without retainer.

"Thanks." He rolled his cigarette in his fingers. He wanted to blow across its tip as he did, I'd come to think, when he was getting to the heart of what mattered to him. But there was no cherry on top to blow on.

"They had this mangy pet monkey in the bar. Everyone got a kick out of it. It could perfectly mimic the sound of an incoming shell. It would do it randomly, to its own delight, to cause those who had never heard it throw their drinks and hit the deck. It had just pulled its little stunt and some people were climbing back up and the rest of us were laughing, and Bishop comes in—

"Wait," Muir interrupted himself. "Let me tell it from where he'd just been. I didn't know at the time. Obviously. But the rest will be easier to understand with that business up front.

"There was this guy. A courier for the PLO. Every week or two, Bishop would trade him a case of bazooka rockets for a copy of their current codebook. Kept us, and those we were sharing intel with at whatever moment, up on their radios. Bread 'n' butter bidness."

Muir reached for the bottle and took a swig. We were sitting next to each other on a driftwood log. Like a picnic. "You know, I really believed he'd hardened to my main rule."

"The 'half of what we do' thumb in the eye?"

"Maybe? And maybe Beirut just kept poking back harder. 'Half of what we do is pointless, and the half that isn't doesn't feel any better.'

"So he dodges his way through machine-gun fire to the meet. It's a tight, doglegged, and high-walled kinda biblical Charlton Heston–style alley. I'd seen it. No windows. Perfect. He gets his codebook. Watches the kid strap the bazooka rockets to his moped and poop-poop off. Tom hears someone behind him. He whirls with his gun. But it's just some granny with two grubby children and baby *à la* carriage.

"He's stuck with two images from that encounter. The stained, broken teeth in grandmother's grin at him. He's pocketing his gun, going for the Bazooka *bubblegum* he always keeps for the kids. Scream of a high-explosive howitzer shell—not like mortars, these come screaming their heads off—it explodes in the mouth of the alley, vaporizing the old woman and the children, throwing Bishop backwards, blasting the baby carriage in flames into his chest as he falls. I don't know why he did it. But he gets up and he looks into the burning carriage."

Bishop has told me all of this. I let Muir continue.

"He was still shaking when he walked into the Commodore. I saw him. I knew something was wrong. I was making my way over, but this American chick beats me to him. He's looking at the monkey, but knows she's come right in at his shoulder.

"He says, 'Someday I'll strangle that flea-bitten dust rag.'

"He looks at her, and she's one of the ones who dropped at the monkey-trick anyway. Her press badge is CBS and she mutters something. She looks twenty-one—just barely.

"He says, 'Your mother know you're here?'

"She says—I hear this—'Fuck you too, very much.'

"But falls prey to his looks, perfume male-model bronzed from the hammer-hard sun. She throws a changeup. 'So you gonna buy me a drink, screw me, or both?'

"I wedged in between them. Tossed an arm around her shoulder.

"'He's gonna screw you, potty-mouth, but later—so beat it.'

"She shucks the big bad wolf paw off her back, says, 'Room 507, blondie,' and tottles off.

"'Well, if that don't make you feel like Roger Moore…' I said to Bishop and signaled for fresh drinks.

"'Wanna know how I feel? I'm dealing with terrorists—kill the lot of us if they could—and I give 'em the weapons they'll do it with. And my government pays me to do that. Why?'

"Our drinks arrived. I'm going on the 'Pride and Ego Up' method—again, I was reading him wrong—so I glossed it with macho cynicism. 'Leave those questions to your preacher. We're protecting American lives.'

"I drank. He didn't.

"'That's just it. I don't see many Americans here,' said Bishop. 'All I see are piles of bodies. Women, little kids. Babies…'

"'Well, buddy, that's part of the reason I've come. President Ronnie's sending in our Marines. See if they can calm the place down. Everything you've done so far: groundwork for the real job of making sure this whole thing goes smooth.'

"'Pride and Ego Up,'" Muir repeated.

"Isn't that an interrogation technique?" I said.

"It is… I don't know where my mind was those days. I…" Muir started another sentence, then decided not to. "Bishop asked where they were going to station, and I told him. Green Beach.

"'Oh, that's beauty. What genius came up with that? Green Beach: the one and single place in Beirut you can hit from anywhere.'

"Bishop picked up his beer. 'Semper Fi,' he toasted me.

"'To fallen comrades,' I responded.

"Bishop asked, '*Part of the reason?* What did you mean by that?'

"'Let's you and I take our drinks to the roof, play dodge-bullet with the snipers awhile.'

"And we did. Up on the roof, I debriefed him. He told me about the grandmother and her toothy smile and all that. You could hear the gunfire—the tracers lighting up the dark streets around us—watch the ripple of shelling off in the distance, always something blowing up with fireballs.

"I said to him, 'Had lunch in Rome with one of our British SIS cousins. Offered this as a freebie,' and I handed Bishop a photograph.

"'Meaning they don't have the assets to do the job themselves,' he said, and was right.

"The target was a senior-ranking Iranian officer. Was going to be in town paying a call on a Shi'ite HQ. Bishop studied the photo by the flame of my lighter, committing the man to memory.

"He asked, 'How reliable?' and I answered, 'Brits say it comes straight from our pal Saddam Hussein.'

"'Doesn't get much cozier than that. How do you want delivery?'

"'Be nice to chat him up a bit, but don't feel you have to be polite about the invitation.'

"As he flamed the picture, I explained that all parties agreed it a great idea to make a play for the bastard. Help Iraq in its war with Iran. Allow the Brits to impress Saddam Hussein, predisposing him to buy some more of the Queen's weapons. In the meantime, it would give us a shot at the Shi'ite command, which would win Uncle Sam brownie points with Israel. Incline them to ease off Egypt, who'd loosen strictures on the Suez Canal, allowing the oil to flow to all. Boy, it always looks good on paper."

Paper is my *bidness.*

His manatee gone, Muir lit up. A breeze had come in off the water, driving the mosquitoes away from me and the smoke right into my face. Muir knew. Preferred to see if I'd adjust or ask him to blow it somewhere else.

I didn't give him the satisfaction of either.

He described the Grab 'n' Go. It was off the books—favor to the Brits—so I wasn't familiar with it, but it went like this: Bishop and a squad of Marine Recons came in, scuba from the sea, and gained entry to a former resort hotel turned military headquarters.

They made contact with the perimeter sentry. Dispatched three. Moved forward.

They leapfrogged their way to a third-story suite; a silenced, low velocity round to take out the guard at the double doors.

Upon entry, they were confronted with two Shi'ite officers at a large table spread with maps, papers, and greasy chicken-bone plates. A bodyguard just inside the door.

Bang. Dead. Down.

The man from the photo stands at the window. At the moment of entry, he was speaking Farsi to the others, waving them to see something. Later, translation and visual confirmation confirmed he'd observed the body of one of their men as Bishop's squad members Two and Three pulled the corpse behind a cabana. Training requirement later.

Squad members Five and Six neutralized the door guard and the first officer as Bishop charges inside. Renders neutral the second officer, before grabbing his target, shoving his silenced pistol in his face.

But someone fucked up.

The target wasn't Iranian. He was a Libyan. Farsi as a second language. Compounding the matter, before anyone can ask him why he'd pull such a dirty rotten trick, three more Shi'ites pop through the door.

AKs firing semi-auto bursts.

Bishop spins, using his Libyan target as a human shield, as his Marines swivel and take down this latest threat.

Exposed and outnumbered, Bishop's capture-target dead in his arms, his squad leader makes the go call. Pissed, Bishop quickly frisks the dead Libyan in his embrace. Finds his wallet. Sweeps the documents from the table into his grab bag and follows his Marine Recons through the door.

Muir finished his cigarette.

"The plans and papers were nothing new, but the Libyan remained a mystery. Langley wrote the whole fiasco off, but for me and Bishop—maybe because it almost killed him, maybe because we both knew a few Marines stationed unsafely at Green Beach—it became our crusade.

"Bishop took it all to his agent inside the PLO. Turned over the Libyan's identity card. His agent recognized the mystery man.

'This man, I have seen. Not with Shi'ite, but with my own people. He brought to us a craftsman. One they call the Clockmaker. Builds most impressive bombs.'

"'He's building bombs for the PLO?' Bishop said.

"'He trained some of our people, but no. He already has taken another job.'

"'With the Shi'ites?'

"That made the guy laugh. 'What do they need more bombs? No. Another Muslem faction. The Islamic Jihad.'

"I'd heard of them. A Shi'ite splinter group. Bishop's source thought they might be planning an action against the United States. I thought it wouldn't hurt to alert the embassy. Bishop thought the Marines too.

"'Their security isn't for shit," Bishop said. "Bunch of kids carrying guns with empty clips.'

"I saw how that disturbed him.

"I said, 'Washington's Rules of Engagement: "A Peacekeeping Force will not carry loaded weapons in a war zone."'"

"Who the fuck decided that shit?" I asked Muir, more disturbed by it and knowing how this all was going to end—and knowing Bishop didn't, Boy Scout that he is—whether on the books or not.

"Tom Bishop worked his network. He watched the edges like Charlie March taught me and I'd taught him, and without Charlie March there to blow Bishop's network behind his back, they survived. That PLO guy is still alive. I've seen him on CNN.

"Bishop got the hit team. He got hard recon on the explosives. Six tons of dynamite in from Damascus. He confirmed the intended target would be American, but he couldn't get the who, where, or the how. And then our own dance card—the Agency's—changed.

"I remember delivering the sorry news. 'We're pulling out,' I told him.

"He thought I meant the Marines.

"'No,' I said. 'You and me.'

"'What?'

"'You got what you got and damn well impressive too. But it ain't gonna be enough. Wind's changed, kid. Official word is Lebanon's a geopolitical quagmire.'

"He was furious. At the Seventh Floor. At me.

"'It's always been a fucking quagmire! What the hell've I been doing this for—two years!—if not for this?'

"I laid it out: 'There's better game closer to home. Last night, Cubans assassinated nine members of this little Caribbean island, Grenada's government. Martial law's been declared. Transports have been flying in all sorts of Russian military equipment. We got Americans trapped there—couple hundred of them. Balloon's going up. First official military action since Nam.'"

"'Not my Marines,' he sniped."

"'No, not your Marines. Pathetic don't-want-the-help college kids. Kind of half-cocks need the most help of all.'"

"'Fuck that and fuck you.'"

Muir stopped speaking. It was after five in the morning. We were kicking the elephant grass from our dead tree, insects stirring. The gray half-light was coaxing life from the jungle shadows and across the water. A pair of herons, or maybe they were egrets—who can tell the difference?—began fishing from the shore, sword bills plunging. I let Muir watch them before lamely trying to coax him back to the topic at hand.

"I've never known Tom to use the f-word in such that way," I said.

"He saves that kinda salty talk for me alone. Lucky, I guess."

"What did Bishop do?"

Muir blows out a big breath like a weightlifter about to grab the bar. "At 6:02 the next morning, while on his way to warn a Marine colonel—same guy who'd been his captain in Nam—a suicide bomber crashed through the gate at the Marine compound. Green Beach. Drove straight into the building."

Muir signaled for the bottle in the grass at my side.

"Two hundred forty-one Marines and sailors were murdered that morning."

"I can't believe we wouldn't have acted on the intelligence," I said.

"Acted on it? They didn't want to hear it. Bishop's intelligence flew in the face of everything else we were getting. Mideast policy was being set. Add to that the tendency with our Directorate of Analysis to value quantity over quality in our ops officers' reports."

"Beg your pardon?"

"C'mon, Russell, Young Turks have made it a priority. An agent-in-place in Cuba submits a month's worth of weekly reports on tobacco production. Intelligence rates all of them as 'fives.' Even if Bishop's one report was a 'ten,' DA ends up valuing the cumulative 'twenty' in cigar-rolling as more important."

"That's bullshit and you know it."

"Maybe you weren't listening. Bishop didn't stop that van."

Muir walked to the water's edge. "Hell, I'm not so sure we didn't provoke the whole damned thing."

He held out his hand again. I tossed him the bottle. He uncorked and swigged. We were making it last. He stared at the water.

I led, "So the two of you went on to Grenada."

Muir glanced over his shoulder at me as if for a moment he didn't know what the two of them ever did after that.

Then he said, "I went in after the invasion. Bishop…? I didn't see him again until he crashed my Christmas, which leads to the problem with my third wife."

I sat up. "The French one. Veronique."

Muir lit another cigarette. Fixed his face with a remorseful smile. "The problem with my third wife? She'd screw anything in pants."

26

THE DISASTER OF BEIRUT didn't weigh any more lightly on Muir than it did on Bishop, but Grenada was a personal success. It distracted Muir from failure's pain. The Pentagon Report of the Invasion of Grenada singled Muir out for having the "temerity to contradict" his own CIA superiors' intelligence product.

Official CIA intel portrayed the Cuban enemy as poorly armed, low in morale, unwilling to fight, and not expected to offer resistance. Worse, they detailed the enemy anti-aircraft as only four guns. Poorly trained and poorly maintained. All of it information that proved incorrect. Even the location of the American medical students the troops were to evacuate was wrong. Muir's "temerity and contradictory in-theater analysis" provided "incalculable benefit" to Air Force, Army, and Navy commanders who listened to Muir instead of the Seventh Floor (clearly Muir's—useless—vengeance for Beirut), and "directly resulted in the minimization of casualties in critical areas and resulted in the timely rescue of American student-civilians."

A compliment for Muir constructed in such a way as to backhand the face of the CIA he served.

The CIA thanked the Pentagon on behalf of Muir. When he refused to reveal his secret Cuban source, Seventh Floor honored the compliment to him by reassigning him to recruitment. They set him up for this round at the University of Virginia with his usual course on "theoretical approaches to the study of philosophy, myth and ritual in ancient systems, their impact on contemporary issues and thought."

For a storyteller like Muir, it was easy two-hours-twice-a-week work. A typical seminar could begin on the concept that, while Socrates could establish a dialectic process of *elenchus* with his Socratic method, and as Plato could inquire into *metaphysics*—immortality, man, mind, and Realism—both fellas came at these thoughts from a robust burnt-offerings-in-the-temple belief system. That belief system held in balance, rather than in contradiction, that one or two heroic gods kept special eye on each Greek city-state to the trumps of their omnipotent strong suit. So, for Socrates and Plato, their Athens was the place to be for Athena's wisdom and they for her guiding hand—especially if you wanted to publish—while Thespiae, where Eros and his sweet-hot mama Aphrodite held sway, was the place both guys went for the kind of good-time inspiration they needed to reach the happy endings of their work. 'Sore was I, ere I saw Eros!' Muir would back his students out from Greece to Spain, joining pilgrims upon the Camino de Santiago racecourse with plenty digressions into his coffee mug of Rioja wine, and fly fishing with Jake Barnes's Hemingway's take on the philosophy of Modernism, and step right up to the tomb of St. James the apostle, before a run at the Valle de Caidos and General Franco's tomb—God as man and a man playing god—Muir giving himself enough connective tissue to end his mytho-philosophical ramble-logue on penises and the Jewish/Arab/Shakespeare King of the Danes conundrum: "To circumcise or not to circumcise, that is the question" of *everyone's* mythologies, which currently fuel the Middle Eastern conflicts across all time to today.

Did you hear the one about the monkey in the Beirut bar? Little furball can whistle the tune of an M-30 122mm howitzer.

Muir's seminars were popular in whatever university the Seventh Floor placed him. Popular with young men who came for the inevitable war stories and sex, the young women who came for the inevitable sexy warrior, and for a group of both, unwittingly earmarked by Agency-sympathetic deans and department heads, as I'd been. Though in my ears' case, clipped as a sheep or as an offender, I've yet to hear him fess up.

Muir's description of his former secretary-transformed-faculty-wife, Veronique, unsettled me to no end. Five years of separating age between them as opposed to the sixteen years I had on Madeline, Veronique's silken hair, long and straight, sparkled in daylight and made mysteries of the moonlight. Hair, he said, created to encourage milliners to go to outrageous extremes of competition. Her face was the shape and the color of almonds—bisque as the shell in the colder months, darkening to the golden brown of the seed as spring warmed to summer—with a narrow, direct nose. Everything she wore on her elegant figure looked chic without having to rely on her nationality to claim the definition. Eyes light brown with flecks of honey that highlighted her pupils and made the black darker and more knowing, secret, promising.

Check, check, check, and check down the Madeline's looks list, though their resemblance was a total coincidence as I'd only seen Veronique once and from afar.

A day before *Strangelove*, at the point I'd come to realize that "those who taught" actually might be "doing" on an exciting, and incredible level, I'd come to kinda-sorta figure out how many humps the camel I followed into caravan had. I was worried though. Muir had been AWOW, Absent Without Word, from lecture hall and campus offices for two weeks prior.

I worked my faculty and parking attendant sources to illicitly acquire the address of his chateau-style townhouse. I had gone there to inquire after him, and of whether my suppositions about him were correct, but after some ringing and pounding on his door, I'd been unrewarded.

Bruised knuckled, I headed across the street to my '68 Corvette Stingray. I opened the door and sat behind the wheel, entertaining the possibility that Muir was only a one-hump camel after all. I engaged the engine. Before I shifted into gear, I gave his house a last look, longing, I suspect like Lancelot, to be part of my imagined Muir's Camelot. I engaged the transmission from the shifter when a flash of light zippered my gaze back to a high, gabled wall dormer. Dark before, now a light burned softly inside. Mrs. Muir, his Veronique, wearing a loosely belted gossamer dressing gown, had stepped to the draperies to pull them shut. Her gown fell open and everything said peekaboo when she reached for the curtains.

She noticed me.

She smiled slyly. Interested, I was sure. I didn't move.

Muir came up, shirtless and perhaps more-less, and embraced her from behind. He pulled her back to disappear into the shadows.

I never told him that I'd stolen his address. I never said that I'd spied on his house. When he bumped into me by the clock on Kogan Plaza across H Street from Rome Hall and pitched me the *Strangelove* ticket the next morning, all I said was—

"Yes."

I always looked at Muir differently—that vision of him possessing Veronique, statuesque mythology incarnate, quite the rubbed-out fantasy for me for years—by the beauty a secret life had rewarded him.

"1983 was a big year for us," Muir said, referring to himself and his wife.

"Martha Stewart had hit a homerun with *Entertaining* a year earlier and Veronique had plunged her hands into its American pages and brought into our Charlottesville home all that she could find. Christmas crafts and candies, cookies and what you could do with an orange: baked, boiled, or porcupined with cloves. Her menu—both Martha's and Veronique's—pure genius.

"Some glen-plaid faculty waistcoats were there, stuffed with my colleagues, their long- and stiff-legged dainty second wives perching on arms of Christmas-poinsettia-fabric-covered armchairs, or their hippo-armored originals, heavy blocking arms clustering around Veronique's holly and crabapple-garlanded, pine-bough and juniper-sprayed *hors d'oeuvre* table because, 'Dears, the buffet table won't be open until my pomegranate-glazed goose has landed.'

"No guest from the Company.

"My dear Welsh friend Digby Livingston in from the Orient—his Livingston Limited newspaper in Hong Kong the longest-running most successful British MI6 cover operation in the colony.

"Digger was raising his glass of Harveys Bristol Cream, extolling it virtues as 'The true, clandestine reason Great Britain joined the Peninsular War against Napoleon in Spain. Anxious to keep John Harvey and his sons—one of whom was a member of the Secret Services Club in Mayfair—in milk sherry, never failing its delivery on schedule from Cadiz to Bristol—'

"I never heard the rest as the doorbell chimed.

"Mystified—her guest list matched her invitations, matched her RSVPs—Veronique sent me, 'See if it's the carolers early, Nathan,' as I'd already taken my fill of the Harveys before even the first of the guests had arrived, and she didn't think at that moment I needed Digger's excuse to have more.

"Bishop stood on the stoop in the snow.

"'You always said if I was in town? I tried to call…'

"'Right, no, *right*... No, the lines've been down since last night.'

"I brought him inside. He handed me a bottle of my favorite."

Muir indicated our Macallan bottle in the sawgrass at my feet. I uncorked and sipped from it. Merry Christmas. I wondered somewhat inhospitably how often Bishop had been in Muir and Veronique's house, then gloated at the thought of the cuckold I could guess this was headed to. I handed the bottle to Muir as he returned to his story.

"I got him wedged in at the table as Veronique, less Martha Stewart cool and more Parisian put out, rushed to set a place.

"'I'm sorry, Ver," said Bishop. 'I don't mean to intrude.'

"But laying out his silver, she turned, practically into his arms, and kissed him suddenly on the mouth to shut him up.

"That drew laughter from all her guests except me.

"'Awright, honey, you know the rules, Bishop's off-limits.'

"A little too drunk. A little too on the nose.

"Bishop quickly introduced himself to the table.

"'Tom Bishop, I'm with State. Tell you one thing, it isn't snowing in Cairo.'

"Digger said, 'Grab some juice, Tommy, old boy, I was just making a toast...'

"Veronique passed Bishop a glass. I watched her fingers linger on his. Her first two on his bottom two around the glass."

Muir gave a faint smile I'm sure he didn't feel at the time. He took a taste from the bottle. We were rationing now. Dawn upon us.

"After the dinner. After the carolers had come and gone. After the guests whisked through the falling powder home, Bishop and I—ten sheets, mainsails, and spinnakers shredded to the wind—sat at the tasting table in my wine cellar. I poured from the bottle Bishop brought.

"'Goose is an improvement from Berlin mutton,' Bishop said.

"'Not by much,' I said, adding, 'So… been back to the camel races, eh?'

"'I found the Clockmaker. Stopped time on his face.'

"'Wasn't sanctioned—was it?'

"'Not something I'm going to lose sleep over.'

"'Well done,' I said, but there was no joy in it for Bishop.

"He told me, 'I came to tell you: it's over.'

"'Glad to hear it. Y'know, I try to put these things in perspective. What really happened? I mean, really? We went for it on the fourth down, missed the pass, but the game goes on.'

"He drank. I realized it wasn't beer. I realized it *was* over.

"'Nathan, I'm sick of you. You make me sick.'

"'Ain't me, baby. Way a'the world. After a while, it stops hurting.'

"'I don't want it to stop hurting.'

"Then you're an idiot.'

"'Then I'm an idiot. Least I'm willing to do something about it.'

"'What? Quit?' I poured him another. 'That what you're gonna do—quit?'

"'You can't stop me.'

"I laughed at him. Real Christmas spite. 'Get serious. You didn't choose this job. It chose you.'

"'That another Rule of Thumb?'

"'Is now. And it'll flick you away when it's good and ready.'

"'When I'm a drunk, self-loathing, woman-hating asshole like you?'

"It took every ounce of courage I had to keep even a drop of kindness in my grin.

"'Yeah. When you're me.'

"'I'll never be you.'

"Bishop got up and headed upstairs. I laughed at him again, then shouted, 'Don't bet on it. You were halfway there the day I rescued you in Vietnam.'

"I dragged myself after him. A maid Veronique had hired did dishes. Neither woman, nor Bishop, saw me lingering in the doorway.

"Veronique said, 'I'm sorry, Tommy. He's drinking more than ever these days.'

"They met in the middle of the kitchen. The maid discreetly left. Bishop took my wife's hand.

"'It's my fault. I better go.'

"I lumbered into the room. 'You're not going fucking anywhere. And get your hands off my wife.'

"'Shut up, Nathan,' she said.

"The French are the best liars in the world because they make their lies honesty.

"I wobbled. Braced against the wall. Was having trouble focusing.

"'You really think you're special—doncha?' I leered at Bishop.

"I lurched forward and poked his chest. 'You dunno shit.'

"'Save it. You're shit-faced. Goodnight, Veronique. And thanks for wedging me in. Merry Christmas.'

"Bishop moves for the door. I lunge after him, but Veronique blocks my path.

"She says something like, 'Don't you dare. Go to bed.' Starts cursing in French—which I hate. Hate French talk.

"But all the ghosts—including the coat-hiding ragamuffin Ignorance and his starving sister Want—had me facing Christmas Present and I couldn't stop if I cared.

"I shoved her out of my way, pushing forward, stammering, 'Before you go, do yourself a favor'n look up EMERALD CITY. Then you tell me how Wonder-white-Bread you feel.'

"I can still see Bishop's honest incomprehension, the fear of not knowing behind it. Then I collapsed in a heap.

"Bishop carried me to a guest room. Dumped me on the bed. They figured I was out till morning. Veronique stood in the doorway, the devil in her eyes.

"'You can't be serious, Ver',' said Bishop.

"She twinkled like Santa's sleigh coming in for a landing. She unwrapped herself out of her dress.'"

If *this*—that Bishop fucked his wife—was the reveal at the end of his secret mission into his please-don't-feed-the-squirrels forest, it was highly anticlimactic for me. What's the big deal? I'd already seen her nude first, in the flesh too, *years* before Bishop had even come on the scene. Muir didn't even know about *that*.

He said, "Didn't you meet her once?"

"No."

"No. I guess you never did."

I laughed, deftly covering my inferiority complex. "He screwed your wife. That is absolutely priceless."

Muir chuckled along with what I'd known in my heart all these years.

"Sorry to disappoint you. Tom Bishop may hate my guts, but he was a gentleman that night. And I'd taught him too well."

He blew smoke.

"You found my address back-when, Russell. Spied in my bedroom window. But Bishop found my address book, and that gave him my mistress. The one who didn't know I was married. He screwed *her*. My third marriage ended thereafter."

27

THE SIXTH HOUR of morning was closing in on us. The scattering of refracted sunlight creeping up the eastern horizon behind us, behind the house, behind Florida and the Atlantic beyond. Sunlight caught the clean air molecules rising from the mangrove swamp, the reef, caught the Gulf beyond, and bloomed violet across the mercury silver-gray of the rolling sea. There was no joy in this brilliance. A motorboat coughed and spit wake.

Muir locked on the craft with an abrupt forty-five-degree shift of his head. Maybe thinking of March's boat. Maybe thinking of someone else. Maybe I, feeling guilty, was thinking of our people or police… He gestured to the path.

He subdued his tone in the jungle closeness. "If they fuck someone you know"—*they* I interpreted as being our women, our wives—"it's to punish you. If they fuck a total stranger, it's to punish themselves. If they fuck someone they know and you don't—until you do—it's to get your attention… or they're just bored and then you've lost everything."

He cleared the same slap-back branches, studying me with an all-too-knowing look.

"So which is it with Madeline?"

"None of your fucking business."

I pushed the branches with my own hand, not trusting he wouldn't let them slap me for not answering.

"My offer still stands to fix it."

His sincerity took me by surprise. My hand slipped, but I bobbed. Instead of my chest, the branches hit my face. Muir dropped the subject.

He continued to the halfway point, the thickest part of his mini-rainforest, with the sound of the motorboat barely audible now. He looked both directions, making sure we couldn't be seen or picked up by directional mics from land or sea. Always operational.

I went too far. Never guessed how far too far could be until there's no good left in stepping back. Madeline, you left me no choice.

Muir looked me in the eye. His anguish remained and maybe saw that it matched my own. If he did, he saved us its distraction by returning to his point.

"I gave you Beirut and Charlottesville so I could give you this. So you'll know why I need you to return Bishop his father's flag. Why you're here. Why I got you drinking."

"You got me drinking this"—and I took more in spite—"to get me down to your level."

"Guess what? I lied. I needed you at Tom's level last time I ever saw him." His words were urgent, his voice almost a whisper. It remained there as he continued.

"Back at the end of December, a month after the Wall came down, I was staring at my wall—blank, no flag—and knowing the Young Turks were already mounting the heads of Cold War dinosaurs on *their* walls. Harker strutted into my office, swinging his arms like Peewee Herman thinking he's Bill Murray popping giant mums in his Cinderella story. He stops. Has the balls to say, 'Man's gone around the bend.' He's speaking of Bishop.

"'Gone around the bend and flapping at the mouth about our business,' Harker claims. 'Been arrested for public drunkenness in Hong Kong. We could let that slide, but this'—and he untucks a *Top Secret*–designated file from his armpit. "He's making outrageous accusations against the Chinese over the Tiananmen Square uprising. Reprisal murders and all that.'

"He waited while I opened it, dipped my toe in the polluted water he was ready to drown Bishop in.

"'He said, 'As if that student uprising is any of our concern… Chinese want Bishop now. Director Folger needs him found.'

"'And?'

"'A field decision made.'

"I shut the file. 'You Young Turks want him eliminated.'

"'We have a Presidential Finding.'

"'Get somebody from the Health Alteration Committee. I'm not doing that sort of thing.'

"'Be reasonable, Muir. Anyone else, it would take months even to find him, and when they did…?'

"'Bishop would kill 'em first.'

"'He trusts you,' Harker said.

"'He hates my guts, Peewee.'

"Harker stared at me a moment, trying to figure me out, then gave his file a pat. 'Just find him. Take care of him.' He smiled his mouthful of hard, gum-shaped teeth. 'For the good of the service,' he added, as if we were in an English play. Then dead serious, 'It's an order.'"

Muir made his face neutral and engaged me with emotionless eyes that made me uncomfortable. "Any comment so far?"

My skin crawled with mosquitos, the sting and itch of their bites. "Why would I have any comments?"

Muir shrugged. "A Presidential Finding. But no Russell Aiken airtight plan, and I didn't trust it."

The sunrise speared through the canopy, the air humid, the light thick from it.

"Stop selling me. Just go on. Tell me what you want to tell me and get it over with," I snapped.

I knew better and know more about how his love story with Bishop is going to end anyway.

"I put out feelers. Waited. Two days later, just after New Year's, Tracy and I are fast asleep—"

"Your fourth wife?"

"Mm. Phone rings. It's Digger. From the Four Seasons' lobby, Bangkok. Tells me, 'He's here. I've seen him not ten minutes ago. Got one of my boys on him right now.'

"'Shit, Digger. Bishop'll spot him. You should've just grabbed him.'

"'I don't think so. He's not himself.'

"So, I took myself to Thailand. Grabbed a taxi. Made my way out to a beach bungalow, spit like a single white tooth from the ever-decaying mouth of green jungle onto the black sand of the beach at Laem Ngop where he was hiding. I was out on its rickety deck as Bishop—hair long, beard"—Muir didn't disguise his distaste and disappointment—"comes swimming in from the ocean.'

"'Beneath his scruffy whiskers, Bishop's face was mottled, paunchy from alcohol. Bishop wasn't surprised to see me. He was barely coherent.

"'You look like a knocked-down shithouse.'

"For a moment, Bishop didn't react. When he did, it was only to shuffle past, dripping, inside.

"Gloomy place. Decorated in empty bottles—beer, vodka, whiskey, wine—bagged as trash that never made it outside or loose on the floor like fallen idols in a Thai temple. And that's just the entry and the kitchen.

"I find Bishop in a bedroom decorated same as the rest."

Muir's faraway tone drew me back to his Seoul. That similar bedroom, Jewel dead as he'd had me see her, stomach bloated as he'd described. The comparison frightened me. I knew who else was hiding out with Bishop whom Muir would soon discover.

"There was a sliding-glass door leading to a Buddhist prayer garden. A ratty bedsheet tacked above: its drapery. Bishop stands there, his back to me, gazing out.

"I say, 'All these years you've watched a pro. You don't even make a decent drunk.'

"'Russell Aiken tell you where to find me?'"

Muir gave me a malicious smile.

I shrugged. "So I didn't tell you I'd heard from him. Write me a ticket. I never told Harker. You know I wouldn't."

"Told Tom I didn't know you knew. Said, 'Goin' AWOL: it's sloppy business telling one of our best legal minds.'"

"You didn't say that."

"So the-fuck-what if I did, Russell? Why do you hate that I like you? And Bishop told me to stay out of your shit. And I said I stay out of Rusty Aiken's shit constantly. I told him Digger Livingston's the one turned him up to me and that's true.

"Bishop didn't care, I don't think. Just leaned there, forehead on the glass. Then he looks at me—corner of the eye—as if he thought I might not really be there.

"'So what're you waiting for?'

"My hand was in my pocket. He knew what it held. What I'd been sent to do.

"'You made me. If anyone's got the right, you do. Do it.'

"So much between us. So much I wanted to say. So much I wouldn't… or couldn't. I pulled my hand empty from my pocket.

"'I'm here because I'm your friend.'

"He gave a single, dubious laugh. 'What? Langley gave you on-site authority? Or maybe you just don't have the balls.'

"'Fuck Langley. Those jerkoffs are clueless.'

"'That's poetic. Seeing how all these years it was me you jerked off in the dark.'

"I dropped myself onto his torn, foam-spilling wreck of a sofa. I didn't want to give up. 'That what this is? All these years and you're still feeling sorry for yourself? Big bad America took advantage of little Tommy Bishop?'

"He lunged at me. Shoved me back. 'Fuck you. It wasn't America—it was you. You with your saving American lives all the times I'm out there murdering people to promote your Berlin Wall, your terrorists, your fucking career.'

"'When I took you on in Germany, you came in with your eyes open. You knew exactly the game you were getting into and you're lying to yourself if you actually think any amount of alcohol-wash gonna sterilize you. Make you blameless.'

"He wasn't talking about Germany. 'I worked with you long enough to know that whole trip was a setup you'd already started on me in Nam. Fucking EMERALD CITY. You came there, and you lied to me, and you destroyed my life.'

"I just looked at him. What he'd become. 'Sure, I lied to you.'

"I remember glancing at my fingernails as if assuring myself there wasn't dirt under them." Muir shook his head, trying to shake out the idea that the respect he'd lost was for himself.

"I said to Bishop, 'Guess it really hurts to find out you're a Cold War hero.'"

"Bishop, one of his real good cracks on the tip of his tongue—he bit it back. Sucked the wind right out of his own sails and all he said was, 'I trusted you. I looked up to you.'

"'I never asked for your idolatry.'

"'Bullshit! You fucking forced it!'

"Bishop suddenly stalks into the adjoining room.

"I hadn't looked inside it. I didn't know what was there. There's this sound of him rummaging through shit. Then a murmur. Then he steps back in with me, clutched in his fist: that old, burnt flag.

"Bishop says, 'I cannot count the days I have sat in cold, empty houses, up towers, lone wilderness hides—countries most Americans never heard of—waiting for some jerk who's gonna walk by. Some jerk I'm going to make the decision to give one more step, one more breath, one more fucking thought about his kids or a bite of an apple before I flick off his lights.'

"He paused there," Muir said. "Awkward, like his train of thought's derailed, but that wasn't it at all. He was seeing faces, and me who's been drunk enough to know that place, the memory lockers we store 'em in, I just wait it out until he says:

"'Afterward. After I tucked one more permanent look of surprise in that hole inside of me, this'd make it all okay. This fucking lie you crafted to replace my father.'

"He hurled that flag into my face. For a moment, I didn't move. Just stared at him. Tom. Tom Bishop. Thomas Bishop, USMC. The flag. His father. The fuck of it all.

"I bundle the flag. I stand up and he shouts for me to get out of there.

"But I'd heard something in that other room. So I pushed the door. Pill vials on the floor with the booze bottles. And I saw her. Her tanned back and golden gleaming waterfall of hair."

Muir turned his face aside. I could see him blink a couple times. His mouth parted slightly. He was doing something, the tip of his tongue filing against his molars and he says:

"'Yeah,' I say to him. 'Leave you to your whining, your booze, your druggie tourist whore,' and bam!" Muir pantomimed a fist in the air. "Kid goes ahead and breaks my nose.

"That's why, Russell, I always recommend a man carry a handkerchief." He pulled the one he had today from his white pants. "Said he loved her. I fucking couldn't believe it."

Muir was fighting to keep that fierce smile he continued faking. I don't know why I felt any sympathy for him, but I pulled the handkerchief from my own pocket like he'd taught me, and we both laughed. Both fake, our white hankies waving false surrender.

"That's how it ended between you? How you got the flag?"

"We weren't completely done.

"'Certain things I hold sacred in this life, Tom. My service in the Marine Corps and my loyalty to you.'"

"God," I interrupted. "You're such a liar, Muir."

"That's what Tom said. 'You're a liar. You've always been a liar.'

"'Not always. And not now.'

"He stared at me. I want to think, but I don't think, he was maybe willing to give me a chance. All he said was, 'Do what you came to, or just get out.'

"I opted for the second.

"I held out the flag. Between us. 'Look, I never wanted to replace your father. But I never had a son of my own, maybe I… went too far.'

"Bishop showed nothing.

"'I won't bother you again,' I said.

"From the door, I added, 'Don't go back to the embassy. You're finished with us. There's nothing I or anyone else will ever do for you again.'"

Muir nodded to himself, recovering, telling himself, I'm sure, if he had to do it again, he'd do it exactly the same.

He pushed his hubris and some plants aside and trekked on through the riotous vegetation.

I remained where I was. I felt as inconsequential as the insects warming and humming around me. I was anything but warm. My thoughts leapt back to the previous morning. What was it Director Folger had said?

Hong Kong Chief of Operations Bishop is no longer associated with Nathan Muir. He is not to enter into this program in any manner whatsoever.

Like I'd known that the "whore" in Muir's story had been Elizabeth Hadley in their last days together before she'd disappeared, I knew that if Bishop had been written off as Folger hinted and Muir now confirmed, Bishop was off the reservation, going into China to get Elizabeth Hadley back.

Don't die. Of all of us, you can't die.

"Sick again? Poop your pants or something? What's going on?" Muir said, coming back.

He stared at me. The silence of his suspicion had the uncanny power of stilling the rainforest around us. I could hear my heart beating.

I could feel its pulse in my throat.

I recovered, wiping my face with both hands. "I'm just wasted. S'all."

He continued with a heavy stare for a moment, then abruptly turned back to the house. I followed.

At the edge of the forest, he gave a sharp look around. Coast clear—for both of us—he took me back to the porch steps. A foot on the first riser, he stopped moving. He shifted his eyes to me as if debating saying something more.

I'm not sure this is what he wanted to say, but this is what he did say: "We train you guys that what you don't know can kill you. That's a First Rule. So here's a new Second Rule of Thumb I put to that and you should think about: What they don't know *can't* kill you."

What Muir didn't know was going to kill him. For the first time in my life, I understood that I'd moved past him. It was an annoying ache I felt for him right then. Sorrowful, but removed, without caring. At this point, his request was both the least that I could and more than I would do for him.

"Muir?"

He glanced back my way.

"What makes you think he'd want that flag?"

"Because I didn't fake it. It belonged to his biological father. That Marine who died in Korea after I was long gone was the hero he should look up to without my contamination."

"Sure. If it means that much to you, I'll get it to Tom."

I won't be able to, Tom, my reckless twin. I'm sorry.

I walked up and past him, not giving him a chance to acknowledge, just saying, "Come on, we need to finish March."

"You sound as if your life depends on it," Muir said.

"And yours doesn't?"

28

WHY HAD MUIR skipped over Bishop's involvement in Panama? That operation defined their real fall: the bridge between Lebanon and Thailand.

An op I know much better than I knew MORNINGSTAR (MORNINGSTAR is the codename for Muir's Bishop operations in Lebanon). After Muir's Beirut revelations, I understand now that Bishop's stories to me about some *mishegoss* with a tragic Egyptian doctor in Beirut were a cover lie concocted to overlay the actual Black Op "Clockmaker" hunt he and Muir were in fact running to a Marine Barracks Bombing countdown failure.

When Bishop left Charlottesville, he left Muir, not the Agency. He went halfway around the world.

Hong Kong station. East Asian operations.

Fueled by the single-minded desire to uncover the phantom sickness Muir claimed had infected Bishop day-one ground-zero of his first CIA mission, EMERALD CITY, he stacked his successes into a tower he would climb all the way to director of station ops, a position I thought, until yesterday, Bishop still held.

Bishop did not discover his EMERALD CITY in Asia. EMERALD CITY found Bishop in Panama. 1989.

I don't feel a need to be fair to Muir. It won't give any benefit of the doubt to his motives. He'd been keeping tabs on Bishop's work in Asia, much as I'd spied on Bishop before New York. Muir knew Bishop was side-saddling DEA interdiction work against the Myanmar–Thailand–Laos Golden Triangle opium trade and had gotten a naive but sincere antidrug stick up his butt, which Muir would use to wag him back to his advantage. He'd

Paul McCartney the band together one last time with a return to their roots.

Muir needed a long-range hitter for Panama and sold Bishop's strong track record of more than two decades' solid work to the Seventh Floor, while selling himself to the Pentagon—who ran the invasion—with a heavy dose of favor-owed for temerity-assistance in Grenada.

It surprised me that Bishop went for it. When he did, I made sure to jump in as the sweeper behind their Patriot Pride Parade's high-stepping palomino asses.

I wrote the CONPLAN inserted into the Pentagon's OPLAN.

I knew it in detail—again, having to Ouija around Executive Order 11905, each word I wrote to disembody all footsteps to all crimes—and for all everyone knows, and history now forever confirms, their operation was a total two-kill/drop-dead success.

It wasn't. Not by—pun intended and specific—a long shot.

Exactly one.

We each have our motives for covering that up, and as in our business where false ends are justifiable by hidden means, we three players, all silently and uncommunicated between, launched the mission from bases of base dishonesty.

So why did Muir gloss over Panama? *Suppressio veri,* to be sure.

Muir had hiked me down to his Captiva Island mosquito coast to build his defense. Not for the taking of Charlie March's life—he didn't seem to care one way or the other about that; and I, much smarter than he'll ever give me credit for, I saw through his cigarette smokescreen and Macallan oil slick. For the first time in his life, Nathan Muir has no secret jack-in-the-box endgame. All this in Florida has been an old man's swan song, needed and pleaded to prolong for the simple purpose that when it ends so too will he.

It's our walk in the woods then, I'm shrewdly guessing, that is the true reason he'd summoned me here. With that walk, with his attempt on Bishop's life and confession about his stolen flag, his avoidance of Panama, he was trying to and failing at erasing his record of the inchoate (*inchoate* in legal not descriptive terms) crimes he's committed against Tom Bishop, which have led to the crushing of Bishop's nobility, the ruination of his career, the breaking of his heart.

Suppressio veri: hiding the truth. Muir attempts to obscure his cruel hand by denying his culpability.

But Panama wasn't their *Abbey Road.* It was their road to perdition.

Then conquer we must, when our cause it is just... Fourth stanza, "Star-Spangled Banner."

The invasion of Panama: Operation JUST CAUSE. Bishop's lethal corner of JUST CAUSE, Muir had me designate it MUST CONQUER. Muir claimed that since Panama was the largest and most complex combat operation since the Vietnam War, President Reagan had insisted all operational designations for the invasion be selected from our national anthem. I dispute that. And I have just cause because it's typical Muir bullshit.

Codenames are required by law to be randomly generated. You connect them all up with a ditty, you might as well be handing the enemy an airline magazine crossword where someone's already done half the puzzle. Honestly, what president—or anyone serious at all—locked in a life-and-death struggle, about to commit troops to combat, wastes time playing word games to amuse themselves?

Espionage isn't an entertainment.

Muir's plan for Bishop was a wildly reckless attempt to bring him back under the wing that Lebanon frayed.

I recall it with certainty: Muir had used that word. *Frayed.* I am not one who takes pleasure in other people's misery. I knew the relationship was important to them, each in their own way.

Like many couples, there's always that one last chance after the initial breakup to "we owe it to 'us' to give it one more try."

Not something I was dumb enough to try with Madeline, "he confessed as he paid the stewardess for three more Johnnie minis."

Things that have happened since confirm that my less than full disclosure to both parties, my choice not to recuse myself so as not to influence events, was the best decision I could have made. Muir may not think I have the killer instinct, but he has no idea how prudent I am with my jurisprudence. All crystal balls reflect backwards. Events that have followed, including the Thailand horror story now revealed as less than a year back, justify my actions in making sure the Panama operation would succeed in the ending of their partnership.

I did what I knew best for the three of us.

When I heard *frayed,* I had no fear that Muir would think I'd be doing anything other than making sure they didn't unravel. What he didn't know is that I'd chosen to approach MUST CONQUER from an altogether opposite definition of *fray*.

Before you run to George & Charles Merriam's word-book to look up *my* definition of *fray*, I'll tell you this, so I can tell you that. "This" is illustrative of the spy game we're forced to live. Appearance *defines* reality. Noah—as in Webster, not the Ark—wrote the conclusive dictionary on our America's language. Begun in 1807 and completed in 1835, to evaluate the etymology of words, Noah learned twenty-six languages, including Old English, Greek, Hebrew, and Latin, so he'd know what he was talking about. Not only did he index and define every word of American English, he classified their idiom, pronunciation, and style.

The Merriam brothers wanted to republish new versions of Webster's dictionary, lured by the dream of having a book that would be a perennial bestseller. Noah refused an offer from the brothers; his book, he declared, was complete. Immutable. Why on earth would anyone need more than a single copy? Over the years, Noah Webster declined numerous bids from Messrs. G & C Merriam. He died correct: people generally only need one dictionary. He also died deeply in debt.

The way the Merriam brothers got hold of Noah Webster's dictionary over other debt litigant-claimants happened in a way Muir not only would have approved but would have designed. They used their years of communication with Webster, counting that its volume over those letters' negative content would—Cuban cigar-rolling over Marine Barracks Bombing—literally weigh in their favor. Estate lawyers being very much like Directorate of Analysis analysts, the Merriam brothers acquired all rights and proceeded to overhaul Webster's work.

The very *fraying* Webster feared.

Not only did the brothers add definitions he'd never have included, but to whitewash their crime, they included his name in the title, invoking his approval from beyond the grave.

Can you guess how this relates to the three of us? Exactly. Me: Webster. Muir and Bishop: the Merriam brothers. Muir is George. How do I know this? One of the additions George made to Webster added a definition for the word *Charlie* [his brother's name] "(n.)—Fool." And that's how Muir would have played Bishop had I not intervened.

In the case of Operation MUST CONQUER, Charlie Merriam and I ended up with the last laugh. As soon as the Second Edition, there is a second definition for *fray:*

> 2. *(of a male deer) rub (a bush or small tree) with the head in order to remove the velvet from newly formed antlers to mark territory before fighting during the rut.*

I'd see to it that Bishop ended this mission with horns frayed into lances.

To ensure the invasion went smoothly, planners elected to eliminate two military targets, both of them generals, one who commanded Noriega's regular army—fellow named Arias—and the other, Miguel Villalobos—who ran his secret police. At Muir's request, I made sure that, legally, this task fell to him. I built my case on two mutually inclusive arguments:

1. *Target(s) neutralization must take place pre-invasion regardless of:*
   - 1.1. *Invasion going forward.*
   - 1.2. *If invasion called off.*

2. *Target(s) oversee Panamanian government contraband/illegal cocaine export.*
   - 2.1. *Seizure of contraband cocaine:*
     - 2.1.1. *U.S. Military will claim for:*
       - 2.1.1.1. *Justification for invasion*
       - 2.1.1.2. *War on Drugs*
     - 2.1.2. *CIA will claim for:*
       - 2.1.2.1. *Future undefined/classified use in Central America.*

I removed the US Military from the op by virtue of 1.2. If the invasion *were* called off, they would have to explain a rogue military sniper punching tickets in a non-war zone. However, I made sure to obstruct CIA with the fact that if the invasion were called on, the eliminations would fall under 11905 jurisdiction and governance that forbids CIA employees from engaging in or conspiring to engage in political assassination. I handed it to Muir by splitting the Company/military difference. CIA would allow the US Military, namely the United States Marine Corps, to call Bishop back to active duty through 10 U.S. Code § 688a: *Retired members: temporary authority to order to active duty in high-demand, low-density assignments.*

Bishop didn't give a damn about how I Merriam-Webster-ed my CONPLAN, but it allowed him to straddle the line in a gray area between 1.1 and 1.2, and avoid a clear violation of EO 11905, his CIA activity under USMC-cut orders. This satisfied both the Pentagon and the CIA, neither of them knowing that Bishop was more hopped up on the "Just Say No" campaign than JUST CAUSE.

To seal the deal, we went off document, using the lesser known but no less effective legal precedent of "Look the Other Way."

When Bishop packed his rig—Muir's father-flag, I now know, inside it—he added a half-dozen thermite grenades Just in Case.

In the beginning, Muir's rehabilitation of Bishop worked like a Vietnam-era ear charm. Foregoing that generation's Winchester to equip with the latest Haskins M500 sniper rifle, he inserted, solo *sans* spotter, from a Costa Rican coffee plantation named Jurutungo—meaning, quite evocatively, "a place very far away and hard to get to"—through volcanic rainforest into Panama.

A five-day hump into a sixth-day ghillie creep brought him halfway down a mountain to a hide he selected two hundred yards above a one-burro, one-burrito village and warehousing facility that had dropped out of the hot coffee business and into the cocaine snowstorm.

DEA-provided intelligence had it that Arias and Villalobos would meet there on the afternoon of December 19. General Villalobos and some soldiers arrived as scheduled, but intelligence was wrong. Bishop waited, but Arias was a no-show.

With crosshairs, Bishop tracked Villalobos—who wore a Kevlar vest—from his truck and into the facility. Two of his bodyguards remained outside with his Range Rover while the other two joined him inside. An hour passed before Villalobos emerged. Bishop tracked him from the warehouse door back to his vehicle, waiting until his target was backstopped by the Rover's armor plating.

He squeezed the trigger.

Back on the Agency range, the round Bishop had chosen, after test-firing all available, was an experimental .338 Lapua Magnum out of Finland. The reason he'd used the Range Rover as a backstop had not been out of any desire to prevent overflight collateral damage, but to explore the secondary penetration the round would achieve after Villalobos's chest exploded, heart-drilled, inside his vest. Twenty minutes later, confident no one was there or coming to challenge him, Bishop located his round six inches into a concrete-filled cinderblock of the warehouse wall—after it had ventilated both right and left bulletproof sides of the vehicle. This information, proof-photographed and later reported, pleased the Finnish manufacturers and increased sales immediately.

Before he did all that, Bishop dropped Villalobos's four bodyguards. Two he tapped before Villalobos had hit the ground; the other two, the moment they understood what was happening beside them had just happened to them. Permanent look of surprise.

He cleared peasant personnel from the structure. It was a distribution point. Bishop tossed in a couple thermite grenades and radioed in his fifty percent mission completion to Muir, who was awaiting his return in Jurutungo.

Muir needed both pieces off the board.

The fallback was Bishop overland to Arias's hacienda five miles deeper inside the Panamanian interior on a three-hundred-acre lowland coffee farm. A widower, Arias lived with his four young children, his staff of servants, cooks, drivers. His tenant farmers. And a small platoon of soldiers.

Bishop crept into position where the jungle came closest to the hacienda, then executed a ghillie crawl of two hundred feet to a silo used for ensilaging coffee pulp with molasses and inoculant to ferment into animal fodder. The vents at the top of the silo offered a perfect view of the back of Arias's Spanish-style home.

Terraces overlooking ponds. A waterfall-set pool area with wet bar. Horse stables and riding ring. A six-car garage where the eldest kid was learning to drive in the roundabout. Two of the general's other children played in the pool. Bishop ran his scope over them. He ignored the crosshairs, and what they represented and guaranteed, as he identified them as girls. One just in, one about to enter her teens and the water.

In the horse ring, an English riding lesson was finishing. In britches, boots, and helmet, earnest in posture, Arias's son concentrated on a course of low-fence hunt-seat jumping. Bishop framed the boy's face in his reticle. The child's cheeks were ruddy, his lips pink and tight with concentration, his eyes blue beneath thick lashes. He was eight years old.

A whistle snatched Bishop's attention from the child. Bishop whipped his point-of-view to the house. He caught General Arias, arms stretched wide, hands beckoning to gather his children to him.

Bishop's finger slid from the side of the trigger to crook onto the smooth front surface. He'd filed his fingertip tender, as the best snipers do.

He regulated his breathing.

I'd known about the *existence* of EMERALD CITY as long as I'd known about Bishop. Like a proper, randomly generated codename, there was no way to see the man behind the curtain; at the time, I was not cleared by the BIGOT-list to access the SCI, Sensitive Compartmentalized Information, that deep-backgrounded why Muir or anyone else associated with Phoenix needed to whack a Laotian general scant weeks before we pulled out of Vietnam. It wasn't until Nancy Reagan got to Just Say No, scaring children with fried-egg brains and pretty, high-diver teens springboarding into empty swimming pool commercials like drug-addled Elmer Fudds, where Bishop started running with the DEA cowboys, that I accidentally stumbled back into EMERALD CITY. This time I was able to read in. I don't mean to mock kid safety vis-à-vis narcotics, but not a lot of kids came home from the Children's Crusade and no matter how shiny red Nancy's Givenchy armor was, beneath it there's no Richard the Lionheart. The bulk of those kids were sold into slavery, which is pretty much what drugs are doing to a whole generation of kids this time around as well.

As Bishop wasn't the only one looking for a real way to fight the war on drugs—the wealth I've enjoyed most of my life a direct result of illegal drugs—Muir wasn't the only one to receive his SCI clearance. Not to be left off the federal money train funding drug trafficking intelligence and interdiction, the Agency had to create an argument for first-class compartments. That meant the Office of General Counsel moved into overdrive reviewing and rewriting CIA drug policy.

I was busy for months ferreting out precedence and writing the clubs of opinion we would use to bash the rabbits of the Washington rival opposition as we drove them from the dark dens and secret holes we now claimed as our own.

In this way, EMERALD CITY came back across my desk. I pulled the curtain, and the Great and Powerful Oz was no better than a carnival huckster named Nathan Muir, desperately pulling levers, honking horns, and roiling smoke. Our job isn't arrest. It's spying. We spied on it and we let it happen. We are only starting to see where the kilo brick road wanders us off to.

When the cocaine industry snarfed its way to the front of the profit line among US consumers—rock stars, politicians, Hollywood, athletes, stockbrokers, artists, writers, and truck drivers… oh, and a minority of kids too, whose parents enabled them to afford it—a meeting took place between the Latin America and South and East Asian drug cartels. Trade deals agreed. Distribution deals contracted. Mutual non-aggression pacts and protection covenants concurred and formalized. General Arias attended the Singapore conference representative for President Manuel Noriega of Panama, his area of expertise: US counter-interdiction.

Arias wasn't worried about DEA agents. Easily kidnapped and killed or, to better effect, paid off with money, drugs, perversion in all imagined combinations, DEA could be contained.

The US military, whose presence in Central America took root with their Soviet proxy wars in Nicaragua and El Salvador and had continued to spread and grow, weren't trained in combating drugs. They were not too much of a worry, but as in the past, behind the US military is their Agency shadow. Arias was keen to know what to expect from us, how and when. In Singapore, he got fed the whole history and took a doggybag home.

With MUST CONQUER written up and signed by Muir in brown fountain pen—always brown with Muir—after Bishop packed his unwritten thermite grenades and shouldered his flag-stuffed pack, I offered him the last stick in my pack of Wrigley's.

"No, thanks," said Bishop.

Muir gave his head a shake. "You ever see Bishop chew gum? Honestly, Rusty."

I continued holding it out. Bishop quick flicked his eyes to mine.

"Might help pop my ears." He quickly concealed the pack in the breast pocket of his BDU camo shirt.

He boarded his transport and flew south.

I imagine he unwrapped the stick of gum as soon as he was wheels up and left the earth, though he's never told me. Whenever he did open it, unwrap the gray stick inside, Bishop found what I wrote on the chevroned surface:

ARIAS = EMERALD CITY

BISHOP'S FINGER took the slack from the trigger. Two pounds of pressure defined Arias's existence.

"Bang," Bishop said.

He watched Arias gather his wet daughters, wait for his scampering son and the other daughter trying so hard to please him by becoming a woman capable of replacing the wife he'd lost to cancer.

Bishop set his rifle aside and rolled onto his back, staring at the metal roof of the silo as he waited in the rank silage for night.

Later, in darkness, aiming his scope on the house, Bishop watched the Arias family dine. He kept his gun sight on them as they ate ice cream and viewed a VHS of *Scrooged!*

He peeped through the windows as Arias tucked his children one by one into bed.

When Arias went into his study to read traffic that had come in while he'd tended to his family, he noticed an open window. When he shut it, but before he turned, he felt the barrel of a pistol against the back of his head.

Bishop didn't shoot General Arias. He didn't stomp on his foot, or pinch him, or even call him mean names. He spoke only three words:

"EMERALD CITY. Talk."

Arias did. He made no excuses for who he was and what he did, suggesting that what the CIA knew of him was hardly the worst of it. He'd always known he would pay it with his life and hoped his time in purgatory would end with reunification with his wife and her forgiveness. Plans for his children had been in place since each of their births.

He asked Bishop if Bishop had been a shooter on EMERALD FOREST. Bishop corrected him on the FOREST–CITY distinction and Arias let him, meeting his words with ironic laughter. It had come full circle.

"Christ said, 'He that is without sin among you, let him first cast a stone.' You realize, surely," Arias said, "the people who used you then and sent you now helped start our drug business here—just as they did so many years ago in Laos and Vietnam."

"I had nothing to do with that. 1975, I took out a Laotian military general who was the architect of the east-flank strategy for the Vietcong's final push on Saigon. I saved my Marines."

Arias said, "EMERALD CITY was the final assassination of EMERALD FOREST. There were a great number of gemstones and geographical features umbrella-ed between.

"1969 through March of 1972? Snipers for the American CIA wiped out the entire Thai and Chinese opium trade. It was the only way to get the Laotian hill tribesmen—their entire existence tied to the opium poppy—to fight the Vietcong and Pathet Lao. Once in a while, though, internecine drug rivalries, or the Chinese, would emerge to challenge the CIA-designed system. EMERALD FOREST would go back into effect. All challengers assassinated.

"Your Laotian General Malo Sayasone planned no offensives. He was an inept general, useless to the Vietcong. He considered himself a businessman. Seeing the wind changing, he stole twenty keys from your tribal allies to finance the rest of his life in Hong Kong—only you put the drop on him.

"Doesn't make you much different than me. Just don't think by killing me and General Villalobos this morning, you're doing anything other than facilitating a CIA takeover like you did back then."

With faint thunder, the American invasion began in the east.

TWO DAYS LATER, having not heard from Bishop, Muir discovered the hacienda razed in a fire caused by strategically detonated thermite devices. General Arias has never been seen again. Although no remains were uncovered of the general or his children, in June, Bishop reappeared at his desk in Hong Kong. The eldest Arias daughter is a democratic politician in Uruguay.

Muir gave him a pass on his disappearing act and a pair of "confirmed" stars for the Panama kills. I finished and filed all legal work. The Young Turks—who'd ascended to power out of the rubble of Iran–Contra—rated MUST CONQUER as true a success as EMERALD CITY.

And, hot time, summer in the city, Watts kids smoke our facilitated crack and die over it.

None of the three of us were yet paying mind to them.

We kept silent and in those days told no one any of the things we'd seen and done. I married Madeline—a love to last my life—Muir misplaced his fourth and final wife, Tracy, busy penetrating the final pieces of Charlie March's treason before the Berlin Wall came down, and Bishop saved the life of the only dictionary definable hero among us: Elizabeth Hadley. Survivor of the

Tiananmen Square student protest and massacre. A Hong Kong British bird, daughter of a currency trader from East Grinstead, at thirty-one she had the guts to ditch her nursing job, cross the Straits, and help because she felt compassion for a Chinese boy she didn't know who stood in front of a tank. The "whore," Muir had called her in Bishop's Thailand beach shack.

That whore was Tom Bishop's wife.

29

ATTRIBUTED TO SAINT GREGORY of Nazianzus and inscribed 537 AD in ancient Greek on the holy water font of Hagia Sophia, the former Greek Orthodox cathedral when Istanbul was Constantinople, were words that translate to "Wash the sins, not only the face" or, maybe better, "Wash my transgressions, not just my face." It has particular meaning for me. It's fundamental to all my work, my beginnings and endings, my alpha to my omega, and my once and future Madeline lost.

Was my inclination to a double life born in me inherited or inheritance; natural inclination or modeled behavior? Or is it an addiction? A psychological pill I found on my own that said, "Take me," and I did and grew larger and smaller for it. The ouroboros of my deceptions.

Madeline made me understand it was all three. Three in one. Each separate from each other, but of each other and impacting the whole as one. As soon as she'd said it, voiced what I'd never allowed even my inner self to voice *out loud*, I was released to a freedom I'd never known I lacked and began to own all three parts of who I am.

So why did I resent her for it? It was revelatory. For the first time, from the first confusion of Sunday school, I finally understood that the Holy Spirit wasn't just the friendly ghost of God Caspering around the earth, but was distinct of God and Jesus, a separate but equal outside presence that imbues divine essence, the intangible spirit between God and Jesus that links it all together.

Purity of Essence.

"Like Superego that unifies the Ego and the Id that stops me from running amok," I said one sunny june-bug-buzzy July Sunday over espressos after lunch at the Cedar Knoll Inn, a restaurant now but formally one of George Washington's farms downhill from Mount Vernon. A shaded table overlooking the smooth, shimmering blue glide of the Potomac.

Madeline laughed. "I'm not laughing at you"—she didn't want to hurt my feelings—"I know exactly how you mean things, how you put absolutely unrelated ideas together and make something interesting and cool and backwards-wonderful, it's just I'm imagining if you'd said this to Father Weaver at church, the look on his face. I love the way I understand you," she said, like she needed to confess it, and held my face that girl-with-her-pony way and kissed me on the mouth, where I tasted her julep. She wouldn't hear of kissing my cheek just because she'd had a drink. And I liked the way our lips fit. But the alcohol put a taste of resentment on my tongue; and I hated it when she laughed at me.

Shut up. She's amazing. You love Madeline and she loves you. You don't build a fort just to knock it down with rocks.

Sigmund Freud would have understood.

We'd been menu sampling for our wedding reception that we ended up having at the Inn that December. The patio closed for the season, we entertained our guests inside the early 1800s farmhouse. Walls of alternating white bands of plaster and dark wooden poles, cramped and even in its simplicity, poorly thought out in its use of space. The antiques were nice and the Christmas decorations were still up—I liked that, as it distracted from the room's windowless aspect and the claustrophobia all historical American buildings trigger in me with an added childhood fear of Indian attack. I'd wanted the patio, forgetting that while you can have Christmas in July, you'll freeze trying for July at

Christmas. Oh well, we had enjoyed the sunset over the river when we arrived; everyone chuckled and enjoyed me when I said, "Same one George Washington watched from his porch," which I'd plagiarized from the brochure.

Muir enjoyed the patio, though, mufflered and puffing smoke in the cold, and Bishop had been the best of best men, coordinating all of the out-of-town travel for our out of town travelers: buying me my tux from Gordon Yao's in Kowloon, paying the priest, and making sure the license was signed and in place in the rectory after the service. Tom's best-man speech via sat-phone from Hong Kong was a riot. My mother was cozy in her wheelchair, parked by the crackling fire (the fireplace large enough for a tomahawk Algonquian to leap down, but I'm sure they'd had defenses for that) attended by my second oldest sister, Paulette, who would never leave Mom's side until our mother's death, waiting for her, tap-tap-tapping its foot, in February. Jeannie, my oldest sister, birthday neighbor's with Madeline's mother, a day and two years apart, shared stories of our awkward childhoods.

All night I watched Madeline. I observed that everywhere she moved, everything she touched, imbued with love's magic, became symmetrical by her presence, fitting perfectly into time and space, and I hoped we'd have a daughter who would be exactly her.

Outside, toward the end of the night, I mentioned this to Muir, thinking he would mock me. He did, but not for that.

"Good thing the girl loves you like a tigress, and you're obviously head over the moon and onward to Mars for her because you took an awful risk taking the plunge on New Year's Eve, my friend."

"We thought—everyone's always looking for something fun and different from year to year."

"It's not everyone I'm talking about. You better hold on to each other. You split up, every New Year's the rest of your life's gonna be shit."

"Shoot for the stars," I toasted him.

"And don't miss or you'll land alone on the cold, airless, and desolate moon."

"Don't know how you do it, but you always know just the wrong thing to say."

Muir appreciated that and toasted me. "I only give dire warnings to people I've a personal stake in and cherish."

He offered me a Cuban Hoyo de Monterrey and I took it and smoked with him in the chill of Virginia and because I was in love, it was my wedding, I couldn't have imagined him not being there.

THE SUBJECT OF DOUBLE LIVES and the inherited/inheritance question came up again, New Year's Eve 1988, our first wedding anniversary. Madeline asked if I had any good stories from other New Year's I'd spent before her. Since all of mine since age twelve were a variation on a theme—how to drink as much as I possibly could, or how to avoid being anywhere where I'd be tempted to drink anything at all—I reached past myself, got my dad to help, and pulled out the New Year's Eve when Dad, aged four, Daniel only child of John and Marguerite, as he told the story, first lost his life.

THE HOUSE DAD WAS BORN IN stood where the house I grew up in still stands, both built by my grandfather's hand upon river-rock foundations carted by horse from the nearby Tujunga wash. My sister Paulette, who's never married, has remained there since Mom's death and I'm sure will remain until her own death tap-dances her way to her. That night, as my grandparents sat up listening to the New Year's program on the standing radio, my father slept on my grammy's lap on the davenport, waiting to be awoken to blow a paper horn and throw newspaper confetti he'd made that afternoon. In October, wildfires swept the San Gabriel mountain range that cupped their community of Tujunga and the neighboring towns of La Crescenta and Montrose. It was a few minutes before midnight now, and it had been raining steadily for two days.

Dad startled awake, not to radio cries of "Happy New Year!" but to a roar in the night as if all of nature screamed in fury. The house trembled at first, then shook violently upon its rocky perch. Power failed. The deafening roar increased in volume, punctuated with explosive crashes and sounds of smashing, cracking, tumbling avalanche destruction. Grandaddy wrapped his wife and son in his huge-muscled arms as a twenty-foot wall of water, mud, and debris howling down from the mountains crashed into his house, tore through it, and carried it off.

Dad was torn from his parents. He found himself tumbling, completely submerged in water, hit by rocks and plant debris, matchsticked lumber, his arms and face cut by glass as a window crashed over him. He'd always said an automobile fender had killed him, ripped from a crushed car, crashing into his small body, breaking the nose in his tiny face and pushing him deep into the mud.

Throughout his youth, Dad was called "The Boy Who Died But Didn't" after the newspaper headline, photo, and article that ran throughout the state. He'd said in the interview that being buried in the mud was his last memory before dying. He returned to life an hour later in the branches of a fallen hundred-year-old oak that managed to hold its roots as other trees both larger and smaller ripped past it. He claimed angels had lifted him and flown him into it—how else to explain waking up atop a tree? Dad pulled himself as high as he could, bleeding and shivering, into the vertical branches. In the flash of lightning and gas explosions, he watched boulders, larger than cars, plow like giants' marbles through the flow of mud ten feet deep that bubbled up with cars and the bodies of the hobos who lived in the canyons and would be found days later thirty miles away by fishing boats at sea. Dad's worst memory, a memory he would recall with a prayer each New Year's Eve, was when he watched twenty families take refuge in the American Legion Hall only to have a seventy-two-ton rock shatter the building and claim the lives of half of them—mostly mothers and children he'd only just started to recognize around the park and at church.

When rescuers found him, one of his hands was clutched so tightly Grammy had to pry open his fingers. Inside was a ball of mushed newspaper, confetti he'd never gotten the chance to throw.

Grandaddy was not a man who gave up to anything. A blacksmith by trade, he owned and operated the local ironworks, and his forge, workshop, and garage had survived. He temporarily moved his family into his business and was the first in Tujunga to rebuild, constructing the house I grew up in out of wreckage he blatantly salvaged from his neighbors and the over one hundred destroyed homes in the three-town community. Height of the Great Depression, you'd think those neighbors would want their own salvage. Instead, Dad recalled them delivering walls and windows, floorboards, sections of rooftop, tarpaper and palettes, a bit of porch, a portion of staircase. Not only that, they helped construct the mismatched, ramshackle two-story mission style meets Victorian craftsman meets ranch house meets adobe-and-rock spare parts house I lived in until college. What Dad learned only later was that his father lived a double life. After the flood and destruction of everything, his neighbors and the community at large needed that other side of Grandaddy more than they ever had before.

Prohibition had been lifted a year earlier in 1935, but the local population, now able to buy beer and wine legally, still preferred local moonshine over the more expensive legal liquors. Twenty-seven stills not only continued operating when the alcohol ban was lifted but increased their local production. Twenty-six of them, located in the hollows and hills of the San Gabriels had, along with their crews, been wiped from the face of the earth by the New Year's Eve Flood. The twenty-seventh still, tucked inside Grandaddy's forge, survived.

My granddad kept it cooking until well into the 1960s, with never a problem from law enforcement. He rode every year with the sheriff's mounted auxiliary in the Rose Parade. L.A. County Sheriff Ed Biscailuz, a semi-frequent guest of Grandaddy's and imbiber of the occasional jar of Old Horsey, sermonized on our front porch the need for time and talent in community service; our family ironwork graces churches, hospitals, and every sheriff's department building throughout the greater Los Angeles.

Dad's own double life, he was fond of saying, began New Year's Day when he was born again in that flood tree. He'd tell my older sisters, Jeannie and Paulette, and me in turn the secret—it was a New Year's Eve tradition, once we each hit four—that his born-again experience wasn't to Christianity (he had Christ since baptism and once you'd caught it, you couldn't catch it twice), but that he'd been born again at age four: a genius inventor. Sure, he drove a long-haul truck to keep incognito, but only because he wanted no credit for those things he'd given humanity. He knew, his identity once revealed, appreciative fans worldwide would descend upon our simple lives and none of us would be able to move an inch from our front door to ever go outside again.

I remember asking, "What did you invent?" And each year he'd add to the list. His inventions had been globally transforming. My sisters, as they got older, asked: if he had invented the things he claimed, why did we live in the Frankenstein House built from flood trash? Why weren't we rich? He'd always say, "When I pass—for the second time—you'll inherit wealth beyond your wildest dreams," and tragically, we did.

You see, Dad invented the hammer.

He invented finger-snapping—correction, "Everyone can snap their fingers," he said. "I invented snapping to music. Get paid every time Sinatra, Elvis, the whole barrel of monkeys do it. Nickel a snap."

Dad noticed before he was yet seven that people going around minding their own business would bust out laughing, donkey braying at nothing. It was an embarrassment until Dad came up with putting something before it happened; that is, Dad invented "the joke." But Dad's triumph of triumphs, one we appreciated each night after grace, was his invention of dinner. Before Dad, there'd been only breakfast and lunch. Not only did dinner end the "quiet hour," that time of the evening everyone sat around the table staring at each other not knowing what to do or say, but no one who adopted his invention ever went to bed hungry again.

Unless they misbehaved. For that, he'd invented the bar of soap.

There was another part of his secret life of little consequence, except I suppose it led to his long-haul trucking career. I learned it first from Paulette, who laughed at me when at thirteen I'd thought of a way to honor President Kennedy, who'd just been shot in Dallas. I would join the Navy like JFK. Problem was, I feared breaking the news to Dad, as he'd never served.

Paulette said, "What're you talking? Daddy was *in* the Navy. You 'member, Jeannie got you out of bed and held you at the window when he came home."

I had no memory of it. Maybe it matches the dream I invented dying from alcohol poisoning in New York—Muir dropping off my father, home from the Navy at the curb of our house—but when I asked Dad back in '63, he just laughed at me. "If I'd been in the Navy, where're my Popeye anchor tattoos? Anyway, I haven't driven a truck my whole life for *that*. Boy, you're going to college."

"I'll go out of state. You won't ever see me."

"Happy to drive you in my Peterbilt." And he did.

After he was killed, I asked Mom. She admitted that he had been in the Navy Reserves, working in transport for four years, one weekend a month, two weeks a year, deployed to that most exotic of ports: Long Beach, California.

There was another thing Dad invented: The Knuckle Trick I'd adapted to profound effect the night I met Madeline. Dad taught it to the girls as a weapon to employ against aggressive boys who push for more than a single front-porch goodnight kiss. He taught them out at the porch railing one night before Jeannie left for college and Paulette started high school. Though I was a boy, Dad thought it useful to know in case I ever found myself positioned against it.

"What you do to defuse the situation," he said, "is offer your Amorous Andys what they're after, but only if they can slam their bent fingers on the edge of the porch railing."

He bent his fingers at the middle knuckle and folded them into the top of his palm. Kind of like a half-closed fist. The bone between that knuckle and knuckle closest to the fingernail is called the middle phalange. Each hand has four of them.

"Very tender. Very weak," Dad would say. "Most refuse right off the bat. Just bending your fingers and looking at that hard edge hurts the mind. It distracts and cools the passions of most of them, but if the enemy remains aggressive, you demonstrate. You take a few practices—that gets 'em nervous—slow, just tapping the edge, then you land one fast as you can and hard enough to make it sound like a gunshot."

Dad demonstrated and Paulette yelped. Jeannie accused me of kicking the railing. I swore I hadn't, and to prove it—having actually figured out the trick—I slammed that railing myself to all three of their surprise.

"Doesn't that hurt, Rusty?" both my sisters asked.

"Nope."

I looked at my dad. He'd never looked back at me prouder. "Well, don't you have more inside you than you let on, son?"

NEW YEAR'S TO KNUCKLES to Madeline, where 1988 had tick-tocked into 1989. Our first year of wedded bliss was in the books. Madeline lay next to me. She ran her fingers through the soft hair on the center of my chest, her palm brushing my nipples and arousing them.

She murmured, "Listening to you talk about your dad, your house, I want to see it—I'd love living in it, I bet. When you were telling me, you know, about your family, it's funny it ended with the knuckle trick you taught me that night—"

"I didn't teach you. You're the only person I've ever known to guess it."

"Besides you," she said and shook the hair from where it had fallen across her face.

I loved Madeline as much as I ever would. She finished her original thought. "That night we met, and just now: the two times you allowed the real Russell Aiken to talk to me."

What? Unfair. You know what I do—I can't tell you what I got going on in my head, in my work, in my real world: the real world. I protect you!

Pissed off, I smiled softly, hiding, and only said, "What about our wedding? I think I was pretty real what I said then."

"Oh, sweet pea, that day wasn't about words between us. The words—we were just repeating things read to us—our wedding day meant a whole lot more than words ever say."

She rolled up onto my chest and smiled at my frown.

"Honey, I'm not getting on your case, I love you all the time—and I know what you're involved in twenty-four-seven is not for me. I just love you so much when the other Russell says hi."

Nice try. You can't get out of this. You had no right to say what you said after I did open up. Screw you.

Disappearing under the covers, that's what Madeline did. That was the night it started to end.

RUSSELL AIKEN, Tom Bishop, Nathan Muir. I'm tempted to say, "Three Blind Mice," scuttling self-built labyrinths to a cheesy reward—"see how they run?" Well, we aren't and know the prize at the end for us. We three dealers in secret death, we engineers of classified hopelessness, our prize won't ever be a rich life, sharp with meaning, aged in truth, and vitalized by a sweet creamy love.

The three of us aren't playing in a maze. We're playing on a crossword. The names of operations, the content of plans, the fears and expectations, the outcomes: all stretching across and dropping down. We only have each other to share these dishonest honesties and because of that we're not maze-blind mice but clear-eyed, bighorn, head-butting rams crashing into one another when our pathways intersect and cross and tumble down the empty mountains of our betrayals.

But the temptation is real. To hide your eyes and run our double lives like a maze. Break the tape at the finish. Collapse into the comforting arms of cheese you didn't find at the bottom of Eeyore's honeypot—anything but the women who wait for us. We do it because we share experience only with each other, and we share truth only once a year with an anonymous technician at headquarters who flutters us with the soulless confessor of her polygraph. To our women, we lie. We wash our hands and face, climb into bed, and substitute sexual release for the Holy Ghost. As Saint Gregory said, νίψον ἀνομήματα, μὴ μόναν ὄψιν.

Wash my transgressions, not just my face. It cleanses in both directions.

PART FOUR

EGRESSION

“Even now the ax is lying at the root of the trees; every tree therefore that does not bear good fruit is cut down and thrown into the fire.”

— Luke 3:9

30

"YOU ASKED WHY I didn't expose Charlie March when I knew for certain," Muir said, back across the table from me, back on the porch.

DAT tape spooled, magnetic digital straw spun into pyrite.

"You suggested that you wanted to uncover the truth about your first wife, Jewel. If she had worked for him in entrapping you."

Muir nodded. "Or if she was merely a victim to his entrapment of my loyalties."

An air of deliberate concern had come over Muir since we'd returned from the forest. An inner calm of self-reckoning, as if everything now was important to get right, paired with an equal unease that it might be beyond his grasp in worthless words.

"I segued to Angola. The Battle of Cuito Cuanavale. Fought August of '87 through March of '88." He scraped a kitchen match. Segueing me back to Marlboro Country, 1991.

"The border bush war that saw South African-backed UNITA forces intent on total democratic independence for Angola, driving the Cuban-armed, led, and reinforced FAPLA—another 'peoples' movement directed from Moscow—into the African township. Over the course of the battle, over one hundred thousand troops, two hundred tanks, and everything in between slugged it out in what was the largest land battle since Stalingrad."

I visualized WWII footage of city rubble, tanks, and artillery, machine guns and grenades, but superimposed savannah grass, swollen-thorn acacia, a couple palm trees. Lingering elephants. Zebras. Makes me think of referees. From that incongruity,

I picture the skin color of the South African soccer team—*not* black. Apartheid white, like their soldiers.

Wish I hadn't thought about soccer. The most insidious of fads. If my Cold War taught me *anything*, it is this: soccer is the communist dream sport worldwide. Fully nationalized. Low to no competition: the most common final score percentagewise is 1-1 followed by 0-0. These egalitarian scores coming from ninety minutes that brainwashed populations believe pure excitement as they root for a team that is state-sponsored and has no in-state national-level competition. Offside rules prevent any individual risk-reward competition—no Hail Mary in this game—each team having to stay behind the ball and take pride in working for the collective. Best of all: no hands allowed, the elimination of the opposable thumb from game play—except for the goalie commissar—the only thing that distinguishes man from beast, and because of this, soccer requires the least dexterity and has the lowest learning curve of any other competitive sport. It is also a sport where cheating—diving, fake injuries, professional fouling, time wasting—is employed as tactic. In America, where youth soccer has taken poisonous root, after an entire season of officially *not* keeping score, every child is given a trophy just for being on the team. Merit and excellence are factored out. Even the kid who misses the most games and chokes in the one match they play gets awarded. Lowest-common-denominator aficionados like to point out there is more soccer worldwide than any other sport. There's also more shit on the ground than diamonds, but I wouldn't bedazzle myself with it.

Let's be clear, I don't wear jewelry. Especially medallions: another fad. I hate fads.

Wait. What am I thinking? Zebra stripes are football refs, not fútbol refs. Whole sport's a sham.

"You need to be listening to this, Aiken."

"Sorry." It wasn't worth explaining.

I took a deep breath. I signaled, *Drinks?* and he measured small ones with his rule thumb and forefinger. From then on, Muir's eyes would go from memory's distance to mine for a dash of understanding, to the recorder's counter for the game clock.

"To find my answers, I needed to get past Charlie March to his control in the KGB. Find the person ordering him.

"We backed South Africa and UNITA. The Soviet Union backed the Cubans. That made this conflict the biggest of our Cold War proxy wars. So that's where I needed to be, because the Soviets secretly needed Charlie March in it and the Young Turks dumbly obliged them.

"I sold the Seventh Floor on an idea to secure a Soviet Su-27 Flanker counter-air fighter we were desperate to get our hands on."

"Where was March in all this?"

"Not sure. He put walls, fences, wire, and landmines around his operational designs, but I knew: if I got that Russian plane, he'd kick rocks to get at me."

"With his foot?" I didn't quite see that one.

"Like a tire does. What is it with you sometimes?"

I couldn't see the old new-car tire-kick trick making much more sense.

"How about we skip the similes?" I smile.

"Metaphor," he said. "Kick rocks; burn rubber."

Then he said, "I embedded with a South African anti-aircraft missile battery. Missile fire-guidance system, radio team, radar, ordnance, support, and perimeter—about ten guys and myself. Their fighters would provoke the Soviet planes.

"*Whoosh!* they'd streak overhead, then turn tail and run, luring the Soviet planes over our ground ambush.

"My crew'd get to work. 'Sir, we have a lock on one... On both.'

"'Fire at will,' I'd give the command.

"*WHOOSH!* Two missiles scream skyward. We fired them without warheads—like big lawn darts. The trick being to cripple one badly enough that the pilot was forced to ditch, and the plane hit the ground without exploding.

"Went on for weeks—hitting 'em, watching 'em blow up every time. We finally smacked one on its stabilizer. Pilot ejects... Plane spins toward the ground."

"It'd be in a thousand pieces."

"Have we met? I'm Nathan Muir: I work for the C-I-A. Pieces are just fine where I come from."

The Florida morning heat coming up was broken by a fast-moving cloudburst. Muir and I reached out automatically to catch some water in our glasses.

Muir described piling into their heavy-duty trucks and racing to the wreckage of the plane. "The pieces were spread out over a vast area. Each time we would find some of it, one of the trucks stopped to collect the prize. I was in the last truck. We came upon the twisted remains of the cockpit. The pilot had ejected. Never did hear what happened to him. But this was the meat of the meal. We deployed our crane and were getting the smashed-up but otherwise unscathed cockpit—learned later the pilot was supposed to hit the self-destruct, it's what all the rest did, so knowing how the Soviets handle mistakes, I honestly hope the Yuri got taken by our side. Anyway, we're swinging the cockpit over our flatbed when we're jumped by a force of Cubans."

Muir checks me, checks the tape, checks back into his memory.

"A firefight ensued. Wiped out my team. All dead. Took me prisoner."

Muir's drink splashed in his glass. Self-consciously, with as much control as he could muster, he set his glass on the table. His cigarette twitched—more like vibrated—between his lips. He angrily crushed it out.

"You got your guts, you got your secret of secrets." He went on with effort. "They say everyone finds God in the foxhole. And you got that… until they pull you out of that foxhole. Before you lose your mind, if you're fortunate enough, you learn one thing most Christians never really believe. About Jesus."

Alleluia. The one guy I'm trying not to think about since last I walked through my front door.

Muir said, "*Eli, Eli, Lama sabachthani?* 'My God, my God, why have you forsaken me?'"

Muir's spirit was paling with what he was remembering and trying to distract himself from. It was clear in the gray color of his face, to which he was trying to pull off one of his ironic smirks and coming up with only scorn.

I tried to help. "The miracles? That he was the son of God and directly spoke to Him."

"Russell, if you *believe* in Jesus Christ, you believe the miracle part already. Jesus's divinity is the believe-in buy-in quotient. The thing we willfully distract from, the thing hardest to wrap our heads around, is that he was also fully human. It's easier to fall into the trap of viewing Jesus as a half-and-half guy—half God, half human. But Jesus was fully Divine and fully human.

"Jesus hurt. And he was afraid. He was a man like you or me. And this guy who was tortured to death, who knew the Divine in absolute, who never wanted to be a Christmas card: he questioned God like a regular Joe. Called and, like the rest of us, Daddy-God didn't drop a comforting hand to his shoulder, didn't speak at all.

"Jesus was suffering in that moment hung up on the cross because of his fidelity to God's will in his life. Get jumped by Cubans in Angola and you get hung up by chains in a blazing-hot tin shack. Every joint slowly dislocates, every tender spot your partner in this electrocutes over and over and over again. Your bones are broken with exquisite care so that the constant pain still rips its path fully from extremity to toenail. Strips of your flesh hang from your shoulders and your back so you can see them—peripheral vision. Your muscles are exposed to biting flies, and you're clear that what Jesus could fall back on as a human—that fidelity? You sold that out long before."

He fingered the inside of his cigarette pack. For the first time ever, there was a last coffin nail inside. He couldn't steady his hand enough to pull it out. Muir huffed air, pissed. Gave up.

"My torturer was a reformed Catholic from the very best KGB school in Havana. His name: Hector Guzman. He had no interest in anything I had to say, but like all good torturers was a bona fide sadist who enjoyed his work.

"What he liked best about that work that day was he'd gotten an American. Made Hector so happy he was making sure I lasted as long as possible, and that I agonized every minute of it... Under his good care, I entertained and pleased him for thirty hours.

"At that point, if you have any faith left in you, one thing is certain. God can only answer on the other side of death. You yearn for it, you beg for it, you scream and cry for it.

"Evil belongs to men and belongs to earth. Guzman was pure evil. He knew all that he was and that what he thrived on is erased in death and doesn't exist with God or heaven so he keeps working to keep you alive and feed evil."

I'd heard Muir's conception of good and evil and Christian afterlife in college before he *Strangelove*d me. Muir's heaven wasn't what I'd been taught in years of Christian school. In Muir's heaven, Hitler is welcome. Muir believes that hell is a human construct. A deception operation run on society by the most evil, who use it to spread fear, which gives them power to weaken their targets with doubt, which obscures the fact they themselves *are* hell.

Did Muir think Hitler was having a lovely all-is-forgiven time napping in eternal sunshine with the lions and lambs?

A *true* Christian, he'd say, must hope it is so. Must hope Hitler is happy and loved in heaven.

But, because evil is the most powerful human construct, it is the most intoxicating existential power a human can control. The more of it you wield successfully, the harder it is to give up and allow one's own soul to transcend from earthly life.

I must say, I do like the idea of Hitler having a pass to forgiveness and blissful immortality freely available for him; I like the concept of a tyrant so wrapped-up-stupid on his former power to take what he wanted when he wanted now trapped in an eternity where all he has to do is release himself to forgiveness yet it is the one thing that he has made impossible for himself. His evil belongs entirely to him. He created it. He fed it. God doesn't know it; and being human, evil has no place outside of human life. Hitler has trapped his own soul and is torturing himself with it and there's no one to unleash it upon, no one to return it to, nothing that understands it or to be effected by it in the infinity-scape of love. Live not on evil, for in Muir's heaven, Adolf Hitler, who did, is hopelessly impotent to time without end in his own self-made hellscape of pure unstoppable horrifying love.

"After thirty hours, there wasn't much left in me for Guzman to ply with his evil. He was prepping to cap me when his boss came in.

"The memory is so permanent." Muir cocked his head as if looking from below. "I still visualize it upside down. When I saw who walked in, a dim little lightbulb of my innate assholeness blinked. I said to myself, 'I know the slut that motherfucker used to sleep with.'"

"If it was Charlie March, you need to identify him for the record now. Repeat what you just said, but with his name."

"It wasn't Charlie March, Dumbo. It was an East German. About a decade older than the photos I'd known him in, and that Ann Cathcart—his former lover—would ever get to know. It was Heinz Trettin of the Stasi. He and Guzman begin to argue. Guzman wanted to blow my brains out. The pistol kept coming up. He really wanted to discharge that barrel, and from my point of view, I'm pretty sure he was ready to discharge in his pants."

"Muir. Jesus. God."

"*That's* the part you're gonna gross out over and invoke God?" Muir gave an acid laugh.

Even the best atheists say "God" when they cum.

"I was pretty far gone, and my Spanish has never been good, but what I remember—and actually found it sickly just…

"Trettin says, 'This isn't how the game is played. There's a rule—unwritten but a rule. We kill each other's agents—fair game—'"

As Muir spoke these words, I flashed back to the Nicosia Country Club. Charlie March. The Johnnie Walker. The exact words to finish it:

We don't kill each other.

"'We don't kill each other,'" said Muir.

"Guzman was furious with Trettin, but he cooperates. Trettin was Stasi—East German Security Service. Soviets ordered them, they ordered the Cubans, and the food chain goes roundy-round at the watering hole.

"They deposited my body with the dead of the firefight for the Russian cockpit—missing, reclaimed by the Soviets. Someone—Charlie March, presumably—had been decent enough to let someone else know to find me.

"They thought I'd been mauled by a lion and perhaps I had. They were tribesmen, not our side, not *his*, just people who bled red and laughed, and fell in love, and dreamed and had compassion like the best of the human race. They took me in. Combination of Red Cross penicillin, native surgical magic tricks, real magic tricks, homeopathy, and prayer: they saved my skin. Literally. And my life..." He checked his hand. The shakes had stopped. He snatched that last cigarette before adding: "figuratively."

Muir crumpled the empty pack and said as he lit up, "One night seven weeks later, after the battle was over, they delivered me to a South African patrol."

He exhaled smoke and considered me with patient eyes, waiting for what? A gotcha moment? I sealed my lips. I wasn't about to say anything.

"I never knew..." My own spoken words surprised me.

I talk in my head, most of my life and more than I want to. It's important and it's soft. Pliable. When I'm thinking and writing legally. The lesser times, I speak out loud. "I remember you took a year off."

"Didn't I come back a little different." He pointed. "My face?"

"The smoking and the drinking, I thought—I dunno." I was baffled. He gets fully tortured and my smile is still more crooked than his? It's that thing with really handsome men: old age, hair loss, now I guess *torture*—they just always remain good-looking.

"I always assumed your sabbatical was because of your falling out with Bishop. The thing with the Chinese and his wife."

Oh.

Fuck.

"His wife?"

This time I stayed silent.

"You just said, 'His wife.' As in Bishop's *wife*?"

I could hear my inner voice running away, *He's gonna kill me! Cartoon feet pattering out of town.*

I reached for my drink. He covered it. He pushed it to the tabletop.

"I shouldn't have, maybe not said that, um," I gabbled.

"I'm guessing probably not, friend."

I went to pick up my glass again.

"Touch that glass, I'm going to break your hand." Muir's eyes were wide, dark with intent. He showed teeth clamped on his cigarette. "What. Do you know. That. I. Don't. Russell?"

"What a fool I am. I told Tom you couldn't possibly have been involved. How would you know who she was?"

"Once I identified her—" Muir started, only to feed me.

"From one glance under bedcovers in Thailand?" I fed.

"Everyone in my line of work at that time knew Elizabeth Hadley. Bishop's life was in jeopardy with her."

"From you."

"I would never."

I was disgusted. I thought I understood the worst about him.

"I couldn't leave Thailand without something or they'd have sent someone else."

"You didn't get your Soviet Flanker jet in Africa," I said. "So you went and got one with the one thing you knew they'd trade for it. You're a hero for that, for doing the impossible." I stared from a turmoil of emotion consuming me. "Talk about evil? Selfishness? Like a no-ticket-into-heaven, you asshole? You're like dancing with a fucking spider. You traded Bishop's wife for an airplane."

"That son of a bitch. He should have told me what she was to him," Muir growled.

"He said he loved her! Why wasn't that enough for you? You'd been sent to kill him. I'm sure he saw that you despised her and hated him for loving her. Whoever she'd end up being."

"Love? Give me a fucking break. She was a mistake. He was making a mistake—That's what it was. *I've been EXACTLY RIGHT THERE.*"

I'd finally penetrated Muir's armor. I worked the knife around a toad-twist.

"Muir, drop Bishop from the equation. Drop yourself. Elizabeth Hadley stands for everything we do all this for. Or we do this for nothing. China is our enemy. She risked her life in Tiananmen Square to save the lives of and rescue freedom-fighting students."

"The need for that plane superseded everything. And she couldn't be trusted. He was thinking with his emotions. She'd helped Hezbollah in Lebanon—not speculation: a fact. Girl like that'd get Tom killed. He had no business marrying her."

I took my drink, daring him to lay a finger on me. He wasn't really seeing me anymore.

A neutral airstrip. Chinese spooks and a Soviet Su-27 Flanker from a Russian Air Force deserter. Muir. And Elizabeth Hadley, a woman who reminded him too much of his own Jewel.

"He knew you did it. Fool I am, I vouched on your behalf; convinced him—like a father to him—you'd never do *that*."

Muir spoke, trying to make a single word as small and insignificant in direct proportion to how much it wasn't: "… When…?"

Not telling him would hurt him. I wanted that, so I didn't speak or move… until I realized: telling him would hurt Muir so much more.

I set the scene for him. Three months back, this past Fourth of July, me and Madeline, and we're not going to the yacht club I'd bought our way into this year to make her happy. She was not looking for that from me. Me preferring a stack of work, she with a red, white, and blue scarf-poncho blouse preferring a screaming, swatting, knockdown-drag-out spat to clubhouse shrimp cocktails.

Madeline breaks open my briefcase and dumps reams of documents over my head. She's kicking them around the room—how important she sees my all-important CIA-bullshit work. Me too impo'tent-with-a-missing-R to make love to her.

You were right, Madeline. I was wrong. Forgive me.

"The doorbell stopped her from killing me."

Muir jumped in. "Bishop was there. He—"

"Don't, Nathan. I'm going to tell this my way, unshaped by you. He was more upset than he'd ever let you see him. His world had ended.

"'Tom,' I said, 'I had no idea you'd be home for the Fourth. We were just about to go to the club for the fireworks.'

"Madeline groaned from behind me. Then I moved and gave her a look and she saw him. Was frightened. And she fake-smile nodded. Said something, like, 'We were. You want to come with…? May I get you a drink?'

"'You should have called.' I didn't know what else to say. 'We'd have really planned something…' I let the words hang.

"I realized I spoke only to prevent him from revealing his pain. I wasn't looking at him, so I did. He gave that thankful grin he has, like connecting with you is the kindest thing in the universe and he's pleased it's happened with you."

Eyes shut, Muir allowed a single dip of his chin, intimately familiar with Bishop's every expression.

"Bishop held out a *Hong Kong Daily Gazette*—your friend Digby Livingston's cover rag?"

Muir stretched a flat, tight, unfelt smile. He speaks an entire language with smiles. With too much mileage on the wrinkled lips to be safe.

"The front-page article was of Hadley's Beijing trial. 'She's my wife,' he said with the urgency of someone who didn't think he'd be believed.

"'Jesus Christ, Elizabeth Hadley? You married her?'

"'Elizabeth and I exchanged vows in Bangkok.'"

I stared. I believed him. Just didn't know what to say.

"'Tom, this is horrible,' I began. 'I mean, first congratulations'—wrong—'on the marriage. That's wonderful'—worse—'but I am *so* sorry. This is—I can't think how devastating. Come in.'

"I tried to draw him inside, but he wouldn't budge.

"He said, 'I need to know something.'

"'Anything,'

"'You're the only person Muir's honest with.' And I thought it funny he'd think that. I never considered it."

I paused for Muir's crack. When he didn't fire one off, I was glad—all the good it'd do him waiting around with Hitler for a Pearly Gates pass.

"'And you've always been honest with me,' Bishop completed his thought.

"'Sure.'

"'Did Muir do this?'

"'No... I wouldn't believe that. I don't. Not even Muir would stoop that low."

"Thanks, Russell," said Muir.

"Shut up. I told him: 'Now come on inside. Madeline: grab that beer?'

Her anger with me had turned sullen and sad on the glide path to lonely betrayal soon to occur.

Madeline loved Tom Bishop. Loved, she told me, how he made her see that all the things she loved about me were precious, things she was lucky to have to care for and to cherish. Things I don't see. I would tell her how I looked up to him.

How Tom Bishop saved my life.

She'd giggle at that. Say I'm gay. Squeeze my cheeks in her hands and she'd tell me how impossible that was when it was Tom Bishop who admired me and couldn't live without me. She called us the twins from different mothers, and that night—after Bishop vanished into the shadows—when we made love, it was better than it had been for a long time because I found hope in her faith in something that made me feel a better man than I've become. It was the last time for us.

Later, I organized my work. I did it to the accompaniment gunshot-sound of firecrackers; the artillery whistle of teenagers' bottle rockets fired on tracer tails; the slap of bright-smile little sisters' sandal-running-feet away from tossed and spark-spinning-to-explosion Black-Cat packs; all into the wee small hours of another Maryland morning. I bastioned my words in my familiar legal clauses and forge-worn iron laws I use to protect American mornings and Lebanese rooftops, and Madeline, who I was too busy to notice, finally headed to the yacht club on her own, and a call to her professor, and a brunch that wouldn't be eaten alone.

"But Bishop," I said to Muir, dismissing Madeline and the locked pasture of my bull-trampled past, "Bishop stood there, staring at his wife's picture. Staring at her conviction for treason. He said—like he couldn't believe, or maybe, like he wished it wasn't true—as if that could somehow help her, 'This really is my wife…'

"Know what he said next?" I honed in on Muir's torment.

Muir blinked at me. Focused. He thought he could take anything. I pulled the knife, pushed back into the wound with my fist, grasped for a heart.

"Bishop said, 'Tell Nathan when you see him: if he did this, I'm going to kill him.'"

The appearance of Muir's face changed. It appeared as if he were dead and whatever soul there'd been had gone so fast it had forgotten to shut his eyes, turn out the light, let his body fall. He sat there, suspended in living death.

I made some housekeeping comments into the microphone. I shut off the recorder and I stood up.

"Fading again. Need to get a shower before we finish up," I said.

Muir didn't see me. Didn't move.

"Muir. Shower?"

He gave me a cockeyed look as if he'd missed not only the story he'd heard, but the story of his life, and now it was past and a dream dreamed alone and without agency. And there was no way to chase it down and catch it. He lifted his arm and flicked his index finger.

"My room's only one that works right. I'll bring a towel in a minute."

31

WHEN YOU'RE BINGE-DRINKING, a hot shower can lock in the drunk at the level you find most pleasant. Believe me, and I'm reminded of that as the *nice* stewardess comes by and collects the last of my little empties. Although we're getting ready for our descent and everyone else is cut off, she's brought me a cup of black coffee. The *mean* stewardess, whose frown wore progressively dour as I cleaned out her Johnnie Walker supply, would not have brought me the coffee.

I thank her and watch her swish away. Same ass. Same stewardess. Good cover—the smile. Try a little tenderness. Learn something new every day. Appearance is capable of reality. People are capable of change. That's why you shouldn't shoot them.

Coffee works the same way. As the shower, I mean. I'll drink that now—save the last Johnnie I stuffed in my pocket for the cab, just before home—be perfectly locked and loaded.

While I showered, Muir came into the bedroom. We spoke through the bathroom door. We talked about paperwork formalities, some other documents he wanted me to notarize, and a codicil he'd handwritten to his will. I promised we'd get to all that. He left the bedroom. I came out of the shower. I dressed. Found the tool of our trade that the shower had actually been my ruse to search for where I knew it would be, in his nightstand drawer.

I'd located it when I first entered his room.

Muir's handgun. I stole it. I had a job to do.

I hiked downstairs.

Muir sat still and weighing up, I imagined, the ruination of his soul begun in Korea.

Listening for that birth echo winging back to you?

"You don't look so hot," I said.

"Time to get this over with."

He reached in and activated the DAT recording device. I gave a little preamble for listeners and later transcribers, and then Muir resumed.

"That speech about 'this isn't how the game is played'?" he said. "It's bullshit."

There was enough for two short drinks left in the bottle. I held it up. Jiggled it, Veronique with the dinner bell at Muir's Christmas. Muir jerked his head yes.

I poured. I did the rainwater off the eaves for both of us. "Your telling of it? Or March's? Or the East German Trettin?"

"All of us. We kill each other all over the globe first chance we get. Charlie March just liked to pretend, and Trettin fed that same bull to Guzman just the way Charlie March fed those lines to me the first time in Cyprus when he encouraged me to meet his pipe bomber. Same lines, just as he'd fed them to Trettin before sending him to save my life."

"I'm more than a bit curious about that. Why did March save your ass? He must have known that you were on to him. And if you weren't—wouldn't his sending Trettin to your torture chamber risk exposure?"

Muir shrugged. "Maybe he thought he owed me. Or Jewel. I *had* been married to his sister."

"You divorced his sister."

"News flash: I'm alive sitting here. How 'bout I finish my debrief and you figure it out?"

Muir knew why. I would figure it out or not in what little time I had left. "If Charlie March sent Trettin, Trettin wasn't March's control."

"Good, Russell. Be like you sending me somewhere. Never gonna happen. But—and this is key—because Charlie March sent him, Trettin would have to report him back to Moscow."

He blew smoke and followed it with a cleansing sigh. He uncrossed his legs and sat forward. They teach you in interrogation to watch for both these nonverbal indicators. Legs open, forward body thrust. True confession usually follows.

"November 1989, and the humpty-dumpty wall came down and nothing would ever put it back together again. Because it played out with students and plumbers, rock bands, pensioners, the gal who cleans teeth. Because it played out with couples newly in love who have their 'Piece of the Wall' on bookshelves in Wichita, or Herefordshire, or Bora Bora. Because it was bus drivers, and pizza cooks, and receptionists, lawyers, heroin junkies; it was bankers, window washers, dry cleaners, school kids, engineers, and mothers with strollers. Because it played out entirely without Harker and his Young Turks, including that nimrod Folger—Troy: Harker will Brutus you in the back first chance he gets, so let me be your 'Ides of March' soothsayer right here, right now—it played out without Bishop, and without you, Russell, and the countless others who have been working the problem since Premier Kissoff faced off with Dr. Strangelove over the Doomsday Machine; because none of us picked up a hammer to whack-a-mole at the concrete, or showed up except to furrow our brows and scratch the thinning hair on our balding scalps: because of this, the worldwide press has taken endless pleasure from pointing out that the fall of the Iron Curtain took the Agency completely by surprise and represents the greatest, most remarkable total failure in the inept history of the CIA, and we now appear to have lost the purpose, if not the heart, of our charter and proven ourselves dinosaurs they would use the Bible to prove didn't exist in the first place.

"I take it in stride. My First Rule of Thumb: Any day we're not in the news is the day we've won.

"In this line of work, it's a bad business practice to advertise our successes, but for those astute observers of the Cold War spy game, this blanket criticism of the CIA has itself one sucking wound of a gaping hole. ROSEWOOD."

"I don't—I don't know ROSEWORD. Is it active-ongoing?"

"Wood. ROSEWOOD. And yes."

"ROSEWOOD. I'm not ROSEWOOD cleared."

"I just BIGOT-listed you." Muir made the sign of the cross, absolving me as well. "ROSEWOOD's the codename we gave our theft of the files kept secret and protected in Stasi headquarters, East Berlin.

"Contained in ROSEWOOD are the names and records and vitals of every enemy agent active in the West, every operational history they ran, and every one of our foreign agents they were on to or up on, if they'd doubled them, and how."

Staggered, I said, "Talk about the Church Committee exposing our Family Jewels—those are the enemy's Crown Jewels."

"Glad you see it that way. The Young Turks don't. They call ROSEWOOD 'Memory Lane.' Only time Harker pays it any mind is to wipe his ass with it.

"An example. I had an East German agent—Bishop would remember him," Muir said, subconsciously trying to keep Tom in his corner. "Horst Bergmann. Great young man. A true believer in democracy and Germany. Bishop took him, hours after he'd made it through the minefield and over the Wall, and convinced him to turn around and go back.

"Horst spied for us about a year. Then he disappeared. Found out later he'd been captured. Bad luck continuing, he got a life sentence to hard labor instead of the bullet.

"Survived the camps. Came across December '89. Presented himself at our embassy. He asked for the American citizenship promised for him and his family by Bishop in '76—though he was the only Bergmann left, as they'd kept shooting his family in front of him to make him talk.

"He checked out through ROSEWOOD, but the Young Turks moving onto the Seventh Floor looking for a purpose denied it—way too much trouble for the transition team, and East Germany was over, so ROSEWOOD was unnecessary.

"But the Bergmann paperwork had to be filed.

"I was ROSEWOOD point. When I got back from Thailand, it was in a stack of shit on my desk.

"I was over in Germany last year—I'm going to get to that, what I was doing, in a minute—but anyway, I delivered for Bergmann and brought him here when I came home. Didn't have the promised house in Frisco, Texas, or the back-pay prize money, but those weren't things he wanted anymore," Muir said, watching me.

"What did he want?"

"He wanted to see the White House."

"That's it?"

"Yep. A photo of the two of us, the House and the American flag flying over it all." Muir sipped his final drink. "The hope for that, the image imagined, is what kept him alive thirteen years in the concentration camps. They'd made him dig graves for his own kids.

"Now that was something the Young Turks paid attention to: the bringing of a foreign compromised spy of unknown allegiance to Pennsylvania Avenue, taking his picture with me, an undercover officer of the US intelligence services, that's a violation—"

"Yes." I said. "Under *Title 50 U.S. Code*—"

"Got quoted by Harker. Got docked pay too, and a check mark in the 'Bad Muir' column on the front of my jacket. And that's everything that's going wrong with this Agency now. Loyalty up, loyalty down. They're killing it.

"But back to Charlie March. ROSEWOOD. East Berlin's Communist Party announced a change in their city's relations with the West. Starting at midnight, November 9, 1989, citizens of the GDR were free to cross the country's borders. East and West Berliners flocked to the wall. They drank beer, champagne, and schnapps, chanting, '*Tor auf! Tor auf!* Open the gate!'

"At midnight, they flooded the checkpoints. Two million would cross that weekend, but only my Black Bag Team and I were crossing West to East.

"We blitzed Stasi Headquarters. Soldiers and citizens arm in arm and drunk. They partied in the street, on the steps, and in and out of that house of horrors, nothing more now than an open-door holiday house on permanent Halloween. They rifled desks, shredded and burned papers. They stole furniture. And fixtures. All electronics. Copper wiring from the walls. They destroyed pictures, windows, unspooled video and audio tapes in streams and tangles of great black and gray webs. Anything—especially anything they didn't know what it was or what it was for, and everything that hinted socialist or Soviet politics—they pitched from the roof to a growing bonfire.

"We knew where we were going. Had the map in our front pants pockets for decades. Their garden of earthly delights ignored, we hustled to the vault room. Detonated thermite charges to burn through locks and hinges, and left the bolts smoking so'd there'd be no doubt it was me."

"Like the Pink Panther's glove," I said.

"Thanks, Clouseau."

He went on. "East Germany's Crown Jewels disappeared from the most secure room in the most secure East Berlin building forty-four minutes and forty-two seconds after the Wall came down. Regardless of what the Young Turks or the press believe or spin it, my team, knowing exactly what was coming and ready to go that night, provided the Agency their greatest Cold War coup. Only I made sure one of those files never reached Langley.

"Within a week I was in Dresden under a black-cloud sky, on a truly shitty block as only Eastern Bloc apartment blocks are stacked. My stolen file led me into the downstairs vestibule, grimy, dust-balled, and water-damaged, of a depressing concrete building with all the warm promise of the parking structure at a chemo center.

"I buzzed the specified address. I announced myself. I waited. After twenty minutes, a solenoid lock snapped on the inner door, my entry reluctantly accepted like the terminal diagnosis of a cancer Hector Guzman should have been allowed in Africa to finish cutting away. Now there was no time or treatment left to rid himself of me.

"The elevator out of order, I climbed nine floors to Trettin's apartment with his file under my arm and a bottle of Charlie March's favorite Johnnie Walker to help him through what he'd have to do.

"He'd put on his best suit: too big, moth-bitten along the thighs, threadbare at the sleeves. His perfectly knotted necktie was last fashionable at the most discerning communist government buffets in the 1970s. We sat across from each other at his kitchen table. Along with fifty pounds, Heinz Trettin had lost the healthy glow of Africa. He wore his age gray and as bone-cold as the grubby building he'd been flushed to in the toilet-spiral of failed totalitarianism. He understood damnation but was pleased to examine the file I'd brought, as it was his official record he had never seen.

"His eyes gleamed as he turned the pages, reading reports and recommendations about himself he'd never known were made, and he relived for the minutes I allowed him—mouth corners twitching small smirks—particular successes of a long and fairly illustrious career. When he finished and returned to the reunifying Western-governed Germany that was leaving him behind his own walls, he aged another decade before my eyes.

"In exchange for clemency from prosecution, Trettin gave me the name of Charlie March's Moscow control."

"You can't offer clemency. You don't have that authority."

"The clemency was in the bottle along with the original file I was giving to him to do with as he chose."

Astounding. "You gave him his file?"

"Harker didn't want it, as had been made clear. And yet they still bug Bergmann's apartment. So fuck 'em.

"One file," I argued, "even the main original, wasn't going to protect Trettin from German prosecution."

"Lookit, having it made the old guy feel better. It represented his life and his destiny, now and for the only time ever both firmly in his own hands. He'd already started drinking—almost half the bottle right off the bat—and was burning pages at the stove when I left him.

"I got into a cab and headed for the airport, where I was meeting Bergmann with his ticket and passport.

"Piecing events together now, I probably hadn't reached the highway when Heinz Trettin stopped burning pages, papers, and documents. There were too many, and you're right: there would be too many more in too many other files, and other men too much more unforgiving than I.

"Heinz Trettin sealed the kitchen window and the kitchen door with kitchen towels. He hasped the dormer above the door with its stick. He sealed it with his suit jacket, but he kept his perfectly knotted tie around his throat. Nice touch, his shirt cuffs bore his ceremonial Stasi cufflinks. All that was left to do was blow out the pilot light and twist open the knobs on all the gas burners."

Enough Johnnie Walker, anyone can get the job done.

"The gas killed Trettin exactly the way he wanted," Muir continued. "But these are not well-built buildings. By the time the gas reached the pilot light in his neighbor's place, it had filled Trettin's four rooms and the corridor. So, either Trettin, or me, or Charlie March, or all three got six more pointless Cold War casualties when the gas found the neighbors' pilot light and blew up the entire floor.

"One of those neighbors," Muir added, "was the young woman who was going to cure cancer."

"You're serious? A scientist?"

"No. A bad driver. She had been destined the next day to hit a pedestrian with her Trabant. Accidental. Bad right turn. A drunken mechanic who was on his way home to murder his wife who *did* have the cancer cure."

What the hell is this?

"Since the young woman in Trettin's building blew up, she was never in her car to kill that asshole and he lived to make it home and kill his wife. And cancer stayed uncured."

"That's the sickest, most twisted Jimmy Stewart *It's a Wonderful Nightmare* you've ever wasted my time with."

"Which is why you never lost your life in the field. That story is exactly what we do for a living. *Exactly.* Clandestine Ops officers like me and like Bishop play that little reel in our head every time we move Company policy forward. Our business is collateral damage. That foot off the sidewalk caught by our escaping car."

Muir wears me down.

"The building didn't blow. Trettin gassed himself just fine and alone and the world was better off for it. Here endeth the lesson."

The rain had stopped. It was almost 9 a.m. and the temperature already at eighty-three degrees. Sunlight beamed through patchy gray, yellow-edged, and fast-moving cloud cover. Steam rising from fresh puddles on the ground, from the stalks and wet trunks, from the broad and variegated fronds entangled with bric-a-brac leafy vines all greens and whites and blackened yellow burn spots, gave the blazing spears of light angling from heaven the solidity of a hundred warriors' lances that trembled and bounced in the constantly shifting grip of the clouds. Muir grabbed a handful of peanuts. He clicked his tongue in so many ways and modulations, I was convinced he was actually speaking "squirrel." The squirrels must have agreed with me. Not only did they come to his call, they answered in complex vocalizations. Muir tossed peanuts.

"You got names for them like your manatee?"

"What do you think I was just calling them by? *Fake* names?"

Pretty sure that was a joke, and it was funny, but laughter comes spontaneously and I'm sitting there choosing whether to chuckle or not—I did a quick squirrel chitter.

"Ah. Chipmunk," Muir said. "Why am I not surprised?"

He tossed the rest of the bowl over the railing, resumed his seat and cigarette. "It took me until last year to find Arkady Olesik."

"March's control?"

"Correct."

I spoke to the DAT. "Let the record show that Arkady Olesik is the name given Nathan Muir by Stasi Officer Heinz Trettin as Charlie March's KGB control. Go on?"

"The Russian was doing a lot better than his German flunky, Trettin. Had set himself up with a Moscow export-import company with a fantastic ambition to become an oligarch. He was in his seventies, so I'm not sure ambition and reality will ever meet. Know what he looked like?"

I didn't care.

"He looked like the fat chicken in a cartoon who gets his feathers blown off and is exposed underneath, this scrawny, scraggily throated, bulging-eyed, plucked-pink, bobbly headed thing. A little bit crazy, but happy enough that he's somehow survived the blast. Very likeable.

"Olesik raised a bottle of vodka in one hand and a bottle of California chardonnay in the other. His wide grin the beam scale between. 'Export the East… Import the West. Make lots of money.'

"'Must take an awful lot of work,' I said to him.

"Olesik bunched and pumped his shoulders, communicating that yes it does, but who is humble-he to complain?

"'You are not in this business,' Olesik said. 'Not a seller or a buyer.'

"'You know exactly who I am.'

"I laid my briefcase on a table. 'And that makes me a buyer today.'

"He saw that all I had was a single document and a brown paper bag. I handed him the doc. 'This is the full value of an unnamed account at a quiet bank in Bern. As you can see, it holds a fair chunk, over three hundred thousand dollars.'

"'This is quite a lot of money.'

"'A settlement. Plus interest. From one of my better divorces.'"

"Tracy?" I couldn't help it, there's something interesting about his chain of wives.

Muir affirmed it with a nod. "Tracy couldn't get over the scars I brought home from Africa and the left foot I left behind."

I gaped at Muir's left shoe.

"Yes, Russell, there's a prosthetic inside. And yes, I can still beat you in a foot race."

"You win, Nathan. Always."

"Only with you—I sincerely hope," Muir said. "But back to Olesik. The document I'd given him. He pointed out the obvious: "'There is no account owner indicated.'

"'Could be you if you tell me what I want.'

"He said, 'Fantastic!' and clapped his hands. 'Tell me, what do you want?'

"'No, no. That wouldn't prove what I need to know. You need to tell me.'

"Olesik scoffed. 'How would I have any idea what you want?'

"'You get one guess.'

"Olesik gestured with his bottles. 'Vodka or chardonnay?'

"He called in Russian for his daughter to bring glasses: 'Right now, Svetlana. Right away!'

"But I shook my head. I opened my paper bag. 'American spies drink this.'

"I produced a bottle of Johnnie Walker and cracked the seal. I asked him, 'Do you have my answer?'

"The daughter, Svetlana—hard-faced and worried behind permanently angry eyes—comes over with small Russian vodka glasses. I poured the American whiskey into them. I allowed Olesik to drink first.

"He smiles, overtly familiar with the taste. 'We were very angry with Charlie when we learned he'd saved you from Guzman. It would have been far better for many on this side to have you die in Africa.'

"'Never was too good at making friends.' I drank with him then, having the answer I needed. I took out a pen. I filled in the account number on the bank document. Olesik took the pen like it was some kind of signing bonus—it was a nice pen, an enamel Dupont that Tracy had given me—but he looked so stupid tucking it into the front breast pocket of his jacket, like prideful, cheap Russians have done since they learned to write in ink, that I let him keep it.

"He folded the letter and put it into his inner pocket—money in the bank—and attempted to caution me. To protect his agent one last time. 'The war is over. What's done is done.'

"'Funny, that's what he said.'

Muir's expression asked me to recall where March had said it. Needed me to recall it as a condition for moving on. I did. It's what Charlie March had said to tee him up about Jewel. I nodded to him. Muir, assured of what I'd just discussed inside my head, did the same back to me with a solemn, thankful look I'd never seen him use before, his eyes narrow and penetrating.

He's giving me a clue?

Nah. Muir was thinking about *her* right now. No more clues to give. I could feel Jewel's ghost and I could picture her the only way I knew how: in colorful *hanbok*. Yellow for earth. My eyes burned when the vision multiplied into three women at once.

Jewel, Madeline, Elizabeth Hadley. The three in one.

Nina.

I couldn't fix what I'd done to Madeline any more than Muir could bring Jewel back to love. Tom's wife still had a chance. I whispered a prayer for them inside my head and Muir said, "Smoke getting to you?"

"Shut up. It's allergies—to *you*." I blinked the burn from my eyes.

Muir stubbed out his smoke and did the magic trick with the butt. "All that was left was to sit down with Charlie March."

This time when it vanished, he didn't bother to bring it back.

"Charlie March taught me that. Took the whole transport ride back from Korea for me to master it. Two days ago, wondering if he'd already vanished, tipped off by Olesik or more likely sweetie-pie Svetlana, I called Charlie March at his place in Key Largo. He answered. He invited me for lunch. I said, 'What may I bring?' and he said, 'We haven't had a pizza in a while.'"

32

THE FIRST LUNCH I ever had with Nathan Muir was pizza and beer after his screening of *Dr. Strangelove*. I'd never been as nervous and as joyously excited as I was at that moment. I could barely contain myself and yet felt more mature than I'd ever felt at the calm, direct, and, I thought, smart way I contained my feelings.

The coolest, most important secret imaginable—

"They have asked me what I"—outside the revival theater, he points to himself—"think of you."

—fights inside me for ego space with the understanding that *Re: Russell Aiken, future officer of the Central Intelligence Agency, United States of America ("Me")*, had ever been selected to receive that secret.

The kid that collected string and threw rocks at trees and busts into his own home with a gun.

Selected not just by my government, but by a man I'd come to look up to with reverence that didn't stop swelling into love.

Muir had just introduced me to honey on pizza crusts—more love that—and he was saying, "No other job on this whole planet, Russell, where you one day might get the opportunity to grab the handle that turns the globe, give it a yank, and spin the whole shebang in a new direction. Think about that, kid."

I did, nodding, munching, dribbling honey like Winnie the Pooh from the Dutch Gold Honey Bear bottle the pizzeria kept in the kitchen for 'Professor Muir,' and the world was a bright spinning golden carousel before my eyes. He peeled the paper ring and handed me a napkin to help me out.

"When you go through training, you'll hear that one plenty of times. They're going to jack you up and jack you off with that globe. There's nothing wrong with it. It's plenty true in its own way, but there's something they're not going to tell you and this is important. So listen: this Company you'll soon be working for doesn't hire bad guys. We go out of our way in recruitment to get the most patriotic, loyal, most honorable, and idealistic recruits we can find. In our opinion, you stand clear-eyed and strong at the white-hat-wearing end of the scale."

He ate.

"At the other end are the black-hearted, black-hat actors this world is full of and we're chosen to fight. Our dear enemies. So what's in the middle? The balance?"

"Clint Eastwood. The gray hat."

He doctored his pizza crust, bit, chewed, and studied me. The place was noisy with the particular white-noise of college campus pizzerias. A trio of starry-eyed sorority girls stole obvious looks at Muir from their gingham-bonneted table. Had been for the hour we'd been sitting there. Muir held only me in his gaze, handing partial ownership of their immodesty my way.

"When we start you out, you'll only operate on the white end of the scale. Business you're asked to attend to will slide around that end, always above Clint Eastwood, until you know how to handle yourself. Then, little by little, at first just a shot in the arm now and then, they'll slap that gray hat on top of your head. You'll be okay with that—you're still gunning against the black, so why wouldn't you?"

"Why wouldn't I," I said. "Right."

"If you're really good at this job—"

"I wouldn't be here if I didn't think I wouldn't be. I—Would be—Good. At it, you know what I mean?"

"I know exactly what you mean, kid. You wouldn't be sitting here with me if you weren't like me."

"I would guess you would make *sure* I—or anyone your Company was looking to hire—would. Would be."

"You're funny. Hold on to that because here's the part you're trying to avoid hearing, speaking your crosswords."

Before I could interrupt and drop the conversation from across to down—

"One day, because your psych evaluation says so, there's going to be a program out in the field where you're on the other side of the gray hat. You see it, over your shoulder. You know the hat you're wearing is darker, but you do it because you rationalize the alternative—what's beyond, down that black end of the scale, is worse. Charcoal looks light enough compared to the impenetrable black of evil. And you're good. You're the most patriotic, loyal, most honorable—"

"Honorable and idealistic," I finish with him, showing my understanding.

"—American we could've hoped to find. It may break your heart, but you can mend your heart. We know that about you. I know that about you right as we're sitting here. And you know something?"

I'd interrupted enough. I shook my head. "Uh-uh," I said, choosing my non-word careful as a thief.

"You'll be okay because the white hat of your innate preference is safely where you left it. Even better? There's a whole lot of the gray area that's become whiter. The gray hat has moved a bit and the black area just got smaller.

"Now there's some men—and women—who think they choose this job. They don't, and they don't last. This job is a scale and it's a sliding scale, and it already has to have been sliding somewhere inside you to get you this far. And, Russell, if it is inside you, and you're able to work it and slide back home from every business trip, widening that white a little more by pushing that gray a little blacker, you'll be in this job that's chosen you for good."

His words came at me rapid-fire, his stare more intense and more magnetic.

"For keeps," I said.

"You like words, don't you?"

I grinned, finished the honeyed crust I'd been gnawing. "I do," bridegrooming my future.

"Good because we don't leave any marbles on the table. Ever. And I guess in that, if you look at each of those marbles as a tiny globe in itself, you're pulling little handles every time you execute each assignment."

I find marbles from time to time. Always green, I always put them in my pocket. Lost by careless children? I find them places children shouldn't play.

"Okay. I get it. I'm up for the challenge, sir."

"Good because I told you all that to tell you this: the black never moves. Black is always black and saying some of it is just dark gray and what was gray is now, in the scope of things, white will Never. Make. It. So."

"Do people who work for your Company get there—get to that place?"

"They do and it happens before they know it and it's a place they can never come back from. I'm not here to sell you that."

He gave himself an assured nod, checking off an item on a list about me in his head. He put his palms on the picnic table and pushed himself to his feet—both pedals real at the time—and he looked down at me with the sympathetic gaze of a man with a dog he thinks has figured out where to go on the paper. He paid with money that somehow, like a magic trick, was in his hand from nowhere.

"We may not work together after training. I can only recommend where I think you should place. But let me tell you: if you ever put that black hat on, I will be the last person you don't see stepping up behind you."

You know real when you hear it. I couldn't trust myself to stand. But a smile can be as real as words and the one he gave me accompanied this: "I expect the same visit from you if you need to knock my hat off of me."

I floated off my bench. As we passed the sorority girls' table, which hadn't been in our path to the door, but now somehow was, the bravest of the bunch greeted Muir.

"Dr. Muir—"

"Professor. Save doctor for the ones who need the practice."

She rushed over his throwaway pun. "You probably don't know me, but I'm in your Wednesday lecture."

"This Wednesday, third row, fourth seat from the left. Last Wednesday, eighteenth row, sixth seat in—"

"I was running late."

"And the other three, the twentieth row—last row—seats one, seven, ten. I don't know your name, I'm sorry for that, but I do know you had a steady boyfriend who was making you late and now you don't."

A cobra hovering over mice.

She nodded and offered her hand like her mother had taught her.

Muir took her hand. "I don't know the right or wrong between you and him, but I hope you threw that big fat sports ring he'd collared you with in the river rather than giving it back."

"Mary," she said, hypnotized. "I will."

"This is Russell. Brightest man on campus. Whether you ever know it or not, you'll be hearing from him one day. Whole world will."

When I finally started breathing again, we'd kicked rocks back to Kogan Plaza, where he'd first set me up.

"Nifty car you got." He pointed out my Corvette. "Going to seem slow once you get started with us."

"I suppose law school is off for me?"

He laughed. "Quite the opposite. The Agency is prepared to help you there."

"That's generous, but I wouldn't qualify for any kind of aid. I'm pretty well set, money-wise."

"I know all about it. I meant in choosing your law school. I've already reserved a place for you here at George Washington, Columbia in New York, USC if you want to be closer to home, or last but I would say best fit for you, Cornell."

"How can you do that?"

"Have we met? Think about it. If there's somewhere else, you'll let me know."

There wasn't, and I'm proud Big Red all the way.

"Before I let you go"—I was his captive then and always have been until now that his hat's knocked off— "answer this: why?"

Why-why?

I stared at him, dumb.

"Why the juris doctorate?" he said.

We stood under the clock post. I looked up. It was somehow already past seven. 7:19. I'll remember the minute after that forever.

"You want the story or the truth?"

"From now on, I'm entitled to your truth. It's a two-way street between us now."

And I've believed that lie since 7:20, Tuesday, April 28, 1970. More's the pity, or as Mr. T would put it a dozen years later, "I pity the fool." More fool me—from Genesis. The band, not the book. Proverbs 29:11.

"It's to do with my father's death back in September."

"The insurance claim. I can see that," said Muir.

"You know about it. All about it?"

"I'd like to hear what you have to say." His face was wholly sympathetic.

"He had an Accidental Death and Dismemberment rider on two policies that paid triple if caused by no-fault manslaughter or someone's suicide. That's what paid out—saved our family's future. Why I have the car and no worries financially for the foreseeable future. It's only because Uncle George found a lawyer clever enough to make the suicide stick."

"It wasn't a suicide who kamikazed your dad's Peterbilt," Muir stated as fact.

I didn't want to voice it, not so directly, and I shook my head confirming he was correct. "The kid and the girl had been broken up for two weeks. He was driving to see his new sweetheart, but he'd made some dramatic and public remarks at the time of the breakup and the lawyer made it advantageous to the first girl's family to testify on behalf of the tragedy and his self-destructive state of mind.

"The other problem was drugs were found in the wreckage. Lots of pills and cocaine inside a lockbox under my dad's seat. Although they couldn't test my father's body for them—nothing much left to test—their presence would have cancelled both policies had not the lawyer brought Kansas State Police and Uncle George together to reverse-engineer an interstate trucking drug investigation in which my dad was part of a sting. My dad did have some military service I never really knew of—Navy transport, or something—and I think they leaned in. Helped. Navy buddies.

"But, without that lawyer, none of those friends could've done it. We would have justifiably—I mean, *truthfully*—lost that leaky, rickety, overcrowded house, and my mom and my two older sisters, and me following, would have had to split up to friends and unknown family and all go to work. You know my mother has constant care for her arthritis? I know if that lawyer hadn't come into our life, she wouldn't have her doctor, her live-in nurse, or her chair, and probably wouldn't be around to need them."

Muir gave my shoulder a squeeze. "How's it all make you feel about your dad?"

"I'd trade every last cent for one more night watching him dance with my mom."

"He was a good man and a good father," Muir said, confident as if he'd known him.

I got in my car. I thanked him for the pizza.

He asked if I'd spot him twenty bucks to pay for it, seeing as to how I was loaded.

My heart dropped until I realized he was kidding, and we both laughed, and then I cried all the way back to my dorm. Told myself they were tears of happiness at being wanted. No more kicking around vacant lots and drinking piss.

Two nights later, I lost my virginity to sorority girl Mary. I dated Mary up through my first year of law school at Cornell until one day, I'll never know why, she was gone.

It hurt, but I was top spot in my class and maintained that off and on to graduate second. Truthfully, third. I often wonder what happened to her—her life, I mean. I don't think anything *happened* to her—but the only permanent relationship I've had from then, until Tom Bishop entered my life, was with Nathan Muir. I wonder if Mary ended up as disappointed as I.

Oh. And disappointing as Madeline.

33

"STANDING BEHIND CHARLIE MARCH in his Key Largo doorway stood Charlie March," Muir spoke into the DAT.

"I beg your pardon?" I said.

"Both of them standing there holding that stupid book. *Now You See Me: A Cold Warrior Steps from the Shadows.* A bookstore standee behind him. 'Likee?' Charlie March said.

"'Tell you what,' I answered. 'Must have been a hell of a magic trick getting half of what you wrote through the Publication Review Board.'

"'Not everyone can be a Trailblazer, Nathan. Those of us who have been recognized heroes—let's just say, in times like these, the old enemies vanquished, they need the war stories from the old warhorse's mouth, trotting him out to remind the masses we do serve a purpose.'

"'I brought some pizzas.' I held up a grocery bag.

"'Mama Celeste's always good.'

"'New Rising Crust.'

"'Story of our lives, eh? Always new, always rising, crustier each year.'

"'Got any honey?'

"'Can manage that. Come on through.'

"I stepped inside, my shoulder brushing the trailing end of the large and clean American flag limp beside his door.

"'I'll crank up the oven and we'll go out to the deck. Enjoy the breeze off the water. Watch the girls on the bike path.'

"He put his book down beside his life-size promotional cutout. He reached out with his arms, loose-skinned and knobby. He pulled me into his embrace. Still quite strong and making a point of that. He smelled of bay rum. He pushed me back. I resisted just enough to make it a push-up for him. His eyes probed mine, not bothering to disguise their cunning. I disguised nothing and I hoped that's what he saw. He turned, facing his replica image. He admired himself in cardboard.

"'Like the way they touched me up in that. The eyes: kind of spooky, kind of daring you to read me—my book. Lot fuller mane. Like the way that looks.'

"He couldn't help it. His hand went to his hair.

"'Put on some music, Charlie. See if he'll dance with you.'"

I watched Muir finger a tobacco flake from the tip of his tongue. He pilled it and flicked it away.

"We worked our way deeply into a bottle of Johnnie Walker double black. Reminisced about old times. Mentor and student. False son, falser father. He was particularly pleased that I had always provided for sister Sandy. That he was sorry we hadn't worked out.

"'She still loves you. Always will,' he said.

"'I know that. The kid thing—we saw it differently in the end. Tore us apart.'

"Charlie March didn't know what to say to that. 'Tough break all the way around.'

"His depression over Sandy, over my refusal of a child, was profound and it was honest, and I said, 'That has to be the one thing we don't talk about today. It fixed itself and it can't be changed.'

"'Agreed,' said Charlie March.

"So we drink and we have our laughs. We enjoy each other as we always had with lies and sarcasm over everyone worse than us, real and imagined. But Charlie March knew why I'd come. He knew what I'd found out."

Muir paused, gathering thoughts. I said, "Why did you torture yourself? Nathan, he killed your wife. I wouldn't have bothered wiping my feet on the mat. Would've just shot him in the doorway and put one through his stupid book."

"You're not that guy, Russell. Never have been and I'm proud of you for that."

You've no idea what kind of guy I've become. Why I'm drunk and keep drinking and carry the gun I stole from you in my blazer pocket.

"I didn't kill him. The same reason he didn't kill me. We were too vested in each other. For each of us, our entire existence was wrapped up in secrets, stealing them, keeping them, selling them, living them, killing them and their jungle beaters. To the rest of the world, we were something false, nothing about us real except to each other. He needed to tell me why, and I needed to hear it.

"We finished the pizza. He poured the last of the bottle into our glasses. I didn't smoke. He'd had that cancer scare after Africa and had written me, while I was in the hospital, that he blamed it on my secondhand smoke."

"You believe all that secondhand smoke rhetoric? They don't have any real science to back it," I said.

"Socrates and Meno's Slave. Doesn't take book learning to comprehend in this cloud we're sitting in, that you're smoking these cigarettes right along with me."

"That's not very nice."

"Nope and I never made the claim to you or anyone else I was nice." He held his cigarette on the horizontal between us. "Want me to put it out?"

"I couldn't care less." Pushed, I guess I like smoking secondhand. I looked at the tape spooling toward the end. "Just let's finish this up."

Muir put his cigarette on the edge of the ashtray. Smoke curled.

"Charlie March said, 'I didn't do it for ideology. I didn't spy for money. Remember old Grivas?'

"'Don't, Charlie: I know it began before Cyprus.'

"He waved away my remark with his showman's flair, pulling back the curtain to reveal the locked and empty steel cage ready for the grand illusion.

"'You remember Grivas hated Communists?'

"'Almost every day. That boy who threw the bombs almost killed me—did kill Miraç Özdemir and six others—kid was one of your agents. You had him silenced against that rock to protect your secret.'

"Charlie March shrugs it off like an annoyance. I'm sitting there: truth facing truth. He doesn't care a bit about the murder of a child. Wouldn't have cared at the time if he'd killed me protecting his secret.

"'He says, 'When I was young—younger than you when I brought you in—I worked for the Agency's father: the OSS. I—meaning OSS—supported and sustained Grivas's guerilla war against the Nazis. The KGB's father equivalent, NKVD, had a counterpart to me in Greece. A Russian agent by the name of…' He smiled faintly, almost pleased. 'But you know his name.'

"'Arkady Olesik,' I said, and say again for the record.

"Charlie March goes on. That magician's cage I'm sitting there visualizing, it's filling with smoke. 'In World War Two Europe, the Russians were our allies. But in Greece… I was caught by them. I was tortured by Olesik and I was given an ultimatum. Spy for Moscow or die.'

"Charlie March took a drink. I did not. A seagull stammered at us from a piling at the water's edge beyond the bike path below

Charlie March's deck. I threw a pizza crust to shut it up. I'm over sixty years old, and sitting there in perfect safety, I'm scared of what I know I'm going to see in that magician's cage.

"'Obviously,' said Charlie March, 'I chose the former. Spy for Moscow. Revealing one of Grivas's guerilla cells, they were rounded up and brought for me to execute on film. Needless to say, I secured my release. I was nineteen years old, Nathan. Younger than you when I met you, and you: it was practically the same thing.'

"I saw him then. Inside the cage. A monster, a gorilla. Fangs dripping blood, hands ripping flesh. If I had killed him, I would have done it then and there."

Muir picked up his cigarette to finish it before it died. "We make other people do that for us. Nature of the beast, beast of nature."

"I lit a cigarette instead," Muir went on, carrying me along. "Blew smoke. Indicated with my eyes for Charlie March to go on.

"'Once Olesik had his claws in me, my crimes kept piling on through the war and on afterward. But it was a two-way street. He funneled information to me, helping me achieve post-war rank. All I could do was manage my career in such a way that I never went for the crucial posting; I never took Berlin; never Western or Central Europe; I never involved myself with Cuba; never Central America or the Middle East. I took the Levant and I took Africa: two places I knew would never stabilize in either side's favor. And they aren't still, Nathan, are they?' He stated it as a fact, pips on the dice he rolled in a children's game of Risk. 'Détente?' he asked and answered, 'Détente.'

"Charlie March told me everything. He was glad to get it off his chest… And we discussed Operation GLADIO."

I jerked upright on the sofa. I couldn't let him go on. I lunged for the DAT. Muir held up a traffic cop's palm.

"Time to shake real dice and let the heads roll where they may." His voice without sentiment. His features set in such a way that I suddenly saw the tiny scars of his reconstructive surgery.

His ice-blue eyes commanded my trust.

On Muir's Florida island patio, I realized I have nothing to lose—anyway, anyhow, anywhere. Ain't life grand. I drank half of what was left.

"Don't worry about our Young Turks, Russell. GLADIO needs to end. It's the only thing Charlie March and I agreed upon. His entire career he stayed away from it to deny it to the Soviets. We both believed it was the West's only insurance policy. And we both were fools not to know that the Soviets had penetrated it from the beginning. My side and his side had played us both. By extension, they'd entrapped you and Bishop. Charlie March was sick about that. As much as I know everything else now, I knew the other then: that the two of you were sacred to both of us."

Oh, fuck you, Muir. Lie to yourself. Don't fucking do that to me anymore. There's too many fucking bodies to bury.

The blood, fired with alcohol, burned in my cheeks, and through and spreading across my chest. All I managed out loud was, "What did March ever give a damn about me and Bishop?"

Muir considered the question. Considered me. That single comment angered him more than anything I'd said the entire time we'd been on his island.

"Take it easy. Not important. Next." All one drawn-out snarl, tiger viciousness behind it.

What the—? What the fuck did we—Bishop and I—have to do with Charlie March? And what did he have to do with New York when Bishop traded GLADIO to me for every drop of booze left in the glass of the world?

GLADIO: the CIA secret-of-secrets implemented by James Jesus Angleton—one of the great OSS heroes and the greatest CIA paranoid—with a little help from former Nazi Reinhard Gehlen: Chief of Hitler's Foreign Armies East – Military-Intelligence. Instead of prosecuting Gehlen for war crimes, Angleton extracted from him Hitler's active "stay behinds," his *Wehrwölfes*. Teams of fiercely loyal Nazi soldiers Gehlen had melted into civilian populations to form secret resistance groups that, were Hitler to lose the war, would activate and bring war to the allies from within.

Hitler lost.

War over, the Werewolves assembled their cells, but with Gehlen's assistance, Angleton and his teams rounded them up and murdered them all. In their place, Angleton created GLADIO.

GLADIO: the CIA and NATO campaign to create, arm, and fund radical right-wing "stay behind" organizations that would, in the event of a successful Soviet invasion of Europe, fight communism to the death. From the end of the Second World War until today, these "Gladiators" have trained in secret, amassing caches of weapons continuously augmented in firepower throughout the '50s, '60s, '70s, and '80s by us. They hide in plain sight in Belgium, Denmark, France, Germany, Greece, Italy, Luxemburg, Netherlands, Norway, Portugal, Spain, and Turkey, as well as the neutral European countries of Austria, Finland, Sweden, and Switzerland.

That the USSR did not invade, did nothing to stop the continued stockpiling, recruitment, and training—all this created a growing vacuum of null purpose.

Muir said, "New York City. The first time in my career I had been duped into violating Executive Order 11905."

"SHINING CITIES was off the books?"

"I thought you'd figure that out at your typewriter. You figure everything else. Yeah. I made up the name from your two's silly book club—*The Shining* and *Tale of Two Cities*," he jeered. "And you so good at crossword talk, I thought you had it, but..." Muir vocalized dissatisfaction with a *ppfff* of smoke. He chained into a new cigarette.

"Stansfield Turner was Carter's DCI in '78," Muir said. "He wasn't trusted by the OSS mandarins who, inside and out, still ran GLADIO. SHINING CITIES was Bill Casey's baby all the way."

Stunned, I asked, "SHINING CITIES was GLADIO?"

Muir nodded. "Casey ran it from his private think-tank. Approved retroactively when Reagan came in and made Casey CIA director in '81."

This was worse than I ever imagined. Worse than what I'd drank myself to death over. Retroactive approval to cover a rogue conspiracy of murder and treason.

Who am I kidding? This close to the end: admit it. Every plan I write is retroactive cover for murder. Even this death shroud.

Muir watched me, waiting for me to reach his same conclusion. He'd been leading me to it all night because this was the real confession both he and Charlie March had lured me to this island to hear. In that, and in Muir's steady gaze, I realized something unusual, something I've never experienced and know I will never experience again: our inner dialogues, Muir's and mine, had found the ability to speak to each other.

He said, "Charlie March and I were duped to believe that the assassination of Aldo Moro was necessary for the greater good of protecting the 'stay behinds.' Truth is, CIA and KGB didn't give a damn about the 'stay behinds' any longer as a world war safeguard.

"*Horror vacui*, Aristotle wrote, and it's come to gently mean 'Nature abhors a vacuum.' Literally, though, it translates to Horror Void, and that's because evil men are always the first to find and fill them. In the absence of Soviet invasion, GLADIO's purpose transformed into the discrediting of left-wing groups and politicians through a 'strategy of tension'—a concept for control of public opinion through fear, propaganda, agent provocateurs, and terrorism. The aim was to instill horror into the populace while framing communist and left-wing political opponents for terrorist atrocities. Only problem was, these played right into KGB desires, and GLADIO groups weren't only posing as communist terrorists: *they became them*." He gave me a hard look. Wanted to make sure I understood. "CIA was doing the KGB's business for them."

I was afraid to ask… "How much business?"

"As much as they were doing for us. How's this for a partial list: Turkey 1960, a coup d'état that kills Prime Minister Adnan Menderes. Algeria in 1961, the French stay-behind army staged and failed in a coup against the French government. In 1967, the Greek GLADIO used the Greek army to stage a coup and impose a military dictatorship. 1969: Italy, the Piazza Fontana massacre in Milan kills sixteen and injures and maims eighty. In 1971 in Turkey, after another military coup, the stay-behind army engaged in 'domestic terror' and killed hundreds. 1977 Spain, GLADIO carried out a massacre in Madrid. 1980 in Italy, the Bologna train station bombing, which killed eighty-five people and in Turkey, a third coup—idiots can't stop. 1985, Belgium, the stay-behinds attack and shoot shoppers randomly in supermarkets, killing twenty-eight.

"Switzerland last year, the former head of the Swiss stay-behind wrote the US Defense Department that he would reveal 'the whole truth,' and was found the next day stabbed to death with his own bayonet."

I asked, "How did Charlie March figure into SHINING CITIES?"

"The Syrians got the notebook from Bishop—that day—right?" Muir prompted, indicating I roll it out. His very own Meno's Slave.

"Yes. Revealing the undercover Israeli agent inside the Italian Red Brigades. What did the Syrians care about Italy?"

Muir cocked his head, patient, anticipating.

"They didn't," I extrapolated. "The KGB did. The Syrians wanted weapons for Lebanon because a war was coming with Israel, and the KGB had those for sale."

"Credit is what credit kills," said Muir. "I think that's an AmEx slogan."

"But you want to protect GLADIO and you suspect Charlie March does as well, even though he's traitorous." I paused. Because I knew. "Charlie March was revealed in that notebook," I said, and marched the beat of the snare to Madam la guillotine: "You knew—because March was a traitor—that they'd be able to verify Silvio Lombardi was a Mossad agent through him. The *four* of us killed that Israeli agent; went on to be responsible for the death of over two hundred and sixty Palestinians; the murder of Aldo Moro's bodyguard and police; and the assassination of an Italian prime minister: all to keep in place a program of CIA and KGB co-sponsored terrorism so the world will continue to shudder and hide their eyes, and both sides can continue to sell weapons. The sides don't matter—it's just the selling of weapons, over and over, more and more of them, all the time, round and round and round..." I whispered, "The ouroboros..."

Palin (Latin: recurrence, repetitious; back, backward, again; returning, repeating) + drome (Latin: running, course; race, racecourse).

"Said Cain to Abel, finding a rock that fit just right in his hand," said Muir. "I'll sign your papers and, like we talked about while you showered, you'll notarize two sets of documents—one for the Italian Parliament, the other, the Belgian government and NATO—that expose the entire GLADIO operation and infrastructure."

I shook off drunken confusion. "No. I don't want those, Muir."

"And I'd never put them in your hands. I just want your official stamp. I'll handle it from there."

"And the addendum to your will?"

"Safe bet. In case my GLADIO files land on the wrong desk. Someone might find me gnawed to death by overfed squirrels."

I leaned back, rubbing my head. My temples throbbed.

No more: I want release from it all. It all hurts far too much.

I was defeated sitting there.

I'm defeated sitting here on this stupid fucking airplane.

"Get it together, Russell. We're just about finished."

My mouth was dry. I finished my drink. "How did it end? Your lunch with Charlie March?"

"That was it. The only thing we didn't speak of was Korea. We sat on his deck. We drank through the Johnnie. Two old spies—me looking like a beachcomber, he like he'd just come off his sailboat. I think, even then, if he'd lied to me about my Jewel, I would have believed him."

Muir dipped his index finger into his tumbler. He swirled it and finished it off. The last of the Macallan 25 mixed, as we'd done it, with rainwater.

"Remember your wedding night, Russell?"

Of course I did. I'd stolen his gun because I hadn't finished the job with my mother's.

"Get that look off your face. I'm not talking about the sex, Rusty. I picture Jewel in my arms, her arms round me. Her face inches from mine. Love, the living thing we'd made real between us. I can still feel her fingertips on my cheeks and hear the tiny scratch of my shave on her fingernails.

"But that's the power Charlie March had over me. The power he had over everyone. There was something neither good nor evil but pure about him. You wanted to be part of it... But her ghost hovered over us as our last day together crept toward night... He walked me to the door. He didn't offer me one from his stack of books. They were only as real as the cardboard cutout of the man."

Now You See Me, and soon you won't.

"I walked to the gate. Charlie March untangled his American flag from where it had gotten hung up on the broad leaves of a giant bird of paradise. We both knew we would never see each other alive again. He considered the flag a moment, then turned his back on it as he'd done his entire life and closed the door behind him."

34

FIRST LIGHT SHONE GOLDEN upon the water. Halyards clanged against masts. Charlie March backed his sailboat from slip 29 at the Pelican Landing Marina, Key Largo.

He passed the jetty and turned toward open sea.

"He was making a run for Cuba."

"And you'd hidden an explosive device on his boat."

"No. This is what you came for, Russell, so listen because this is important. Something else you're certainly not cleared for is HOUNDFOX."

"Cool. 'Random' or 'ego-generated?'"

"Superego. Thank you very much. The Agency has long held an agent in Cuba deep within Castro's impenetrable inner circle."

"One of yours?"

"No, he set himself up as an independent contractor. His daughter brokered the deal for him through me. I have never met him. No one has. Our only contact has ever been the daughter."

His eyes drilled into my soul. I was beginning to realize: I'd never crawled out of that cage inside the coffin and I suddenly knew the worst thing he'd done to me: "Was every single thing between us a lie? Everything I've done, everything that's happened to me with you? Have I always just been the pawn of your opening gambit?"

"Remember what I told you about lies?" His voice was gentle, more gentle than father or uncle. Gentle like Nina in New York. "Hell, you're a lawyer. You understand lies better than any of us. How many times have the lies been yours worked on paper for me? Are you sitting right here, right now on a lie?"

"What? This sofa? Yes, Nathan."

"Sure. This sofa. That's the *sofa lie* you're telling me right now, Russell. And I'm okay with that because with a good lie, a lie we tend with a gardener's care to keep alive, everyone ends up better and the thing called life grows more meaningful."

Motherfucker knows my plan.

"And yes. Nina's father is HOUNDFOX."

"Nina's father is dead. Executed."

"Anything but. I put her on you in New York because I knew you were jealous of Tom. I was breaking four ops and probably a hundred laws worried about you."

"Nina was your plant."

"She was only to watch you, keep you safe, keep her distance. She was the courier, Russell. She took your CONPLAN and OPLAN, then she made the run to the UN with Bishop's disguise kit. She was to keep an eye out for you in case you showed up. And you did. Once the op was over, she was to walk off."

"She didn't. We dropped acid."

"So I heard." He flicked ash. "Y'know, you've always been a problem for me in this department."

"It was you who called my room. To make her leave me."

Muir grimaced. "Couldn't risk her getting involved with you. Every woman I've ever put on to watch you has this crazy habit of falling in love with you. Nina, Nancy, Mary..."

"Mary and I lived together for a year."

"She quit the Agency to do that. Right after meeting you at pizza."

This whole short, stupid life of mine has been a charade, and dammit, I'm mad: the son of a bitch is proud of this shit.

"Then why did Mary leave me?" My voice was small. It was unfamiliar because I said something out loud I'd only said a million times in the noisy silence inside my skull.

"Because try as she might, you loved a future with the Company more than a future with her. This job chooses the man."

My chest hurt. My lungs were constricting. I had one final question: "Madeline?"

"Fuck you. What do you think?"

"I don't know."

"You do, kid."

"Tell me, Nathan. I must know," I said. "I have things to do."

Muir shook his head. "You do know." He smoked, blew it at the DAT. "Now we're not going on any farther with this—you're gonna make Harker cry."

And what did it matter anymore? I centered myself with a few deep breaths. "Finish your story, Muir. Give me HOUNDFOX."

Muir's expression was one of approval. "Good. Violating every procedure, every rule of the Agency, I used HOUNDFOX to do the work for us. Cubans have long memories. The torturer Charlie March saved me from, Hector Guzman—in the intervening years—has made a career for himself with Castro's Dirección General de Inteligencia. Last week, he was given information on how he could settle an old debt with me. The name of a boat I would be aboard yesterday morning."

Muir told the story in detail as HOUNDFOX had reported it to his daughter, as Nina had briefed Muir yesterday from the ugly-wedding-present-Yamamoto assassination sofa.

And all these years I'd kept a longing eye on the mail for a picture frame from the sea; a photograph from a place, a life, parallel and better.

"Guzman activated two Cuban sleepers in Miami. Kids in their twenties. Stasi-trained in Havana in explosives and black bag work. Dead of night, they made it down to the Key, temporarily disabled marina security, and made it undetected onto March's boat named like a slap in the face to the service and the nation he betrayed: *No Regrets.*

"Once inside the cabin, they accessed the engine compartment. Laid out their tools. Pulled the explosive device from the gym bag they'd brought. Set the timer to the ignition. Set the fail-safe—a pressure plate inside the engine compartment hinge so that if for some reason Charlie March—or me, they thought—had wanted to look at the engine before he pulled out from the marina, he'd detonate the bomb the instant he lifted the hatch.

"Charlie March motors quietly past the jetty. I watched him turn toward open sea. He unfurled his main sail, feeding it to the wind. He breathed deeply—I saw through binoculars—thankful to be alive to experience this moment the bomb intended for me took his life."

Muir spread his hands before me like Christians do when opening to God, or the guilty when surrendering to handcuffs.

"That's everything: how it was and how, my friend, I didn't do it."

I waited for more, but it was over.

In every way possible.

I shut off my recorder.

Muir did some cleaning up of our interrogation table. I brooded, drunk and disillusioned. Hot and sticky from the unwelcome humidity. I looked to my saddlebag briefcase, ready to receive his required signatures. Realization came slowly to my alcohol-fogged mind.

"You don't need my documents."

Returning through the glass door from inside, Muir flashed a close-lipped smile. "Charlie March was the very best. I was everything he wanted me to be… Only problem was, Charlie March was the enemy."

"And you didn't know it or believe it until it was too late."

"Don't let anyone tell you different: in our line of work, it's not how you play the game; it's how the game plays you."

"Because HOUNDFOX is involved, and HOUNDFOX is an active and ongoing asset inside the government of an enemy nation, you're covered. Everything you did. Everything you've said. All covered by the National Security Act."

Muir wasn't smiling anymore when he nodded his checkmate.

"I told you, Russell. I'm finished now. I'm out. And I want your word because—and I've always known this about you—when you give your word, you keep it."

Our rings exchanged. My left hand tied to her right with thirteen-strand hemp. I lift Madeline's veil. Kiss me—I'm thinking the same words as Muir to Jewel—Kiss me. You're my wife.

There was the tiniest bit of scotch in the bottom of the bottle. I lifted it.

"Don't." The word a bullet. "It won't be good for you."

But I tilted the bottle and drank the last drop. "What you don't know, Mr. Muir."

"Leaves space on the head of a pin. The game's over. No winner. All losers 'cept you..." He gave a definite look from me to my saddlebag briefcase. "Maybe."

In deep silence, Muir read and signed his retirement papers. Fountain pen: brown ink. Always the same. And I, Russell Aiken, legal counsel to the Central Intelligence Agency, United States of America, countersigned and stamped with special black ink that can't be counterfeited, then provided Muir with his copy.

He watched me pack them back into my briefcase. Then he saw me to my car and we exchanged the words about Charlie March getting what he wanted, the two of us splitting the thirty pieces of silver.

I gripped the steering wheel. Drizzle fell, obscuring the glass before my eyes. He braced his arms through the open window on the ledge of my door. He didn't want me to leave and I didn't want to stay.

"I meant to tell you. We finally got that Doomsday Machine."

"What?" I said, annoyed, my mind already walking me through airport security, my Agency credential allowing Muir's gun through with me. "*Strangelove* again?"

"SDI. Star Wars Initiative. The Soviets' fear of it, their inability to continue the arms race, allowed Reagan the Cold War win."

I allowed Muir a begrudging smile. I started the engine. He played my smile to his advantage.

"Hold it. We got one more thing I promised I'd do for you."

Madeline.

"Forget it. There's nothing to be done about that cunt anymore."

Muir stepped away without another word. Without a goodbye and without a wave. *Finito.* Moro would know that one: Italian for "All washed up."

35

I'M OFF DOCUMENT.

Computer powered down for the landing, safe in my saddlebag where they'll find it and the DAT and all there is to tell. My silent voice, that other man inside me, finally met in volume.

I'm in the cab rolling up my street to the 1938 brick-built Tenleytown, American Traditional townhouse Madeline fell in love with after we started dating and that I bought for her as a wedding present.

I'm on my own.

No cops waiting upon landing—I'm drunk, but not stupid enough to call ahead and tip anyone off—and there are no squad cars or undercover vehicles anywhere I can see. I have the driver pull around the near-corner, the place where I'd hidden in my car and watched Madeline and her lover leave her mini-SUV together for the first and last time.

I pay him. I get out into the night. In the darkness between streetlights, I play a little game. I allow myself to believe that none of it has happened. Charlie March, CIA Trailblazer, is going sailing tomorrow; Nathan Muir is finishing his vacation; Madeline is baking a cherry pie. That what's to happen next won't. Then I shoot the last Johnnie Walker mini and bounce it hard on the asphalt street.

A Charlie March vial of poison.

I walk to my front door. And I'm thinking now—not of Madeline, not of me—I'm thinking of Jewel.

She walks into her Seoul garden cottage. Charlie March waits inside. He kills her.

Where's Muir?

I open the door. This time I'm the one carrying Muir's pistol.

Jewel was carrying a pharmacy bag. Why did Muir tell me that? He said "grocery bag," then he Yamamoto-sofa-ed it to "pharmacy bag."

The bullet-shattered lamp lies in untended wreckage on my living-room floor. I see the two bullet holes in the sofa where I fired above their heads.

Chickenshit.

Muir was right but not anymore.

I notice a light burning in the back guest bedroom.

"Russell?" Madeline calls timidly from within.

I'm not worth it, honey. You deserve better.

I put Muir's pistol against my heart—a tip of my gray-faded white hat to Jewel—and I pull the trigger. It's the fraction of a moment between the trigger's release of the firing pin spring and the firing pin punching the primer.

I know why the pharmacy bag.

I know why Jewel was bloated.

Why Muir would never try for kids again.

I know the very last lie between us.

"Because while I've killed for my country and never thought twice about it, murder is an unlivable thing."

Jewel didn't kill herself.

"Tell Nathan he never murdered a soul."

I know Charlie March wanted to take the credit away for it because Charlie March didn't kill Jewel. Charlie March needed Jewel alive. He convinced Muir of Jewel's betrayal as a way to get them out of Korea, break Muir, create a vacuum inside him, preparation to turning him to the Soviets and treason. But Muir went further than Charlie March had anticipated. It's why Muir held on to Charlie March's secret so many years.

It's why Charlie March would never turn Muir.

It was his guilt: Muir's guilt.

Muir murdered his own innocent wife and his unborn child and that's the cardboard cutout of himself he's been hiding behind forever since.

I've made a terrible mistake and the pin hits the primer.

36

CLICK.

I'd done it. I'd aimed a gun at a living soul and I'd pulled the trigger to take the life.

Ha!

Muir thought it couldn't be done.

Madeline stood naked and backlit in the spare bedroom doorway, her body lithe and frank. "You sweet fool. He took the bullets when you were in the shower."

I'd never been happier in my life.

"No cops?" I said.

"You scared the shit out of Dr. Finley PhD. He was ready to take it the whole way."

"Why didn't he?"

"Oh, trust me, he tried. So I called that boss of yours. Your Nathan-this, your Nathan-that you're always going on about. I didn't know him at all when we got married. He was just that guy who smokes you work for. But he told me the night we got married, after you smoked that cigar: if you were ever in trouble—real trouble you could not get yourself out of—even if you were on the moon, he said that—I was to call him and he'd fix it for us." She shrugged. "So I called him."

She walked over. "Will you forgive me? Can you? I only did it because I got bored with you. Nathan says that means—"

"You're just trying to get my attention?" I stared at her.

"Don't ever shoot me again?" she said.

"I shot *at* you. It's me I shot."

"Well, you might've used the knuckle trick."

"You might've called Muir earlier. Before you let Beardy-Baldy—"

"You call him that?" Madeline smirked.

"What?"

"I say Baldy-Beardy. In my head."

"Liar."

Caught, she gave a playfully innocent shrug as if she could get away with what she'd done. But Muir's words came back to me:

"How horrible it is to feel hatred for someone you love more than life itself."

Speaking of Jewel, he'd been speaking directly to me.

"Madeline, the guy was fucking you. I'm still furious," I said, but I don't know why I wasn't furious.

That's a lie. I do know. I thought I'd be dead and I wasn't. It's called euphoria. I suddenly understood the attraction of Russian roulette—there's euphoria in the certainty of death self-inflicted and self-denied. Though I don't plan to join a roulette league or anything like that.

"You get bored again and want to get my attention—" I went to the other Russell inside me, the one she liked better, the one I let narrate life in the silence of my mind while it passes me by, but my alter ego was gone. I had to finish the thought for myself: "Walk out that door and never come back, because if I let your heart get even a single covert footstep away from mine, I'll deserve it."

She placed her fingertips to my face. In them, I was conscious of the in-out steady beat of the tide of life inside her, the pumping heart that charged her mind, that let her know her soul, that proved itself to me with her tears and mine: both pure. Both clear.

Life cannot be lived a game of words inside our heads. I would be one man, now and forever, and I would be Madeline's. I dropped Muir's pistol. With my left arm around her shoulders, like a dancer

I reached with my right hand down her hips and across the firm, smooth curve of her rear. I scooped her into my arms, then committing to my lies and promises, my failures, embarrassments, and regrets owned and owed—my Life—I marched upstairs to our bedroom and rolled with her onto the bed.

"I've loved you since the moment I saw you," I said as I competed with her eager hands to remove my clothes.

"All I ever wanted to be was yours," she said.

I LAY IN the close darkness. The darkness plays tricks on you. The darkness in the human heart, the worst tricks all. Tomorrow, I'd go in, hand over the recorder and the tape, the signed documents sealing Muir's fate but not his future. I would collect Bishop's flag from Muir's office and fly with it to Tom in Hong Kong. A worthy purpose for my first overseas mission.

I didn't think I'd see Muir again and as I thought that, his words from when I'd arrived the day before came back to me.

"The Baluba believe that contained within that first gasp of air—our first infant cry—is the story of our entire lives. We're born and we cry out, and that cry echoes from hut or hospital or home, from behind the plow-ox, rice paddy, taxicab, or whorehouse—wherever we're born—across time and space. It echoes all the way to heaven, where heard by God it is judged imperfect as all of us are—even you, fancy that—and He returns it to earth, where it echoes along the path of our lives until it finds us and slays us."

Charlie March's path was the essence of imperfection; for that, he was truly and mercilessly slain. But what about the rest of humanity? Every single one of us dies, but I won't believe the imperfections along life's path for the vast majority of humanity, young and old, aren't self-laid paving stones of their lives, but the pebbles in their shoes, the asphalt cracks that stub their toes;

mistakes, shame, regrets, large in guilt, but little more than embarrassment in scope. Most lives are spent landscaping our paths toward perfection.

1. *CONDITIONS PRECEDENT:*
   - 1.1. *From birth to death humanity's obligations to Life's Path hereunder are conditioned on the following:*
     - 1.1.1. *Our First Cry contains our entire life before it's led.*
     - 1.1.2. *God pre-judges that life imperfect and returns our First Cry directly in pursuit of us.*
     - 1.1.3. *That First Cry follows the path of our life, measuring us in strength and weakness as we strive for the Good or fall to the Evil.*
     - 1.1.4. *When that First Cry catches up to us, it carries us to the home it left God to prepare for eternal life.*
   - 1.2. *Muir said, "It's not 'their' God. It's God. God, Aiken—*
     - 1.2.1. *Western God*
     - 1.2.2. *Eastern God*
     - 1.2.3. *African God*
     - 1.2.4. *Agnostic maybe-God*
     - 1.2.5. *Atheist non-God*

       "—His one and only—it's what we're all in business to fight over."
   - 1.3. *God/maybe-God/non-God dignifies all humanity with the precious gift of free will.*

> 1.3.1. *With free will, we are given the chance to change that imperfect path, to steer that echo from the natural chaos of unthinking entropy we're born into, the path of the selfish and the cowardly, the greedy, dishonest, and cruel—human evil—to a spiritual choice to blaze a path toward grace with strength and compassion, our best morality, our humblest forgiveness, our purest love and truth.*

Parsing it out, alongside Madeline in the darkness, in the manner best suited to my path, I smiled. I know now what Muir knew all along. Why he'd asked if I could differentiate spirituality from religion. It was of utmost importance to him. What he lived by, and why everything he'd told me after he'd first told me this could only make sense the way he'd wanted me to understand his life, his path, his horror—all the rubble along it he'd fought and lost against, so many times, bullets smacking stone hearts, but always, always kept at the fight—knowing this: there is nothing in life worth striving for if there isn't imperfection to strive against.

In a few hours, Muir would arrive at headquarters. He would quietly say goodbye to Gladys, tell her to expect me and to give me his flag. He would turn in his credentials, process out, and return to his island. The Captiva Island house would soon be his. I'd seen the evidence in his bedroom, after my shower. An offer accepted. Escrow papers ready. He'd had a bunch of satellite photos of the island—a year of tides and weather—that he'd illegitimately tasked through Imagery Analysis and would have to return and hope nobody did an audit on his GEOINT requests.

There had been boxes of other belongings—a photograph of Bishop, oddly, his high-school graduation, no photo of me, but he'd kept a ticket stub from the revival theater, although he'd used the *Strangelove* recruitment more times than I care to count. He had also moved in a set of green leather-bound journals—one for every year of his service—written in a code I'm sure anyone could crack with a little elbow grease. If I hadn't been planning to steal his weapon to kill myself, I'd have reported it. I'm glad I didn't. I wasn't going to tell. My blackness toward him was safe now and velvet.

For Madeline and me to make it, I'm going to need every one of Muir's always unsolicited First and Second Rules of Thumb. And all the toes. While I showered, he'd given me some encouragement through the bathroom door.

I smile in the dark, recalling.

The only real compliment he's ever paid me. Couldn't do it to my face. Waited until I was shouting distance behind two doors and under a water spigot. Doors that lock from the inside.

My phone interrupted my half-dream state. Probably Nathan checking up on me, in which case, I wouldn't answer.

It was a number I didn't recognize. A California area code.

The bedside clock glowed a devil-eye red: 5:22.

I opened the clamshell and crept into the living room. I hit the light switch, but the lamp was destroyed so I tripped, barked my shin, moved to the ruined sofa from Slagermann's. I sat and let it ring out. I rubbed my face, my fingers through my hair, and assessed my level of sobriety. The throbbing in my temples and behind my eyes indicated a fair level of alcohol pounding its way out of my system. And that awful body smell.

The cellular phone chirruped again.

"Hello?"

The woman at the other end, voice tight with emotion, asked me to identify myself.

Obnoxious.

"Who wants to know in California?"

"Are you Russell Aiken? I have your number from my ex-husband, Nathan Muir."

After all these years? The chateau dormer window. Veronique? I knew I'd seen interest.

"My name is Sandy. He told me if I was ever in serious trouble and I couldn't get ahold of him, I'm not to call anyone but you."

And probably the six other names at the top of the list smart enough not to answer at the crack of dawn.

"I've been with Nathan these past couple days. We had a time of it. I'm sure he's sleeping now."

Like I should be.

She said, "In over thirty years, he's never not answered my call within two hours when he wasn't operational."

"You're divorced. You call him that much?"

"No. Not that much, but some things divorce doesn't erase. Our son has been arrested. It's all over the news. In China. For espionage."

"Nathan doesn't have a son."

"I just told you he did."

"Does he know that?"

"What do you think? I'm calling you to surprise him?!"

Does anyone else know—at the Agency? Does anyone know?

"Does your son work for the Company?"

"Why are you being obtuse? I just told you that."

Aha! That's it. That's wrong. The numbers don't match.

Muir told me: inducted into the CIA in 1951, and I hear Muir take over my inner voice:

"I wouldn't see Charlie March for three more years, wrapped up as I was in training-wheel assignments in Asia."

"Nice try, ma'am. You weren't married until 1954. Flag trick wouldn't have worked on Tom."

"Happy to give you the cook's tour of those, but none involved Charlie March so you won't find it pertinent to your purposes."

"So you *know* my son, Mr. Aiken."

"Tom Bishop's last name isn't Muir."

"What's with the word games with you? Tom Bishop is my son. With Nathan Muir. *My* ex-husband. We were married March 31, 1951. We had our reception the next day at the Washington Hotel."

"Why the next day? No one does that."

"God, you're insufferable. How does anyone put up with you?" she said. "*Because* he'd knocked me up. I was embarrassed enough by the wedding. He threw the reception as an April Fool's surprise brunch."

Then she laughed to herself—but I heard it, so it wasn't *really* to herself—and she said, eminently tender, "He loved me. He did. He really did," and I realized how closely tears sound to laughter.

"Mrs.—uh, Sandy—please don't cry."

"God! I'm not crying. Nathan loves Tom. Loves him. Nathan just never left Korea. My brother did that to him. I don't think *he's* such a good person or I'd call Charlie."

I wasn't about to tell her about her brother. Bishop's uncle. Charlie March. Dead. Traitor.

"Mr. Aiken, you're supposed to know Nathan. Every day of the year is April Fool's with him. It's the only way he lives with himself."

She threw a sigh. It hit me across ten thousand-plus miles. The number of hours between my birth and Bishop catching up to me alive. The numbers actually did work.

"The Chinese have arrested our son for espionage," she repeated. "I don't care what your goddamn Agency wants. I don't care what the president wants. I don't care what kind of incident this creates. When Tommy ran off to Vietnam to chase after the dead Marine Corps father I'd invented for him, Nathan promised to look after him. Find Nathan. Have him call me, Mr. Aiken. Thank you. That's all," she said and hung up.

Her call could mean only one thing. Bishop had gone after Elizabeth in China and failed. And all the time he was doing the work, winging his own CONPLAN without legal consultation, I was legally assuring, illegally, that the one man who could save him would have no power to do it.

Tom Bishop's father. Nathan Muir.

What have I done?

"Russell?" Muir shouted through the bathroom door, and I'm back this morning on Captiva Island, Muir's house, Muir's shower.

"What now?"

"Well, I hesitate to pay you a compliment…"

"You've never paid me a compliment. Why start?"

"I think I remember paying you one in New York City."

I rinsed shampoo. Went for the conditioner, sorting out one from a half-dozen little bottles from a half-dozen countries I'd never visited.

"That was over a decade ago," I said.

"I liked your CONPLAN."

"Thanks heaps."

I realize now, this chitchat was probably used to track my position by voice while he thumbed the bullets from his Sig-Sauer's clip.

"You ran amok after that, at the UN and in the City, so you can understand why I've been hesitant."

Well, screw Nathan Muir anyway.

"You're a legend at The Farm," he said.

"Why?" I shut off the taps. Staring at the tiles. Head against them. Resting. Not weeping.

"Your secret. You fucking locked yourself in that cage." He laughed.

I grabbed a towel. Dried my eyes first. "Biggest humiliation of my life."

"How you look at things. For those subjects with claustrophobia, the sight of the cage breaks them. Some do get in it and get the buried-alive treatment, but you are the only person, in history, who ever had the guts to lock the gate. On themselves."

"Isn't that giving up?"

"If it was a real abduction. But there's another test they're administering at the same time of the simulation."

"What's that?" I looked at myself in the mirror.

I didn't want to use his dirty hairbrush. I ran my fingers through my hair. I found my jockey shorts. My mouth was sour. I grabbed his toothbrush and scrubbed my teeth with Crest.

The fluoride cancels out the toothbrush germs.

"How far you're willing to trust the people you've entrusted your life with. No one has ever shown the level of trust you showed for me when you locked that cage. I tell you every time I can, Rusty. It's all how you look at things. That's what's real."

Dressed, I came out of the bathroom. He looked at me from where he sat on the bed. The gun in the drawer. That was real. I would steal it in a few minutes—all the good it would do me.

He said, "If we never get a chance to speak again, it's been a privilege serving with you."

I watched him out of the bedroom. Appearance just can't get by without reality. Or are my words backwards?

I tried Muir's number on my phone, but like Sandy, I couldn't reach him. I'd try again in a few minutes.

I walked over to the turntable. To the cupboard where I keep my dad's vinyl. Before I found and selected *Nice 'N' Easy*, I thumbed some of my and my older sisters' records. When my mom died, Paulette put them all in a box in the order they'd always been. I took them out like that and put them in my cabinet.

Next to the last Sinatra, my hand stops on *Dumbo*. In black Magic Marker in the upper orange corner above the little gray, big-eared guy soaring with the crows, I'd crossed out Jeannie and printed my name in shaky first-grade letters, *R-U-S-T-Y*. Muir had busted my secret of secrets; he'd chosen Sinatra for my burial. But he's always called me Dumbo. My record cozied up against my father's. I understood. The elephant who got drunk on a flood of Old Horsey only to wake up at the top of the tallest tree; the lay of the land, the subtle ways of the world: sleepy eyes see it all now, and plainly, laid across the cross-stitched pattern of boxed fields and down the railroad tracks stretched and stretching into sunshine.

ABOUT THE AUTHOR

In 1989, Michael Frost Beckner's script for *Sniper* launched a military-thriller franchise now in production on its eighth sequel. Three consecutive record-breaking spec script sales and three films later, Tony Scott directed Beckner's original screenplay *Spy Game*. An international blockbuster that paired Robert Redford and Brad Pitt as CIA partners and rivals, it is now a classic in the espionage genre. Branching into television with his CIA-based drama *The Agency* for CBS, Beckner's pilot predicted Osama bin Laden's terror attack and the War on Terror four months before 9/11. In that series alone, Beckner would go on to predictively dramatize three more international terror events. Having penned more than twenty-five pilots for network and cable television, miniseries and docudramas, and dozens of original motion picture screenplays, adaptations, and rewrites, he is a Hollywood institution.

Now, in conjunction with the twentieth anniversary of *Spy Game*, Beckner returns to the world of Nathan Muir and Tom Bishop with the release of his trilogy of *Spy Game* novels: *Muir's Gambit*, *Bishop's Endgame*, and *Aiken in Check*.

CPSIA information can be obtained
at www.ICGtesting.com
Printed in the USA
LVHW101814031122
732305LV00015B/527/J